DAY OF NO SHADOWS

Enjoy the journey!

♡ Sonia

Edited by Jennifer Clark-Sell

Cover art by Lee Ching at Under Cover Designs

Search for

DAY OF NO SHADOWS

playlist on Spotify

♪♫♪

PART ONE:

2012

CHAPTER 1

Spring, 2012
Yucatán Peninsula, Mexico

A GENTLE GULF BREEZE flows past, carrying the scent of the sea, but it does nothing to tame the unforgiving wildness of the Yucatán heat. My long black hair clings to the back of my neck. I regret not braiding it before getting off the plane.

The taxi driver had repeatedly assured me this office in the town of Progreso was the place I wanted to be, and the small sign attached to the building that reads 'Casa Mestizo' confirms this is true. I don't remember it looking this dismal all those years ago. While I had hoped to find a modern brick building with glass windows, air-conditioning, and a simple door, this place is none of those things. The hut stands like a defiant piece of decaying history amid civilization.

Wooden beads clack and seashells rattle as I push aside the strings layering the entrance of the shack. My gaze sweeps the space. Not much has changed from fourteen years ago. In one corner rests a simple desk with a large computer on top. Chairs line the wall near the windows. A small hallway leads to other doors, where I assume there's a bathroom and office.

I struggle to pull my wheeled luggage over the uneven ground. The tiny hut could be called quaint or cozy with its open-air windows, thatched roof, and lack of a door, but this place bespeaks stark poverty, not of quaintness for the sake of it. Looking down at the dirty cracked floor, I can barely contain my huff of exasperation. Once again, my dad hired the same, cheap tour guide.

Last time, a father-son duo working out of this office led our tour. That twelve-year-old boy became my first sworn enemy. I was only nine, and just wanted a friend. He barely spoke to me unless it was to tease me about my long, skinny legs, or to yank at my braid in passing.

Swinging my sweat-dampened hair over one shoulder, I crouch on the floor before sliding open the zippered luggage compartment to remove a folder containing my travel documents. The first several pages have my flight itinerary, and I skim past those until I find the one I'm looking for.

"Bueno," comes a deep voice above me.

I force a slight smile before glancing up. "Hi, I'm looking for—"

My voice wavers mid-sentence as my gaze meets his. In front of me is the most handsome man I have ever seen. A strange expression ignites in his eyes, and he seems to pale slightly.

I clear my throat and glance down at the opened folder in my hands. " … um, someone by the name of Guillermo."

A muscle in his jaw clenches and he scrubs one hand over his face, wiping the odd look away. "Hablas español?"

"No." I lie, squaring my shoulders. "No, I don't."

Strange, dark eyes twinkle from a set of thick lashes. "Es la idioma de tu corazón."

The language of my heart? Nah. More like a curse weighing on my life. I exhale a short breath and spread my hands in helpless appeal. "Look, I can't speak Spanish."

"Can't?" he repeats in heavily accented English, raising one thick brow. "Or won't?"

Instead of answering, I thrust my reservation paper in his direction. "I have a tour booked with Guillermo."

The man sits on the edge of the desk, crossing long legs encased in dark jeans in front of him and not taking the paper. "Guillermo isn't here."

I scan the reservation page again, looking for the second name I saw. "How about Ig … um … Ig—"

"There is also no one named Ig-um-Ig here."

He's not even trying to be helpful. The man sits with the bearing of someone utterly relaxed, but his tightly folded arms and the fingertips tapping on his bicep hint at tension simmering beneath the surface.

Perhaps he can be convinced to help. I stand, flip my hair behind my back, and walk over to him. My jean shorts hug my hips perfectly, ending just below my butt, and my blush pink, cropped halter top doesn't allow for a bra. His gaze drops slightly, but in the same instant he blinks, bringing his eyes back up to mine. I lean in and point to the name Ignacio on the paper.

"Maybe you can tell me how to pronounce this name." I force a sweet smile to my lips.

He spares the page half a glance, then pins his strange eyes back to mine. They're not brown. They're a deep, dark blue, much like the night sky beyond the rising moon.

"Ignacio," he says, pronouncing it Eeg-nah-see-oh. "But you, señorita gringa, can call me Nash for short."

"Nash?" My eyes widen. The memory of a dry, hot summer

spent wandering the Yucatán as children flashes in my mind. I wonder if he remembers me too. I control my features before they reveal anything. "I'm not a gringa."

"You pronounce 'gringa' really well for a gringa who can't speak Spanish." He unfolds his arms and pushes off from the table.

Even though I'm unusually tall for a woman at nearly six feet, my eyes only meet the level of his chin. I don't like the way he's looking at me. Like he knows some secret I'm not privy to. I swallow, moving one foot behind the other in a half step away from him.

"Can we get the tour started? I'm told you'll have a package or something for me at the end of this."

Amusement lights up his eyes. "This is not that kind of tour. No, ehh … how do you say … 'funny endings' here." He winks, one side of his mouth curving in a smile.

The old me would have enjoyed the flirting, and maybe even joked back about funny endings versus happy endings, but I am not amused by whatever stupid game he's playing with me. I know his type already. I'd fallen for him countless times in other faces and different names, but all the same arrogant personality.

Speaking of faces, Nash is painfully gorgeous. His aquiline nose ends with the slightly wider nostrils that distinguish Mayans. Most men here in the Yucatán are shorter, but his stature is that of a professional athlete. Instead of the shorn, dark locks other men in this area have, his golden bronze hair falls around his shoulders. His strange eye color completes the uncomfortable contradiction of his being. I only feel a strong need to get away from him.

My eyes drop to my gray low-top Converse as I dig my toe into a crevice, dislodging a small rock. Clearing my throat, I sneak a glance at him. Immediately, I sense he's recognized my discomfort.

14

His eyes are pinned to mine while a smirk spreads across his face. If there's anything I can't stand, it's a man who knows his own appeal and uses it as a weapon against unsuspecting women. In my experience, it's an unspoken rule that men like this are no substance at all, only a brittle, beautiful shell.

Impatient, I rattle the paper in my outstretched hand, waiting for him to move toward it. My features tighten in annoyance, and my chin thrusts out in a stubborn tilt.

He plucks the paper from my grasp and peruses it, reading my name aloud first. "Ines de la Luz. Your father is Jose de la Luz?"

"Was. He died three months ago." I wait for recognition to appear in his eyes, something to show I'm not the only one remembering that summer all those years ago.

An indecipherable expression crosses his features. "I'm truly sorry ..." he says, shadowed blue eyes raising from the page to meet mine.

"Thank—"

"... but your father is the man who booked the tour, and he booked it in Spanish. Asi, voy a hablar en español por todo el duracion. Ven."

So he's going to talk Spanish the whole time.

Dumbfounded, I watch as he breezes past me, picks up my luggage, and walks out the doorway. He almost had me fooled. I had thought he would act like a normal person and be kind by offering condolences for the loss of my father, but of course, he behaves like a complete barbarian.

I make my way through the cascade of shells, wildly shoving at the offending strings. If only there were an actual door to slam. Outside, an open-air Jeep stands waiting. Nash tosses my bag into the trunk and then waves his hand to the passenger seat. "Esperate, aqui," he orders, telling me to wait here, and then keeps walking. I watch as he jogs across the street and pulls open the door of a restaurant.

Well, I'm hungry too.

Bells tinkle as I open the door to the colorful building advertising traditional Yucatecan dishes. A blast of gloriously cool air conditioning hits me. Nash stands in front of a middle-aged man, arms crossed over his chest, immersed in conversation. Both men are nearly identical in height and build. I hear sounds of exasperation from Nash, complete with angry gestures as he talks in rapid Spanish. The older man looks up and sees me standing at the door. My mouth spreads in a grin at seeing Nash's father, Guillermo.

"Ines!" He greets me with open arms and a smile. I rush to him and enjoy the brief squeeze of his hug. Guillermo holds me back at arm's length. "It is so good to see you again. What has it been? Fourteen years?"

I nod, looking into his warm, brown eyes. "So good to see you again, too. My dad booked this tour for me a while back, and I was hoping you'd be able to take me."

Guillermo glances at his son, then shakes his head, while chuckling softly to himself. He signals to a man behind the counter and says, "Una platito más," to order one more plate.

He guides me over to a table, then pulls out a chair, inviting me with a wave of his hand to sit next to him. Nash sits on the opposite side. His knee brushes against mine as he pulls his long legs under the table. He reacts instantly, scraping his chair backward. The waiter returns, bringing everyone at the table a bottle of beer. Beads of condensation form on the dark glass.

Guillermo gives me a look of utmost patience. "I am always the one at the desk when people come in. Always. I just left now to get lunch for me and my son. It looks like the gods have chosen who your tour guide will be."

The gods. I resist the unbidden urge to roll my eyes. The Yucatán Maya are deeply rooted in their ancient beliefs and traditions, but it's preposterous to think a god would stoop so low as to dictate a person's tour guide.

I try again. "Your name is first on the reservation though."

"And my son is the first person you saw. The gods have decided. Who am I to say different?" He shrugs, as if his explanation should make sense and it really is out of his hands.

His smiling eyes settle on his son, who leans the chair onto the two back legs and crosses his arms. Nash's stance brings to mind a pouting child who's been told he has to share his toys. He, too, must have been trying to convince his dad to switch places. Maybe the both of us together can make a convincing argument. I'd rather not spend the next seven days with him.

I lean in toward Guillermo. "Look, I'm willing to pay you extra."

"Your money is no good with me, hija."

I soften upon hearing him call me 'daughter' but I refuse to be charmed by his fatherly ways. "Guillermo, your son won't even speak English," I say in exasperation, gesturing to Nash, who rolls his eyes to the ceiling. "I'm not taking no for an answer. The customer is always right, correct?"

Guillermo tilts his head. "The customer … que?"

He directs his attention to Nash, who gives a rapid translation of the saying into Spanish. They look at one another for the briefest of

17

moments, and then both men explode in laughter. My eyes flit back and forth between the two in confusion. I don't see anything funny about what I said.

Guillermo slaps the table, and roars, "The customer is always …" The man can't even get the last word out with how hard he is laughing-crying.

Eventually, the two men calm down, and Guillermo reaches over to pull a white napkin from the metal holder. He dabs tears of laughter from his eyes, breathlessly chuckling. He then sets the napkin down, looks at me, and very seriously says, "No, not here."

Now it's my turn to pout. I sigh heavily and sit back in my chair. Nash frowns at his father, arms crossed over his broad chest, his lips tightened in frustration. Guillermo tries to diffuse the tension at the table by asking about my dad, and his face falls in sadness at the news of his passing. At least someone in this family shows an appropriate amount of sympathy.

A waiter sweeps in from the kitchen, and places identical dishes in front of each of us. Several pieces of fish are coated in a reddish seasoning, each alongside a scoop of white rice and a simple salad of tomatoes, onions, and cucumber. The men put a scoop of lime-flavored mayonnaise on their salad. I resist the impulse to grimace, but then decide to try it for myself. When in the Yucatán, do as the Yucatecan do, I guess.

I drizzle the creamy dressing on top then stab my fork in. My eyes close in delight as I chew. I cut off a piece of the seasoned fish next and pop that in my mouth. Everything is incredible and the red seasoning is on the fish is like nothing I've ever tasted. We devour our food in silence. Nash orders a second bottle of beer, and I hold up my hand for another icy brew.

Guillermo wipes his mouth with his napkin, smiling at me.

"Your hair is still so long and beautiful, Ines. Ignacio always thought it was very pretty."

"Ay, papá," Nash groans, ducking his head as he rubs the back of his neck with one hand.

When he looks up again, our eyes meet. He then affixes his attention on his beer, scowling darkly at the drink. How interesting that he told his father he thought my hair was pretty. Maybe there's more to him than meets the eye. But probably not. I catch myself already trying to make excuses for a man's irritating behavior. I'm not going down that self-destructive path again.

Nash pushes away from the table, unfolding his large frame from the chair. "Me voy a pagar," he says, pulling his wallet from his back pocket.

"Here." I shift in my chair and dig into my bag for some pesos.

Nash shakes his head then heads to the cashier to pay. I speak my thanks to his retreating back, but he makes no sign of acknowledgement. I turn my attention back to his father. Time to try begging.

"Guillermo, please." I speak softly, and reach over the table, putting my hand over his large, tanned fingers. "It would mean a lot if you'd do this. I just lost my dad, and it would be nice to have someone familiar around." My eyes are filled with sincerity and I'm pleading with the man, giving it all I've got.

He looks over at his son, then back at me. "Ay, the two of you still don't get along," he murmurs sadly. Guillermo presses his lips into a thin line, shaking his head. "Ines, if you walked in five minutes earlier, I would be the one taking you. But the gods have chosen. You will go with my son."

"But ..."

After pushing his chair back, he stands from the table, ending my last-ditch attempt at getting a different tour guide.

"A donde van, hijo?" Guillermo questions his son, asking where we are going.

I listen with interest, as I have no idea what's in store.

"X'tambo, Tatun Cuzmal, Tulum, Coba, y Chichen Itza."

He may as well have been speaking Dothraki. Out of the odd string of words he says, I'm only able to recognize the obvious Chichen Itza, one of the Seven Wonders of the World.

The two men face one another. Guillermo grips the back of his son's neck, and they press their foreheads together, speaking softly. I avert my gaze, uncomfortable to be intruding on what looks to be an incredibly intimate moment. This is the most intense "goodbye" I've ever witnessed, and we will only be gone for a week. I'm up next, and Guillermo pulls me into his large arms for a bear hug. He squeezes me so hard I feel breathless afterward.

"May the goddess Ixchel be with you and guide you on your journey," he says warmly.

"Um, thanks," I say. I have no idea who this lady Ee-Chell is he's talking about. I wave, tossing one backward glance over my shoulder as I walk out the door. "See you later, Guillermo."

He solemnly places one hand on his heart and does the sign of the cross with his other. I cock my head at the oddity of it. How strange.

Nash doesn't have the decency to wait for me and is halfway across the street, pausing briefly to let a pickup truck pass by. Quickening my pace, I hurry after him. I'm already tiring of this man, and it has only been thirty minutes. I climb inside the Jeep, and he peels away. I yank at the black strap several times before I'm able to get it buckled.

After several turns, we leave the small town of Progreso, heading east on a two-lane highway. My stupid tour guide immediately begins to fire off observations about the foliage and random landmarks in Spanish. The fact he is speaking a language other than English makes it much easier to tune him out. I have nothing to say to him, anyway.

CHAPTER 2

HOT WIND WHIPS MY hair into a frenzy around my face, but I make no move to lasso it in with a hair tie. The strands become a dark curtain shielding me from Nash. I can't believe I'm stuck with him for the next week. Closing my eyes, I try to drown out the sound of his voice. Admittedly, there is a rather soothing quality to the lilting way he speaks Spanish. It reminds me of the way my dad spoke.

My father would burst out in Spanish in moments of emotional highs and lows. It was the language of *his* heart, never mine. If I scared him by jumping off the top of a slide, it would be Spanish he'd shout out. At night when he'd tuck me in, the stories he whispered would be in Spanish. The language had been a small, but precious part of my existence. Life felt almost perfect before that summer I turned nine.

We had just gotten home from a long vacation in the Yucatán, where I'd climbed pyramids, swam in cenotes, and learned about the vast number of oddly named deities the Mayans worshipped. Our tour guide brought along his bronze-haired son who had strange blue eyes. The twelve-year-old boy barely glanced in my direction when I'd been eager for a friend. My dad promised we'd visit every year and immerse ourselves in our newly found culture. As it turned out, we never returned to the Yucatán.

I stop the flow of memories. No need to rehash the past. Instead, I return my mind to his final letter to me. I'd read that precious piece of blue lined notebook paper so many times I recall every word. I thought I was in the clear, ready to leave this sad chapter of my life behind, when a month after the funeral, the attorney handed over various documents, along with a hand-scribbled letter from my father. I'd hiked to my favorite waterfall, Abrams Falls, and opened the envelope there. I read my dad's words while the rush of water calmed my shattered nerves.

Mi hija linda, it started, using the name he always called me ... my pretty daughter. I had closed my eyes to compose myself. It was almost as if I heard his soft, gentle voice again. Fingers trembling, I continued reading.

If you are reading this letter, then that means I am dead. I don't have much time to write. I am sorry for everything. I cannot control any of it. Sometimes I am myself again for five minutes, and then I'm gone again. I wish you didn't have to spend so much of your life caring for your crazy father. It wasn't fair you bore the burden of my illness. I don't fully understand why this happened to me, but I have some idea.

I fear my condition is genetic, and I pray you find the answers before you experience it. They lie in the Yucatán. You must go back. My last gift and final request is that you experience the land and love it once more. At the end of your journey will be another letter, possibly a package. I am slowly writing a bigger explanation as I gain moments of clarity that leave me too soon. The fate of our world rests in your hands, mi hija. Siempre, te amo. Espero que nunca me odies.

That had been it. I could tell he was losing it at the end with the whole "fate of our world" crap. And my suspicion was confirmed when his language regressed to Spanish, saying he hoped I would never hate him. My dad's condition was no fault of his. I could never hate him for it. But my first reaction was an anger so intense I shook with it. How dare he think he could just send me on some random journey alone, to the place where I almost died. And I knew I would have died if he hadn't been there to save me.

Yet now, I really am completely alone. But there's a short thread of comfort knowing he provided me with a guide, a familiar person, even if I don't particularly like the man.

My guide turns and smacks me on the arm.

"Mira, muñeca." Nash points one long, bronze arm across my face. "Flamencos rosadas."

I don't like being called nicknames, especially something like "doll" by a man like Nash.

Pushing his arm away from my face, I glance in the direction he's pointing. "My name is …" My voice trails off as my eyes lock onto what he sees. In the distance, flocks of pink flamingoes stand in rose-colored water. My mouth drops open. "… holy schnikes."

His lips spread in a smile. "Te quieres parar, Holy Schnikes?"

I ignore his new nickname for me. "Yes, please. Let's stop."

Rocks crunch under the wheels of the Jeep as it slows, pulling off onto a gravel shoulder. I unbuckle my seat belt and push the car door open, my rising excitement reminiscent of my nine-year-old self.

"Quita los zapatos," Nash orders, pointing to my shoes.

I would have protested being told what to do, but I'm already busy untying and slipping off my shoes. The sharp rocks on the embankment make me wince as I step over them with my bare feet. I slow to a halt, but Nash grabs my hand and pulls me through native grasses, then red dirt and clay, until we're calf deep in shallow

24

water. Pinkish salt swirls up with every step we take until we're surrounded by impossible colors. My toes sink in salty clay.

About fifty yards away, the flamingoes glance warily in our direction, giving short honks of protest at our nearness. But we don't impose any further on their dinner and simply watch in silence as they dip their long necks and curved beaks into the still waters. The crisp, azure blue of the sky contrasts against the coral lagoon. Gray herons dive overhead, and white storks dip their tangerine beaks into the water.

I envy their freedom and lack of worry. I could stay rooted in this spot all day, if only to absorb the absolute peace of this place. My mind has been clouded with so much confusion and hurt. Maybe if I stayed here long enough, these magical waters could push the weariness, the anger, and the pain from my body, replacing darkness with calmness and clarity.

Nash and I stand there for maybe a quarter of an hour, simply watching the flocks of birds. I marvel in awed silence as some of them take flight, their bodies stretching to even longer lengths and their wings flapping strong. I breathe in deeply then release my breath in a whoosh. Nash has stood still next to me the entire time, saying nothing, doing nothing. I'm grateful he doesn't feel the need to chatter on about the Laguna Rosada, understanding some things don't require words and are only meant to be experienced.

"Listo?" he finally murmurs, reaching his hand out.

Ready?

I nod, fitting my palm against his for balance. When our hands connect, his eyebrows furrow slightly as he glances down at our linked hands. His eyes raise to meet mine for a moment before he breaks eye contact and turns, pulling me through the living poetry of the Yucatán.

Nash and I bump along the road, him saying random pieces of information in Spanish, and me looking in the complete opposite direction. Even though I pretend to ignore him, I still listen. There's so much poverty here. I see homes that are simple covered huts with just wooden posts and no walls. People walk down the road without shoes on their feet. At one point, I even see a man running through the trees wearing what looks like a loincloth. I sit up, raising my sunglasses so I can see better, but the rays of light from the setting sun wash him out.

"Do people around here seriously wear loincloths?" I blurt out, interrupting whatever Nash has been saying about the dumb trees.

His eyes slide sideways to me, and the hint of a smile twitches on his lips. "Si te quieres pagar, yo puedo."

I roll my eyes. "Horrifying."

What nerve he has suggesting I would want to pay to see him in a loincloth. Though if I'm being honest with myself, I'm sure it would be a spectacular sight. Dude is built like a bronzed Ares brought to life, all tanned skin, broad muscles, and flowing hair. That body would be a great diversion from the aching sorrow lodged in my bones.

And yet, I have no interest in exploring the ways this man could break my heart. I'm all too familiar with, and addicted to, the tingly rush of obsession and lust. It's a powerful, potent drug. Every relationship starts out that way, but in my experience, all are fated to dissolve into unspeakable sadness. I'm already sad. No need to compound it.

"Where are we going?" I shift in my seat, drawing my knees together as I face Nash. The setting sun is a blinding glare behind him, creating a halo around his head.

Silence is my answer.

"Nash," I say firmly.

He turns to me, an innocent expression on his face.

"Where are we going?" I repeat.

One shoulder raises in a shrug. "No entiendo."

He doesn't understand?

Right.

I know what he wants from me, and I'm not willing to give it. I refuse to speak Spanish when he can speak English perfectly fine. So in silence we sit, zipping along the flat road.

Just before sunset, we leave the main road and turn onto a narrow, dirt path. Within the lengthening shadows ahead lies a small village. There are no homes with four walls and a sturdy roof. These are the homes of the Maya: oval-shaped wooden huts, topped by a thatched roof. They're called palapas, Nash tells me in Spanish. Usually two stand side by side, one for cooking and one for living. We slowly drive past huts with people peering out, their faces alight with curiosity.

Nash parks the Jeep and gets out, then walks to the nearest hut. His tall frame bends low so his head can clear the doorway. My seatbelt remains buckled as I can't imagine why we're stopping here. I don't even know where our final destination is. I should have demanded an itinerary from him.

Nash's head pops out of the doorway, and he waves me over with his heavy, dark eyebrows raised in impatience. "Ines, vente."

He could have asked nicely, instead of saying "come" like I'm a street dog.

"Ordering me around … " I grumble, unbuckling my seat belt.

I'm not sure whether I should bring my bag or not, so I leave it. He should carry it for me anyway, being the tour guide and all. I slam the Jeep door behind me and stretch, squeezing all the aches from my cramped joints. Dim light of stars overhead is beginning to bleed through the cover of the darkening sky.

"Ines!" comes the impatient, male voice from the hut.

My eyes narrow. I dislike being ordered around, especially by a man like Nash who seems to think his easy-on-the-eyes appearance alone commands a woman's obedience. But I'm tired and hungry, and more than anything, I want this day to be over. Dragging my feet, I walk toward the hut, then duck my head to move through the low doorway.

In the center, an older woman sits low on the floor, expertly laying tortillas on flat rocks settled over a fire. Two hammocks hang from the walls. Nash and an older man speak softly in a language sounding nothing like Spanish, yet somehow it's familiar. There are a lot of T, L, and X sounds, and I don't understand a bit of it.

I crouch next to the older woman, and I smile in greeting. She returns my friendliness with a look of something between derision and resentment. I tilt my head, immediately offended, and move away. I can't understand the unspoken hostility. As the tortillas cook, she hands one to Nash and then another to me. Nearby lies a pot of pork covered with red sauce. Nash uses his tortilla to pick up a chunk of meat, and I copy. The meat is so tender it nearly melts away when I go to grab it. I eat three of the tacos while Nash polishes off six.

"Thank you." I meet the woman's dark eyes to convey my gratitude. "Um, gracias?"

I wish I could express my thanks in her language. A warmth brushes against my hip as Nash crouches behind me, bracketing my body between his widespread thighs. The gentle contact causes an electrical feeling to rocket up my spine.

As if he heard my unspoken thoughts, he speaks low into my ear, "Dios bo'otik."

"Dios bo'otik," I repeat, doing my best to ignore the pulsing wave in my body in response to his nearness.

The woman raises her chin and gruffly responds, "Mixba'al." The tiniest smile lifts the corners of her mouth.

"That was interesting." I pull my door shut and buckle my belt, then turn to face Nash.

He climbs in and starts the truck. As expected, he responds with his usual shrug, and begins driving carefully down the dirt road. The headlight beams illuminate the now heavy darkness.

I forge ahead, undeterred. "You *did* have me say thank you in Mayan, right? Not something ridiculous like, 'Nash is a god among men.'"

Straight, white teeth flash as a wide grin splits his face. "That wouldn't be ridiculous."

Hooting loudly, I pump my fist in the air. "Ha! English! You're speaking English! Winner, winner. Thank you, thank you." I bow to my imaginary audience.

"Cálmate. We're calling it a ... how do you say ... even Esteban." He jabs a finger in my direction.

I swat at the offending digit pointing at my face. "It's even Steven."

"Meet me halfway, Ines," he says in a low, serious voice.

Even the way he says my name with that accent, Ee-nesss. If I weren't a changed woman, I'd ask him to say it again, but more slowly. I clear my throat and shake my head, attempting to dislodge the traitorous thoughts I can't seem to control. *I am a changed woman*, I repeat my new mantra. Maybe I'll actually believe it if I say it enough.

"Why is it so important I speak Spanish, anyway?"

"It's part of your heritage, just like the language of the Maya. Your father wanted this trip to be about you learning who you are."

"I already know who I am."

"Tell me, then. Who is Ines de la Luz?"

"I am twenty-two years old and will be turning twenty-three in July. Um, I like doing yoga and I love dancing. A koala bear is my favorite animal—"

"Why?"

"Because even though it's really cute, it could kill you with its claws."

He shouts out a laugh, turning to me. "Like you, no?"

I only stare back at him, my breath going shallow. A warm glow unfurls in my chest at seeing joy move across his face. He doesn't only laugh with his mouth, he embodies laughter. It completely changes his demeanor from something harsh and brusque to something welcoming and pleasant.

"So who is Nash, um … What's your last name again?"

"Dominguez."

"Who is Nash Dominguez?"

He doesn't immediately respond, but pulls off the road and onto the grass, then puts the Jeep in park, leaving the engine idling. He regards me with a serious expression. "What you said." He grins, spreading his arms. "A god among men."

I make a huffing sound of exasperation. "All men think they're gods."

He leans in, one hand reaching for me and his arm pressing against mine between our seats. In one delicious moment of anticipation, I imagine him gripping the back of my neck and pulling my mouth to his. It would be rough, and frantic, and perfect. But his fingers only touch a few pieces of hair hanging across my face, before pushing the black strands behind my ear. I've stopped breathing again, as his hand lingers a beat too long near my jaw.

"You could be a goddess too," he says softly.

Time stops briefly but then speeds back up into reality.

"Please." I lean away. "Flattery doesn't work on me anymore."

He has the audacity to look wounded, but then he recovers. Turning forward, his hand flexes as he grips the steering wheel tightly.

"You will learn something about me, Ines." He faces me once more. "I do not flatter."

Nash kills the engine then opens his door.

"What are we doing?"

He extends a hand into the darkness. "Home for tonight."

Squinting, the shape of a thatched hut comes into view. I sit back in my seat and cross my arms. "I'm not sleeping in there, Nash."

"Sleep in the truck, then."

He slams the door and strides to the hut.

CHAPTER 3

FRUSTRATION BOILS IN MY veins. This man is the epitome of hot and cold. Why would my father do this? This entire journey feels like one big betrayal from the only person in the world who loved me. It's asking too much.

That little girl who dreamed of a life filled with grand adventures died a long time ago. Even when I was supposed to be fantasizing about fairytales, somehow I knew those things wouldn't be part of my life. Instead, I'd submerged myself in the social scene of college—partying, dancing, and drinking, getting lost in the oblivion of shallow hook-ups and random dabbling in illegal substances.

Something about arrogant, bossy men drew me in. I loved everything about going head to head with them, and seeing raw emotions explode when I pushed them over the edge. That odd fascination came with a price. I landed in the ER with a fractured collar bone at twenty years old. The first man to whom I'd uttered the words "I love you" decided punching me was a good way to communicate his jealousy. It wasn't the first time I'd been hit by a man, and truth be told, I usually had no problem hitting back. Maybe that would always be the endgame for an outspoken, stubborn woman like me. After dating a few guys, I realized my taste in men was not to be trusted.

My heart had cracked, and the fissures dug by my tears widened to an unrepairable degree. What once had been a soft, yielding thing soon frosted over, hardening into ice. The idea of finding safety in love became akin to belief in mermaids and unicorns. Some people believed in the silly notion of true love, but I no longer could. One-night stands got me what I needed from men, all while saving me from the inevitable heartache inextricably linked with a relationship. I would never put my happiness in the hands of another human being. Men became useful only for what their bodies could provide—a few moments of fleeting pleasure.

I walk to the rear of the Jeep and begin rummaging through my luggage. Once I find my toiletries, I walk into the hut where Nash has banked a small fire in the center. He lay with his eyes closed, sprawled in a hammock. A second hammock hangs across the small, circular room.

"Nash."

His eyes crack open.

"I need to use the bathroom and take a shower," I say.

"There's no bathroom and no shower." He shuts his eyes again.

"What?" I fling my arms out. My voice rings shrilly in the dark hut. "Why are we here then? What am I supposed to do?"

"You'll figure it out."

Useless man. I stomp out of the hut ineffectually, since you can't really stomp properly on dirt floors, and I glance around, looking for a good place to pop a squat. Behind the hut might offer more privacy, so I begin moving that way.

"Watch out for snakes," Nash mutters from inside the palapa.

"Oh God." I turn and go back inside, chewing the inside of my cheek as I try to figure out what to do. I squash my pride and resort to begging. "Nash, please."

"Mm?" He doesn't open his eyes.

"I can't … no snakes. Please. I really gotta go. I don't know

33

what to do." I bounce from foot to foot, part nervous energy, and partly because I need to pee so badly.

"I don't know either." Yawning, he shifts in the hammock, turning his back to me.

I wait a full ten minutes, focusing on the flames of the fire to try and distract myself from my near to bursting bladder, but I have no choice in what I do next.

"Did you just pee inside the palapa, Ines?" comes an amused voice from the still hammock.

"Um, no." I swiftly button my jean shorts, then sweep my foot across the ground, vainly trying to cover up the wet spot with loose dirt. "Go back to sleep, Nash."

He sits up, a halo of bronze hair mussed about his head. If I wasn't so mortified about the fact that he was about to see the seeping wetness on the ground, I would have mused about how freaking adorable he looked. I stand still, attempting to use my shadow cast by the low glow of firelight to cover my ghetto port-a-potty. He lifts up from the hammock and walks over to me, squinting at the dirt floor. Glancing behind me, I make sure the area is indeed in shade.

"Move," he says in a deep tone that commands obedience.

This man will learn I am not the obedient type. He's tall, but I'm also tall. I lift my chin higher, jutting it out at a stubborn angle, and set my lips in the chola sneer my friends say looks like I'm gonna shank someone with a homemade blade. I know saying no to him outright won't work, so I go for distraction. It'll buy me a few moments of time until the inevitable embarrassment follows.

"You're really tall for a Mayan. What are you, like 6'1?" I aim low, knowing his pride will force him to respond.

"6'5, and I could say the same. You're really tall for a wannabe Mayan. What are you, like 5'8?"

He's playing the same game.

"5'11 and a half, cabrón."

A look of utter surprise crosses his face upon hearing me call him a bastard in Spanish, and then he laughs loudly, eyes crinkling shut and gripping his abdomen with one arm. Heat fills my belly and spreads out to my limbs, and my heart feels both shattered and mended in that moment. I'm flooded with confusion at my response.

He steps even closer, until our chests are nearly touching.

"Step back." he says in that same tone he used earlier.

"No." I speak loudly and with force, but my voice trembles.

He fills my vision then, the wide expanse of his chest fully pressing against mine. A moment of lunacy overtakes me. Something about the size and heat of his body makes me feel both weak and protected at once. I want to throw my arms around him and burrow against his chest like a rabbit. Those big arms would be strong, and the space right above his heart would be a perfect spot to lay my cheek. Human comfort has been a weakness I thought I'd discarded long ago.

I keep my chin lifted and then raise my hands to push against the corded muscles of his chest. Stronger hands wrap around mine then pull my arms down around my back. He encircles my wrists with his thumb and forefinger before wrapping his other hand in my hair, twisting the length around and around his fist until my head is pulled back at an uncomfortable angle.

He traces his nose along the line of my jaw. Gooseflesh breaks out over my arms and ripples down my legs as his breath tickles the skin of my neck. I hold as still as possible, not even willing to breathe.

"Admit it," he whispers, warm lips against my throat. "You've thought about this all day."

Finding humor in wrong moments is a really bad habit of mine, but if I'm uncomfortable or sometimes even really sad, I end up laughing. And I happen to be very uncomfortable. It's not the position he has my arms twisted in, and no, not even that his hand is wrapped in my hair and steadily pulling with just the right amount of delicious pressure. The discomfort is in feeling myself unraveling. I imagine myself relaxing, letting my head fall further back and giving in to him. I'd be putty, warm and moldable, between his palms. And then, he'd destroy me. Laughter bubbles out, then explodes from my mouth in a loud, throaty sound.

He releases the grip of both hands at once. I take a stumbling step back, attempting to distance myself from this current state of mind.

He runs one shaky hand down his face then a derisive expression curls his lips. "Anyway, I don't sleep with women who don't know who they are. Are you a gringa, a Maya, or a dog who pisses on the floor of someone's home?"

"Screw you, Nash."

"Ah, too bad. You lost that chance."

He moves back further then turns away, shoving his hand through his hair. He drops into the hammock, fidgeting briefly before standing again.

His eyes meet mine. "All that sound of pissing ... Vamanós."

That ordering tone again, telling me let's go. It makes me want

36

to throw a clump of dirt at his head, preferably the one I peed in. But for some reason, be it utter stupidity or sheer curiosity, I follow his wide back out the doorway.

We walk in silence through tall grasses. The gibbous moon grows rounder with each passing day, but lights up the night with enough of its lunar glow to reveal a footpath. I tilt my head up, and my eyes fill with the blackness and light of the Mayan cosmos. Darkness sprinkled with tiny bits of history and future. Ahead, a small building comes into view.

"I will now piss like a civilized man," Nash says with a smirk.

There's an outhouse.

My mouth drops open in disbelief. "You jerk."

The door slams shut as he steps through, sealing his chuckle of laughter behind the thin wood. I fume for a moment. There probably isn't a lock on that flimsy wooden door. I reach down for a nearby clump of tall grass and pull, bringing up the grass along with roots caked in sandy dirt. Sure enough, when I tug on the handle, the door opens easily. In the darkness, I can't see, but I throw my wad of dirt and grass, then release the door so it bangs shut. A hiss of exclamations and curses in Spanish follows.

"Ines!" comes a roar from the other side.

The door flies open, and Nash explodes from the outhouse in a furious rush, while buttoning his jeans.

I don't even try to run from him. It would be useless. But with every step forward he takes, I shuffle back, all the while speaking in a rush.

"That's what you deserved, Nash. You knew this was here the entire time, and you said there was no bathroom. You freaking bastard! I humiliated myself by peeing on the ground in the palapa. Is there really no shower too? Or are you also lying about—"

He rushes on me then, lowering his head to catch my waist with his shoulder. And then he's running, me tossed over his back like a blasted cavewoman, his hands firmly gripping the backs of my thighs. I scream and kick and howl, beating ineffectively on his back. I'm not going down without a fight.

After about a minute of my airborne tantrum, something changes, and he begins going down a set of wooden stairs. For my own safety, I stop kicking. I decide to give him a good old-fashioned wedgie by reaching in the back of his jeans. My fingers shove down the waistband of his pants, but I find only warm, smooth skin.

The man apparently goes commando.

He hisses out an exclamation. "Jesu Christo, Ines. I already said no."

There is no good comeback for that. I sag in defeat, all while wishing I were dead. I'm glad he can't see my face, because my cheeks heat with embarrassment. The sky retreats above, set in a circular outcropping of trees and roots.

Fear slams into me as I realize where he's taken us. We've descended into a cenote, which is a natural limestone swimming hole. The clear water reaches hundreds of feet deep. The Yucatán is littered with countless beautiful, hidden cenotes. However, the last time I swam in one of these, I almost died.

Panic flies into my chest then comes out in a rush of words. "No, Nash, please. I'm sorry. Anything but this. Please don't, please—"

And then I'm airborne, only for a second, but in that moment the nightmares plaguing me for years unravel before my eyes. I hit the water with a screaming splash, then go under. Silence and liquid darkness envelope my senses. My head breaks the surface, and then I'm clawing for the nearest dock. The moon illuminates the space just enough to see Nash there, pulling his shirt over his head, then kicking off his jeans and diving in.

I scissor my legs and reach for the dock, filled with that intense, gripping fear of something chasing me. It's coming so close. I can feel it on my feet. And then it wraps around my ankles, pulling me under. I scream, but it's silent as oxygen escapes in bubbles from my lungs. I don't care that I'm letting out all my precious air. I just shout and kick and kick until my head breaks the surface. My hands connect with the dock, and I cling to it, harshly sobbing out screams that echo in the hollow cavern.

"Ines, what is—"

"Please, get me out, Nash." I gasp, my voice a throaty shudder. "Please. I can't—"

One of his hands reaches under me, gripping my thigh just under my butt, and then he hefts me into the air to deposit me firmly onto the wooden dock of my salvation. I shake and sob while lying on the rough wood. I feel so weak … so unlike myself. I'm soaking wet and having a mental breakdown in front of the most gorgeous, arrogant guy I've ever met. This may be the lowest point of my life. All my shame transforms into anger. I sit up and unleash my fury on him.

"How dare you," I hiss, tears streaking my face.

I'm certain I look a terrifying sight in the glowing moonlight, since my carefully applied eyeliner and mascara from that morning have probably run down my face.

"You wanted to bathe." He crosses his arms, resting them on the edge of the dock to hold him steady in the water.

"What if I didn't know how to s-swim, Nash?" I hiccup out a sob mid-sentence.

"I just saw you swim."

"That's not the point, tonto!"

He rolls his eyes. "That is the second time in my life I've been called a fool, Ines. I don't like it."

"And I don't like … everything *you*!" I shout, then slam my fists on the dock. I'm so embarrassed to be crying in front of him. "This isn't me. I don't freaking cry! I've been with you for all of what? Five, six hours—"

"Five beautiful hours, *in k'áat*."

"Eeen cot back at you," I grit out through my teeth with as much anger as I can muster.

I have no idea what he called me in Mayan, but I just threw it back at him. Hopefully it's something terrible.

He responds with laughter and shoves away from the dock. I draw in a deep, shaky breath, calming slightly. I look up at the sky, nearly chandelier-like with the amount of visible stars. It's one of the most beautiful sights I've seen. That is, if I weren't near the depths of hell. I tuck my feet under me so not even my toes can touch the water.

To my right lay a pile of abandoned clothes. Nash's jeans and t-shirt. The ball has entered my court. Now I can humiliate him by making him run back to the palapa butt naked.

I stand, stretching my arms and arching my spine as I peek over at him. Nash floats peacefully on his back in the water. I make a quick sidestep, grab his clothes, then jog up the two flights of rickety stairs.

When I get to the top, I glance around looking for the glow of fire from the palapa. There it is, about a hundred yards away. I sprint away from the cenote and head straight to the Jeep for my spare change of clothes, knowing I don't have much time.

I strip off my wet shirt and shorts then shimmy into my pajama shorts and tank top. After wringing out my soaked clothing, I drape them over the Jeep door. A moment later, he's there, appearing next to me like a phantasm from the underworld. Water streams from his hair and rivulets run down his chest and stomach. I keep my widened eyes pinned to his face. And he just waits for me to say something.

"Um … here, uhh." I turn and grab the wad of his clothing from the trunk then thrust it in his direction without turning to look.

He rips the clothes from my grasp and uses them to dry off, moving as if he has all the time in the world.

"If you wanted to see me naked, Ines, all you had to do was ask," he says in a low, dangerous voice.

A short, hysterical laugh sounding like a dying mouse escapes me, and I stand frozen. Nash reaches into the trunk to find his bag, then he unzips it and pulls out spare clothing. Taking a step back, I slide slowly away from him.

Well, that fine plan backfired. I walk into the palapa then head to the second hammock and lower myself in. Nash's presence fills the room shortly after, but he says nothing as he drops into his own hammock. Fire crackles and pops, casting dancing shadows along the walls. Minutes pass and neither of us speak. While I was comfortable with the silence earlier, now it's just a pressure I need to pierce.

I clear my throat. "Nash, I need to explain what happened at the cenote."

I inhale and cast my eyes in his direction, waiting for him to say something snarky.

A grumbled murmur from him signals me to continue speaking.

"You remember when my dad and I came here, right?"

"How could I forget? I was being stalked by a nine-year-old."

"Why were you so mean to me anyway?"

He sighs and rubs his hand over his head. "I was just acting like a dumb kid, Ines. I thought you were pretty."

His confession renders me momentarily mute. I'm suddenly flooded by the simple but awkward feelings of a girl who just wanted a boy to be her friend.

"So what happened?" he asks.

I clear my throat. "The last day, on our way to the airport, my dad stopped at some random cenote. Not one of the touristy ones. The sun was straight overhead and shining into the water. You could almost see to the bottom. I jumped in and then something happened." I inhale sharply, squeezing my eyes shut as the memory fills my mind. "It—it … The water got really bubbly. I don't know how to describe it. Almost like a hot tub. Something wrapped around my ankles then pulled me under. The sound … I'll never forget it, like the earth was screaming. My dad grabbed my arm and we were just descending so fast to the bottom. Thankfully"—I laugh slightly— "my dad is so old school. Well …" I pause for a moment, feeling like I've been sucker punched in the stomach. "… he *was* old school, I mean."

Saying that aloud hurts.

I swallow hard, then continue. "He always kept a pocket knife in his shorts, and he went to town on whatever dragged me under. He even cut me a few times. I still have the scars." My fingers brush the raised, sensitive marks around my ankles. "But he got me loose. I lost all my air by screaming, so he had to do CPR on me when he got me to the dock. It was … yeah. That's why I'm so afraid of cenotes."

Nash doesn't say anything for a few moments, and his dark gaze drops to the ground.

Until finally, "I'm sorry."

The words seem difficult for him to get out. I have the feeling it's rare to hear those words from him.

"Even Esteban?" I say tentatively, searching for his eyes.

He rewards me with a smile. "Even Esteban."

CHAPTER 4

A WARM, DRY BREEZE blows through the hut, and the scent of tortillas cooking over a fire carries on the air. Nash's hammock lies empty. The Jeep is gone, but my luggage stands inside the doorway. After using the outhouse, I brush my teeth then change into a pair of linen shorts and a turquoise tank top.

Running a comb through my hair, a soft chuckle escapes me as I remember Nash's embarrassment when Guillermo said his son always thought my long hair was pretty. Usually, the promise of heat would have me putting it in a braid or wrapping it into a high bun on my head, but today I leave it loose.

After waiting a bit longer, I chew the inside of my cheek and experience the briefest moment of panic, thinking Nash has left me entirely and he's driven back to Progreso. Maybe my dramatics at the cenote were too much for him. But even as I fret, I hear the rumbling engine of his Jeep. He's installed the top and sides on the vehicle, so it's no longer completely open.

The engine stops and the door shuts with a soft thud. Nash strides in, dressed in dark wash jeans and a black t-shirt. The fluttering sensation low in my stomach reminds me I'm not immune to his good looks, and I instantly loathe him for his beauty.

In his hands he carries a bowl and a cup, along with a folded white cloth in the crook of his elbow. He hands me the food and drink, and I murmur my thanks. Two corn tortillas lay on top of the bowl, and underneath is a mixture of beans, eggs, and plantain. I tear off a piece of the tortilla and scoop up the mixture, then chew happily, before sipping carefully at the hot coffee.

"So what we doing today?" I use a piece of tortilla to grab another bite of the slightly spicy mixture and stuff it in my mouth.

Nash sits on the opposite hammock, still cradling the white cloth, elbows resting on knees. "Today, we help the villagers call to Chaac, the rain god. There's been a drought, and this is what will end it."

"You really believe that stuff?"

The haughty look returns to his face. "You really believe in God Almighty who created the earth in seven days?"

I look down at my bowl, sopping up the last of the food with my remaining tortilla. "Honestly, I don't know what I believe anymore, Nash."

"You need to understand something. My belief in multiple gods is no different from you believing in one or three, or whatever you people believe. Both are based on something we cannot see, and a record we choose to trust."

He has a point, but I'm not about to admit that aloud.

I set down my bowl then point to the bundle in his hands. "What's that?"

He waves his hand like it's not a big deal, but the way he looks down and chews his lip for a moment tells me this is something of importance to him. Reverently, he unfolds the cloth, then holds it up to show me a dress. The long gown is designed in the traditional Yucatecan manner.

"My offering of peace to make up for yesterday." The heaviness of his gaze pins on me as he weighs my reaction to the indigenous design. "This is a huipil."

The white dress is composed of three panels, with yellow, coral, red, and blue flowers. Various lacy designs border the bottom of each panel and line the square cut neckline. I stand from the hammock and move toward where he's sitting, then run my fingers along the silky fabric and brightly colored flowers. "It's incredible."

"This dress was made on a loom by one of the women in this village. It's a lot of work. The flowers are even stitched by hand. I thought you might like to wear it for the ritual today …" He hesitates for a moment then says in a rush, "… if you want to. If you don't, I understand."

I grab the dress from his hands and smile as I hold it against my chest. "I'd love to wear it. Thanks."

In his eyes, I can see this means more to him than he's letting on. He inclines his head then walks backward a couple steps to the entrance of the hut, before turning to lean against the doorframe. His back turned to me, he begins to whistle a tune I don't recognize while waiting for me to change.

After pulling off my shorts and tank top, I slide the cotton dress over my head. The garment whispers down my body, where the hem rests below my knee. On a Mayan woman, the dress would probably be ankle length, as most of them are around five feet in height. Regardless, I feel beautiful in this cultural treasure.

"How does it look?" I ask Nash, letting him know I'm done.

He turns, still whistling. The tune dies on his lips, and he raises his sunglasses so he can look at me fully. Momentarily self-conscious, I run my hands over my hair, then smooth down the dress.

A smile transforms his face. "Perfect."

Pleasure sparks in my chest upon seeing his reaction, and I can't help but return his smile. "So step one, we summon Chaac. Then what?"

"Then it rains."

At 7 a.m. the full sun promises dense heat. Nash gives the slightest jerk of his head as a signal for me to follow. I bristle at the silent command but trudge after him. We pass the cenote from the night before then follow a well-worn path through the verdant jungle. Overall, the entire Yucatán peninsula is a dry, infertile land, but this area is different. Low lying palms and heavy stones line the carefully laid path we tread. In the distance, tops of stone structures rise above the treetops.

"Is that a pyramid?" My voice raises in unconcealed excitement.

As a nine-year-old girl, the pinnacle of our vacation had been climbing the steep pyramids.

"Sí," Nash says, smiling at my enthusiasm. He stops at the end of the palm-lined path and sweeps his arm toward the stone ruins. "This is called X'tambo. It is small, but it is one of my favorite sites."

"Sh-tam-bow." I repeat, rolling the odd sounds over my tongue.

"Also called X'tampu, depending on who you ask. Maya was not a written language. It was repeated, and then depending on who translated it, that's how it was written."

Pale stone structures lay scattered around a massive, grassy clearing. Young palm trees outline the inside of the manicured center, with some mature palms scattered throughout. I hurry to the edge then turn to Nash.

"Is it okay to climb it?"

He gives a slight bow of his head and a gleam enters his eyes. "Can you beat me up there, gringa?"

"Probably not." I narrow my eyes at hearing him call me a white foreigner again and point behind him. "What's that?"

When he turns, I push him as hard as I can then bolt up the stairs. The small steps feel unnatural and uncomfortable, so I skip them, taking three at a time. Nash blows past me with incredible speed. Needless to say, he beats me to the top.

"Can't even cheat and win," I whine, breathing raggedly as I rest my hands on my knees.

Nash laughs, looking smug. His breathing isn't altered in the slightest. We are above the treetops, and to the north is the gulf coast. The ocean is a brilliant ribbon of blue stretching across the horizon. In the center of the platform, a weathered, crooked cross is set in a pile of stones, stacked around the wood to hold it in place. The Christian idol seems out of place and doesn't look to be original to the design of the structure, but rather something additional.

I point to the relic. "What's with the cross?"

He lifts one corner of his mouth in slight grimace. "Survival. Spanish came in 1500, which forced us to co-exist with Catholicism."

That explains why Guillermo mentioned a Mayan goddess one moment and made the sign of the cross in the next. I move around the top of the structure, examining the edge. None of the pyramids come to a point like the ones in Egypt. Rather, they are truncated, looking like someone lopped off the tops, but the design is intentional.

"They built temples up here." Nash shoves his hands in his pockets and walks along the edges of the platform, showing me where wooden posts would be placed in order to create a thatched frame covering an altar. He gives me a measured look. "Then they would do rituals and sacrifices."

"No." My lips curl in disgust. "You guys really sacrificed people?"

He scoffs. "Who didn't? Everyone sacrificed people. Even now, you sacrifice people."

"Americans do not sacrifice people."

"What happens to the people sent to war? Isn't that human sacrifice?"

I shake my head, slightly stuttering as I protest. "That—that's war. It's for the greater good."

He looks down at me. "And preventing a drought isn't for the greater good?"

"What you're talking about is straight murder, though."

"And war is your government murdering sons and daughters without getting their hands dirty. What is the difference, Ines?"

He asks the question, not gently, but harshly and pointedly. For some reason, it's really important to him that I think about this. So I ponder for a few moments, imaging the ancient Mayans on the uppermost heights of their temples, spilling the blood of countless numbers of men, women, and children. I'm sure they believed their gods looked down on them in approval. Delusion and superstition fueled those murders. I can't compare war to heartless bloodshed; however, I imagine the weight of lives lost tips the scales more against wars fought over millennia.

"Life is life," Nash insists, his gaze fast on me.

I purse my lips, nodding my head in a slight concession. "So it is. If we're going to look at it that way."

"What other way is there to look at it?"

"Motive, reward …" I throw up my hands in frustration. "I don't really know!"

"Calm down, Ines." He grins at me, then. "The Maya do not sacrifice humans anymore."

"Came to your senses, huh?"

He shrugs and purses his lips, a look of resignation crossing his features. "No. It's illegal now."

We trot down the steps of the pyramid to explore the rest of the site, continuing to walk through the ruins as the orange Mayan sun climbs higher in the sky, casting off a rising, thick heat. A fat iguana meanders around the grassy clearing, acting like he owns the place. Off to the side, a white building catches my attention.

We come to the front of a small white chapel with a thatched roof. The small building is adorned with modest, three tier towers topped by crosses on both sides. Nash ducks his head to enter the squared doorway, and my head barely clears it. Ahead lies a sacrificial table about hip high, with a large stone slab as the top. I slide myself on it then lie down, crossing my arms over my chest.

"Look, I'm a human sacrifice," I say to Nash.

He walks up to the table and looks down at me with a wide smile. "Don't tempt me."

We leave X'tambo from the opposite side we arrived and walk through the deciduous forest once more. A large palapa filled with women comes into view. We've returned to the village entrance in a roundabout way. Children run around outside, oblivious to the rising heat. Women sit on low rocks next to fires scattered throughout the hut, busily rolling out tortillas and laying them on flat rocks. The heat rolling from the fires combined with the natural Yucatán heat must be intense. Sweat drips from their faces and sizzles onto the stones.

A short way in the distance beneath the shade of several tall trees, a wooden table fashioned from sturdy branches is adorned with leafy vines and garlands of red, pink, and fuscia flowers. A fire sends up smoke beneath it, and wooden bowls lie on top.

"Only men do this ritual," Nash explains as he leads the way to a bench against the outer wall of the palapa and motions for me to sit. "No women or children should be present, but they can watch. Over there"—he points to the wooden table—"that is the kanche', or altar bench, to Chaac, god of rain. Do you see los calabazas on top?"

I nod, seeing the gourds. Each are filled with some food or drink.

"What's in them?" I ask, squinting slightly. There's a bowl of water, another bowl of darker colored liquid, and something wrapped in leaves.

"Different drinks and foods for Chaac."

"What's the point? He can't eat it."

The full weight of his attention shifts to me, and then he sighs out a long-suffering exhale. "In your Christian religion, the first man and woman were created from what?"

"Dirt."

"The Maya story of creation says the first humans were made from white and yellow corn. Corn is sacred. It feeds us. The gods give it to us. So we show our thanks by returning it to them and hope they will answer our prayers."

"And if it doesn't work?"

He rubs his jaw with one hand and leans against the palapa, crossing his arms and grinning. "Humans are made from corn, remember?"

I nod, unsure where he's going with this.

"If the original source doesn't work, then we try a different form."

"Ah, here we are again. Human sacrifices," I murmur. "You heathen."

He winks then walks away to join the other men.

CHAPTER 5

RAIN WOULD FALL, HE had promised. I wait in expectation throughout the heat of the day with the other women in the palapa. The children maintain a respectful silence, but sometimes one or two would slip out of the palapa and run toward the village. Part of me wishes I could run back there with them and kick a ball around, while my cynical half wants to watch the failure of this senseless ritual.

A crystal blue sky, clear and cloudless, stretches as far as the eye can see. The sun shines high overhead. No rain will fall from those heavens, of that I am sure. I wonder what Nash's explanation for the derelict rain god will be. I smile as I chew a warm, soft tortilla filled with meat and chiles, imagining him flustered and making excuses for his absent god.

I glance over at the altar and see Nash crouched near a rock, holding a gourd in his hands. He cradles it with the reverence one might use when holding a newborn, his dark head bowed over the bowl. Minutes bleed into long, still hours, and yet the men persist in their low chants. The dense heat from both the cooking fires and the unforgiving sun has the women's hair plastered to their necks and foreheads with sweat. And still, they continue their work of nourishing the village.

A sudden, strong breeze blows through, the wind peeling off a layer of the burdening heat. Everyone seems lighter as the women look up, smiling and chattering excitedly. The sun appears to be swallowed up as the sky darkens.

I step tentatively from the hut. Wind whips even harder, ripping dry leaves and small twigs from surrounding trees. My long hair wraps around my body like a cocoon. Shielding my eyes from the billowing dust and debris, I look up at a once blue sky that has now filled with angry, roiling clouds. Thunder booms directly overhead before the clouds split open, scattering down torrents of rain. Within seconds, fat raindrops soak my hair and seep through the fabric of my dress, but I stand in awe, arms spread and face turned up to the heavens.

Everyone rushes out of the palapa, save for a few women who have no time for this kind of nonsense. Once parched, dusty ground turns into squishy mud between my toes. Children slide around, screaming in joy. Men run into the hut and grab their women, tossing them over their shoulders or dragging them into the rain.

My gaze wanders the clearing, searching for Nash. I find him standing still at the altar, eyes locked on me. My initial impulse is to turn away, but I feel pulled to him by some unexplainable force. Rivulets of water stream down my face and drip from my hair and eyelashes as I walk toward him. His black shirt and jeans are soaked, clinging to his large, muscular frame. I can only imagine how I look wearing this thin, white dress. A flicker of heat ignites in his eyes as his gaze runs over me.

"It's raining," I say stupidly.

"Eh?" He cups his hand around his ear like he can't hear me. "What did you say? Nash was right?"

I laugh and shake my head. "No. You're going deaf."

A shout of deep laughter explodes from him.

We leave the village and take a narrow road southeast. Nash says it's about three more hours of driving until we reach Playa del Carmen. A ferry will bring us to our next destination, the island of Cozumel. I look around the now enclosed vehicle, remembering he installed the soft top roof right before the Chaac ritual. Purely coincidental. He didn't know it would rain.

Nash notices my inspection of the interior. "You okay?"

"You checked the weather forecast, didn't you?"

His eyebrows raise as an amused expression comes onto his face.

"How? It's not like I have a laptop, or the village has internet service. And my phone is just a regular one." He reaches into the storage section above the radio then holds up his flip phone.

I breathe out a huff of exasperation and cross my arms. "That was a whole lotta coincidence."

He shrugs. "Okay."

It's odd how easily he gives up trying to convince me of the validity of his rituals. I narrow my eyes, trying to figure out where the trap is. But he doesn't say anything for a while as we pass village after village.

Nash finally breaks the silence after ten minutes in the car. "Tell me about your father's parents."

"Easy," I respond with a shrug. "From what my dad said, they were killed in a car accident when he was seven. He was with a neighbor. After that, a family in the United States adopted him. But they couldn't handle him. He ended up getting moved from foster home to foster home for a while. He met my mom in foster care when he was seventeen. They ran away together. And then lived happily ever after until I came along."

"Why until you?"

This is a painful part of my past I don't ever, *ever* talk about. I'm not sure why I choose to do it now, but I do. I'm trying to be a changed woman in many ways. Burying my pain has only served to sprout more sadness. I grip my hands together, squeezing my fingers as I gather my thoughts.

"Well, they struggled for so long to get pregnant and then gave up because they thought they would just never be able to have a baby. My mom was thirty-seven when she got pregnant with me." I laugh softly. "She was already four months along when they found out. And then, I ended up being a huge baby. My mom pushed for three hours before they did an emergency C-section. I weighed eleven pounds, four ounces. Anyway, my mom ended up hemorrhaging inside her body. They didn't even know until she was already dead." I open my arms, trying to dispel some of the heaviness of what I said. "And ta-da, here I am. No more happily ever after."

"Ines …" Nash says softly, shaking his head. "You know your dad was happy to have you and that he loved you, right?"

I shrug one shoulder, biting my inner cheek as I stare out the window. "He would always say, 'Muñeca, I would never trade you. Ever.' But I can't help but think how I'd feel if my baby killed the person I loved. There's gotta be some resentment, right?"

"No. Sure he was sad, but you were a gift. I don't think someone can really understand until they are a parent, but I'm sure even your mom was happy to give her life for you."

My jaw hurts with how hard I'm clenching it, trying to keep my emotions under control. I turn toward the window and lean my head against the glass. As much as I appreciate him trying to make me feel better, they're just words I've been told before. But it doesn't change the fact that in my coming to life, I murdered my mother.

We travel for another hour, when I notice we're driving through a town where every single building is a golden yellow color, a seemingly intentional design. The small and humble town is well-manicured and clean. Block after block of houses and buildings of yellow pass by. And then we come to an intersection where ahead to the left is a massive pyramid, its base beginning mere feet from the roadway.

"Oh my gosh." I sit up straight, leaning over the armrest as I stare out Nash's window.

We continue driving down the block, yellow houses along the right side of the street and a gigantic pyramid to the left on the east side. My eyes soak in the strange sight of this pyramid in the middle of a town. It's so surreal and seems like it doesn't belong, yet somehow the structure fits in so perfectly in this small, golden city. The base is huge, at least 750 feet on one side. Nash turns left, leaving the pyramid behind us, and there are only yellow buildings once more.

I hold up my finger. "I know you did not just drive past a pyramid and not let me get out and climb it."

"I did."

"Turn around!" I yell, smacking his arm.

"So demanding." He chuckles but then turns left at the next street, heading back to the pyramid.

Nash parks in a shady spot, and we get out. No rain fell over here, so the hard-packed earth is covered in brown, dry grass. Some trees have leaves, while others are bare, their brown bark cracked and parched.

"Looks like they need some Chaac up in here," I say cheekily.

Nash shoots me a glance and snorts out a short laugh, shaking his head.

"So, give me the history on this one," I say as we skirt one of the wide, crumbling staircases.

"This city is called Izamal, and it honors the god of creation, Itzamná, and the sun god, Kinich Ahau. That is why the entire city is painted yellow, to honor the sun god. This pyramid is for Kinich Kakmo, the bird form of the sun god." Nash stops just before the second column of stairs. "Mirá."

Look.

He hops up on the large slab and crouches, extending his hand to me. I take a high step up and grab his hand to pull myself up beside him. He motions for me to crouch then points to the underside of the next level of overhanging bricks. Yellow paint.

"This pyramid used to be covered in smooth stucco and painted yellow."

"Amazing," I say on an exhale. "So tell me more about this sun god of yours."

As we walk along the massive base, he randomly kicks trash and loose stones away from the pyramid and toward the street. "Kinich Ahau is considered the god of medicine and healing. He looked like a guero, with his pale skin, blonde hair, and blue eyes."

I glance at him. "Says the blue-eyed guero." My lips curve in a teasing smile.

He grins, but doesn't rise to my baiting. "A little known fact about Kinich Ahau is that he was a shaman. It is said that some shamans were so powerful they could turn into animals."

I snort out a laugh. "So he could become a werewolf and howl at the moon?"

Nash raises his eyebrows. "Something like that."

As we continue walking, I try to imagine what this massive structure looked like a thousand years ago. What were people's lives like? Did life just carry on around this thing, much like it does today? At the top of the pyramid, I can make out figures, and from my vantage point, I swear I see someone wearing an elaborate headdress.

"Look!" I point up to the top.

Nash glances up, then back down at me in question. "What did you see?"

"They must be doing something up there. Did you see that massive thing on that guy's head?" My hands frame the ridiculous dimensions of the feather headdress I saw.

We reach the north side of the pyramid, but the stairs are in no condition for climbing. I jog around to the west side, where the steps are more defined and secure, and then begin making my way up. Something is definitely going on up there, because I hear a faint drum beat and hushed chanting. I move faster, and my thigh muscles burn. This pyramid is so much bigger than the one in X'tambo.

Finally, I reach the top, breathing raggedly, but nothing is there. I race to the opposite side of the platform, thinking maybe they're going down the other way, but I see nothing. Eyes wide in confusion, I turn, and Nash is standing there, having just reached the top. I squeeze the bridge of my nose between my thumb and forefinger.

"I'm sorry," I say on a soft laugh. "I'm going crazy, apparently."

He doesn't say anything but continues looking at me, eyes squinting and lips slightly pursed as if he's trying to figure me out. I turn away, feeling silly and stupid for running up this blasted thing.

Nash comes up behind me and gently squeezes my shoulders, then drops his hands to his sides. Standing behind me, he points forward to the east, where a huge yellow plaza is framed by a wall with cut out arches. Beyond is the wide, flat expanse of the Yucatán. He points in each direction, naming ancient and modern names of cities. This is my history and my culture. I feel the familiarity in my bones, and my heart is slowly catching up.

"Ines."

A firm shake on my shoulder pulls me from my sleep. I come awake, a short gasp escaping me. My heart beats wildly and a familiar ache throbs between my legs. Rubbing my eyes, I sit up.

"You okay?" Nash says, an odd, half smile on his face. "You're looking at me like this." He opens his eyes wide and crosses them.

The silly expression makes me smile. I relax a little bit. I probably *was* looking at him like that. What a weird dream I had. I shake my head trying to clear its remnants from my mind. We must be in Playa del Carmen. The Jeep is in a parking lot and turned off.

"Our ferry leaves soon," Nash says.

The clock on the dash reads 18:00. It's already 6 pm. We spent long hours in the hot sun exploring the city of Izamal, which completely zapped my energy.

After boarding the ferry, we head to the open-air upper deck. Nash watches with critical eyes as the ferry workers drive his Jeep onboard. The sun is close to setting, but I'm wide awake after my long nap. Nash dozes on the seat next to me for the thirty-minute ride, and I think about the odd dream I had while we were driving.

It was like I was in another person's body, but I wasn't me. When I looked down, I was completely naked up top and only wore a skirt tied around my waist. Instinctively, I tried to cover my breasts, but I had no control of my body. The woman was sitting at a stone table, sorting leaves. And then her head lifted.

She knew he was there. Warm, large arms came around her chest. That feeling that rose inside her felt as potent as any drug. She loved being in his arms. His hands pulled her hair to the side, and his lips found the back of her neck. Every day it was like this when he returned to her. She closed her eyes, reveling in the feel of him. His hands found her waist, and he spun her about to face him. His blue eyes met hers, and he grinned before capturing her lips with his. Her fingers tangled in his hair as he laid her across the stone slab, crushing her precious leaves beneath her now bare body. She didn't mind. She knew where to find more of the medicine later.

And then Nash woke me up right when it got to the good part. The only "problem" with my dream is the man looked like him, yet I knew it wasn't him. It was odd. The woman's intense feelings for the man make my heart ache just thinking of it.

When the ferry docks, it's my turn to shake Nash awake. He groans and leans forward, resting his elbows on his knees as he scrubs his palms against his tired eyes. Bronze strands of his hair fall over his forehead, and my fingers itch to move them away. His gray T-shirt stretches to accommodate the width of his shoulders. Rays from the setting sun stretch out over us, and his skin glows golden in its dying light.

I give a few friendly pats on his broad back to encourage him to get moving, and then my hand settles in the space between his shoulder blades. My fingernails lightly trace a line halfway down his spine. I tell myself to stop, not to touch him because it's weird, but it's like I have no control over myself. He freezes but doesn't stand or shrug my hand off. I press in harder, rubbing up to his shoulders, alternately squeezing the thick muscles near his neck. I end by running my fingernails up his scalp then giving him a little slap on the back of the head, forcing us from the moment.

I stand. "Let's go. I'll send you a bill for that massage later."

CHAPTER 6

THE HEART OF COZUMEL thrums with the beat of activity from restaurants, nightclubs, and resorts. We pass signs advertising snorkeling, zip lining, and even swimming with stingrays, which does not sound fun to me.

The coastal highway leads to the southeastern part of the island. A glorious ocean breeze tangles my hair through the rolled down windows. The lights, sounds, and busy activity of the city fade in the distance, and then it's just Nash and me with the sound of waves crashing against the rocky shore in the distance. The sun falls completely below the horizon, spreading a divine palette of colors throughout the sky.

My dad and I hadn't come to the island of Cozumel when we were here fourteen years ago. The realization makes me ache with missing him. He would never see this beautiful place.

The memory of the week we returned home from the Yucatán fourteen years ago rises in my mind. That was when our lives changed forever.

"Dad?" I called as I knocked on the locked door.

My father wasn't waiting for me at the bus stop. Usually, he was there, because he didn't like me walking the winding mountain roads to our home alone. It was unlike him to forget me. I rummaged around our rickety wooden porch until I found the key stashed in one of his old work boots, and let myself in, noting his jacket hanging on the hook in its usual spot. So he was home.

The low rumble of his voice drifted from upstairs, as if he were talking softly on the phone. An uneasy feeling settled in the pit of my stomach. I walked up the stairs and peeked into his room. He sat on the edge of his bed speaking in Spanish, eyes staring unseeing, but he held no phone in his hand. It wasn't until I stood in front of him and clapped a few times that he came out of it. But for an hour after that, he could only speak Spanish.

The strange episodes continued at random throughout my teenage years. Afterward, he'd only be able to speak Spanish for a couple hours. The language that once seemed so comforting had turned into something I feared. Sometimes he'd come back around holding a piece of notebook paper full of odd symbols inside square shapes. My father claimed he was having confusing and frightening visions of the past. He couldn't make sense of what he saw.

Thanks to high school Spanish class, I understood more of what he said. He spoke complete and utter nonsense. One time I even made an audio recording of him talking and played it back to my Spanish teacher, hoping maybe I missed something with my basic understanding of the language. My teacher furrowed his brows and said it sounded like fairytales.

Little by little, the bouts of insanity outweighed the moments of lucidity. He completely lost his ability to speak English. From then on, Spanish became the only language spoken. Communicating became difficult, but I adjusted. By pure necessity, my ability to speak Spanish caught up to his. But sometimes he'd speak a language I'd never heard before, and I assumed he made it up.

When I turned seventeen, he received a diagnosis of stage five Alzheimer's disease. My father moved into a care facility, while I left for college on the other side of the country. I'd fly back home to Tennessee and visit for major holidays, but it seemed pointless. Heavy doses of anti-psychotics removed the last traces of the man I knew. Sometimes he'd get violent, engaging in a battle with some unseen foe. The first time I watched him be subdued, restrained, and then sedated, I thought I would never recover emotionally. And maybe I never did. My father, my rock, my everything, became reduced to a man who couldn't speak coherently and lost control of his bowels and bladder.

I still remember that first time he looked at me when I came to visit. He smiled politely and asked my name. My words choked out of my throat like I'd swallowed a lump of sand.

Tears prickle behind my eyes as the memory releases me. I sniff in sharply and stare out my window at the darkening sky as spots of starlight emerge. The Jeep slows and turns right, pulling into a gravel driveway. A circular driveway leads directly to the front door, where small plants in colorful pots decorate the entrance. Mature palms are scattered all over the property. The two-story house has a white stucco exterior with large glass windows lining entire lengths of the first level. We come to a stop.

"Wow," I say on a soft breath, shutting the Jeep door. "This place is gorgeous."

"Thanks." Nash shoots me a sideways smile. "This is my place."

My eyes dart to him in surprise. I didn't expect a young bachelor to own a house.

"Two bedrooms upstairs with their own bathroom. Rooftop patio. The beach is right out the back," Nash says brightly. "It's not sandy though. It's all rocky cliffs, but there's a dock with stairs leading straight into the water."

Nash pushes open the black entrance door, motioning me to pass in front of him. On the entry wall is a large, gilded mirror in the shape of the sun, with a crescent moon inset within the face. I stare at the beautiful bronze color while tracing the edges of the sun's rays. My eyes meet my own reflection, and I hastily smooth down my windswept hair.

The first floor is a great room, with a living area to the left and an open kitchen to the right. The U-shaped kitchen has cherry wood, black granite countertops, and stainless steel appliances. The wall leading to the back is made entirely of glass. In front of the glass wall is a large, farm style dining table with seating for eight. Out back, a manicured lawn is scattered with potted palms and colorful plants. And beyond lies the sea.

Nash grabs my bag and points to the wide, marble stairs next to the entryway. "Let me show you your room."

I follow him up the stairs and to the right. He sets my bag on the floor, gives me a brief smile, then leaves. My bedroom has a queen size bed with a brilliant blue comforter. A wall of glass faces the ocean with doors leading to a balcony.

After sliding the glass doors wide open to let in the sea breeze, I meander down the hallway to find Nash's room. He is facedown on a king size bed, arms and legs spread wide. I plop down on the white comforter next to him. He lifts his head then shifts to his side, a tired grin on his face.

"If it wasn't so late, I'd suggest we head back to town and go dancing," I say, hoping he'll claim he's not too tired to go out.

"What kind of dancing do you like?" He rolls to his back and spreads his elbows wide, clasping his hands behind his head.

"Salsa, cumbia, bachata."

"Ah, so you do have some Latina in you," he says, nudging me with his thigh, indigo eyes sparkling in amusement.

She aches for him in every part of her body. She's not used to feeling so frantic about catching a man's eye. At times, he behaves as if she doesn't exist. It hurts to be ignored by the one whom her heart beats for. But when he finds her in the night, when it is just him and her alone, he is transformed into a different person, the person she knows he really is. His eyes are filled with so much love, and longing, and always the burning desire. She comes alive underneath his hands. Is it possible to love someone so much and survive it? "Ixchel," he whispers, his voice adoring and hushed as his lips find hers. All through the night he worships her body with his. She will love him forever, and even that won't be long enough.

Light rain pitter patters on the thatched awning, as cool ocean air blows in from the open balcony. Shivering, I wrap the blankets around me. The slightest hint of daylight illuminates the gray sky, as waves gently lap at the cliff-like shoreline.

Last night, the moment I closed my eyes, a dream reel began to play. My body and mind became immersed in the most exquisite passion. The couple from my earlier dream in the Jeep visited me again and again in my sleep.

I inhale the scent of the sea and close my eyes, fully intending to fall back asleep. And then the aroma of spiced cooking meat and brewing coffee hits my nose. My eyes ping open. Nash must be making breakfast in the kitchen. I guess he's not a completely helpless bachelor after all.

After pulling on some jean shorts and a t-shirt, I wander downstairs. Through the wall of glass leading to the back, I see Nash walking down the dock toward the sea, not fazed by the light drizzle. A gray sky outlines his wide, bronze back. He's only wearing a pair of short, navy blue Speedo bottoms. His hands frame his face, adjusting what appear to be goggles. Only briefly does he stop at the end of the dock and peer down, and then in one smooth motion, he dives off the edge into the water below.

I walk around the low counters covered in granite and enter the U-shaped kitchen area. After guzzling down a tall glass of water, I head outside, following the path leading to the ocean. The drizzle has slowed to misty droplets. Smooth wood of a well-maintained dock replaces the concrete under my feet. To the right are stairs leading directly into the water, but straight ahead is where Nash dove off. I walk over and look down. Below resembles a lagoon, with clear water buttressing against the rocky limestone face, and fish darting around.

My gaze moves across the surface. He's nowhere to be seen. It's been several minutes since I saw him dive in, maybe even five. I chew my lip, unsure what to do. He seemed like a strong enough swimmer when he threw me into that cenote two nights ago. Perhaps I'm worried for no reason. But I keep staring into the water, hoping to see him. Anxiety rises in my chest. Too much time has passed. How long do I wait before running back to the house to call for help?

And then I see a dark form moving up the rocky, underwater face from far, far away. He's gone impossibly deep. No one can survive that long under water.

I rush down the stairs leading into the ocean and jump in fully clothed, ready to pull him out. And then his head breaks the surface as he pulls in a massive lungful of air. He pushes his goggles up from his eyes and removes a clip holding his nostrils shut.

"Hey, I didn't think you'd be up already." He takes in my terrified expression then looks down, seeing the clothes I'm wearing in the water. "You didn't bring a swimsuit?"

"Oh my God, Nash! I thought you drowned or something. I saw you dive in and then you didn't come up. What the heck?" My voice sounds hysterical to my own ears.

"No, no. I'm a freediver."

My eyes are wide and my heart pounds hard in my chest. "What?"

He then explains to me he dives without an oxygen tank.

For fun.

"I don't ... Why ..." I'm stammering, unable to think a coherent thought over the adrenaline racing through my veins. "What?" I repeat stupidly, grabbing onto the wooden rail of the stairs to hold myself steady.

"I really scared you, didn't I?"

"Yeah!" I blurt out. "I mean, I was trying to figure out how long to wait until running back to the house to call for help. And then I'd have to call your dad and let him know ..." I pull in a shaky, hiccupping breath then reach out to grab his arm. "Don't do that me."

"Sorry I scared you." A genuine expression of remorse moves across his face. He gestures to the stairs. "Let's go in. I made breakfast."

I strip off my wet clothing and jump in the shower to rinse the salty ocean from my skin and hair. After putting on white shorts and a sky-blue tank top, I run a comb through my hair leaving it to air dry into loose, flowing waves.

When I return to the kitchen, Nash is standing at the stove, also freshly showered and dressed, heating a corn tortilla over an open flame. He flips it using just his fingertips then slides the warm tortilla inside a folded dish towel.

"Doesn't that hurt?" I stand next to him, peering over his shoulder as he sets another one over the fire.

"No. As long as you move fast. You'll be a true Mayan if you can warm tortillas like this."

He moves back, waiting expectantly for me to take his place. I accept his challenge. We switch spots, and he stands directly behind me, bracing one hand on the counter next to the stove. I'm way too aware of him leaning over my shoulder, and with each small move I make, my arm or shoulder brushes against his torso.

I grab the tortilla between my fingertips and move to flip it, but I go too slowly.

"Ah!" I yell, dropping the hot tortilla to the floor as it burns my fingers.

Nash laughs, and I feel the vibration from his chest against my back. "Try again."

He steps away to grab another tortilla. Once he hands it to me, I drop it over the flame. Nash gives the signal, and then with a quick movement, I successfully flip the tortilla. I beam a proud smile at him, and his eyes crinkle at the corners as he returns it.

Nash moves to the counter and starts putting the food on plates. We work side by side, me heating the tortillas, and him filling them with the chorizo and eggs he cooked earlier. After sprinkling on chopped cilantro and crumbled Mexican cheese, Nash brings our plates to the table. I grab mugs from the open shelving next to the fridge and pour coffee into each one before sitting.

The clouds thin out overhead, revealing swatches of a bright, blue sky. We eat in companionable silence and sip our coffees, enjoying the ocean breeze rustling through our hair.

"What's on the agenda today?" I ask.

"There's ruins on this island at a place dedicated to Ixchel, one of the most important goddesses of the Maya."

Ee-Chell. I cock my head slightly. That's the name from my dream. And thinking about it, that's the goddess Guillermo mentioned. What a strange coincidence.

Gravel crunches under our feet as we follow a long, shaded path through the trees. San Gervaiso is home to many ruins. Nash describes the structures and what they once looked like. The love for his history and culture is clear, because he describes the past as if it's actually visible to him. Birds sing to us from the branches, and sunlight filters through leaves, creating a mosaic of shadows to play on the white road. Ahead lies a large pile of what looks like rubble from a distance. Closer, it appears more like a three-layer cake. Nash calls it the altar of Pet Nah.

"Maya women come here at least once in their life to ask Ixchel for guidance," he explains.

I stare at the pile of stone, wondering how something so

insignificant can be of great importance. "Like what?"

"What do you want, Ines? Are you happy with your life? Do you want it to stay the same, or do you want different?" He rattles off the questions, not expecting an answer, then inclines his head to the stones. "Go on. She listens."

Nash turns, shoving his hands into his pockets, and continues further down the white road, giving me privacy to consult with his non-existent goddess. It seems this woman, be she born from reality or fairytales, was viewed as a wise grandmother figure.

Admittedly, I have wished for a woman's guidance in my life. Having only a father made for an awkward adolescence. He did the best he could, but I always wished I had a woman to ask for advice on how to deal with inevitable blood stains when I first got my period and then later in life, how to make better choices when it came to men.

"What would a Mayan goddess know about abusive men anyway?" I murmur at the pile of ancient stones as I walk away.

We come upon another temple called the Tall House. Ka'na Nah is what Nash calls it. This well-preserved building is almost entirely whole. A wide set of six stone stairs lead up to a circular platform, with a square-shaped building on top. Through the doorway, a bench and an altar are visible.

Nash grips the stone lintel above the doorway, then steps back, viewing it from a different angle. "This wasn't originally here. The doorway was higher." He looks at me then makes a mark on the wall just above my head. "It would have been about this high. She was tall like you."

"Who?"

"Ixchel," he says, as if it's the obvious answer. "She and the sun god, Kinich Ahau, had a"—he hesitates, searching for a word—

"difficult relationship. He was jealous and abusive. One day she decided enough. She left him and came here to Tantun Cuzmal. That's the Maya name for Cozumel. This became her sanctuary. The outer walls were blue and the inside was yellow."

My one eyebrow raises in disbelief. I want to ask how he knows for sure, but I'm sure I've already caused him enough offense with the doubtful questions I've asked all day. So I quietly try to have an open mind instead.

Our last ruin of the day is what Nash says was an elite residence. As we follow the path, he explains that the elite class lived inside the city in homes made from durable materials like stone. Middle class merchants resided just outside the city in huts plastered with stucco. The lowest classes, the laborers and slaves, lived even further out, beyond the city walls designed for the sole purpose of keeping them away.

Not much remains of what was the home of a ruler. The footprint of the home is large, but there are no side or back walls. Stones making up the sides of a doorway remain intact, along with maybe half the height of what used to be the front of the residence. I cross the threshold, and then all at once, limestone walls rise high in front of and all around me. A beautiful shade of ochre spreads over the wall, and the dirt floor is suddenly clean and smooth under my feet.

To the right, he stands, filling the space with rage. He once made her heart swell with so much love she thought it would explode from her chest. But her heart is fearful this time. She backs away and a firm wall stops her escape. He is angry again. His eyes are full of unshed tears and his lips are drawn in a tight line. She'd caused him hurt by running away in the night, and somehow he's tracked her here. Something bitter and twisted got hold of him again. Love guided them through so much, but for him the anger always reigned supreme. More than love, more than even their passion, the anger was what energized him. It had taken her too long to see, but it filled him. She foolishly thought her love could heal him. Now, he would hurt her again. His large hand wraps around her throat, and he holds her pinned to the wall, making it impossible for her to draw in a breath.

"Ines!"

The angry features of her lover transform into Nash's face right before my eyes. I scream and put my hands in front of myself for protection. The house melts away and is only crumbled ruins again. Mouth agape, I look around then feel my throat where I swear I can still feel the pressure of an impossibly large hand. It was the same people from my other dream. I look around in confusion, grabbing my temples where my head is suddenly pounding.

I forgot my water bottle in the car. Dehydration is causing me to hallucinate. I stumble as I walk out the doorway, and Nash grabs my arm to steady me. I rip my arm from his grasp. "Don't," is all I can manage to choke out.

And then I'm running. Tears stream down my cheeks as I hurtle along the white path, passing wide-eyed tourists along the walkway. I reach the parking lot, where I find the Jeep, then promptly puke behind it. The pressure left by his hands throbs on my neck. I don't know what happened back there, but the experience of being choked by a man holding me against a wall has triggered my own memories. I pull in a shaky breath, one hand rubbing my throat as I try to reign in what's about to become a full-blown panic attack. This is my third day in Mexico, and I've already had too many emotional breakdowns. I shove my palms into my eyes and promise myself this will be the last one.

The beeping sound of the Jeep unlocking brings me back from

the edge. I drop my hands to see Nash standing at the driver side, cautious eyes studying me. I inhale deeply, then spread my arms in a helpless gesture.

"I think I'm dehydrated," is the best explanation I can come up with.

An awkward silence fills the air as we drive along the highway. I don't understand what I just experienced, but I can't help but think of my dad's letter when he said he believed his condition was genetic. Maybe this is how it all began for him … people living out lives in his head until delusion overtook reality. I squeeze my eyes shut, hoping hard my father was wrong. I'm too young to have my mind crumble. But so was he.

The emotional drain of that experience has me wishing I could sleep away the afternoon. But Nash begins to excitedly chatter on about how it's a perfect day for swimming in the ocean. And he's right. I need to pull it together so I can enjoy the backyard sea. Perhaps I'll drink my problems away with some beers later.

Once we get back to the house, I head to my room and pull my red bikini from the black dresser. After braiding my hair, I tie on the skimpy swimsuit.

"Vamanos!" Nash's voice comes up from the kitchen, telling me *let's go*.

I roll my eyes at his impatience as I stand in front of the floor length mirror, adjusting the bikini fabric to fit the small triangular cups over the middle of my breasts, and tying the bottoms tighter over my hips. When packing for this trip, I had envisioned myself lying on the beaches of Cancun, not freediving with an arrogant, beautiful man.

Nash's eyebrows soar into his hairline as he watches me walk up. "You're going swimming in that?"

"I have smaller bikinis. Would that work better?"

He gives a short, nervous laugh and a quick shake of his head. "No, no."

As we head to the dock, he glances down at me. "Smaller? Really? I mean ..." He cups his hands around his chest as if feeling imaginary breasts. "I can already see almost everything, Ines. Are your other ones just strings?"

"You'll have to wait and see," I say with a raise of one eyebrow, resisting the urge to laugh at his wide-eyed expression.

The sun is framed by a clear blue sky, and my skin warms under the strong rays. Nash insists I dive down with him, so he teaches me a breathing technique designed to pull oxygen deep into the lungs. At first I feel silly breathing in such an exaggerated manner, but his expression of patient determination wears down my self-consciousness. Goggles in place, I practice floating face down, holding my breath as long as I can. Next we do a few dives a short distance down. Coral reefs filled with life line the shore. Blue fish dart through the water, while a school of small gray ones Nash calls grunts weave around. Seeing the abundance of life in the sea makes me wish I could hold my breath as long as him.

I rest on the steps of the dock, watching Nash dive deep down and disappear from view. He returns, holding a pink conch shell about the size of my head, then turns it over to reveal the dark shape of the creature living inside. I scramble away, and he laughs.

"I'm going to dive some more. You don't have to wait. Go

shower, nap, whatever." He adjusts his goggles and attaches the clip to his nose again.

The excitement shining in his eyes is contagious, and an odd jealously stabs me. I can't help but feel betrayed by the ocean, commanding all his attention with her splendor.

I give a small frown and stand. "I'm going to check out the rooftop."

Nash nods, then draws in rapid breaths before taking in a single deep gulp of air and pushing off backward into the water to descend. I don't know if I could ever get comfortable being without oxygen for minutes at a time.

After grabbing a book from my room, I find the stairwell to the rooftop patio. I reach the top, and the warm breeze rustles the roof thatching. The view over the sea toward the Yucatán peninsula appears to go on forever. Sailboats float in the distance.

A wet bar with four simple barstools lies in the shading of the thatched palapa. Two red hammocks sway as the ocean breeze rocks the ropey fabric. Off to the side in the full sun are a pair of lounge chairs, perfect for attempting to get a tan.

After flopping down on the chair, I lie on my belly and untie the strings of my top to expose my back. My book keeps me company while the sunshine heats my skin. I imagine myself darkening to a beautiful golden shade under its strength. Try as I might, I've never been able to get my skin even a shade darker. It's always remained a pale alabaster, which admittedly is a pleasing contrast to my dark hair. But maybe what I've needed all this time was the Yucatán sun. After twenty minutes, I set my book down and flip over to work on my front, resting my arm across my face to shield my eyes.

"Ines?" Nash's voice floats up the stairwell.

I grab my towel and cover my exposed breasts. "What's up?"

"I'm gonna get some tacos. Want anything?"

"Fish tacos, please," I yell. "And a beer!"

The sound of his soft chuckle makes a smile come to my lips. Hearing him laugh makes the lonely, aching feeling inside me ease up a little. I imagine what it would be like if that feeling left entirely. Once I hear the hallway door shut, I drop my towel to the floor, then return my attention to the thriller I'm reading about a woman who's gone missing. Obviously, the husband did it. After a while, the words blur on the page. My eyes open and shut in long, lazy blinks under the narcotic rays of the sun. My mistake is thinking I can close my eyes for one moment. And then the dream begins.

CHAPTER 7

THE DARK HEAD OF her lover rests in her lap, his tears soaking her skin. He makes the same promises he won't be able to keep, because the anger will always win. She doesn't have the heart to tell him what she's thinking, and she holds him as he weeps, begging her to let him stay in her arms for the night. She should say no, but in her heart she knows the craving her body has for him will win out over her fear of him. She promises herself this will be the last time, and then she will disappear. She will let the Whole One God decide her fate.

The dream releases me, and I startle awake. To my left, there is a scraping sound as glass slides across stone followed by a bottle cap popping open. Nash is sitting at the bar, beer in one hand, taco in the other, and I'm lying here topless.

"Dude!" I yell, snatching up my towel to cover my breasts.

He glances over at me with a raised eyebrow and an unrepentant grin across his handsome face. "You can't blame me for enjoying a good view, Ines. There is a sunset *and* mountains." He laughs before dropping his head back and pulling a drink from his beer.

"Oh, real funny." I use my chin to pin the towel to my chest, trying to tie my top on.

There are no actual mountains visible from this rooftop, unless you count my breasts. I stand, then toss the towel at his head. He catches the white terry cloth in one hand. Not making eye contact, I settle in the seat next to him and pull my tacos from the paper bag, then I rip open the bag of chips with salsa. An odd emotion twists in my belly. Inside, I feel like a guitar string wound so tightly that I would break if strummed.

"Thanks," I mutter.

"Oh, no. Thank you."

I give him a hard stare, and he grins back at me while sliding a bottle across the counter. Keeping eye contact, I bring the top of the beer to my mouth, then use my back teeth to pry open the crimped metal. I spit the bottle cap onto the floor and tilt the bottle to my lips.

Nash responds with a wide-eyed stare and a low whistle. "Marry me."

Beer shoots out of my nose. I cough and slap the counter as Nash pounds on my back, his deep laughter rolling over me. He chuckles breathlessly while passing me a napkin, his blue eyes lit in amusement.

After wiping the beer from my face, I shoot him a side eye glance. "Really, Nash? That's what gets you going? A woman opening a beer with her teeth? Such a savage."

He spreads his arms wide and raises his shoulders. "I'm a simple man, Ines."

"I can see that." I grin and shake my head before taking a swallow of beer. "Personally, I need more than that. At the very least, a ring. So, proposal denied."

He clutches his hand to his chest in mock pain, then chuckles softly. We eat while watching the horizon dim to pink and purple hues.

After taking a bite of my taco, I decide to lay into him. "I can't believe you waltzed up here and thought, 'Oh, yeah, Ines would love if I let her lie there topless.' You should have said something."

"No." He points the mouth of his beer at me. "I thought, 'Ines knows I'm coming back. Might as well get a look at what she wants to show me.' No?" He shrugs, eyes locked on mine in defiance.

My mouth drops open. "I would never—"

"But you did. So I did. And here we are again. Even Esteban." He reaches over and grabs a chip, then pops it in his mouth and crunches loudly.

"Not even close to even Esteban."

"Okay fine. How about this? There's a place in town we can go dancing. The live band plays rumba and salsa."

My eyes widen. "Really?"

Nash nods.

"Do you think they play bachata too?" My voice rises in excitement.

He frowns. "I hope not."

Long, thick curls cascade down my back. I rarely ever curl my hair due to how labor intensive the task is, but salsa dancing in Cozumel is a special occasion.

Nash comes in my room every five minutes asking if I'm ready yet. After fifteen minutes, I barricade myself in the bathroom away from his incessant pestering.

Outside the door, I hear dresser drawers slide open then slam shut. "Wow, Ines. Crotchless thongs? Okay."

I shout out a laugh before cracking the door just wide enough to throw a bar of soap at him. And no, I didn't bring crotchless thongs. Those are safely at home, thank you very much.

While I haven't worn much makeup due to the fear of it melting off my face in this dense heat, tonight I darken my eyes with eyeliner and mascara, then swipe on cherry red lipstick. My dress is a clingy cobalt blue lacy thing hitting just above mid-thigh, with a deep V plunging neckline. Thin straps criss cross several times over the low back, making a bra impractical. After sliding on a black pair of stilettos, I tug open the bathroom door and brace my hands on the frame, waiting for him to turn.

Nash glances up from where he is bent over—legitimately rifling through my drawers like a perv—and straightens, letting out a low whistle. "Wow, Ines. Really, I mean … you are a beautiful woman."

Inside, I preen like a peacock at the compliment. "You look amazing too, Nash. We're gonna blow Cozumel away with how hot we are."

Grinning, he extends an elbow to me. "Vamanos, muñeca."

My gaze sweeps over his choice of outfit. He's paired black, slim-fitting pants with a tucked in button up black shirt. The sleeves are rolled up, and his pants are masculine, but tight enough to showcase his muscular thighs. A dark brown leather belt pulls it all together. The simple look is stunning on a man with a build and face like Nash. As we leave the room, I lean back and take a sly glance at his butt.

Very nice, indeed.

We get along for all of three steps down the stairs until he grumbles something about me suffocating all the short men with my breasts while dancing. And then I tell him he should have worn a skirt with how visible his junk is through his pants. We bicker like an old married couple while we walk out to the Jeep, and then, gentleman as always, he opens the door for me, but then shoves me inside before slamming it shut behind me. He pushes his hand through the front of his hair as he walks around to his door.

I'm getting used to his mercurial moods, but truth be told, I'm mostly entertained by them. I pull down the visor and check my teeth for lipstick in the mirror. All clear. I sit back in the seat and cross my legs, settling my gaze on him. His eyes drift downward to where the lacy edge of the dress meets my thigh.

"So rumba? I don't know how to dance rumba."

He turns forward and starts the engine. "It's not too different from salsa. You'll see."

The little club is packed full of people. It's difficult to even get through the door, let alone find somewhere to dance. Many people move along to the music, not really sure of the style, while other couples perform complicated steps and spins. Nash laces his fingers through mine and the intimate contact makes me feel as if a hummingbird has taken residence under my ribcage. He firmly pulls me through the crowd toward the bar. I signal to the bartender and order us two double shots of tequila, opening a tab on my credit card.

"So it's going to be that kind of night, eh?" Nash downs his shot with a backward tilt of his head.

In front of the dance floor on a small platform, a group of men perform live music. One man plays drums, another strums a guitar, and another man blows a trumpet. One uses a stick to play an instrument resembling a hollowed-out gourd.

Nash begins to shimmy his shoulders to the tapping beat of the guiro instrument, extending one hand to me in invitation. I place my hand in his, and he pulls me onto the dance floor. It's a character flaw of mine that I don't like giving up control, but when it comes to dancing, I allow myself to be moved exactly as he wants me.

We move effortlessly around the dance floor. Nash is a strong lead, and I follow every cue without hesitation. A slight change in pressure from his fingertips on the palm of my hand, or a tightening of his arm against my waist tells me which way he want me to move or spin. Song after song, we move in a perfect union, between the fast spinning cumbias and merengues, and the more intricate footwork of salsa.

After the band leaves at midnight, a DJ takes over. He spins a popular salsa song, then a cumbia, and we don't stop dancing. Sweat soaks through his shirt under my fingertips, and strands of my hair cling to my back and neck. And then the tropical beat of a bachata song bleeds through the ending of the cumbia. Nash drops my hands, leaving his raised in a clear "I'm not touching it" gesture as he backs away.

"Please, Nash? Please?"

He shakes his head and walks away to the bar. Another man is quick to step in his place. He's a decent lead, however, Nash was right. The shorter man's face is pretty much smothered between my boobs as we sensually sway to the bachata beat.

I glance toward the bar and see Nash down a double shot of what is likely tequila. We had been too busy dancing to drink anything more since our initial tequila shot. He wipes the back of his hand over his mouth then raises his fingers in a gesture to the bartender to bring him another. My attention stays glued to him. Nash is a big guy, but he needs to slow down if he's going to be sober enough to drive later.

A reggaeton song starts, and a taller white man takes the shorter one's place. This man pulls me against his hip, with his arm tight around my waist. I hope he can't understand the lyrics, even though you'd have to be dense to not understand what "noche de sexo" means. But I love this song and am really feeling it until he turns me around and pulls my bottom against his groin and grinds into me.

Perfect cue to leave. I turn and push away from Sir Humps A Lot, shooting him an angry look of disgust. Heading toward the bar, my eyes lock with Nash who is leaning both hands on the counter, glaring darkly out at the dance floor. Three empty double shot glasses lay upside down in front of him.

I lean against him to talk in his ear over the loud music. "Hey, you okay?"

He nods, putting one hand on the small of my back as he turns to me. "Want another shot?"

A new, languid look coats his eyes and his demeanor is more loose. Even though I don't like the fact that he drank so much alcohol in such a short period of time, I trust he knows his limits. Regardless, I would still like another drink.

"Sure."

We each down another double shot as a salsa song begins playing. I wrap both my hands around one of his, then drag him away from the bar and onto the dance floor. He's a bit sloppier, but still very much in control of his and my body. Inevitably, after a few more salsa and merengue songs, the slow tempo of a new, popular bachata song begins. Everyone cheers at hearing the initial beats, and couples leave their seats to rush to the dance floor.

I cling to Nash, wrapping my hands around his triceps. "Please? Please?"

He shakes his head, but he's not as quick to pull away as he was before. I can tell I'm wearing him down. The presence of Sir Humps

A Lot at my side ready to step in forces Nash to stay with me on the dance floor. I wrap my arms around his ribcage and tighten my hold around him in a "thank you" hug as we begin moving to the first slow beats of the song. I pull back to look at him, and his eyes are closed with a pained expression, as if he can't believe he's doing this.

His eyes open, and he meets my gaze. I mouth along with the words of the song. "En tus manos yo caí, tienes control sobre mi."

A small smile lifts the corner of his mouth as we slowly move side to side. Then the beginning stops, and it speeds up into the normal rhythm of bachata. He pulls me in tight with one arm around my waist, and our hands clasp together as we start to move. And this man can absolutely dance bachata like a king. I can't believe he held out on me. He's got the turns down, the fancy, quick Dominican footwork, and all the sensuality that's supposed to ooze out with bachata. It's oozing. Big time.

He turns me to face outward, my back against his front, and his palm spanning the space of my belly between my hips as we step side to side. His face is buried against my neck, and I feel his lips moving along to the words. Clearly, he loves bachata. It's evident in how he dances to it. But I can't understand why he refused so adamantly at first.

Nash turns me to face him, and we're in close, my arm high around his neck as we move, and our faces pressed cheek to cheek. Our legs are juxtaposed together, his thigh tight between mine. His hand slides up my back to my neck, and I bend back for a low, sweeping dip, my left leg high by his hip. He pulls me back up to standing, but our bodies remain anchored in the center. There are no steps with the next move, and just our hips keep the rhythm. And then we're back at a respectable arms-length for a variety of complicated turns.

The song ends, and we move smoothly into the next one, another bachata he seems okay with. I'll have to wheedle out of him later why he was so hesitant to dance this style. We go back and forth between the dance floor and bar for shots until lights come on in the club and the owners start kicking everyone out.

We stumble arm in arm through the doors to the outside, and are at least responsible enough to get a cab. We are probably the most obnoxious passengers of the night, because the cab driver keeps shooting scathing glares at us through the rearview mirror. Even though we think we're conversing at a normal volume, we're pretty much yelling in one another's face and laughing hysterically in the back seat.

When we get back to the house, he grabs me around the waist and does some Dominican footwork to imaginary music. I laugh and respond with some of my own footwork. Nash grabs me by the hand and pulls me up the stairs, then toward his bedroom. I pause at the doorway, unsure about what's going on.

"Fine, fine," he says, slightly slurring his words as he turns to me in the doorway. "I will dance with you more, Ines, but you can't tell anyone. Prométeme!" He points a finger in my face, demanding that I promise, and I sink my teeth in. He yelps looking injured, and then begins laughing the most adorable, boyish belly laughs. "She bites!" he exclaims, shaking his hand out. He crouches next to the bed and looks up at me, holding one finger up to his lips. "Shh."

After pulling out a case holding sleeves of CDs, he rifles through. Finding the one he wants, he slips the disc out, then walks over to the bedroom stereo.

Bachata streams from the speakers, and he opens his arms to me. I can't resist. Smiling, I step into his room, then move into the circle of his body. We spin, and sway, and dance deep into the night with the moon shining its luminescent glow through the open balcony window.

A groan to my left wakes me. My head spins from the amount of tequila I drank the night before. I crack open an eye and look around. Garish rays of sunlight stream in the open balcony windows, and then it's my turn to groan as my head pounds. I'm lying face down and not in my own bed. I'm still in my dress, though historically that means nothing in my experience.

"Ay, Dios," Nash says.

I push onto my elbows and cast my eyes in his direction. He is shirtless, but at least his pants are buttoned. My eyes linger on the smooth skin of his chest.

"What happened?" he asks, looking around his room in confusion.

"We danced bachata all night long." I smile.

A horrified expression enters his eyes. "We did not."

I nod. "Did too."

"Oh, no."

I lift an eyebrow in his direction. "Okay, fine. We went at it all night on your bed like a pair of rabid bunnies."

He inclines his head. "Ah, okay. That I can live with."

I throw my head back and laugh loudly, then grab my pounding head.

"But a bunny?" he says, grinning. "Can't it be more like a jaguar?"

I crack one eye open, the corner of my mouth lifting in a smile. "Rawr." I swipe my nails at him. "That was the worst sex ever, Nash. You didn't even get your pants off."

We both laugh in short snorts.

"Your dress either. That's how good I am."

My mouth opens on a loud shout of laughter. "Oh my God, stop. My head is about to explode if I laugh one more time."

Turning to the right, he rolls off the bed then heads to the bathroom. He returns with aspirin and grabs a bottle of water from his nightstand. The muscles in his chest flex as he loosens the cap. I am definitely thirsty, and in more ways than one. Nash pops two pills and chugs half the water, then hands me two pain killers, along with the remainder of the bottle.

Once I swallow the pills, I do the smart thing and leave his room.

After starting my shower, I sit on the closed toilet lid, head in my hands. I almost made a big mistake last night. Even though I was mostly in control of myself, I'm not sure if he was. I test the water temperature then pull my clothes off. Looking in the mirror, my reflection stares back at me. I tilt my head back and run my hand down my throat, right to where his lips touched me last night. I close my eyes, remembering the sound of his voice in my ear after that last song ended in his bedroom. The deafening silence between us felt like a ticking bomb.

"Stay with me tonight, Ines," he had said.

His hand tangled in my hair as he moved flush against me, pressing his cheek to mine. He turned his head and sealed his lips to my cheek. A whisper of his breath moved across my ear, sending a shiver down my spine.

"Stay with me."

His dark head moved lower as his mouth found my neck. His hands roamed all over me, cupping my bottom, then slipping inside the lacy V of my neckline. Looking down, I marveled at the image of his bronze hands against my pale skin. Even as my mind protested with my 'changed woman' speech, my body stopped listening. My head fell back as he drew the most exquisite sensations from my body, and my fingers curled in his thick, dark hair. I felt my dress slide up around my thighs and then I snapped back to reality.

"Wait, wait." I pushed him away. The gleam of hunger in his dark eyes almost drew me back in. But I came up with a quick excuse to get away before I did something I'd regret. "Let me go to the bathroom."

I had gone into his bathroom and took the exact same position I'm in now—head in hands, sitting on the toilet, and madly aroused. I'd waited a full ten minutes before cracking open the door and peeking out to find Nash fast asleep, legs hanging off the side of the bed. I walked over and bent next to him to pull his heavy legs onto the mattress. And then something, be it loneliness or the simple desperation to be next to another human being, made me crawl into the bed beside him and sleep.

Today, I'm filled with equal amounts of regret and relief. I shake my head, berating myself for being so stupid. After showering, I pull my pajamas on. Hopefully he has nothing big planned today, because I do not plan on moving far with this hangover. I go downstairs and start the coffee, then make us toast and scrambled eggs. Nash comes down, freshly shaven and showered, wearing only shorts.

"So American," he says. "Toast and eggs. Gracias."

I grin and take a bite of my buttered, jellied toast. We eat and sip our coffees in companionable silence, and then I've waited long enough.

"Can I ask you something, and you be honest with me?"

His eyes shoot to mine, and I can tell he's not sure what to think of my request. Then he lifts his shoulder in a laconic shrug. "Sure."

"Why do you have a love-hate relationship with bachata?"

He grimaces and looks at his plate. "Wow, Ines. You went straight for the neck." One finger slices an imaginary line across his jugular.

I pull my bare feet onto the chair and wrap my arms around my knees as I wait. Nash rubs one hand across the back of his head, and it's obvious he's uncomfortable with the question. I decide to make it easier for him.

"Okay, how about this? I'll guess and you tell me yes or no."

He purses his lips for a moment, thinking, and then gives a quick nod of his head in agreement. He lifts his fork and stabs the eggs for another bite.

"Bachata was playing when you lost your virginity, and you cried right after." Eggs shoot out of his mouth, and then he holds one hand over his lips, his shoulders moving in silent laughter. But then he shakes his head no as he grabs a napkin and wipes the splattered egg off the table. I smile and move on to the next guess. "Your mom and dad would put bachata on anytime they had sex, so when you heard it, you knew you couldn't come back home."

A gagging sound comes out of his throat. "Ah, yuck." His eyes sparkle in amusement as he shakes his head no.

I lean forward on my elbows, going in for the kill. "You used to dance bachata with the woman you loved."

He pauses just as he's about to put another bite of food in his mouth. His entire demeanor changes, and it feels like that moment when the sun has been covered by clouds. Not meeting my gaze, he nods yes. Everything darkens, and I sense him closing up behind rows of intricate locks. I immediately regret pushing the issue. He stares over my shoulder out the window as he continues eating, but he doesn't smile again.

"Her name was Alma," he says softly, and that's all he says about it.

Once he finishes his food, he leaves the table and starts washing the dishes. I can tell he needs space, so I go to the rooftop terrace with my book, but I can't concentrate enough to even turn a page.

An hour later, he finds me up there and lies on the lounge chair next to mine. I turn on my side to face him, studying his strong jaw, straight nose, and perfect lips. I wonder what that mouth would feel like against mine. His kisses felt heavenly everywhere else. He stares up at the sky, watching the clouds intermingle and merge.

Nash clears his throat. "We were together for two years. She was a dance teacher … taught bachata. I walked by, saw her teaching, and watched through the window. When her class ended, I went in and signed up for the next class. I already knew most of the other dance styles, but bachata is what she taught me. Anyway, I have a bad temper, Ines." The muscle in his jaw ticks.

My lips part, and I already know what he's going to say next.

"I loved her so much. I swear I did. But one day I hit her."

He turns his head to face me, and I freeze my features, desperately trying to control my reaction. This deeply personal confession is painful for both of us, because I've been on the receiving end of a man's physical abuse.

Nash focuses his attention on the sky, squeezing the bridge of his nose between his thumb and forefinger and sniffing in hard. "Our first year together was like heaven. You know?" He glances over at me, and I nod. "And then it started changing. I would yell a lot, and that moved to pushing. One day I got jealous about something stupid I thought she did, and I hit her." He pauses and looks down at his hands. Those long, strong fingers that could bring a woman the most incredible pleasure, or the most heartbreaking pain. "I … I broke her nose. Her face was all bruised up. It made me sick to see what I did. I begged for forgiveness, but she was a smart woman." He gives a short, bitter laugh. "She knew I couldn't change. And that's it. The last time I danced bachata was with her. And last night I danced it with you."

Regret fills my heart. "I'm sorry I made you dance, Nash."

He looks me in the eye. "I'm not. I had fun dancing with you, Ines. But you should know what kind of man I am."

With that, he gets up from the lounge chair and leaves the rooftop. I tighten my hands into fists, forcing myself to stay put. Even after that confession, some sick, twisted part of me wants to run after him and reassure him everything is okay. But it absolutely is not. Nash is the culmination of everything I hate in a man—the arrogance, the temper, along with the fact that he's an abuser. This attraction between us is undeniable, and I know if I entertain it in the slightest, we will 100% hook up before this trip ends. I cannot allow that to happen.

"I am a changed woman," I whisper, my voice shaking.

But clearly, I'm not, as I've quickly fallen for an abusive man yet again.

CHAPTER 8

AFTER THAT DAY, THE energy between us changes irrevocably. He's not as playful or flirtatious, and I do my best to no longer flaunt my curves. We continue our days with a kind cordiality, taking turns cooking meals and washing dishes. If I'm being honest with myself, I miss the tentative friendship we'd built.

We leave the island, and the ferry ride back to Playa del Carmen passes quickly. Soon, we're in the Jeep driving south on a two-lane highway. A steady rainfall pours the entire hour of our drive. The heavy storm passes, leaving behind thin, wispy feathers of clouds overhead. Patches of blue peek through in some spots, promising sunshine for the rest of the day.

"Tulum?" I say, reading a sign as we pass.

Nash nods. "We'll stay here for a few days. Tulum ruins tomorrow, then Coba, then Chichen Itza."

"And after Chichen Itza?"

Nash glances over at me. "That's pretty much it. Unless there's something else you want to see."

A strange sadness fills me thinking about this trip being over. Part of me wishes we could keep driving around the entire Yucatán peninsula, exploring every little city, and each seemingly insignificant ruin. He's been an amazing guide, and has somehow shifted from someone I intensely disliked into someone I consider a good friend.

"Anything you suggest?"

He purses his lips in thought. "There's cenotes I'd love to dive in. But I know you hate them."

"Hey," I say gently. "I don't mind tagging along. I'll find ways to occupy myself. Anything you want to do, let's do it. Okay?"

Nash gives me a brief smile and nod, before returning his attention to the road.

"And Nash?" I rush out the words I've been thinking for the past couple days. "I'm sorry I didn't say much about what you told me the other day. I needed time to process." I grip my hands together. "The thing is, I've been on the other end of abusive relationships, so it's hard to hear you did that to someone."

He blows out a deep exhale as his hand flexes on the steering wheel.

I continue. "What you did was wrong. But don't let it define you. Don't let it be who you are. You're the only person who has the power to change that. You're allowed to do better. You're allowed to change. You know that, right?"

His eyebrows knit together as he presses his teeth into his bottom lip. "Sometimes I don't know, Ines. It's like my heart has anger all the time, and that's who I'm meant to be."

"You can be more than that. And you have to forgive yourself."

We come to a stop at a light, and he turns to me. "But do *you* forgive me?"

I narrow my eyes in confusion. "You've done nothing to me."

"Sometimes you act like I have."

His simple words are like a slap in the face, and I recoil at the weight of the accusation. "What do you mean?"

The light turns green, and Nash begins driving. "I know you've been hurt before, Ines. But since we met, you've treated me like I'm all the men who hurt you. The way you act is like this huge sign on your chest."

This is unexpected. I wasn't prepared to talk about myself. My initial reaction is to deny, but I say nothing. I know I've become a bit of a shrew from my past relationships, but it's unsettling having it thrown in my face.

"I don't know any other way," I finally say.

"We're friends, right?"

I nod. "Yeah, Nash. I think we are."

"Treat me like a friend. That's all. Don't assume I have other intentions. When I have other intentions, you will know."

When he has other intentions?

I clear my throat, shifting away from the uncomfortable subject. "So how long ago was Alma?"

His eyes squint slightly as he thinks. "It's 2012 now … eh, so three years ago? And to be honest, I haven't been in a relationship since then. I find a woman I like, I go home with her, and then I'm gone when she wakes up in the morning."

"One-night stand, huh?"

"It's the safest."

"I do the same thing." I pause, reflecting on everything that just passed between us, then take a deep breath. "But look where that's gotten us, Nash. We're two adults who can't cope with conflict, who are avoiding long term human relationships because they challenge something inside us. I don't know about you, but I'm tired of it."

Nash makes a low sound of agreement in his throat.

And I'm lonely.

The unspoken words in my mind cause an uneasy feeling to expand in the pit of my stomach. Crossing my arms, I lean my head against the window and watch the greenery go by. A year ago, I wasn't even close to recognizing any of this. But when my dad died, something in me shifted. It was shocking to be reminded how impermanent life is. Having Nash see through me and kindly put my failings center stage challenges a different part of me entirely.

We turn off the main highway and take a small road through a quaint beach town. To the left is the blue of the ocean, and we turn off onto a sandy drive. The two-story beach house is a narrow thing, with white stucco walls, oddly shaped windows, and a brown thatched roof. Instead of it being a declaration of civilization at the end of a vast, wild ocean, the house blends in seamlessly with the palm trees shading it all around.

The Jeep doors softly thud shut, and we grab our luggage then make our way inside. My hand runs along the flat, beige walls. The interior with its open floor plan is simple and minimalist, reminding me of a tiny home. To the right of the entry door is a small room with a double bed. Inside the room, a set of stairs lead to the second floor, but we pass those and walk to the kitchen. A wall of dark wood framed glass doors lead out to the brilliant blue expanse of the ocean.

Nash walks over and tugs open the doors, bringing in a fresh, saltwater breeze. A wide set of limestone stairs lead directly to the sand, where hammocks hang from palm trees.

Nash turns to look at me with a sheepish shrug. "This place is smaller than it looked in the pictures."

"No, it's perfect. It's just us. We don't need a lot of space."

I follow him to the first floor bedroom. It's an oddly located room, since the stairs leading to the second floor take up one wall of the space.

"I'll take this room," Nash says, throwing his backpack on the double bed.

I pointedly look at his 6'5 frame, then at the bed, then back at him, knowing there is no way this man will fit in a bed any less than a king size. He smiles then points up the staircase. I follow behind.

The stairs lead straight up to a dark wood door. Nash pushes it open to the master bedroom, which occupies the entire second floor. The entire ceiling is gabled and thatched like we're inside a modern hut. I walk to the wall of windows and pull open the balcony doors, letting the ocean air circulate through. In the center of the room is a king-size bed on a raised concrete platform.

"We can just enjoy the beach today," Nash says. "Then first thing in the morning, Tulum."

The high sun glowed hot overhead. Water sparkled blue beneath the heavy rays and pulsed through her like a heartbeat. Xibalba called to her, and she was ready. She missed his eyes most of all, that color of the sky that promised heaven. If only he would find her again. Closing her eyes, she fell forward.

With a start I awaken, a hiss of agony escaping me. An odd pain accompanied the ending of that dream. It felt like my entire body was filled with the pins and needles tingling of a limb that fell asleep. I flex my feet, then clench and release my hands, trying to shake the sensation.

The sun has not yet risen, but the glow of its promised return lights up the horizon. I roll over and try to go back to sleep, but then throw back the covers as I decide to get a jump start on making breakfast. Nash is an early riser and is probably jogging all shirtless and glorious on the beach already. He's usually famished once he's done exercising. It's strange getting to know a man's routines and preferences. Odder yet is my unfailing urge to fill those needs. I recognize the feeling for what it is.

Hopeless, impossible infatuation.

As I head down the stairs, I glance over at Nash's bed. He's still in it, one arm over his face. His blankets have been kicked off and his feet hang over the edge. He is also stark naked and spread eagled. I stumble on the stairs, then fall down the last two steps. My shriek wakes him up, because he's suddenly beside me picking me up off the floor.

"I'm fine, I'm fine." I shield my eyes as I limp out the door. "Jesus! Put on some clothes."

Cheeks aflame, I head for the small kitchen. The refrigerator has been stocked in advance with our requested groceries, a convenient service. After putting a pan on the stove flame with a harsh banging sound, I pull out the chorizo and eggs. The phallic-shaped tube of sausage in my hand causes a giddy, hysterical noise to bubble out of my mouth. I shake my head and start muttering psychotically to myself as I cut open the sausage.

Nash enters the kitchen, jeans pulled on and no shirt. He stares at me while I use a spatula to angrily stab at the meat in the pan to break it up. His eyebrows soar up high, then he skirts cautiously around where I'm standing at the stove and starts fiddling with the coffee maker. He glances over at me and scratches at the growth of beard on his jaw.

"Ines? I'm ... ah, sorry you saw that. I didn't sleep well last night. I thought I would be up before you."

"Oh, you were up all right." I chuckle humorlessly as I shake my head.

He blushes, then stutters. "I—I …"

"Look." I whip around, pointing the spatula at him, and he flinches away. "That thing needs to" —I gesture angrily with the cooking utensil—"not exist in my space." Breathing out, I center myself, saying, "I am a changed woman."

His demeanor shifts from one of caution to concern. "Are you afraid of me, Ines?"

"No … Yes!" I throw up my hands then grab the eggs and a bowl. I crack some eggs and furiously start beating them with a fork. "Nash, you remember how we both said we haven't been in relationships but had one-night stands?"

He nods, putting some coffee grounds in the machine. I pour the eggs into the pan of sizzling meat and start mixing.

"I had lots of one-night stands. That"—I point my spatula in the direction of his pants—"is a distraction."

Nash tilts his head, and his expression gentles as a half smile touches his lips. "Ines, I mean, it wouldn't be so bad if we—"

"NO!" My voice explodes harshly. "Do not say it. I'm not gonna let you say it. I am no longer that woman, Nash. I have more respect for myself." My eyes are pleading as I look at him. "Help me have more respect for myself."

A resigned look comes on his face, and he nods his head in agreement. He starts the coffee maker, then grabs two plates and sets them on the island. Next, he grabs the tortillas from the fridge and starts heating them over the burner.

He looks sideways at me while placing a tortilla over the flame.

"So you were tempted by me, eh?"

I center myself again and breathe outward slowly. Failing, I turn to him and begin beating the heck out of him with the spatula. He laughs and ducks under my arm then grabs me around the waist. We end up in an unfair wrestling match ending with me on the floor underneath him.

The forgotten tortilla burns to a crisp.

We are among the first to arrive at the archaeological site of Tulum. Nash calls it Zama, which he translates to "dawn." The name is appropriate, because as the dawning rays of sunlight reach out over the sea, the first place they touch is Tulum.

I peek down from the rocky border of stones overlooking the beach. Vivid turquoise waters glisten against a long stretch of sandy shore. In the distance, multitudes of massive wooden canoes line the shore. People in odd clothing busily load and unload cargo.

I nudge Nash, pointing to the odd scene. "You think they're filming a movie over there?"

He glances at me, then at the boats, then back to me again, pausing longer than normal. "They're traders," he finally says, giving me a measured look that makes me think he's weighing my reaction. "Honey, salt, vanilla, amber. Lots of good stuff."

"I can't believe people use boats like that still." I shield my eyes to get a closer look. "Let's go down there."

Nash grabs my hand. "Later."

He pulls me away from the bluff, but as we walk he doesn't release his hold as I expect him to. Rather, he shifts his grip. Our two shadows stretch away from us in the rays of the rising sun, linked hand in hand. Seeing us touching so intimately makes anxiety explode in my chest. The morning light casts a vision of something I desperately want but senselessly fear. The warmth of his palm against mine is like a small flickering beacon thawing the frozen spaces in my chest.

I can only wonder what the rest of his skin on mine could do.

I release a harsh exhale, shaking my head. Madness is consuming me and I blame this entire peninsula. With a slight twist of my wrist, I slip my hand from his then cross my arms as we continue down the path. Our once linked shadows continue down the path side by side but no longer touching, and I can't help but think how lonely they now appear.

An odd movement catches my eye. I turn to look at the large castle site at the forefront of the bluff. Vivid colors of blue and red appear then fade as if a spotlight is shining around. I blink, cocking my head to one side.

"Do they have a light show here or something?" I turn to Nash, pointing to the building. "Do you see those colors?"

He looks at the castle, then at me. "Yes, sometimes there are light shows. Come this way." He grabs me by the elbow and pulls me away from it before leading me down another path. "There's a palace over here where the elite lived."

My mouth opens in hushed awe when I see the palace. It's been completely restored. Stucco covers the walls, painted in vivid green and red shades. Thatching mounted on top of wooden posts provides shade. I turn to look at Nash, but he is no longer there. He must have walked ahead while I was busy gawking at the magnificence of the building. I move around to the rear, and a breeze blows through the site.

I look down and gasp aloud. Oh no, it's happening again. I'm topless and in that woman's body. This time her arms have red designs painted on them. She's moving without my permission, looking left to right for him.

Her king. Her husband. No, she doesn't love this man like she loved Kinich Ahau for all those years, but he saved her life then asked her to be his queen. How could she refuse? In any case, she is no longer a young woman. She needed a place to live, and he had been kind to her. His people already heard of her through stories, many real, and some embellished, but her abilities with healing made them think she was divine. And now, he has requested her presence on an urgent matter.

She follows the path behind their home and finds him sitting in their garden. He is not nearly as handsome as Kinich, and seeing him doesn't make her heart ache, but she has learned that to love someone like that is nothing but risk, and it is not necessary for happiness.

"Chaac," she says, walking up to him.

His wide face lights up when he sees her. He stands, his head rising just a few inches higher than hers.

"Chaac Chel, my queen." He smiles, holding his hands out to her.

As his wife, she has taken on his name. He leans in and presses his forehead to hers, and she smiles and closes her eyes, accepting his affection.

The air shimmers, and then I'm back. I'm by the palace, walking beside Nash with my arm linked in the crook of his elbow as he chats on about the history.

" … the different ways Ixchel is shown is confusing. Young and old, creation and death. Whoever she was with, she made them that much more powerful. The good became better, and the bad took on a life of its own."

I come to a stop, and I'm looking at the palace again. It's no longer a restored building with a colorful facade. It's a gray, faded stone ruin. Tears spring into my eyes. My dad was right. My mind is disintegrating just like his did.

CHAPTER 9

THIS TIME, I SAY nothing. I do nothing. I become stone, crumpling my fear into a ball then swallowing it down. We don't tour Tulum much longer, and next we drive north to a cenote where Nash has been dying to go freediving. The passing trees and flowers become a blurred canvas through my window. I stare, unseeing, my jaw clenched tightly as I try to control my emotions, when all I want to do is curl up in a ball and cry. How fast will this disease eat away my mind? Will it destroy my brain faster than it did my dad's?

A tear slips down my cheek, and I squeeze my eyes shut, pressing my forehead to the window to hide from Nash. When I get back home, I'll have to see a doctor. Maybe medication can slow the decline.

"Ines, mirá," Nash says softly, telling me to look.

We're driving slowly on a single lane dirt road in the middle of a jungle. Multitudes of butterflies fly all around … hundreds and hundreds of winged, beautiful creatures. There are black butterflies with red circular patches, ones with zebra stripes, another one with iridescent blue in the center of its wings, and butterflies with completely red wings. They flutter all about, and some land with a soft thud on the windshield.

My eyes look around, widened at the beauty around me. I forget about the shining tears on my cheeks and listen while Nash tells me the names of the ones he knows as he carefully moves through the horde of flying wonders.

The Ruta de las Cenotes is a strip of road with cenotes marked at various signposts. We see many such signs, but drive past. After a turn at Kin Ha, we continue until the sign for La Noria, where Nash turns off the road and parks.

I grab my towel from the trunk and wait while Nash rifles through his things. Hopefully there's a place where I can lie out and attempt to tan, since my last session did absolutely nothing but redden my pale skin for a day. A low sound of frustration comes from Nash's throat as he continues searching.

"You lose something?" I move beside him to help look.

"My suit." He shoves his hand through the front of his hair. "Must be back at the house, or I left it in Cozumel."

After a few more minutes of both of us looking, he slams the trunk shut then braces his arms against the Jeep. "I'm sorry." He presses his lips together in frustration. "This was a waste of a drive."

"Let's at least go see it."

He shoves his hands in his front pockets and then nods.

The jungle around us is alive with activity. Birds chirp and swoop from tree to tree, while monkeys make short howling noises. This cenote looks like hole in the ground and is probably about twenty feet in diameter. A flight of wooden stairs to the side leads to a dock stationed in the center of the tranquil surface. Nash gazes wistfully at the cenote then trots down the two flights of stairs into the cavern. I follow carefully behind.

Stalactites drip from the limestone top, and the water reflection shimmers on the uppermost parts of the cavern, dancing about like a mirage. Two ropes hang from the ceiling nearby, with a wooden swing attached at the bottom. In the distance, bats chirp and dive around the black edges. Sunlight pours straight in through the opening, igniting the intense blue jade color of the water. A yellow fish swims past before disappearing below the dock.

Another groan of frustration comes from Nash, and then he say, "Ines, close your eyes."

I sigh heavily and squeeze my eyes shut, turning my back to him. It didn't take Nash long to decide to forego the swimsuit entirely and go at it all native like that first night at the cenote he threw me in. I hope no one else finds their way here, because otherwise they will be treated to the sight of a giant, naked savage; a sight from the morning I can't seem to erase from my mind, and one I secretly wish I could see again. Just the remembering has my head turning of its own accord. I am completely powerless to stop it.

My eyes sweep down the broadness of his bronzed back, then to the narrowing of his waist, to the curve of his buttocks, and his long, athletic legs. He stands facing away from me at the edge of the dock, ready to dive in, but at the last moment, his head turns and those dark eyes connect with mine. And still, I can't turn away from the sculpted artistry of his body. Two heartbeats pass with our eyes locked, and then in one smooth motion, he dives from the dock into the water. I move to the edge to watch him descend with fluid grace. He goes down so deep I can no longer see him.

Today, I wore my crocheted bikini. The top is golden yellow, trimmed with red and turquoise blue. The bottoms are turquoise blue with a cheeky Brazilian cut. I drape my white sundress across the nearby wooden ledge where Nash hung his clothes. Sunlight pours in from high above, almost searing in its intensity.

I spread out my towel then lie at the edge of the dock, my face peering over into the water below. Small fish dart around near the surface. I know Nash will be down there for several minutes, exploring the bottommost parts of the deep. Closing my eyes, I focus on enjoying the heat beating down on me, and push away thoughts of the impending certain doom of my future, but they rise to the surface.

If I could live my life over, what would I change? If I only have a few years of sanity left, how do I want to spend them? In the past, experiences have always made me feel most alive. Travel, friends, food. Do I go back to the States and find a doctor who will put me on various medications? It might prolong my lucid state, or it could be like my dad where many of the drugs made him irreversibly worse. Or do I just blow the small amount of money I have left and travel? I don't want to be alone.

A flicker of a thought passes through my head, and I wonder if I should ask Nash if he'd want to go traveling around the world with me. I push that idea away. That would lead to a relationship, and I don't want to drag someone down with me through my unavoidable demise. This, right here and right now, will have to be enough of him for me.

And then the sensation of soft, wet lips press against mine. Somewhere low in my belly tightens in response. I inhale, and immediately return the pressure. My eyes open and Nash's face is in front of me. The color of his eyes matches the deep, dark blue behind him. He doesn't say anything and just takes in another lungful of oxygen before pushing himself backward and rotating into the water again. My fingers graze over my lips, certain that did not just happen.

He'd been down there for at least five minutes, which I know isn't a lot for him based on his stated record of eight minutes. He kissed me before he even filled his lungs with air again, as if my lips were more important than his next breath. That simple sensation of his mouth against mine made me feel cherished. I'm starved for more.

"Ines." Nash's voice comes from the right side of the dock where he's resurfaced once more. He's pulled the hanging swing over. "Try the swing. Only your feet will touch the water."

He's weighing my expression, and both of us say absolutely nothing about what just happened. I push myself up from the wooden dock then stand and walk over to the swing. With my feet at the edge of the platform, I move the swing behind me and give a slight pull with my arms, testing the strength of the ropes.

I glance down at Nash. "If this breaks, you better be ready to get me out," I say with a nervous laugh.

"Of course, *in k'áat*," he says with tenderness.

"What does that even mean anyway?"

That's the same thing he called me after he threw me in the first cenote and I had a complete emotional breakdown.

His lips twitch as he holds back a smile. "It means rabid bunny."

I laugh. "Liar. You better not be calling me something mean."

And with that, I take a deep breath and sit back fully on the swing. I keep my legs straight so they don't cause drag, and then I'm swinging over the surface of the blue, blue water. Laughing, I straighten my arms and lean all the way back. The end of my braid dips in behind me. For about a minute, I glide from side to side over the expanse of water.

I slow to an inevitable stop, leaving me calf deep in the cenote. I wait for fear to take hold, but holding ropes and sitting on a swing gives an illusion of control. The cold water refreshes my heated skin, and part of me wishes I wasn't so scared. But then I look around and realize the dock is now about ten feet away, and there is no way for

Nash to pull me back while I'm sitting on the swing. He notices it at the same time, because I hear him curse softly.

He moves in front of me, treading water. "Will you be okay swimming back?"

Both my hands tighten on the ropes as I look behind me where the dock is. I close my eyes and nod my head once. Swimming is not a problem for me, it's just my psychological fear of this watery deep that makes it so much harder. Even the mere thought of my entire body being submerged has me tucking my feet up tight underneath my bottom. I've got to do this before I psych myself out and become paralyzed up here.

My eyes widen as I stare into the water below and breathe in short, shallow breaths. Before I can think a moment longer about it, I release my hands and lean forward, dropping in. I go under for a split second and then twist around, kicking hard as I reach my arms toward the dock. The piercing anxiety feels like thorns swelling in my lungs, but I'm okay. I've got this. Then something brushes against my ankle. I shriek and kick wildly then slip under the water. Nash pulls me up.

"It's a fish!" he shouts. "It's just a fish!"

I grab onto him, fully intent to climb him like a tree to get myself the heck out of this water. He goes under, and then his arms grip me tight around the waist before he gives a mighty kick, bringing us back to the surface.

"You're gonna drown us both, idiota!" he yells in my ear, our cheeks plastered together.

"Don't call me idiota!" I shriek back, still clawing to get up his body.

"Turn around and climb out now," he says in a strained voice.

We've reached the dock, and his hands are gripping the wood, holding us steady in the water. My arms are fully wrapped around his head, and my legs around his ribcage. My heartbeat thunders loud in my ears.

"Jesu Cristo, Ines, get your tits out of my face," comes his muffled voice spoken from my cleavage.

"Oh—oh, sorry," I say dumbly.

The ladder is just to the left. All I have to do is let go of him and move over. I release my legs first and slide down him, but I dare not let go of his neck yet. For a moment, we stare at one another, our faces so close that if I turned my head our noses would brush. The air between us sizzles and fills with energy.

"You … you kissed me," I say softly, my eyes darting to lips that had been soft and tender.

"And I'll do it again if you don't get off me."

I believe him. He's ready for that and more, the fact of which is becoming very, very evident below the water. I release my hold around his neck and turn to grab the platform. And then he's behind me. One of his hands releases the dock and grips me around my ribs, just under my breasts, pulling me back against him. His lips touch the back of my neck, and my chest rises and falls in harsh, uneven breaths. I've got to get the heck out of here. But I close my eyes for just a second and memorize the sensation of his skin against mine, reveling in the peace that fills me.

Nash takes us out to dinner that night in Tulum. I wear a two-piece silvery gray dress. The crop top looks like a simple bra covered by lace extending to my ribcage, and the matching skirt is high-waisted, with a high slit starting at my hip.

We eat at a little beachside restaurant. Nash orders the filet mignon and I get the sashimi. Yes, we feel so fancy, but we balance out the boujee by ordering beers to drink. For a moment, I fantasize about what it would be like if we were a couple and this was a real date. Would he hold my hand all night? After dinner, would we take a romantic walk on the beach while the sun sets? Dance in the moonlight? Make love all night on silken sheets with the sea breeze cooling our sweaty skin? I know I'm not doing well sticking to my changed woman mantra, but being faced with the impending decline of ones sanity combined with Nash's looks tends to have that effect.

His long, sinewy fingers absentmindedly twirl the frosty beer bottle. I'm mesmerized by them as I remember the sight of his tanned hands on my pale skin that night in Cozumel. Nash tells me of all the amazing stuff he saw at the bottom of the cenote, and of a hidden cave he found down there. I tell him it's risky, and he could die, to which he responds by chugging the rest of his beer and then ordering another.

"Ines, you could die walking out of your house, or driving in your car, or slipping and falling when you get out of the shower. If I die doing something I love, then so be it. What does it matter to you anyway?"

I give him a hard, angry look. We've been in one another's company for a week now. Truth be told, I can't pinpoint the moment my feelings for him transformed from hostile resentment to friendship. And now it's a full blown crush. He'd laugh in my face if I ever confessed that to him, and my ego couldn't handle that.

"Just promise you'll take care of yourself, Nash. Please? I want to be able to come back again and have a friend to visit."

"Or you just stay here with me," he says casually, popping the top of his next beer as he keeps his gaze pinned to mine.

His eyes give nothing away. No flicker of hope, no sign of joking. The words come out as easily as if he were asking what I want for breakfast the next morning. My eyes drop to my hands on the table. I don't understand what he's suggesting. And I doubt it means the same to him as it does to me. Is he asking me to live with him? Does he want me to be his girlfriend or his roommate? I don't have an answer for either of those, so I don't ask him to clarify.

"That's just silly, Nash," is all I end up saying.

Stars glimmer high in the inky blue sky as we lie in the hammocks outside the house. The day has been stifling hot, and the ocean breeze is nonexistent. We stubbornly refuse to turn on the air conditioning units in the house and have just let the sea air blow freely throughout the small space. Tonight we may have to finally concede to the Yucatán heat. Nash stands and pulls off his shirt.

"Close your eyes, Ines," he says in a teasing tone. "Or watch, cochina. Whatever."

"Oh, Christ," I say, squeezing my eyes shut and putting my hand on top for good measure.

He has some nerve to call me a dirty girl, when he's the one stripping at every opportunity. This dirty girl is only human.

"C'mon, Ines. We're in Costa Maya. It's hot. Let's go skinny dipping." I hear the sound of his jeans unzipping, and then the soft thud as they fall on the hammock. And then there is silence.

"Did you walk away yet, Nash?"

I peek one eye open through my spread fingers, and he is halfway to the ocean, running full tilt. A huge grin spreads across my face. I have a bit more sense though, and I run inside to grab towels first. I take my clothes off then wrap the towel securely around my body before walking to the water's edge. The full moon illuminates just enough to see my way, but much is still cast in shadow to make me feel less brazen.

Nash stands waist deep in the ocean, with the moon high and bright behind him. I drop my towel and wrap one arm around my breasts, then rush into the water, shrieking as the cool wetness hits me. We move away from the shore until I'm shoulder deep, and immediately get into a splashing match until my hair is soaked.

Laughing, we swim and float around while Nash howls some good old-fashioned ranchera love songs to the moon.

He stops mid-song and turns to me. "What was going on with you earlier today?"

I blink rapidly, startled by the sudden transition and surprised he even noticed. I decide to play dumb. "What do you mean?"

He sighs, swiping his hand over the surface of the almost still water. A wave of gentle ripples moves to the shore. "You were crying while we were driving."

Okay, guess I didn't hide it well. And the fact is, I really don't want to talk about it. Having Nash view me as someone who is mentally deteriorating is not something I want. He should always remember me as I am now, vibrant and full of life, instead of thinking of me with pity. This is also why I cannot allow anything romantically to happen between us. On the other hand, if I do tell him what's happening, perhaps he won't kiss me again, especially here in the silken rays of moonlight with absolutely no physical barrier between us. That thought solidifies my resolve.

"You remember I said my dad died from Alzheimer's disease?"

He makes a low sound of acknowledgement.

I continue. "It hit him hard, and he lost his mind fast. He would have dreams and visions of the past, he said. In the letter he left, he said he believed the condition he had is genetic, and he's afraid I'll get it."

"You're still young though, Ines."

"No, you don't understand. It's happening. I'm—I'm seeing things! At the pyramid in Izamal, at the house in San Gervaiso—I thought I was being choked, Nash." I take in a shuddering breath. "And then yesterday in Tulum, that one lasted longer. But it's happening. And every night, I'm having these intense dreams. I'm too young for this," I say, my voice barely choking out the last words.

Nash reaches through the water and grabs my wrist then pulls me to him. He stays aware of our nakedness and holds me against his side, his hand around the back of my neck, muttering words meant to give comfort. But the words don't comfort me as much as his arms do. I wish I could be fully enclosed inside of them instead of this awkward half hug thing. The waves lap at our waistlines, and we move side by side to the shore. He gets out first and grabs one of the towels, then wraps it around his waist. Gentlemanlike, he holds the other one up for me, turning his head. I move quickly and wrap the terrycloth around my wet body.

Instead of heading inside, I collapse on the sand, knees pulled together to the side, watching as the water washes over my toes, then recedes. The stars above are brilliant and so much more visible than I've ever seen back home. Nash sits next to me and heaves out a sigh.

"Nash, my dad said there's another letter he sent that has an explanation for this, and maybe a solution. Do you know anything about that letter?"

He looks at me, then turns away, hesitating. "Mi papá has it. The instructions were not to give it to you until we get back."

"Did you read it?"

Nash shakes his head. "No, it's still sealed."

I don't want to put all my hopes on that letter, because my dad wasn't ever coherent for long periods of time. As far as I know, the entire thing could be absolute gibberish.

Nash reaches over and grabs my hand, then gives a gentle squeeze. That slight, insubstantial contact of touching skin seems to be an unspoken promise that he will never leave my side. I shut my eyes, chiding myself for my desperate thoughts. If I'm not careful, I'll be assuming he has feelings in his heart that aren't actually there.

As if he can sense my discomfort, he releases my hand, then moves to standing. I accept his proffered hand, and he pulls me up beside him.

"Do you want me to call mi papá and have him open the letter? He can read it to you over the phone."

It's a tempting offer. For a few moments, I seriously consider saying yes. It would provide the answer right away. Is there something to hope for, or is this mystery letter full of nonsense? But no matter what it says, I need to see my dad's words with my own eyes. I would want to re-read them over and over again, and cry in privacy over whatever the letter reveals.

I shake my head. "No. I can wait a few more days."

"If you change your mind, let me know, okay?"

I nod, then decide to reciprocate the offer of comfort. "Hey, Nash? Sleep in the bed upstairs tonight."

He lifts an eyebrow, flashing a now familiar wicked smile. "With you?"

"Ha, no," I say pointedly. "I'll sleep downstairs. I'll fit better in that bed."

Nash laughs softly. "Neither of us will fit in that little bed. It's designed for tiny people." He presses his lips together, and I can nearly see the wheels in his head turning. "If I wear shorts for sleeping, will you share the bed with me?"

"You promise to behave?" I tease.

A brief smirk crosses his features before he responds. "Only for as long as you do."

I manage to behave myself for the entire night. At one point, though, I wake up when Nash wraps me up in his big arms and curls his long body around mine. I stiffen briefly, but then relax into him. It's healing to be held in such a way, and a foolish part of me would like to think maybe I could heal him too.

The next day is nothing but heavy rains, so we sleep in then go out for a late breakfast. Afterward, we restock on groceries and beer. The little house doesn't have a TV, so we while away the afternoon sitting in bed, listening to the rain and talking. He asks about my previous relationships, and I'm painfully honest with every amount of abuse dealt to me, and that I also gave back at times.

Nash reveals that he grew up watching his dad abuse his mother. My eyes widen in surprise, because Guillermo always seemed to be a kind man.

"This"—he points to his beer—"can bring out the worst in a

good person."

I pull my knees to my chest, leaning back against the headboard. "What about you? We've drank almost every day here. Is that normal for you?"

"No, not usually." He shrugs, shifting his attention to the open balcony door. His legs stretch long in front of him, crossed at the ankle, and one foot bounces in a nervous rhythm. "But I should hate it, shouldn't I?"

I don't have an answer for that. Some of the things he described seeing would absolutely make me hate alcohol.

"You think it's genetic, Ines? To be an abuser?" He turns his intent gaze to me.

"I think seeing those things affects your brain, yes. I think you learned unhealthy habits from watching that, yes. But do I think because of that you're fated to be abusive? No. I hope not, Nash. It's a choice only you can make."

CHAPTER 10

THE ANCIENT RUINS OF Coba boast one of the highest pyramids in the Yucatán. It's one of the few big pyramids people are still allowed to climb, so we scale the 120 steps and stare out at the vast, green carpet of jungle stretching all around. Seeing the Yucatán from this viewpoint makes it easy to imagine what the past must have been like for the people who built these lasting monuments of stone to mark the passage of time and the movement of celestial bodies.

Thankfully, I have no strange hallucinations while touring the ancient site, but I remain on edge. Nash keeps his hand linked with mine as we walk around. I think he's doing it to protect me in case one of the episodes begins. In any case, I enjoy holding hands with him more than I should. That cold, aching feeling in my stomach seems to melt away whenever we touch.

We come upon a well-preserved stone court. The Mayan ball court looks like a long, wide hallway with sloping stone walls on either side. In the uppermost middle parts of the walls is a hoop made of stone.

I turn to Nash. "Have you ever played this?"

He rubs his jaw and smiles. "Yeah, it's difficult."

What he describes sounds like volleyball with a heavy rubber ball weighing anywhere from six to eight pounds. Instead of using forearms, hands, and wrists, the players use only their hips and thighs. Nash marks out imaginary lines on the stone court, where teams would have to get the ball across to win. Getting the ball through the stone hoop would be an automatic win ending the game.

I shake my head. "That sounds impossible."

Nash gives a short laugh, nodding in agreement. "Wait until you see the court at Chichen Itza tomorrow."

Shadowing my eyes with my hand, I stare down the Great Ballcourt at Chichen Itza. At 545 feet long, and 215 feet wide, it's bigger than a football field. If I thought it would be difficult to get the ball in the hoop at the Coba court, this court makes it a complete and utter fantasy. The hoop here is an impossible twenty feet from the ground.

"Was this court designed for giants?" I ask, my mouth agape.

Nash snorts. "Maybe. Sure looks like it."

Everything at Chichen Itza is beyond imagination. The detail, the carvings, the precision. Nash points out pictures carved into stone near the bottom of the ball court wall, depicting a ball player being sacrificed. The team captain kneels before a priest, awaiting execution.

The great pyramid, Kukulkan, is a massive, yet intricate monument, designed for both aesthetic and acoustic show. I stare in wonder at these fragments of history formed from stone. Nash says there are actually two more pyramids built inside the current one, and the entire thing is built over a cenote. Groups of tourists stand at the bottom of the long flight of stone stairs, clapping their hands. The chirping noise echoing back from the top is the sound of the quetzal, one of the most sacred birds to the Maya.

"Was that an accidental thing?" I ask, as we begin moving toward the Sacred Cenote.

He shakes his head. "No. It was carefully designed to be that way. Even the ball court makes special sounds. A man once spent four days there trying to figure out how it worked so he could design a theater. And yet, no one has ever been able to replicate it."

My eyes widen in wonder. "How did the Maya go from being these freaking genius architects and mathematicians to being dirt poor people living in shacks all over this peninsula?"

An intense look comes into his eyes. "Exactly, Ines. Many people wonder what happened."

"What do you think happened?"

Nash's eyes twinkle. "The reason for every man's downfall." He shoots a teasing look at me, a slight curve to his lips. "A woman."

I give him a hostile look but ruin it with a soft smile of my own at the end.

Nash's voice takes on a low, almost reverent tone. "Legend says the king of Chichen Itza, Kaan Ek, which means Black Snake, met a princess named Sac Nicte. They had one passionate night together when he became king of Itza. She left before he awoke and he never saw her again. Some time later, the rulers of Itza were invited to a wedding in Uxmal. There he saw Sac Nicte again, and found out she was to wed the prince of Uxmal. The moment he saw her that second time, Kaan Ek fell in love."

"Love, ha." I snort out a harsh laugh. "That's just lust wrapped in rainbows. It's an ache that burns away and all you're left with is ashes. The end."

Nash cocks his head in my direction, dark blue eyes full of surprise. He remains silent for a moment, then releases a breath.

"Wow, Ines. You really are cold hearted." His brow creases in a look of disappointment, but he shakes his head and continues his story. "Anyway, the day of the wedding, Kaan Ek arrived with sixty of his best warriors. They charged at the altar as if going into battle. Kaan Ek shouted, "Itzalan! Itzalan!" and grabbed Sac Nicte. The Itzas left their palaces, their homes, their temples, all for the love of their king, with Kaan Ek and Sac Nicte, hand in hand, leading the way."

"If he would have controlled himself, maybe Chichen Itza would still be a great city."

Nash makes a negative sound in his throat. "Ah, it's just a story, Ines. Kaan Ek's battle cry of "Itzalan" doesn't appear anywhere else in Maya history. Maybe there is some truth to it. But there were a lot of things going against the Maya of old."

"Such as?"

He kicks a stone off the raised, white path. "They burned so many trees to make the temples and roadways. Trees keep temperatures low and protect the dirt, then absorb water during the rainy season. If the heavy rains came and there weren't enough trees to absorb it, the water would wash everything away. They didn't understand that. Another big problem was similar to any government or ruling power. The elite would keep everything. They would get richer while the poor became poorer. You remember I said they built walls around a lot of the sites?"

I nod.

He continues, "Many of the walls built weren't to keep invaders out. They were to keep the lowest classes out. Add to that, you'd have droughts, and then in order to end the droughts, there would be many human sacrifices. Who do you think they'd use most often for that? I don't know about you, Ines, but if my rulers were going to kill me and my family in order to keep their own lives comfortable, I don't think I'd stay."

This is an interesting perspective, and I turn it over in my mind for a few moments before responding. "So you think the people started leaving because they weren't being treated well by their rulers?"

"Maybe, but it's impossible to really know." He stops suddenly and turns to me with a strange intensity. "If you could go back in time and change their fate, would you?"

I laugh out a sound of disbelief. "Like how? Just walk up, and be like, 'Hey guys, it's me, from the future. Can you stop killing everyone and just be one big happy family?' And then, goodbye to you. They've found their next human sacrifice. And let's not mention the impossibility of time travel."

"Of course, but just play along," he says with frantic gleam in his eyes. "Say you had a way to convince them to listen, and you knew they might listen and change. And then"—he snaps his fingers and casts his hand in an arc in front of us—"this entire peninsula is different."

My eyebrows knit together. "Yeah. I'd think anyone would want to prevent the collapse of that amazing empire. But maybe it was just their time, you know? Nothing lasts forever, Nash."

"Can you put this in the glove box?" Nash hands his cell and keys to me.

I close both our phones safely behind the hatch then grab my chapstick. Finishing our Chichen Itza tour yesterday was bittersweet. Today marks the end of our tour, and we're driving back to Progreso. Back to where I'm hoping to find answers in my dad's letter. But first, Nash begged to come back to this spot near Chichen Itza where there's a special underground cenote.

"You planning on swimming?" I swipe chapstick on my lips before setting the tube in the cup holder.

It's nearly noon, and the Yucatán heat makes my hair stick to the back of my neck. I gather my ink black tresses to the side of my head and begin braiding.

He slants his eyes in my direction, a smirk on his lips. "You planning on watching?"

"Probably." Smiling, I return the flirtatious look.

When the day comes that I lose my mind and memories entirely, I pray the vision of that bronzed, muscular body visits me in my dreams. I smile softly in remembrance, even while he sits next to me. So close, but impossibly far from reach. Our time together has almost reached its end, and I'm filled with the hopeless desperation to prolong it somehow.

The heat of Nash's eyes travels over me as I combine thick sections of my hair into a long plait. His heavy gaze soaks in my every move. Finished, I tie an elastic band to the bottom of the braid. Nash reaches over and wraps his hand around the section closest to my head, then tugs, letting the length pass through his fist.

I meet his gaze, making a split decision as I give in to my impulsive nature. "Do you want to go on an adventure with me, Nash? Travel the world?"

He doesn't hesitate in his response. "Yes."

A brief chuckle escapes me. "You don't even know where I want to go."

"It doesn't matter, Ines. I'll go anywhere with you." His eyebrows draw inward. "Do you want to go on an adventure with me?"

"I asked you first, so obviously the answer is yes."

"Let's go."

I cock my head with a slight smile, curious about what impending adventure he has in mind. From a short distance away, the low hum of motors pass as cars zip along the highway. On the other side of that highway lies the famed Chichen Itza and its Cenote Sagrado. I'm still not sure why they call it that. Yesterday, it didn't look so sacred with its murky, leaf-littered water. We slam the Jeep doors shut and walk in the opposite direction, away from the highway.

"Will it be okay to leave your truck here?"

"Si." Nash glances over at the white building near the gate and raises his hand. "They are friends."

An older woman lifts her hand in return greeting. I'm surprised he doesn't stop to chat like he typically would. When I turn to him, he's begun walking. A banked, burning energy simmers within him today. I'm not sure what has him in this odd mood. I follow his broad back to a line of trees beyond the small gravel clearing. He moves so quickly that even with my long legs I have trouble keeping up. At the edge of the forest, he stops and turns, waiting for me to catch up.

"Vente, Ines." Nash thrusts an impatient hand in my direction, slipping back into that old ordering tone again.

I imagine myself asking him to speak more nicely to me, to be more patient and more kind. Or maybe I'll respond by slapping his hand away. But I do none of those things, because more than anything, I ache to feel our hands locked together. I reach for him, and his large, warm hand encloses around mine.

We move through the dry, brittle underbrush that covers so much of the upper part of the Yucatán peninsula. The blades of grass are so sharp and dry they stab into my calves as we walk. I can't imagine how so many people were once able to live and thrive in such hostile conditions.

Nash comes to a stop, releases my hand, and then peers forward. Ahead of him is a gaping hole in the sandy dirt, only about four feet in diameter. Wooden beams create a small, sturdy frame on one side.

"Is this it?"

He turns to me with a quick nod and blue eyes shining with contagious happiness. "Right now is what the Maya call Day of No Shadows. The sun is directly up, casting no shadow."

I look at my feet, and sure enough, there is no visible shadow. Glancing up with one hand shading my eyes, I see the sun reaching its zenith, and I also note the pale outline of the daytime moon drawing closer to the sun.

Nash nudges my arm, then points into the hole. "*Mira*. Look down there."

While Nash leaned directly over the open drop, I have a bit more sense. Slowly, I shuffle to the wooden beams where a cogwheel and pulley system is set up. I brace my hand against the wood and lean forward to peer into the dark cavern below. Dizziness consumes me, so I straighten to standing.

"Did you see it?" Nash asks.

"No, that hole makes me nervous. How far is that drop?"

"Maybe forty feet." He waves his hand like it's no big deal.

"Here, try again. Give me your hand and I'll hold you."

The ultimate sign of trust. For a beat, I stare at him, then extend my arm. He wraps one hand around my forearm and the other clasps tightly to my palm. This is, by far, the stupidest thing I've ever done.

I lean over the open hole, while Nash shifts his weight in the opposite direction, his hands gripping tight. My heavy braid swings forward, dangling toward the water. The light cast from the sun is one single, heavy ray shining straight into the cenote like a flashlight. Incredibly clear, turquoise water shimmers below. The light pierces straight through, and I swear I can see the bottom.

It's inviting and almost pulsating with life.

I have the insane urge to wriggle my hand from Nash's and fall, fall, fall into the gentle blue waters below.

They would envelope me and take care of me.

"Ines!" Nash shouts, and pulls me hard against his chest.

I'm trembling, filled with some strange energy I can't describe. It's like starlight is trapped in my skin.

"What are you doing?" His eyes search mine as his hands grip my arms. "You were pulling away from me."

"I don't know … I don't know. I feel so odd, Nash."

His body against mine mimics the same buzzing energy threatening to spill out of me. It's not uncomfortable. It's inviting. I let my head fall forward, resting my chin against his shoulder. I love the scent of him.

"I don't know," I whisper again.

Nash turns his face to me, and his lips brush against my cheek. Instinctively, I turn to meet him. Seeking. Wanting. But he stills, and doesn't seal his mouth to mine. It's only a brief brushing of our lips as I turn.

"Ines," he whispers, then moves back so he can look me in the eye. His direct gaze is strong, unwavering, and intense as always. "Are you sure this is what you want?"

Turmoil rages in his eyes. The struggle is visible. Nash isn't the type of man who holds back from what he wants, so I don't understand his hesitation.

"It's just a kiss, Nash." I fist my hands in his white T-shirt, pulling him closer.

He moves in, and I run my hands over the strong planes of his chest, then drag my fingertips down the ridges of his abdomen until they find the spot where his jeans meet his hip bones. A soft groan escapes him.

"*Solo un beso.*" His gaze drops to my lips that are parted in invitation to his. "It's never just a kiss, Ines."

His thumb traces a line up my throat, before he captures my chin and turns my head so his lips find my opposite cheek. The warmth of his nose and lips is an exquisite sensation that has me craving more. I try to turn. I want his mouth, but his grip on my chin is firm, holding my head immobile. Warm lips nuzzle my cheek, then he traces his nose toward my hairline, before sliding to my jawline. There is brief pressure as his mouth seals to the space where my earlobe meets my jawbone. A lightheaded sensation follows, and I grip his arms to keep me standing. His breathing is harsh and rapid as his heart pounds an unsteady rhythm against my chest.

I itch with the need to bring him closer, to finally give in and connect with whatever this insane magnetism is between us. But he merely brushes his lips feather light over my face, skimming my nose, kissing the space between my eyebrows, and pressing his lips below the fullness of my lower lip, all while keeping my head in place with his hand. This dance is maddening.

He speaks again, slowly, enunciating each word. "When our lips touch, that's it. You're mine."

One day, this man will learn that I am not the type to belong to someone. But today, I only want a kiss.

"Just … shut up and kiss me already, Nash."

He laughs softly, then removes his hand from my chin where he's held me immobile, giving me my power back. His head dips as he nudges his nose against my cheek once more. "Your move."

My response is immediate and visceral. I couldn't stop even if I wanted to. And I don't want to. I turn to him with hungry desperation. My single focused need is to feel the realization of what my imagination has promised. My lips catch his, and he exhales raggedly before cupping my face with his hands. His hands are so large his fingers wrap around the back of my head as he holds me, crushing his mouth to mine.

Our lips meet and part, demanding and hungry. The length of his body presses against mine. My hands cling to his forearms as he holds me steady, drinking from my lips like a parched man who has been wandering a hot desert. And I give back to him in full measure. I empty myself to him, all my longing and years of yearning for some nameless force he seems to possess.

He pulls away, staring into my eyes, seeking or memorizing something. I don't care which, I just want more. I lean forward to taste him again, and for many moments we get lost in a savage, passionate assault on one another. There is no relief to be found, and it's as if we've thrown gasoline on smoldering coals. We ignite and burn and completely combust.

In one quick movement, Nash wraps his arms around my waist, lifting me from the ground. My legs encircle him, while his large hands move to span my hips and bottom, holding me in place. He stops kissing me and rests his chin on my shoulder, breathing unsteadily.

"Perdoname," he whispers.

Forgive me.

"What?"

"Don't let go," he says.

And then while still holding me, he moves to the edge of the cenote and leaps into the blackness below.

PART TWO:

ITZALAN

CHAPTER 11

I AM BEING DRAGGED from the depths of a deep sleep. My body convulses as my lungs wrack, expelling inhaled water. I heave and cough, then turn onto my hands and knees to vomit the contents of my stomach onto the smooth limestone beneath my hands.

Limestone?

My brain seems to expand inside my skull, and I open my mouth on a silent scream, falling sideways as a splitting pain explodes in my head. My hands shoot up, squeezing hard to offset the pressure. The pain is so intense I can't even scream. Only a hollow moan escapes my lips. Inside, pieces of thought float like a scattered puzzle drifting on water. I grasp at the convoluted chunks, but they drift and shift out of reach.

Wet hair clings to my face and water drips from the soaked strands. Another wave of pain rockets through my head. I curl my body inward, rolling into the fetal position and pressing my forehead against the stone floor. A noise comes from my throat that sounds like a dying animal. Squeezing my eyes shut, I gasp in lungfuls of air as the pain recedes.

I open my eyes and crane my head around to see the grayish yellow stone above and around me. There might be enough room to stand, but it still feels like a coffin with how close the walls descend around me.

The only sound I hear resembles static. It's a loud, pulsing, relentless noise. Confusion and pain are the only constants right now. Even my own name doesn't come to mind. All I know is I'm soaking wet and in a tremendous amount of pain. From a short distance away, sunlight filters through a small opening in the rock.

The light. La Luz.

Ines de la Luz. A piece of comprehension falls into place, flooding me with relief. I roll sideways, sudden fatigue washing through me. My back lands against a large, motionless body. I suck in a short, fearful breath of air and scramble upright to move away. Long legs encased in dark jeans lie eerily still. He, too, is soaking wet.

Nash.

The name comes easily to mind. My swirling thoughts slow and begin to juxtapose from jumbled confusion to tentative comprehension. The only visible part of him are his legs, while the upper half of his body is hidden in shadow.

"Nash," I croak out, coughing at the end.

I crawl to him and push against his thigh in an attempt to shake him awake. It's like shoving against wet sandbags. He remains motionless and silent. Alarm snakes up my spine as I reach for his shoulders. My hands touch water, where his upper torso and head are fully submerged.

"No, no, no," I whisper in a broken tone.

As I stand, pain pierces my skull, but I keep moving. Gripping under his chest, I straighten my legs and pull. His deadweight is heavy, at least 220 pounds, so I can only shift him a few inches. Moving next to his head, I crouch in shallow water deep enough to be his grave.

Panic floods my body at the thought of him being dead. I shove my hands under his chest, the limestone floor ripping skin from my knuckles. I brace my feet under me and again straighten my legs to try and flip him. I'm only able to raise him slightly, so I put my shoulder against his, then push forward.

I succeed in turning him onto his back. His right arm dangles limp to his side, while his left arms lies pinned beneath him. After pulling his arm free, I lean over and put my cheek against his mouth to feel for breathing. Nothing. All I feel is the chilling coolness of his lips. I press my fingers to his throat, feeling for a pulse.

Nothing. Not a flutter, not a murmur. Not a single sign of life.

My heart stops alongside his. For a few moments, I do nothing. I panic, patting his cheeks with my hands and smoothing his hair as if I could wake him. And then common sense kicks in.

"Nash," I sob out, getting myself into position.

I lace my fingers together, palms facing down, and start compressing his chest. Tears stream down my cheeks, and my life reduces to this man in front of me. I can only hope I'm doing this right. An unspeakable, almost paralyzing sorrow takes hold while I press harder and harder on his chest. I ignore the ache that spreads across my lower back and the burning pain in my wrists as frantic sobs and mumbled pleas slip past my lips. I move to his mouth, pinch his nostrils shut and puff in two breaths of air. I repeat the compressions then push my oxygen as deep into his lungs as I can.

What happened to us? How did we get here? My short-term memory is gone. I keep compressing and my lungs ache as I continue breathing into his mouth. I wonder if I can make it out of here somehow to make a phone call for help, but I know those precious minutes could mean his death.

If I'm not already too late.

"Please, please, please, Nash. Don't." Sobs of incoherent nonsense accompany each downward thrust I make against his chest.

And then he coughs. I roll him to his side as he heaves and expels the water in a loud racking sounds that echo in the chamber. Like me, he ends by vomiting on the ground. A strangled sound of pain comes from his throat as his hands shoot up to his head. He writhes, and the torturous expression of his features momentarily frozen in agony frighten me.

As the pain subsides, his dark eyes lock on me kneeling near him. His eyes widen, and he appears just as shaken as I feel. He shifts upright and away.

"Quien—" He can't get the "Who are you?" question out before the pain slams into his head again. Sounds of anguish choke out from between his clenched teeth as he falls to the ground again, jerking helplessly.

My throat thickens with the acidic taste of fear. Something is seriously wrong with both of us. Memory loss, splitting head pain, vomiting. I wonder if we're being exposed to some sort of natural gas leak in this chamber. And what is that sound? The loud pounding, rushing noise makes me think we're under a waterfall.

My attention refocuses on Nash, who is lying on his back, eyes wide and breathing in huge lungfuls of air. My man of macho bravado is scared to move and feel that head pain again. I don't blame him. It felt like my head was being bashed in by a hammer.

His eyes dart toward me. "No se …" he begins in Spanish, then swallows hard. "No se mi nombre."

Just like me, he doesn't know his name. I crawl forward until I'm in front of him. I have the urge to pull him into my arms and comfort him through the fear and pain, but I know he'd pull away.

"Se llama, Nash." I tell him his name. "Ignacio Dominguez."

He gulps in air then nods his head. "Gracias."

I sit quietly beside him for several minutes, waiting for him to get his bearings. Hopefully his memory returns to him at the same speed mine did. The seconds pass with the pulsing waves of pressure in my head, though they're not as shooting and intense as they were before. My eyes trace the profile of his handsome face, attempting to distract myself from the discomfort in my skull. I almost lost him. Gratitude fills me, knowing we've been given the gift of another chance.

For what? my brain whispers, but I push that nagging voice away.

"Ines," he says on a quick exhale, glancing over at me.

"Nash, thank God."

I move closer, and he sits up. He pulls me toward him with one arm and holds me against his ribs, pressing his mouth to the top of my head. The relief of being close to him causes a strange emotion to expand in my chest. I'd weep if I weren't so confused.

The sound of his voice rumbles through his chest. "What happened?"

"I don't know." I pinch the bridge of my nose. "I remember us putting our phones in the glove box. We were going to see the other sacred cenote. And that's all I remember. I think …" I hesitate and sit up so I can see his face, knowing what I'm going to say will sound crazy. "I think we're underground."

An expression I can't place moves across his features. Guilt maybe?

"La cenote sagrado," he whispers.

His breaths come faster as he leans forward to rest his elbows on his knees, clutching his head between his hands. His wide back expands and contracts with every breath. I lean my cheek against his shoulder, taking comfort from him even though he seems like he's about to have a panic attack. After a while, his breathing slows. He turns, moving his arm around me again and pressing his cheek to the top of my head. I snuggle in, enjoying his closeness more than I should.

"We need to figure out how to get out of here," I murmur.

"I know how." Nash speaks softly with a slight waiver to his voice. "You were right in a way. We're underground between two cenotes, but in an air pocket. We have to go through that opening there"—he points to the dark space where his upper half had been submerged—"swim down about ten feet, then back up and out."

"What?" My mouth widens, then shuts.

What he's talking about isn't possible. First of all, there is no way I would have willingly swam deep into a cenote in the first place, let alone done some underwater spelunking I don't remember. He's not thinking clearly. His brain must still be scrambled from whatever poisons are in this place.

"That's not possible, Nash." I smile in patience.

He closes his eyes. "I've been here twenty-seven times. I dove deep, found the entrance to this cave, memorized every detail."

Truth rings heavy in his words, but what he's saying not only sounds nuts, it's beyond the realm of what is humanly possible for myself. I would've had to swim INTO an underground cenote air pocket in order to be in one.

My eyes dart around the mostly blackened cave, and my gaze latches on the faint glow of light coming through a small opening.

"What about there?" I point to the light. "Can't we find our way out by going up?"

Nash shakes his head, thinking for a moment. "Do you remember cenote La Noria?"

La Noria brings to mind the image of his bare, muscled body, and the memory of a brief, stolen kiss.

A blush heats my cheeks. "Of course."

He hesitates a beat and tries to suppress a smile by running his tongue along the inside of his cheek. "Over on that side, it's the same type of cenote as La Noria. The opening is a hole at the top of the ceiling. There is no way out without a rope at the top." He turns to me, sitting with his feet flat on the floor, knees spread. Resting his elbows on his knees, he makes a U-shape with his hands, thumb touching thumb as if to play a game of paper football. "Imagine my fingers are the water in both cenotes. My thumbs are where the water meets at the bottom, running under this air pocket. The space between my fingers is limestone. We came in on this side"—he wiggles his left finger—"and the only way out is the opposite side, which is the cenote at Chichen Itza known as La Cenote Sagrado. It is the same water, just opposite sides. At least we can use rocks to climb out over there."

I widen my eyes, surprised he hasn't considered the obvious. "Um, or we climb out using the stairs. Don't most cenotes have stairs?"

Nash tilts his head back and exhales. "Ines, there will be no stairs." He straightens his head and looks me in the eyes. "We are no longer in 2012."

CHAPTER 12

MY LOUD LAUGHTER VERGES on hysteria. Not only because Nash made the ridiculous suggestion that we've time traveled, but what seals the deal is the complete and utter sincerity in his expression. Deep indigo eyes stare back at me, unblinking. My laughter slows. I wait for him to smile and tell me he's actually joking.

"Do you have any questions?" is all he says.

"Yes. How much crack have you been smoking?"

Not even a trace of humor flickers in his eyes. "None. Next question."

"Oh, okay," I say mockingly, deciding to play along with his game. "What year are we in?"

"Not sure. Whatever year we are needed to make a difference. The Whole One God decides that."

"Whole One God, really?" My voice drips with sarcasm. "How did we get here?"

He knows I'm not taking him seriously. I can tell by the way his heavy brows raise slightly, and then the sighing sound he makes as he answers me. "The cenote is a time portal."

My eyes widen in exaggerated surprise. "A time portal? Oooh, that sounds serious. So is there a purpose for this trip, or are we just going to randomly time hop for fun?"

"The purpose is to make a difference." He sits cross-legged and rests his elbows on his knees. "My family is from a long line of

Maya daykeepers. Our ancestors wrote many of the records. When the Spanish came, they burned much of our written history. Thankfully, oral history kept it alive, so it is still up here." He taps his head. "According to the Maya, history repeats itself cyclically. A Universal Cycle lasts about 5,125 of your solar years. The Maya divide that into thirteen sections of 394 years called bak'tun. Within each of these bak'tun those who have the power get called and are able to travel back to another bak'tun to change something major in Mayan history. Once the Universal Cycle ends in December of this year, that cycle is sealed, and history becomes permanent."

"So it's true? The world is going to end in December 2012?"

I purposely avoid giving attention to his crazy statement about people being able to travel back in time.

He shakes his head. "A new Universal Cycle will begin, but the one we're in now will become unchangeable. The true value of the Mayan calendar is incomplete without the holy books, which the Spaniards burned. The holy books are a map, and the calendar is the key. Together, they reveal the truth about the time portals. You remember cenotes are called Xibalba, right? The underworld?"

I nod.

He continues. "Ancient Mayans noticed when they'd sacrifice people, some would disappear entirely. We now know some of them traveled through, but most probably drowned in the process because they didn't know what was happening. Over time, the Maya figured it out and recorded it in our holy books."

My disbelieving gaze stays locked with his. I still don't believe him, and he can tell.

He leans forward. "Ines, remember that story you told me about how you almost died in a cenote? It had to be a day the portals were open. The snakes dragging you to the bottom, that's how it happens.

Snakes are sacred."

"Why don't I remember time traveling through a cenote?"

"You will. Your brain has undergone trauma with the time jump, which affects short term memory. The head pain is another symptom. Even now I feel my brain like a heartbeat. Do you?"

My eyes narrow as I'm able to feel what he's talking about. I'm uncomfortable with what he's presenting me. The answers don't align with my perception of truth. I press my back against the damp limestone, trying to figure out how to trip him up and prove he's joking.

I sit forward in a sudden movement. "Okay, prove it to me. Let's go out there. Show me. We're right by Chichén Itzá. If what you're saying is true, we'll see an actual, living city."

He points up. "Do you hear that?"

The rushing, pounding noise.

"It is the wet season, so it's raining. It will be too hard to climb wet rocks out of the cenote. We'll wait in here. As long as the water doesn't rise too high, we'll be fine."

"And if it does rise?"

"We swim out and wait in the water." He says it with a nonchalant shrug, as if it were a good, alternate choice.

I press my back against the wall again, my breath coming out in short gasps. "Nash, I won't be able to swim out. I just ..."

"You know how to swim, Ines. I've seen you swim."

"I'm scared though."

"I won't let anything happen to you, my love."

The last two words efficiently stop my threatening panic attack. I tilt my head at the very serious term of endearment I never expected to hear from a man like Nash. "Did you mean to say that?"

He looks back at me, the picture of innocence. "Say what?"

"You called me, my love."

An expression of shock moves across his face. I wait.

"Ines, I—I spoke Mayan at the end. You ... you must be understanding it somehow." His eyes are wide and incredulous. He straightens up and recites. "This is an account of the beginning, when all was stillness, silence, and water." He stops, then looks at me. "Repeat what I said."

The words roll easy from my tongue. I hear my voice, but the words coming from my throat are not English. I gasp and clap my hands over my mouth. I'm speaking a Mayan language, having never been taught it.

Nash beams with excitement. "The time travel must have triggered the language in your genes somehow. I worried how we'd handle the language once we got here—"

I hold up my hand, my features marked with confusion. "Wait, wait, wait. You said you worried about once we got here. Did you plan this?"

Guilt flickers in his eyes. "I had a plan for me alone. You were never part of it, but you showed up at the right time, so, eh."

My lips curl in an expression of disbelief at how casually he says that. "First off, there is no way time travel is real. Second, didn't you think to ask my permission?"

That question hits a nerve. His jaw clenches and he breathes out sharply through his nose, but his eyes pin mine with a stubborn look. "Hey, Ines, let's jump in a cenote and change history. Oh, and snakes will wrap around your ankles and pull you all the way down. You'll probably drown, but don't worry. I can hold my breath really long, so I'll keep you safe. Okay?"

He holds out his hand in mock invitation. I slap it away, then draw my arms tightly across my chest as a meager shield against the feeling of betrayal coursing through me.

I unleash my fear and anxiety on him in the form of anger. "If you're joking with me, it's cruel. You've taken it too far. And if you aren't joking, then that's unforgivable. I thought we were friends, Nash."

Hot tears prickle behind my eyes. I sniffle and rub my nose with my knuckles, mortified to be showing weakness to him. His gaze drops downward, and he is silent for several moments. At least he has the decency to look ashamed.

The cool dampness of the cave combined with my wet clothing sends a shiver through me. I clench my teeth tightly then hug my arms around my raised knees for warmth. The pounding in my head has reduced to such a faint pressure that I have to focus to feel the sensation. My head feels so heavy, and I just want to close my eyes. I don't know exactly what Nash has done, but this whole thing, whether it's the truth or a charade, feels like an ultimate betrayal. Grief wrenches at my heart.

I loosen my arms from around my knees then turn away and lower myself to the ground, lying sideways with my knees pulled into my chest. Another shiver runs through me. My clothes will never dry in this dampness. A sound rustles behind me and then his warmth envelops my back. I squeeze my eyes shut. I wish I had more pride or even the desire to push him away, but I don't. Instead, I accept the offer of his warmth and close my eyes, succumbing to exhaustion.

The sensation of falling jerks me awake. Nash's arm tightens around my waist. Like bubbles coming to the surface of water, my memory fills in. The kiss. My fingers reach up and touch my lips as an electrical feeling moves up my spine at the recollection. That may have been one of the hottest moments of my life. I smile softly, feeling his body shaped around mine. The heat of him against me is delicious.

And then the rest of the memory comes through. Him picking me up and saying 'forgive me' before jumping into the cenote. The forty-foot drop. Looking up as we fell, seeing the sun directly overhead, and plunging deep into shockingly cold water. And then the slithering sensation of snakes wrapping around my legs, pulling us impossibly deeper, leagues deeper it seemed, all while that shaft of sunlight followed us down.

There was a moment when that single ray expanded, filling the entirety of the space with its heat and blinding light. The last part was excruciating. Water filled my lungs, as it felt as if my body were being ripped apart. His arms remained tight around me, his own body jerking as the pain tore through him as well. My last conscious memory is him pushing off the floor of the cenote.

"Nash," I whisper. "I remember."

He exhales and presses his forehead to the back of my head, his hand tightening around my waist. "Me too."

He doesn't apologize. It doesn't matter, because I can't ever forgive him for that. The choice he made was heavy and life-altering. I deserved to have a say. Of course, I don't know whether we indeed did traverse time or if my experience was a side effect of hysteria and drowning.

Neither of us speak for a long time. The pounding sound of the heavy downpour outside has slowed to a steady rainfall. With good timing too. The water level from that shadowed hole inches closer. Soon, we'll leave this hollowed out place that has held us in limbo between two worlds. I don't know what I'll see out there. Either it'll reveal the extent of Nash's trickery, prove his delusions, or we'll truly be in a different time. For now, I need more information.

I clear my throat. "How did you know it would work, and we wouldn't just drown?"

He sighs, and I can't tell if it's from relief I'm speaking to him or because he's hesitant to answer the question.

Finally, he says, "I didn't."

I roll away from him and sit up, so I can see his face. "Are you kidding me?"

He pushes off the ground and also moves into a sitting position, but then he looks away, rubbing the back of his neck with one hand. "No, I'm not kidding. I've never done it, so how could I really know? The closest thing I know about it is what you said happened to you. It made sense of a lot in the holy books we didn't understand."

I am wide mouthed and incredulous at his stupidity. Just jump in and hope it'll work. What an idiot. I keep my opinion of him to myself, continuing my line of questioning.

"Can anyone do it?"

He shakes his head. "Only those of certain bloodlines."

"Bloodlines? What does that mean?"

"This is difficult to explain." He purses his lips in thought, then his eyes light up as he leans forward. "In your Christian religion, God sent a flood. Why?"

"Because people were bad." It's more of a question than a statement.

He inclines his head in a brief nod. "Not only that, but some angels came down and had children with human women. Those children grew into giants called the Nephilim. The flood killed them all. But do you believe the angels never did that with human women again?"

I frown. "I never really thought about it. But what does Christianity have to do with Mayans?"

"Everything, Ines. It's all connected."

"Nash, how do you know so much about the Bible? That's more detail than I know."

He shrugs. "I do not limit my knowledge. I make it a habit to study many religions and histories. But I speak of the Bible because it is the holy book you are most familiar with. If you were Buddhist, the conversation would be different. So the angels made their giant children with women all over the Earth, Maya too. These giants became revered in cultures all over the world. For the Maya, they became our gods. And those who have genetic links to these divine ones are the ones who have the ability to time travel."

"So you and I have genetic links to divine ones."

He nods once, his deep blue eyes holding mine in a gaze that imparts truth.

I put one finger up, needing clarification. "So you're saying my great grandfather to the hundredth generation was the child of a fallen angel?"

"No. It was a woman. And her name was Ixchel."

The Moon Goddess, who we learned about on Cozumel. The woman appearing in my dreams.

I lean forward. "How could you possibly know that?"

"I have dreams of her too. You are a mirror image."

"What about you?"

"My recorded ancestry goes back to Kinich Ahau, known as the

Sun God."

The man she loved. The one who looked almost exactly like Nash. My brows knit together as I ponder his words. But this story is just too fantastic, too mystical to be true. Things like this just don't exist in my practical world.

Nash continues. "The dreams and visions, how you feel a bit crazy ... It is not dreams. It's genetic memories, awakened by the land and by each of the holy places we visited. Every place we visited had a strong significance to our ancestors. Your dreams are their memories, imprinted in DNA, and passed down each generation. During sleep, conscious thought is not in control, which lets the memories come to surface. So you are remembering the lives of Ixchel and Kinich."

"So I'm not going crazy?"

"No."

"What about my dad?"

"Our best guess is your dad should have been taken that day, but you were grabbed instead. So his mind started the time jump but remained fractured since he didn't complete it."

I sit in silence, remembering the years of misery that followed, and how much he suffered as a result.

"The information should have been passed generationally, but like you told me, his parents died."

That's why he asked me about my father's parents when we were driving to Playa del Carmen. This entire time he was calculating, planning, and manipulating. He even used that kiss as a means to an end. I wrap my arms around my knees and turn my face away from him, a hollow ache expanding in my chest.

After a few minutes of drawn out silence, I ask, "Why didn't the memories or whatever start back then?"

"From our understanding, they don't start until puberty hits. You need to be near the sacred sites to activate them."

A bit more clarity. I didn't start my period until age twelve.

"Did my dad ever learn about the time travel?"

Nash looks down. "The only thing mi papá told him was we knew why it was happening to him, and we might be able to help you. I don't know why he never told him more. But that's why your father sent you here. As far as we know, he didn't know anything about the genetic lines or time travel."

I set my head in my hands. "He fed me to the lions," I moan.

"Ines, the truth is when you showed up, I was about to leave and do what I needed to do. Alone. My own trip was already planned to come to all the ancient ruins so my mind could absorb as many different ancestral memories as possible. I never planned to bring another person with. All we had was a floating reservation under your dad's name. We didn't know when you'd come. And then some moon goddess looking gringa"—he shoots a grin at me—"walked in during the five minutes mi papá left the desk. My heart stopped when I saw you." He gives me a heavy look. "Ines, this is bigger than you and me. Maybe it was God."

"I don't know if I even believe in God, Nash."

"It's obvious he believes in you."

Crossing my arms, I lean back against the stone. What he's describing about genetic memories sounds crazy. And yet, I've read fascinating articles about genes passing epigenetic information. Scientists can confirm that certain events incorporate into the genetic code. But what Nash is suggesting is beyond that. Could the lives, emotions, and experiences of those who lived before etch into our DNA? I imagine what would pass are the most significant events. I'm experiencing exactly that. The strong connection between our ancestors is causing vivid dreams and visions. They were so strongly connected that their love story and tragedy are at the forefront.

I glance sharply up at him. "Do you have the same dreams?"

He stares back at me, and I know he understands the root of my question. He exhales and nods slowly. "I do."

My lips tremble. "But Nash, those dreams … in my dreams it feels like it's us, but in a different time."

"It isn't us. It's them. Their story."

A chill moves down my spine. I draw my knees into my chest and wrap my arms around them. "He was terrible to her," I whisper. "Abusive, controlling, evil."

He nods. "And she loved him anyway."

"Well she was wrong to love him," I shoot out. "She didn't deserve to be treated like that."

"No one does." His voice is so soft, I barely hear him.

We are both silent for several moments, lost in our own thoughts. I wonder if he feels any kinship with his abusive ancestor. Ixchel's strong sense of goodness kept her faithfully loving a man who harmed her repeatedly. And Kinich Ahau, for all his passionate love for her, seemed stuck between good and evil. And the evil won.

"I was a jerk to you that first day," he finally says. "And it was because of their memories. Most of my life I dreamed about a woman who looked just like you. Of loving her and nearly killing her. And then my own temper. I wanted you to hate me so I could never hurt you."

I stare levelly at him. "It didn't work."

He gives a short, caustic chuckle. "No. Our ancestors' blood has made sure of that."

I'm not sure what to make of his statement.

"Nash, what now?"

"We present ourselves to the inhabitants of this place. One of us alone makes it easy for another god or ruler to dismiss our claims. But the two of us together, returning as Kinich Ahau and Ixchel, is more convincing."

I shake my head, not fully understanding his line of thinking. "Wait, so we're going to lie to them?"

"Throughout all Mayan history different versions of many of the gods appear. Ixchel especially reappears many times as a young woman. We suspect it was various generations of her ancestry. She has so many roles in Mayan history, as I'm sure you remember from the places we saw. You will now create your own role."

"It feels wrong. Like we're tricking people."

Nash leans toward me. "This is what we are destined to do. You will understand in time. But for now, you have to follow along with me." He stops talking briefly to listen. There is only silence, meaning the rain has stopped. "It's time to go."

He reaches for the hem of his shirt, and in one move, pulls his shirt over his head. My eyes widen. I don't understand what he's doing. He gives me a patient look as he bends forward to pull off his shoes.

"The Maya know we get birthed from the cenote. Clothing is not a part of birth."

Nash moves over to an area of the cavern where the limestone is higher up and dry. He lays his shirt over the top then unbuttons his jeans and slides out of those next. And with that, he is ready for his ancient Mayan birth. He keeps his back to me as he arranges his jeans over the rocks, draping them so they will dry. An important question pops in my head as I watch him do this.

"Nash, will we ever go back home?"

He freezes, the muscles on his back and shoulders flexing as he

151

grips his clothing. His head turns slightly, and I can only see his profile as he answers me.

"I will not return. But I promise you, Ines, when you want to leave, I will help you."

"Tell me now," I say, my voice trembling. It's not that I don't trust him ... I did once. "When and how can I return?"

As expected, there is reluctance in his expression as he turns to me fully.

"Can you ...?" I gesture towards his groin and turn my head, closing my eyes. I hear movement and then feel his presence in front of me. I open my eyes, expecting that he would have grabbed the shirt to cover himself, but no. He's just as naked as before, but this time standing half a foot away from me. I squeak out a noise of shock and move back, but he gets closer.

"Ines," he hisses, eyes aflame. "As a divine one, you cannot act like this when it comes to a naked body. You are no virginal girl. You are a woman. This has to be a natural sight to you. If you make that"—he mimics the hiccupping chipmunk sound I made—"noise every time a naked man comes near you, we are in trouble. So you need to look, and be okay with it. So, look." He raises his arms to the sides and waits for me.

Obviously, I've seen naked men before. Their bodies are beautiful, and the raw strength from their long, muscled limbs is intoxicating. I've seen plenty. But it's always been for a singular purpose, and usually I'd have had several drinks by then. Right now, I'm painfully sober, and not about to jump in bed with him. It's remarkable how comfortable he is in his own skin. My eyes trace the planes of his body, appreciating his design. He has no reason to be ashamed of a single part. Flawless, is the first word I'd use to describe him, with gorgeous being a close second. Blessed, would be the third.

He gives me a wary look. "I'm going to tell you everything about how to go back. But promise you won't leave without telling me, okay?"

"I promise."

The words come out effortlessly and actually mean nothing to me.

"It's dangerous, Ines. You can die. Promise me." He moves close, putting us eye to eye.

"Fine." I cross my arms. "I promise."

"En verdad?"

"Yes, for real."

"You remember what day I said it is, according to the Maya?"

"Yeah, something about no shadows."

"The Day of No Shadows is a solar zenith. It is a powerful celestial event which opens the portals. There are other combinations of events that can do it, but the guaranteed ones are the solar zenith, during the equinox, and with an eclipse. Each event lets one person pass through. If two tried to go, only one would be taken, and the other person's mind would become permanently fractured."

I blink slowly. "So how did we both do it?"

"Today was rare. We had both the solar zenith and an eclipse in our favor."

"When does it open again?"

"Next zenith. Middle of July."

My shoulders sink. Two months stuck here. It's going to feel like a lifetime.

"But you can't jump in just any cenote. Only some will work. The most dangerous parts will be the going down and coming up, so I have to teach you."

It's just like freediving. Nash did the descent on one breath, while I pretty much screamed all my oxygen out in the first ten seconds. I have a lot to learn before attempting it on my own. At some point in the future, I will plan my return home. I refuse to stay in a primitive past. But for now, I need to focus on what lies directly ahead.

"How deep are we?"

"Only sixteen, maybe seventeen meters. So, ehh, about fifty feet."

My head spins at the thought of swimming up from the bottom of a cenote. Just imagining myself surrounded on all sides by water makes my lungs ache.

Nash grabs my arms as I begin spiraling into despair. "Sixty seconds, Ines. That's it. You just have to hold your breath for sixty seconds. I'll be right next to you."

For some twisted reason, I don't doubt that I can trust this man with my life, but I would never, ever trust him with my heart.

"Depending on what time we're in, clothing will vary. Sometimes women wear nothing up top. Men usually have a ..." He scrunches his eyebrows, wracking his brain for the word. "A cloth? Un tapabarro?" He gestures to his groin.

"Loincloth," I supply, not actually looking down, but seeing enough from my peripheral. "What if ..." I pause, not sure how to word it. "What if they don't know who we are?"

He tilts his head, as if he never considered my question. "Ixchel and Kinich Ahau are among the most known of Maya gods. They will know us."

"Is there anything I need to know about my role, or ..." I shrug my shoulders. "I have no idea what to expect."

"The Whole One God will direct us."

I close my eyes and clench my jaw to keep my mouth shut. This entire thing is frustrating. Believing in one almighty God can be a trial of faith, but being forced to play the role of a Mayan goddess further weakens my belief in any type of divinity. I don't know what to believe or trust anymore.

Nash extends one hand to me. I comply, fitting my hand to his palm. A brief expression of regret moves across his face as his eyes drop to our linked hands. The way things have changed between us is undeniable, and I fear, permanent. How could I ever again fantasize about someone who's deceived me about something so important and unchangeable? I refuse to emotionally tie myself to a person who could make such a huge decision about my life without consulting me. Silence permeates the air, and for several moments neither of us say or do anything.

Until finally he says, "It's time."

CHAPTER 13

HE DOESN'T HAVE TO tell me, but I know what I have to do next. I move over to the rocks where he laid his clothing and remove my shirt, then sneakers, and jeans. I sneak a glance over my shoulder, and he has his back to me. Not like it really matters, but I'm grateful for that small measure of dignity he provides me. After removing my bra and underwear, I carefully lay everything flat on the rocks, my hands grazing over these precious pieces of fabric that give me so much security. My braid drags across the wet limestone floor as I crawl toward where Nash waits.

I sit back on my heels, clasping my hands together in my lap. "I'm ready."

He turns, careful to keep his eyes on mine. "Use the rocks to pull yourself along the tunnel. You won't be able to use your arms to swim because it is not very wide. After going down about ten feet, you'll be out of the cave and at the bottom of the cenote. Push off the bottom and go straight up. I will be right behind you. Count to help you keep track. Every second is about a foot."

Fifty feet. I nod, feeling my heart rate increasing.

"Wait," Nash says, then reaches for my braid.

He pulls off the elastic and gently unravels the thick plait, then runs his fingers through the length, spreading my long black hair like a curtain around me. For a moment, his eyes sweep over my bare body. Even though my instinct is to fold my arms over my breasts and use my hand to shield the dark apex of my legs, I don't. I let him look. And I watch him as he looks. His breathing goes shallow as his gaze roams over me. He clenches his jaw and closes his eyes before extending one open hand to me. I settle my hand against his.

Fingers press into my wrist as he feels for my pulse, eyes still closed. "Too fast," he says, frowning. "Cálmate, cálmate."

I shut my eyes, attempting to move myself to a serene, meditative state. After a few minutes, he taps my wrist, a signal to start the breathing technique to fill my body with oxygen. I sip in the air, knowing these are my last seconds of breathing freely. It's only going to be sixty seconds in the water, but I know it'll feel much longer. I don't have the same experience as Nash. For him, this will be an easy ascent.

"One last breath in," he says.

I inhale deep, bending forward to the liquid blackness.

"Go. And don't stop."

Cold water envelops my head, and then I immediately back out, dripping wet and gasping.

"No, Nash. I can't do this. I can't."

"You can. And you will. Breathe, breathe, breathe," he instructs me to take in several short breaths of air. "Now one big breath. Hold it. Go."

The water comes over me like a curtain of night. I resist the urge to back out of the cold liquid abyss, because I have no choice but to get out. Trying to see is futile in the darkness. My hands find the rocks and grip tightly, and I use them to pull myself down the narrow tunnel leading to the water of the Cenote Sagrado. Ten feet down, he said. I count down in my head to keep track.

... seven,

... six,

157

... five,

Nash's fingers brush my ankle, and his presence behind me relieves some anxiety.

... four, three, two, one.

The immensity and weight of the water above encloses all around my body. I straighten out, then sink like a stone about three feet. Mushy clay meets my toes, and I bend my knees, coiling inward, then spring straight up, pushing off the cenote floor. I synchronize my arms and legs, swimming with strokes like a frog. Open and close go my legs, while up, out, and down sweep my arms.

The danger of swimming up from so deep is that at around forty feet of depth, the weight from the water above pushes down, so going up is like swimming against a current. If I stop swimming I'll sink. Thankfully, this cenote is not as deep as some of the others. I count to twenty seconds in my head, all while struggling to propel myself upward. And then I feel the pressure let up some, and my body becomes more buoyant.

I've still got about forty feet to go. I look up periodically, making my way to the pale green glow of light up top. My lungs burn from the exertion of my body eating up my oxygen.

I can't imagine how Nash does this for fun. This is terrifying. It feels like an endless struggle to the surface. I just want to breathe, and fill my lungs with oxygen, but if I open my mouth I'll drown. So I clench my teeth together and keep moving and counting.

... nineteen, eighteen, seventeen ... almost there. The expanse of the murky green surface looks so close. In my periphery Nash is right next to me, and I imagine he's enjoying this leisurely swim from hell while I'm about to pass out. I know he can swim a lot faster, yet he keeps pace with my clumsy, awkward strokes that probably appear like I'm clawing my way to the top.

And then our heads break the surface, and I gasp in a sweet breath of air. The expanse of sky is above us, colored in the purplish indigo of impending nightfall.

"You okay?" Nash immediately swims up next to me.

I nod grimly as I glance around, looking for something, anything, to confirm or deny Nash's claims. From my vantage point, there are no differences. The sky is the same, and if anything, the trees might appear a bit thicker and closer to the cenote. But that could also be due to nightfall. And then I see the area Nash told me was their sacrificial altar. It had been a shapeless heap of crumbling gray stones. What stands there now is a scarlet colored building with a stone altar.

A clatter of rocks comes from above and Nash and I turn our heads toward the sound. Three round faces of children peer over the ledge. Nash waves his hand. The kids shriek, and then disappear, the patter, patter of their feet retreating.

"Come, Ines."

I glance over where Nash has swam to the edge of the cenote and is reaching to grab hold of the flat rocks to climb out.

Naked rock climbing. Great.

I sigh and move forward before reaching up. My fingers grip the smooth stones as my toes find leverage below the water. I begin to pull myself upward. My hair hangs long and wet behind me, long enough to cover my butt. Nash's head appears at the top, and I continue climbing. He reaches a hand for me, and I grip it with mine, then he pulls me up the rest of the way.

"Okay?" He nods his head.

I don't know what he's asking, but I nod dumbly along with him as I wring water from my hair. None of this is okay. I am naked and wet and have no idea what is about to happen. We begin walking side by side down the raised white path.

"What happens now?"

Nash answers me in Mayan. "Try the language. Practice it."

My tongue stumbles some, but then the words roll out. "What happens now?" This newfound ability to speak a language I've never learned is one of the most undeniable facets of this that has me convinced he may be telling the truth.

He continues speaking in Mayan. "We present ourselves to the priests."

"And then?"

"We trust God will lead this the way it should go."

Trust. I'm not good at that. And God? Don't get me started.

Ahead, voices rise in commotion. The children have notified the village of our presence. Torches flare to life, lighting up like fireflies from a distance, then begin converging and moving in our direction. My shoulders draw inward, my chin drops, and I pull my hair around me to curtain my body.

"No." Nash stops and turns to me, then pushes my hair back behind my shoulders and lifts my chin with his hand, holding it in place. "You are a goddess, Ines. Divinity is in your blood. Carry yourself as such. Bow your head for no one."

I exhale, nodding my head in understanding. We turn forward, continuing the walk to meet the chattering crowd of people. My mind attempts to draw upon the memories of my ancestress. She was a proud stubborn woman. I lift my chin even higher and pull myself to my full height of nearly six feet.

"I'm scared," I say to Nash in a hushed voice.

"Me too, muñeca." He throws the Spanish word in there, and I smile at the comfort it supplies. "But it is time to live our destiny."

Faces alight with curiosity float around our torsos. The tops of people's heads reach no higher than my collarbones, and these are the adults. Hands briefly touch my body and my hair, but not in a lewd way. They touch to see if we are real.

"Who are you?"

"Where are you from?"

Questions rain down on us, spoken in a Mayan dialect with harsh X, T, and L sounds, but I understand every word. My eyes dart around, settling on their brown, intelligent eyes staring out from tanned faces. I can't believe these people are living, breathing beings. We continue walking forward. The natives part as we move along the raised, white path. The term sacbe immediately comes to mind to describe this type of road. Nash says nothing, and I follow his lead.

"Dzonot! Dzonot!" the children shout to any adult who will listen, tugging on their hands. "They came from dzonot!"

People crowd the path in front of us as we move toward the heart of Chichen Itza, but they continue parting to the sides, allowing us to pass. In the trees on either side of the path, firelight flickers, illuminating the frames of many raised, thatched huts. We cross a road running perpendicular but continue moving straight into the heart of the city, surrounded by a mob of at least fifty people.

This section of the city no longer has homes. It seems to be more of a business district, with each building surrounded by a low, fence-like wall. Directly to our right is a massive building with pillars.

Straight ahead lies the great pyramid of Chichen Itza, one of the Seven Wonders of the World. One day, it would be called El Castillo, with the great snake, Kukulkan, running down the side stairs. But there is something different about this pyramid. It's smaller. Nash notices at the same time I do, and I hear a sharp intake of breath from him.

He turns his head to me, talking low in English. "You remember the Temple of Kukulkan?"

I nod. The pyramid we saw at the Chichen Itza ruins was said to have been built over another pyramid, effectively replacing it. That massive structure we saw is not here. Only the smaller pyramid exists.

"This must be the pyramid of the Red Jaguar King," Nash says, speaking of a person who must have ruled in a not so distant past.

When we toured Chichen Itza, Nash described how Toltec influences began to seep into the Maya religion, introducing human sacrifice to appease the gods. It appears we have arrived at a time perhaps directly before these influences have begun to infiltrate the Maya beliefs. It's somewhat comforting to know we won't have to observe the horrors of human sacrifice.

While El Castillo, or the Temple of Kukulkan, towered at about ninety-eight feet high, this pyramid is smaller by about a third, so it's maybe sixty-five feet high, and is painted a rich red color. Still an impressive monument.

The raised white path leads to a massive clearing holding numerous buildings and pyramids, temples and platforms. The floor of the entire clearing is made of the same smooth, white material as the path. Fires contained in large clay pots give light in the fast fading daylight. Men wearing what I can only describe as kilts patrol the structures. It is indeed a living city.

I sneak a glance at Nash, and his expression is filled with just as much wonder as I imagine mine is. But this means so much more to him. His entire life has led to this moment.

To our left lies one of the smallest structures in Chichen Itza, but it still stands about ten feet high. When we saw it as a ruin, all the bricks were white, and all their shapes were exposed. Now, everything is smooth, flattened by some sort of plaster, and painted a brilliant red cinnabar color. Other colors define the shapes and stone art—rich golds, brilliant blues, and verdant greens. Various stalls are scattered throughout this open area surrounding the base of the pyramid. I imagine this is a busy market during the day.

People buffer us on all sides, controlling our direction. We continue past the pyramid of the Red Jaguar King, then past the circular Venus platform. Trees close in around us as the sacbe narrows once more. It appears we're being led to the observatory, a blue and yellow cylindrical building about three stories high, resting on top of rectangular platforms. I'm not sure who we'll see here. Nash said we'd be presented to the priests, but it's also likely we'll meet their king or ruler.

Upon reaching the observatory, we begin to climb the three flights of smooth stairs leading to the top. My nakedness makes me feel exposed and more vulnerable than ever.

The crowd waits, and they do not follow. I glance back, and there has to be at least a hundred people now gathered below, with more streaming in from the main square. The commotion of our arrival is garnering much attention.

When I look forward again, a figure stands at the top of the stairs. The setting sun glows behind the figure, so making out anything of significance is near impossible.

A man's voice rings out, and the crowd goes completely silent.

"The heavens revealed the moon and sun in the sky as one with the morningstar. And now, the sacred well has given them to us. The gods have received our sacrifices."

Nash and I reach the top, and finally the building comes between my eyes and the setting sun, allowing the owner of the voice to come into view. I nearly gasp aloud at the resplendent man in front of us.

He is even taller than Nash, reaching at least seven feet. Tied around his hips is a loincloth dyed in various colors—blue, red, and orange. Layered on top is a blue, circular cloth with a white hem, folded in half. The ends meet at the waist, and then everything is held together by a bright red woven belt. Over his shoulders is a short orange cape, knotted against his throat, and decorated with brilliant blue circles with red symbols in the middle. The white hem is covered with blue lines drawn like a fringe, and notches nicked in the cloth every few inches. Various jewelry decorates him, the most obvious piece being a long jade bar through his septum. More intricate jade jewelry hangs from his earlobes and neck. One necklace has large jade beads, and in the center is an obsidian disc with a snake carved into the glass. Three red dots, painted on, follow the downward slope of his cheekbones, and more red designs adorn the bronze skin of his arms. To top it all off, literally, is an elaborate headdress adorned with the long, golden green plumes of a quetzal.

A yank on my hand shocks me from my reverie, and I glance to my left, seeing Nash kneeling before the man. Immediately I lower my head and sink to my knees. My damp hair falls about my body, providing a temporary shield to my nakedness.

"The Whole One God has sent us Lady Chel and Kinich Ahau!" he roars.

Lady Chel? I hear a sharp intake of breath from Nash. The muscles of his forearms flex, and I see the movement of his jaw clench. The crowd has at least quadrupled in size now, and they erupt in cheers. The man holds out his hands to us. "I am Lahun Chan, king of Itza. Come, my friends. I will show you to your home."

Thankfully, Lahun removes his orange cape and hands it to me. I move to put it around my shoulders, and Nash gives the tiniest shake of his head. Apparently I'm supposed to wear this as a skirt. I grumble inwardly as I tie the cloth around my hips. All I need now are Mardi Gras necklaces. I choke back a giggle, and Nash shoots me a disapproving glare.

Lahun Chan, we learn, is one of the two rulers of this place. As he leads us down the observatory steps, he talks animatedly about their day long ritual in the rain.

The king of Itza points to the sky. "The stars said you were coming."

I can only wonder what language the stars speak, and how this man can understand it. We follow the white road east, where it leads to another small clearing surrounded by trees. The mass of people respectfully part as we pass, speaking in hushed tones, but they do not continue down the road with us. It seems this place is off limits. Four small, colorful buildings come into view, and I remember this was one of the best preserved ruins when I saw it in our time.

The Red House. Several neighboring structures appear similar in shape and size, but they only looked like crumbled mounds of rock when I first saw them. Now, they too are impressive residential buildings. One house is painted red, and sits on top of a platform about sixteen feet thick. The other houses also lay atop massive platforms and are each painted a different color. One purple, one blue, and one yellow. Even the roofs are made of similarly painted stone.

The short steps to the red house are awkward to climb, so we take several at a time. The platform serves as a large, open air front porch, in a sense. Huge timber beams covered in thatch create a tall slanted frame, providing shade. Fires burn inside large clay pots on the terrace, casting a glow of firelight and making shadows dance on the stucco walls.

"You will stay here," Lahun tells me. "Your servant will be coming soon."

Servant? I'd rather not have a servant, but I have enough sense to keep my opinions about slavery to myself.

On the terrace floor are several square-shaped thatched, filled cushions. I take a seat on one, drawing my knees to the side while I watch Lahun lead Nash to the yellow house next door. Once Nash enters the yellow house, Lahun strides away, heading to the center of the city, likely to summon a servant.

Nash leaves the doorway of the yellow house, loincloth tied on, and returns to where I'm sitting. Everything is peaceful and so quiet, and yet he appears completely shaken up. I pat the cushion next to me in invitation, and he sinks cross-legged to the floor.

"Where did you learn how to put one of those on?" I point to his new undies.

He grimaces and reaches behind him, giving a small tug. "I'd rather not wear anything at all."

I grin. "Ah, finally found a place where your chronic nudity is permissible." I lower my voice to a whisper in case someone I can't see is standing nearby. "Why did he call me Lady Chel instead of

Ixchel?"

His impassive features reveal nothing, but the low tone of his voice is tightly controlled. "Because as Lady Chel, you are eligible to be his queen."

My eyes widen. "Uh, I didn't come here to be a bride."

"We don't get much of a say in what happens. It would be a high honor to marry a descendant of the Morningstar god."

"Then you marry him." I cross my arms over my breasts. Several seconds pass before I glance up at Nash again. "Morningstar god?"

Nash nods. "The planet Venus is the morningstar, called Lahun Chan in Maya. Our king must be a descendant."

I couldn't care less that this guy's ancestor was the god of Venus. So far, I see nothing godlike of the man, apart from his unusual height. The awe of seeing Itza caused me to somewhat forget my anger at being tricked by Nash and having no say in coming here. Now I'm seething, because I've forgotten how the past has never been all that kind to women. We are viewed as vessels for pleasure and a commodity to be traded at whim. If this Mayan god slash ruler wants me, there is nothing I can do about it but submit.

And yet, in the few moments I've known him, Lahun seems to be a decent man ... or god ... whatever. Funnily enough, he and Nash have similar features. Both have the long narrow Mayan nose, with slightly flared nostrils. The same wide, full lips too. But unlike Nash, Lahun has dark hair and dark eyes. He also sports a beard, which, according to Nash, is highly unusual. Even though Lahun is about half a foot taller than Nash, their builds are similar. Their bodies are those of men destined for power and glory and pleasure.

A tiny girl runs up the steps of the red house. She looks to be no more than eleven years old. Her long black hair is braided and cut into blunt bangs at her forehead. She wears only a simple, colorless cotton skirt and is barefoot. Around her forehead is a woven belt allowing her to hold a basket against her back, and she carries a platter shaped dish containing folded leaves and gourd bowls. After placing the food between Nash and me, the girl bows her head and moves to the edge of the terrace to wait.

I look over at her with a smile. "Thank you."

She stares at the floor.

Nash removes the tie from the banana leaf holding one of the packages closed. Inside is what appears to be a leaf rolled up and filled with a paste made of masa corn dough, white beans, and meat. There is one for each of us.

I bring the taco-tamale hybrid to my mouth and take a bite. My gaze shoots up to Nash's and we look at one another, both of our eyes widening at the combination of the sauce, meat, and beans. It is definitely an actual leaf we are eating, but the unique flavor is unlike anything I've ever tasted. The bowls each hold a mixture of onions and a spicy salsa to drizzle on the food. Our cheeks are stuffed to the brim like a pair of chipmunks as we efficiently obliterate the meal in front of us.

"This is really real." I glance up at Nash, waiting. "It's actually real."

He nods and smiles. "Thankfully. Otherwise you'd be pretty upset with me by now."

Blinking slowly, I drop my eyes to the thatching. I'm already pretty upset. Either he's an inconsiderate person, or he truly has no idea. I press my lips together, holding back the curses and angry words I want to hurl at him. They will do no good now.

Once we finish eating, the girl takes the platter away and motions for us to follow her. The white sacbe road gleams in the moonlight. We come to the main intersection, for lack of a better word. On the other side of the sacbe is the observatory. Continuing, we pass the Venus platform, and then go past the Xtoloc temple, where Nash says is another cenote.

The girl leads us to a small building just behind the Xtoloc temple. Inside the low doorway are several small fires safely contained inside clay pots for lighting purposes. She sets down her deep basket along with the one holding the remains of our dinner on one of the stone slab benches, then points to a small entryway in the far wall.

Nash's eyes light up. He immediately removes his loincloth then drops to his hands and knees to crawl through the entrance. After removing the orange skirt-cape thing Lahun loaned me, I hand it to the girl, asking her to make sure it gets cleaned and given back to him. She nods then picks up the food tray and leaves the building.

I crawl through the small doorway, where heat and steam thicken the air. A bench runs all along the circumference of the circular room. On the end opposite the tiny door is a large furnace type structure with a hot fire blazing inside. Attached to the front of the furnace is what appears to be a shallow stone basin. Nash crouches at the side, using a tool to remove large stones from the fire and placing them in the dry vessel. My eyes scan the line of his body. The way the heavy muscle of his thigh is bared brings to mind the image of a condemned Titan forced to shoulder the world. I'll never get used to the sight of him.

In the center of the room rests a huge stone sink filled to the brim with water. Underneath the sink are shelves notched out of the limestone, filled with empty wooden bowls. Nash fills a bowl with water and pours the liquid over the hot rocks. Steam hisses from the heated stones. He moves over to the tiny doorway and places a woven screen over the entrance, preventing precious steam from escaping.

I move near the steamy heat and sit in one of the hollowed-out chairs. They're perfectly butt shaped. Nash sits opposite me, leaning forward, elbows resting on his knees. He uses his thumb and fingertips to rub his forehead.

"Look, Ines," he finally speaks in hushed English. "I didn't know what to expect. To be honest, based on the history of our ancestors, I thought if you had to marry anyone it would be me." He looks over at me, and for the briefest of moments, vulnerability appears in his eyes. "And I hoped it wouldn't be such a horrible idea for you."

He's trying to make me feel better, but all he's doing is irritating me further. To think he could meddle with my life, as if he were God and direct my major life choices all for what he believes is the greater good ... It angers me. My life has been a series of events I couldn't control, and so much has been taken away from me. Now, my future feels uncertain. This is the last straw. I want to hurt him just as bad as he's hurt me.

I cross my arms and lean back in my seat. "Actually, if Lahun asks, it's fine. He's hot. And I mean, look at the size of that man. I'm sure he'll be good in bed ..." I wave my hand casually. "Or whatever we'll be sleeping on. What more could a girl want?" I pin him with my eyes, daring him to say something.

Hoping he'll say something.

"Oh," is all he says. He stands and moves to the vessel holding fresh water and pours handfuls over his head and body, using his hands to scrub.

He sits again, then apparently having thought of a good comeback says, "I thought you weren't so simple. I thought you wanted more out of life."

Upon hearing this, I stand and march over to him, my eyes burning in anger. I lean forward until I'm nose to nose with him. "More out of life? Like what? Like not being kidnapped and drowned? Like not being forced to travel back to the freaking Dark Ages? Like what, Nash?"

I've completely snapped and my voice comes out in a hysterical shriek. I slide to the floor of the steam bath, my shoulders shaking as I attempt to reign in my cracking emotions. The softer, weaker part of me wishes he would try to provide some comfort, while the betrayed half wants him to never touch me again.

He remains motionless, staring down at my curled body on the floor as I come completely unraveled. I want to kick my legs and flail my arms like a toddler in the midst of a tantrum. But I just wrap my arms around my knees and hold myself together. Loneliness and despair flood my body. I'd almost forgotten what they felt like.

CHAPTER 14

WHEN NASH AND I leave the bath house, the girl is waiting for us, head bowed and small shoulders drawn in. If she takes notice of my reddened, swollen eyes, she gives no clue. From her basket, she pulls out a colorful loincloth for Nash, and attempts to move the cloth between his legs to dress him. He lets out a strangled sound of shock and sidesteps her, then ties the cloth on himself. She hands him a few more colorful pieces of fabric, then turns her attention to me.

For me, she has a skirt. The cloth is mostly red, with a white, notched hem. There is also a narrow ribbon of black, blue, green, and orange squares next to the hem. Straight around the middle is a wider band containing blue and yellow geometric designs. I tie the skirt on, and the length stops just under my buttocks. It's clearly meant for a shorter woman.

While we walk back to the colorful houses, I try and ask the girl questions about herself. But she walks faster to get ahead of us, keeping her head down.

"She'll probably get punished if she talks to you," Nash warns in a low tone.

Apparently we are considered the "elite class" while the girl likely comes from a lower class. I don't say much in return to him, but I promise to be careful. I plan to treat the girl like an equal, not a lesser person. She will have much to teach me.

When we arrive back at the houses, two young women wait on Nash's terrace; likely a welcome gift from Lahun. A small thread of jealousy burns in my chest, but I push it away. Nash doesn't belong to me, and he never will.

The more I think about it, the more irritated I become at the unfairness of it all. Why can't two muscular men be sent to me for my own fun? But I remind myself that I'm a changed woman. And besides, my ancestral memories aren't providing me with a Mayan word for condom. I'd rather not be knocked up when I leave this time period.

I leave Nash to enjoy his diversion, while the girl guides me into the red house. There are four rooms in total. The first room is the entire width of the house, and it acts almost like a hallway or even a living room, because all three back rooms are accessible from it. The center room holds various bowls, leaves, and tools. Wooden beams frame the inside of the stone room. This space looks to be mainly for food preparation. The doorway to the left opens up to my room. It is spartan and plain but has everything I need. Along the back wall is a platform of raised stone with a mattress on top made of woven thatch and filled with something soft enough to be comfortable. Various colorful blankets lie on the bed. This room, too, is framed with wooden beams, and a woven hammock hangs diagonally between two thick posts.

Small vent holes cut into the wall allow for air flow. The jungle breeze brings in the ripe, damp scent of impending rain along with a variety of giggles and sighs from the yellow house. I quickly usher the girl away and send her to her own home to preserve her innocence.

The day has been tiring and long, but falling asleep proves difficult. The jungle itself is full of strange noises, but on top of that, the sounds coming from the other house just don't stop. For hours. At one point, they finally quiet for about twenty minutes. I nearly drift to sleep but then get woken up again to the sounds of the women, one after the other.

My own feelings of loneliness rise fast to the surface, and a bitter regret boils in my belly. Desperate for sleep, I flip to my stomach and plug my ears with my fingers, finally succumbing to the night.

The same sounds awaken me as dawn is rising and now I'm ready to murder him. Raw arousal and pure anger fuel me. I sit up and throw my blanket to the floor, then stomp out onto my terrace.

Lahun's handsome face is coming up my stairs, sans the quetzal feather headdress. He looks much more human than god at the moment. I quickly smooth my snarling features into something more befitting a moon goddess.

I am demure, I am poised, and I am the embodiment of serenity.

"He is enjoying my gift?" Lahun says with a laugh, inclining his head to the decidedly ungodly noises from my neighbor.

"The entire night," I return with a smile, eyes squinting as I barely suppress a yawn.

"You and him are not ..." He frowns, his gaze moving quickly between me and the yellow house. "I failed to ask before."

"We are not," I say quickly, then add with a coy smile and bow of my head. "I am accepting gifts as well."

Lahun's look of confusion is quickly replaced with a shout of laughter. "Your spirit animal is the rabbit for good reason. Say the word, Lady Chel, and I will have strong, capable warriors lined up solely for your pleasure."

My mouth hangs open. I was not expecting that response. Well now.

I clear my throat, blush heating my cheeks. "I will let you know if the need arises."

"Anything for you," he says. A hesitant expression comes onto his face. "I know the sun is not yet in the sky, but I am going to the observatory to see the rise. Would you join me?"

I beam in happiness at his kind request. "I will."

The city is mostly asleep, but the sky begins to come awake with pink and violet hues in the east. As we walk, I ask Lahun questions about himself, to find out more about this enigmatic ruler. He is twenty-two years old and does not yet have a wife. Tiptoeing away from that topic, I shift gears and ask about his co-ruler.

"Chaac is twenty-nine and also without a wife. He has travelled to a great king in the west to secure an alliance for our city."

Is he talking about *the* Chaac, god of rain? I don't want to appear stupid, so I don't ask. But I can't wait to tell Nash about this to see what he thinks.

Lahun and I climb the three levels to get the observatory. The structure looks like a three-tiered circular cake, set atop a two-tiered rectangular cake. He tells me the building is newly built, and he commissioned the best architects and artisans. He speaks enthusiastically of the design and is animated in his telling of how it was built.

What he's describing astonishes me, as many of the things seem far too advanced for this time period. But I watch in awe as he shows me two curved wall compartments resting in slots on either side of the observatory; moveable walls, if you will. The king sets each of the walls to his desired position and then guides me inside the circular building.

At the top of the flat ceiling is a cut-out hole, likely to mark the zenith sun. Running along the wall is a spiraling ramp that goes up two levels. There is a ledge holding various leather-bound instruments, and Lahun selects one, then leads the way up the ramp.

"The sky tells me of the future and reassures me of my path," Lahun says as he stares through the instrument set in one of the notched out viewing holes. "Every morning and every night, I come here to view the heavens. Two nights ago, the moon and Venus rose with the sun. And here you are next to me. The goddess of the moon in the flesh." The king turns from the inset window, giving me a kind smile.

He hands me a long tube made of leather using the same care one would use in cradling a newborn baby, making sure I use two hands to hold it. At the end is a heavy disc of polished crystal. It's a telescope.

For the next hour, the king guides me around the observatory, showing me how to use the instrument and making remarks about what's in the sky. And before we know it, the sun is over the horizon, blotting out the stars.

I thank Lahun for sharing his sky with me, and then he walks me back to the colorful houses. The city comes alive as people begin setting up stands in the market. Lahun points in the direction of the great pyramid.

"You are welcome to enjoy the market. The people will know to send me the cost of anything you or Kinich want."

"I thank you for your kindness, my king."

The young women come down the path from the yellow house, soft giggles and laughter preceding them. One carries a large bowl with wet cloth inside, that had likely been used to wash after the night's and morning's activities. They move to the side of the raised sacbe with their heads bowed to allow us to pass.

Apparently it's okay for them to bang a god all night but never look one in the eye. Got it.

"Please come to the observatory any time," Lahun says with a warm smile. "I am there almost every sunrise and sunset."

I smile up at him and pull my hair over one shoulder, running my fingers through the strands to detangle them. "I will."

He turns and retreats down the path, and I climb my stairs, where the young girl is waiting in the middle room with wooden bowls of food. I kneel on the floor and begin eating the mixture of root vegetables, tomatoes, and beans.

"What is your name?" I ask.

She doesn't answer and only stares at her small hands clasped in her lap.

"My name is Chel," I say. "What are you called?"

I wait, hoping she'll speak soon. The girl glances up at me, but drops her eyes, murmurs an apology then slaps her hands over her mouth. Her eyes widen in horror, as if she can't believe she's transgressed so severely by both looking at a goddess *and* speaking to one. Large brown eyes fill with tears that spill over onto her round cheeks.

"Child," I say soothingly. "Please do not fear me. I want you to speak to me. I will tell no one. Only the trees and birds will know we talk."

She sniffles and wipes the back of her hand under her nose.

"What is your name?" I whisper, hoping maybe she'll be more willing to respond if we whisper.

Her eyes dart nervously around. She licks her lips, then

177

whispers, "Calalu."

Amaranth, my brain translates.

"Calalu," I repeat softly.

Returning my attention to the food, I continue eating, all while quietly asking her questions. Calalu moves behind me to style my hair. I learn she is twelve years old. This is her first position as a servant. Serving one of the elite class is a great honor for her family. She is a well-mannered, bright girl, and her gentle female companionship is a balm to the soft, feminine part of my heart.

Once I finish my meal, she grabs the empty bowls and leaves the house. Two more hollowed out gourds filled with food lie in the middle room. Upside down gourds cover the tops to keep curious insects out. They must be for Nash. I want to share with him the information I gleaned from Lahun, so I grab the bowls, leave my house, and climb the yellow stairs.

He too has a thatch-covered terrace, but no front room. There are three doorways straight ahead, and the center is similar to mine, with the interior wood framing, and bowls for water and food. The room to the right is where Nash lay sprawled out over his well-used mattress, sleeping in the nude as is his preference. My eyes sweep over his sleeping form, and a sudden feeling of regret passes through me. It is the missing of something gone that never existed. The thought unsettles me.

My bare feet move silently over the stone. I crouch near his head and brush his hair off his cheek with my fingertips. "Hey, Nash," I say softly.

He comes awake almost instantly, then he reaches for my hand and brings it briefly to his lips. A dark look shadows his eyes, but he closes them again and just rests his cheek against my hand. An odd feeling slams into my chest, almost like anxiety, and yet I keep my hand in his with our fingers loosely threaded together.

I missed him.

There. I've said it.

We've been practically arm in arm for days upon days, sometimes falling asleep together, and often waking up near one another. Last night was the longest we've been apart.

"Lie down," he says softly.

I shake my head violently, giving a short laugh. "This entire room needs to be burned after last night."

"We were in the other room. Lie down." He tugs on my hand, pulling me to him.

And I don't know why, but I do it. I slide down to the rough mattress. One of his arms goes under my head, while the other hangs over my hip. It just feels right being next to him like this. There is nothing sexual about it, even though he is completely naked and probably still covered in his and their sweat from an arduous night of lovemaking. I push it from my mind, because to simply lie next to him feels as important as taking my next breath.

And just as necessary.

When I awaken, Nash is no longer curled around me. He is sitting in the bed, his back leaning against the wall while he eats the food I brought. I sit up next to him, and he tilts the bowl in my direction as a silent offering. I shake my head and lean back against the same wall, crossing my arms over my bare breasts.

"So I talked with Lahun this morning. He said the other ruler here is Chaac. You think he's talking about *the* Chaac?"

179

"Definitely a descendant, at least. It's impossible to know, though, because with the first several generations it's believed divine ones lived a lot longer than a regular person."

"He said Chaac is visiting a great kingdom in the west to create an alliance."

Nash looks puzzled for a moment, and then understanding comes into his eyes. "It must be why they'll build the Kukulkan pyramid."

"I don't know what you're talking about."

"The Toltecs in the west are who came before the Aztecs. You think the Maya were bad" —he gives a short, harsh laugh— "well the Toltecs were worse. From what I understand, we didn't start the sacrificing until we accepted their influence. If we've gone to the time directly before the Kukulkan pyramid gets built, then we're in the 9th century AD. Or CE, whichever you prefer." He stands, setting the now empty bowls off to the side, then ties a new loincloth onto his hips, before sitting down across from me. "And from what I've heard, the Maya here are still a peaceful people."

"I don't know," I say dryly. "Sounded like someone was getting murdered last night."

He snorts out a sound of surprise, and a flush of red moves up his neck.

"Um, sorry about that." He looks down. "It won't happen again."

"Nash look, you can do whatever you want. I'm not going to judge you for having human needs ... I mean, I have needs too." I sigh, and glance down, tugging at the embroidered hem of my skirt.

He looks at me, weighing my expression, then says with a smug grin, "You could have joined. There is enough of this to go around."

I exhale out a choked laugh and lean forward to give him a light shove on the shoulder. "Oh, that is just sick."

His expression looks wounded at my comment.

"Not that the thought of being with you is sick," I clarify. "I mean … I just don't share well with others."

Our gazes lock for a moment, and he searches my eyes. I look away first.

"Ah," he says softly.

We sit in silence for several moments following that awkward exchange. I keep my arms crossed over my chest, still not fully comfortable being topless. A gentle breeze blows through the room, as light rain begins to fall outside. It must be close to noon by my guess.

We begin talking at the same time.

"Ines, just so—" he says, while I say, "I want you to—"

We stop.

"Go ahead." I nod encouragingly for him to continue.

He looks down and fidgets with the colorful hem of his loincloth. "Tricking you to come here was wrong of me. I hope one day you understand why this is important, but I should have given you a choice."

"Thanks for saying that."

The apology isn't a magical salve to fix the hurt, but it's a start, and for now it's enough.

He takes in a deep breath. "And I really am sorry for what I did last night. I was just hoping to feel something."

I frown, my eyebrows scrunching together. "You don't feel anything down there? That sounds like a medical problem, Nash."

He coughs out a laugh, shaking his head. "I feel just fine down there, Ines. I just …" He exhales out a groan, dropping his head back to look at the ceiling. "I wanted to feel something here." He raises his hand, pointing one finger to his head, eyes flicking over to meet mine. "And I didn't. Now I just feel empty."

181

I know exactly what he's talking about, because I've been there too. Sex for the sake of release is fun at the moment, but if a person's heart and mind aren't being filled, it's as futile as pouring water into a broken glass. The good feelings disappear fast, leaving an emptiness that yawns deeper than before.

"Ines, I need you to know something." He leans forward and looks me in the eye. "That kiss? Before we jumped in the cenote? That messed me up bad." He shakes his head. "Not even an all night threesome made me feel what that one kiss did."

My face cracks into a smile as I breathe out a short laugh. I scan his eyes, waiting for the humor to appear, to see that beautiful laugh of his, and for him to say he's joking. But he doesn't. My smile fades. He stares back at me, soul bared and effectively dropping all this emotion in my lap.

"I ..."

Words fail to come from my throat. I don't know how to handle the weight of what he's thrown at me.

"Listen," he says. "I'm not saying this to try and convince you to be with me. Because I don't think it's why the Whole One God has us here. No matter what happens, I just need you to know. Understand?"

I nod dumbly. How do I even respond? I've kept my heart tightly shuttered, and then plastered an extra barricade of derision on top. He's been charming and flirtatious, and while I've enjoyed the attention and even returned it, I never expected to hear words like this from a man like him. I think back to the number of times I've thought the words "man like him" about Nash. Countless. I've been prejudiced to him from day one. This entire time, I wonder if everything he's said and done has actually been sincere, while I've been busy keeping him in a neat, stereotypical box for my own protection. I stare at him, the tangled ball of yarn in my head loosening, allowing me to unravel a bit more truth about him.

He stands, grabbing a circular yellow and green cloth from a basket next to the bed, and busies himself by folding it in half and wrapping the ends to meet at his waist. I reach in the basket and pull out a blue woven belt, then slide myself to the edge of the bed, my feet on the floor. I wave him over with a gesture of my fingers. He moves to stand in front of me between my spread knees, still holding the two ends of the hipcloth together. I thread the belt around his back, then tie it at the front.

Nash kneels in front of me, a pained look in his eyes. I trace my fingers down the side of his face, and he closes his eyes, grabbing my hand and turning his face into my palm.

An intense pain erupts in my chest, and I want to cry for some reason. What is happening to me? I don't like the way this feels one bit, and yet I don't want him to move away. He eventually puts his arms tight around my waist and lays his cheek against my bare chest. I wrap my arms around his head, just resting my chin on top as I run my fingers through his hair.

Something tender and sensual and foreign lingers around the edges of this moment. My brow furrows with confusion as invisible dots in my heart connect, forming the picture of something I never hoped to imagine.

CHAPTER 15

THE JADE BAR IS about as long as the length of my hand, from the wrist to the end of my pointer finger, and about as thick as my pinky finger. I hold it up to my septum, eyes raised in a questioning manner to Nash. His arms are folded over his wide, bare chest, while his right hand holds his chin in contemplation. He looks at me, then at the jewelry designed for piercing, but smiles softly and shakes his head.

That sadness still lingers in his eyes after the intimate moment in his house. I hate seeing him sad.

I move the jade bar from my septum and bring it lower, right in front of my nipple and raise my eyebrows again. I am the picture of innocence. This time he covers his mouth with his hand, his entire body moving with laughter as he shakes his head no.

Pleasure blooms in my chest as I watch him laugh. I grin back at him then thank the merchant for showing us his wares as I set the jade bar back in his hands. The merchant, bolstered by my interest, draws my attention to several other pieces.

"For the lady of the moon," he says, unveiling a special stash he keeps in a wooden box hidden inside his cart.

One of the sets catches my eye. I carefully lift a hoop from the box. The small piece of jewelry is carved entirely from jade, filed to resemble a crescent moon. Nash looks over my shoulder at the pair of earrings.

"Get them," he says encouragingly. "You said your boyfriend offered to pay for anything."

I throw a scornful look over my shoulder at him, but I have the merchant package up the hoops, along with a jade beaded necklace and a set of gleaming bracelets Nash calls tumbaga, which is an alloy blend of gold and bronze.

We take our time wandering the market. I habitually use one arm over my breasts at random moments, and Nash gently elbows me and shakes his head. It's not an easy thing to get used to my upper half being on display like this.

The grinding sound of soaked corn kernels being processed into masa dough draws our attention. A woman kneels on a thatched mat, wearing a simple long skirt with a notched hem. She wears a red, folded hip cloth over her white skirt. The long, smooth stone in her hands continually scrapes against the shallow stone bowl on the ground in front of her. Over and over, she moves the stone until the corn is reduced to a pulp, but she stops and stands when she sees us.

"Kinich Ahau and Lady Chel." The woman speaks to us with her eyes lowered. "It is my honor to serve you. Please sit." She extends one arm towards a leafy tree where several thatched mats lay.

"You hungry?" I murmur to Nash.

It's been several hours since our light morning meal.

"Always," he responds with a short laugh, leading me by the elbow toward the mat.

After maneuvering a hot rock from the homemade oven, the woman scoops it into a stone pot which is holding a mixture of white beans and spices. The mixture smokes and sizzles as it cooks from the heat of the hot rock. Soon after, she brings us the mixture, along with several corn tortillas.

Grinning at one another, we eat a small meal of what is basically tacos.

"All we need is a beer now," Nash says on an inhale when he comes up to breathe from shoveling food into his mouth.

I nod in agreement. This food reminds me of the meal at that small Mayan village the first night we were together. So much has changed since then. He's become a part of my life that I never wanted, nor could I ever be without. The thought is discomfiting and so unlike me.

"You all right?" Nash asks, his eyes fixed on mine, then without waiting for my response. "You gonna eat that?" He points to the last taco.

"No." I shove the food toward him, but I don't know which of his questions I actually answered.

An old man sits motionless at a simple stall while I peer around his little shop. Nash has been summoned by Lahun Chan, and I'm left to wander the open market on my own. I glance over at the elderly herbalist, and he appears to have fallen asleep. Dried herbs, chunks of bark, and chopped lengths of roots are laid out in woven baskets. A stone pot sits inside a banked fire, some liquid potion simmering away. I've always been interested in herbal medicine but never had the opportunity to learn. I smell the various items and nothing smells familiar. My nose wrinkles at a root emitting the sharp, musky scent of skunk.

"You have aching bones?" comes the aged voice of the man.

Turning around, I see the once slumbering healer is now awake.

He has the bearing of a younger man and his weathered face retains a youthful light.

I shake my head. "No. What is this?" I point at the musky root.

"Powerful, powerful medicine. Let me introduce you to my friend, *pay'che.*"

Alarmed, I glance behind me, expecting to see another person who's crept up. A chuckle of laughter turns my attention back to the man, who has now stood from his seat and is shuffling over. Though stooped with age, his head is still far above mine.

"This." He grabs the basket of the stinky root and extends it to me. "This is my friend, *pay'che.*"

Smiling, I greet the root with the traditional Mayan greeting, then turn to the old man. "Who are you?"

He draws himself to his full height. The old man is even taller than Lahun. "I am Tato. I am One Who Knows." He uses the Mayan word H'men to describe himself, which can be loosely translated to mean shaman. I spend a long time there with Tato, sniffing, examining, and greeting all his plants … or friends. My eyes are lit with wonder and knowledge, and I yearn to know even more.

The market activity gradually ebbs, and soon Nash returns for me as the sun is setting. He finds me with Tato, the old healer filling my head with as much information and I can take. I feel such an odd sense of comfort with this old man and decide to take a chance.

"I want to learn everything you know, Tato. Will you teach me?"

He smiles widely, revealing several missing teeth. "Follow the west sacbe early in the morning. Before the sun returns. There you will find me. You will know."

I wave goodbye to the old man, and Nash and I leave, heading back to our homes. People trickle out of the market, baskets attached to their backs with tumpline straps around their forehead, carting their goods back to their huts. The sky is awash with streaks of orange and blue, rising upward as if they could overtake the entire sky.

"He says he is One Who Knows," I say to Nash, telling him about my new friend.

He nods. "Not many shamanic healers exist in our time. And if they do, they keep their gifts quiet. People who don't understand it call it the work of the Devil." He shakes his head, a bitter twist to his lips. "Plant medicine is a gift from the Whole One God."

"I'm going to learn it." I square my shoulders with pride.

"Your ancestress, Ixchel, was also a great healer. Maybe even that will be in your genetic memory."

We pass the sacbe leading to our homes, but instead of going to our colorful houses we continue ahead in the direction of the observatory. I raise an eyebrow to Nash in question.

"Lahun would like to speak with you," he says, then sets his jaw tight.

"What did you guys talk about?"

"He asked if I have the intention to make you my wife."

My heart stops. "And you said?"

Nash turns to me but doesn't meet my eyes. He only stares at the white road, kicking a stray stone from the path. "I told him my goal here is to support his rulership in whatever role I'm needed."

Thickness moves into my throat. The words he said earlier this morning ring hollow in my ears. Clearly, I make him feel something, but not enough to save me from marrying a man I don't lo— I stop the errant thought in its tracks. That word is not in my vocabulary anymore.

"If he asks you to marry him, it would be wise to accept."

"I already said I don't want to marry anyone."

"And I already said that neither of us get much say. I mean, Lahun is a good man, Ines. He would make you a better husband than I would."

I blink slowly and square my jaw. Apparently, what I might want means nothing to Nash. Again. I straighten my neck and pull my shoulders back.

As casually as I can muster, I say, "Well, I'll see you later, then."

With that I turn and walk away from one man, and toward another, yet with the nagging feeling I'm leaving something important behind.

The observatory is quiet, with only the light rushing of the evening breeze coming through the wall notches. Flickering candles set on stone ledges cast a soft glow of light throughout the hollow sanctuary.

"Lahun?" My voice spreads throughout the dim space, and I wonder if he is even here.

"Lady Chel," he responds from the topmost parts of the observatory. "Please, come up."

One foot moves in front of the other, and then I follow the spiraling ramp to the second level. It's been difficult for me to reconcile everything that's happened. We entered Itza a mere twenty-four hours ago, and the fact that Nash spoke the truth about time travel only serves to confirm the existence of the forcible will of a Whole One God directing all of this. I wonder what would happen if I refuse Lahun.

But I've made up my mind. If Lahun seeks to make me his bride, then that's what I'll do. I'll leave here in two months anyway. I have no problem going through the motions until I can go back home. This is purely survival.

I reach the top platform where Lahun waits. He smiles as he watches me approach. As far as unwanted marriages go, I could do worse. The king is tall and solid muscle. He and Nash could be distant cousins, as their features are remarkably similar. Whereas Nash remains clean shaven, Lahun has a short beard, making him look a bit more serious. The effect of which is ruined by the two dimples in the creases beside his smiling mouth, making him appear boyish.

I can't help but return the king's smile and extend my hands to the ones reaching for mine. His large hands virtually engulf mine. I feel tiny next to him, and I've never in my life felt tiny.

"We have much to discuss, Lady Chel. But first, let me show you something." The low timbre of his voice is gentle and almost melodic.

He guides me to a wall and with utmost care hands me the leather wrapped crystal. I set the telescope in the narrow window, designed to fit just its size, then put one eye up to the cylinder. I can clearly see the morningstar, Venus, emanating its steady glow.

"Do you see the big lion?" Lahun's voice is close, and I can feel the heat of his body against my skin, even though we aren't touching.

I've never been one for astronomy, but I can only assume he's speaking of the Leo constellation. I make an affirmative sound, even though I'm not really sure what I'm looking at.

"Then the virgin, do you see her?"

"I'm not sure, Lahun," I say, feeling helpless.

"How about stars in a row that look like a vine?"

I see a smattering of stars all in a row, but on a gentle arch. "Yes, I see it!"

"Keep following that, and then at the end, what does it look like?"

The star vine curls around, ending in a splatter of stars, forming what looks to be a flower.

"I think it's a flower," I say, not too confidently.

"It is!" He reaches for the telescope, and I move to the side so he can look again. "It's so clear that's what it is. Except, I don't know what it means. It's always next to the morningstar … my star."

He stares through the telescope for a moment, then pulls away, shaking a dreamy expression from his eyes. "I am sorry. That's not why I asked you to come here." Giving me his full attention, he puts his hand under my elbow to guide me back down the ramp, then wastes no time. "I'm asking you the same question I asked Kinich Ahau. Do you want him to be your husband?"

I nearly trip over my own feet, and Lahun steadies me with one hand. Mumbling out my thanks, I keep walking. What if I say yes? What then? Does the Whole One God allow me to exert my will? I shudder when I think of how Nash would react. He'd think me a silly, pitiful female prone to fantasies. Our purpose here is singular, one I can't say I understand, nor care much about. But I'm here.

Clearing my throat, I turn to Lahun, giving my most brilliant smile. I parrot Nash's words. "I am willing to support your rulership in whichever way I am needed."

His eyes narrow. "That's the same thing he said. But you didn't answer my question, Lady Chel. I have watched you and him. I can tell you are good friends. Maybe more. Do you want Kinich Ahau to be your husband?"

"No," I say truthfully. "I do not want Kinich Ahau to be my husband."

For I do not know Kinich Ahau, is my unspoken thought.

Lahun breathes a sigh of relief. "Well, then. That's settled."

We've reached the bottom of the ramp and Lahun turns to me. Hesitation enters his eyes, a questioning look, before he leans forward and presses his lips to mine. I'm startled by the sudden intimacy, but I don't pull away. The kiss is not unpleasant. The king's lips are warm, and the fullness of them could almost leave me wanting more. Almost.

Lahun pulls away and his look is not what I'm expecting. Dark, heavy brows are drawn inward and his lips are curved in a small frown. My ego nearly cracks at what I see. I can tell I didn't meet his expectation.

He gives a short laugh. "I apologize for that."

I lower my lashes, casting my gaze to the floor. "I'm sorry it wasn't to your liking, my king."

His eyes widen, and he gives a quick shake of his head. "No, Lady Chel, no. You are beautiful. Your lips"—he brushes one thumb over my lower lip—"are perfect. I just …" Lahun's large shoulders collapse, and he glances up at me with a sheepish smile. "You will think me a fool."

What could possibly make this enigmatic ruler feel at the risk of ridicule?

"Try me," I say, lifting my chin.

"I wish for love." His brown eyes soften wistfully. "And I imagine I'll feel it in a first kiss."

My eyebrows crease in question. "Have you ever felt it, my king?"

Lahun smiles softly. "Maybe. When I first became king of Itza, we celebrated an entire week. Many people came to the city. I met a young woman after sunset while I was alone in the observatory. She came to see the stars. We never said our names, but we watched the sky together the entire night. I honestly don't think she knew I was the king. As the sun was rising, we kissed, and … we didn't stop there," he says with a boyish grin. "The next day, I searched for her, but she was gone. No one knew who she was, and so many women fit the description of small with long, black hair. I never found her. But that first kiss was the best experience of my life. I haven't felt it since. Did you feel anything like that with me?"

Love from a kiss? I shake my head. Lahun's kiss was nice, but he's right. It lacked something important. Unbidden, the memory of Nash's hands spanning my jaw as our mouths moved together comes to mind, and my belly heats in remembrance. The kiss left me with a wide, aching gap in my chest that I fear will never be made whole. But love? That's not love. That's just an urge. It's chemicals and hormones drugging the brain.

Lahun's soft sigh brings me back. "I guess it doesn't matter anyway. I just had to be sure before the matches are made."

I cock my head. "Matches?"

"When Chaac returns within the next uinal, he will bring a Toltec princess."

If I'm remembering correctly, a uinal is twenty days. The Toltecs from Mexico greatly influenced the late Maya and gave way to the Aztec nation.

Lahun continues. "We seek to form peaceful bonds throughout all the land, and connect our people in order to ensure peace. I became king of Itza a year ago, when I was twenty-one years. And I've only recently brought Chaac on as a ruler. We've decided the best way to continue this rulership is to bring in others to co-rule. We will be the Itzaes. Our wives will rule alongside us. We set up marriages with a matchmaker. She will study each of our day signs and find our best matches."

"Lahun, I—I …" I pause momentarily, hoping my words don't anger him. "I would rather not be someone's wife."

"Lady Chel, it is absolutely necessary. You are the moon goddess. Marriage ensures your protection. Otherwise, any man can take you for his."

My brow creases in annoyance. I continue to forget I am residing in a time where marriage and breeding are the ultimate goals in life. If the king were a crueler man, he wouldn't have even asked my opinion about any of this. As grateful as I am for his kindness, I can't help pushing further.

"So if any man can just choose to take me, then I can choose to take any man I want for myself?"

Confusion clouds his eyes. "I guess that is possible. It is why I asked if you and Kinich had a connection. If the moon goddess chooses the sun god, that is permissible and even ideal. But it is not usually done that way for the elite. We submit to the gods direction."

I sigh. Like it or not, I'm about to become a bride. Unless I can stall somehow.

"My king, once the matches are made, when will the ceremony take place?"

"The matchmaker will choose an auspicious day. Could be the next day, or it could be several uinals later."

My eyes brighten. This entire thing will be a gamble, but I'm hoping the marriages will be scheduled after the portals open next, because then I'll be gone.

CHAPTER 16

THE WHITE PATH GOES on much longer than I expected. When I set out to find the old healer's palapa the next morning, I imagined a brief walk down the roadway. Now, close to twenty minutes have passed, and the sun is reaching its first tendrils of daylight over the treetops. Hurrying, I pick up my pace.

A few minutes later, a lush garden comes into view—neat, tended, and carefully separated into sections. I walk through rectangular areas neatly framed with stones. There are bushes and vines, flowering fruit trees, and herbs. Mature palms provide areas of shade, but much of the garden gets sun throughout the day. I notice what appears to be a water collection and transportation system, with hollowed out wooden tubes connecting one to the other, working with the natural, gentle slope of the land to provide valuable water to all the plants.

Tato's house is humble, but finely built. Two buildings stand side by side. The smaller one has a workbench with baskets of chopped plants and herbs. The large, oval shaped building rests on top of a wooden platform and is covered with a thatched roof. Two hammocks lie inside, and one is occupied.

"Tato?" I call out.

A woman sits up from the hammock. She is young, but still a good decade older than me. She must be his granddaughter.

I greet her and say, "I'm here to learn about plants from Tato.

Where is he?"

She shoots me an angry look then points down a path that leads into a thicket of trees, before flopping back down on the hammock. I incline my head in thanks, not certain why she seems so unhappy with my presence. The well-worn path is easy to follow. If I don't find him, I'll easily be able to make it back on my own. But five minutes later, I see his tall figure, slightly hunched, with a basket hanging on his back.

"Tato," I call out, hurrying to catch up.

The old man turns, and he smiles upon seeing me. "So she remembers." He adjusts the woven strap on his forehead from the basket.

"It took me longer than I thought to walk here, but I won't be late again. May I?" I hold out my hands, offering to carry the basket.

He waves my hands away with a "pah!" sound. "I may be old, but I am strong." He squares his jaw and juts out his chin in a strangely familiar way.

"You look very strong."

I say the reassuring words not just as a means to soothe his male pride, but because he truly wears his age well.

The man looks to be in his mid-80s at least. Even though he stoops at times, the framework of his bones is solid. Sun-browned skin sags with age, but the muscles on his body are ropey and lean. I imagine when he was a younger man, his build was similar to Lahun's.

A flurry of twittering erupts in the trees near us, and then two brightly colored flying creatures veer out. The vermillion birds spin and flap, diving and soaring as they fly about, but remain in close contact.

Tato laughs. "The oldest dance there is. Soon there will be eggs in nests."

The birds' mating dance reminds me of something important I need to know now that marriage may be in my future. "Do you know of something for a woman so a man's seed doesn't take root in her womb?"

He nods, and shoots me a curious look. "Every woman knows of it. We will find it today."

As we walk, Tato mumbles under his breath, but I can't make out the words as they're not spoken to me. Several minutes later, a rabbit bursts from a thicket of trees. Tato immediately turns and walks straight into the forest, leaving the path behind. I follow carefully and the canopy thickens. The shade is a cooling contrast from the rising heat. Tato wanders for a few moments, scanning the tree trunks, then makes a soft, pleased sound.

"Here she is." He extends his hand to a thick tree with vines wrapping all around. The vines reach high into the uppermost branches and extend out into the canopy. "This is Ix Ki Bix. She grows beside her lover, Ki Bix. See"—Tato points to one side of the tree where an enormous vine has taken root in the ground—"he grows here on this side. And she"—Tato moves to the other side of the tree, where another vine emerges from the earth—"grows here. Always together, these two lovers. Now notice this." He returns to the male vine and pulls out a dark blade. The obsidian knife gently scrapes into the bark, and Tato pulls it apart, revealing a white inner core. Next he returns to the female and does the same, but the inside of the female plant is a deep red shade of layered colors. "What does that remind you of?"

"A woman's blood," I say, my voice hushed in amazement.

Tato nods, his intelligent eyes gleaming. "The plant often tells us what it can do. We just have to look and listen. And now, because she is our friend and helps us, we say thank you to her gift."

The old man crouches at the female root. "My friend, I thank you for your power and the valuable medicine you share with us on this day." Upon finishing his words of thanks, he chops away at the vine, tossing the pieces behind his head where they neatly land in his basket. "If you do not thank the plant, and only take, it can choose not to help you. It is alive, just like you and me. Honor it. That is the most important thing I will teach you."

We walk a short distance through the trees before emerging on the foot path, Tato again murmuring softly to himself. Every few minutes, he makes a joyful exclamation, then rushes away from the path to collect his findings. He shows me leaves, and flowers, and how to identify poisonous plants. We cut more roots and collect wide leaves, narrow leaves, and bark, throwing them all into the rapidly filling basket attached to his back. The names he rattles off for each of his "friends" pile into my brain, settling like little index cards of information I file away.

My hair lies like a thick carpet on my neck and back. I'm helpless without hair ties. Calalu has been doing my hair each morning, and she hadn't arrived before I left an hour prior to dawn. I twist my hair into a serpentine tail then move the end through a loop to create a knot.

"I saw your granddaughter in the hut when I arrived. She didn't seem happy to see me."

Tato quirks an eyebrow in my direction. "My granddaughter is on Tatun Cuzmal. The woman you saw is my wife." He laughs at the surprised look on my face. "I may be an old man, but this body works just as well as a young man's. I have energy to walk these paths and work all day, and I still have energy to play all night."

At first, I'm somewhat shocked at how casually he talks about his virility, but then laughter bubbles out of me. Tato chuckles in amusement, pleased with having gotten a reaction.

"So be it," I exclaim, breathless from the laughing. I turn to him. "How old are you?"

"I have seen one bak'tun, my daughter. Since then, I have stopped counting. I am very, very old." Tato sighs, as if the weariness of old age is a heavier load than the one he is currently bearing.

After returning to his home, we chop roots, boil potions, and sort leaves, setting them in the sun to dry. Tato's young wife supplies us with food and water while we work, and she regards me with a curious stare. I suspect she thinks I've come for her man. A smile crosses my face at the thought.

Tato gives me some of the Ix Ki Bix vine along with detailed instructions on how to use it. He is confident in the herbal contraceptive and says he has never had a woman become pregnant while using it.

"Unless the Whole One God wills it, a baby will not grow in your womb while you use Ix Ki Bix," Tato says while I drink the bitter potion he brewed. While this dose won't prevent immediate pregnancy, it should become effective after my next period.

When the sun moves closer to the treetops, I thank Tato for his time and head back to the heart of Itza. The return walk passes quickly, and soon I reach the market where sellers are packing up their goods. I stop at a food stall, where I grab the interesting leaf-taco-tamale thing we ate on our first night. As I walk back to my house, I eat my dinner.

Just as I reach the sacbe leading to the colorful houses, a strong hand grips my arm and spins me around. My food slips from my grasp and falls to the path. Nash stands in front of me, bewildered anger brewing in his eyes. I feel as if he stares forever, his gaze sweeping my body from head to toe. I'm not sure what he's searching for, but he's hurting my arm.

"Ow, Nash." I twist away from him.

"Where have you been?"

My eyebrows draw inward. I don't like the demanding tone of his voice. "Well, hello to you too." I grab his bicep and dig my fingers in the tender inner part of his upper arm until he jerks from my grip. "Is this how we're greeting one another now? Jesus, Nash, you ruined my dinner."

"What, he didn't feed you?"

"Of course he fed me, but the day was tiring. We did a lot. I'm hungry and I need a bath."

Something flares in his eyes, and he exhales sharply through his nose like an angry dragon. He turns on one heel and stalks away. Dinner forgotten, I run after him and grab at his wrist. He is swift to shrug out of my grasp, and it's like trying to clutch at a stream of water.

"Nash, what is your problem?"

He continues to ignore me, shaking his head and avoiding my eyes while marching up the stairs to his house. I dart in front of him, blocking his path.

"Why are you acting like this?"

"Move." His low tone trembles with anger.

I step aside and let him pass through the doorway, then immediately turn to follow him in. He throws himself facedown on the thatch covered pallet in the side room. The pose reminds me of a pouting boy who's been told to go to bed without dinner. I move around his spread legs and lie by his side, facing him. He turns his head the other way, so I slide myself over his back, putting us face to face again. His eyes remain closed and tension draws his features in tight.

"What's going on?" I ask softly.

His jaw clenches, and he opens his eyes to glare at me, before jerking himself away from where my breasts have pressed against his side. After a few moments, he says, "I guess we're even now."

"What?"

I search his eyes. Hurt and pain are apparent. The last time we saw each other was when he left me with Lahun. Afterward, I walked back with Lahun from the observatory to his palace, and he showed me around. When I returned to my house it was late. I went straight to sleep, then left early to spend the day with Tato. But Nash thinks I spent the entire night and the day with Lahun, and the words I spoke were heavy with the same meaning. The realization hits me like a hammer to my chest, making me breathless.

He's jealous.

The notion floods me with an odd, fierce joy, but then I remember two nights ago hearing him have sex all night and into the morning with two women. How dare he treat me so harshly, when I did nothing to deserve it. I've found a weak spot, and I'm ready to dig into it.

My lips spread in a lazy grin. "I am so tired. He worked me hard."

Nash's nostrils flare like a bull ready to charge. I really should stop before I push him too far, but I can't resist one more jab.

"My back and thighs are actually aching from how long we went at it." I breath out a short, surprised laugh, and reach around to rub my lower back.

It's like I set a flame to the fuse of a cannon. With an angry roar, he explodes from the mat, rolling himself on top of me. I shove against him, but I'd have more success pushing against a limestone wall. At least the wall wouldn't be pressing closer. His hand tangles into my hair, before he smashes his lips to mine. The kiss is nothing like the passionate one from before. It's cruel and punishing and near bruising in its force. Shoving against him does absolutely nothing, and I'm suffocating under his mouth. When he pulls away for air, I whip my head to the side, gasping in ragged breaths.

"You are mine, Ines," he grates harshly in my ear. "Remember? I told you that before I brought you here. Mine."

"I belong to no one but myself," I hiss.

I shove the palm of my hand against the side of his head while bucking my hips upward. I succeed at knocking him off balance, but he grabs my wrist as he rolls, pulling me with him. We wrestle for a few moments, me straddling his chest, while attempting to claw at him, but he holds my arms immobile. I don't even know what I'd do if I got my hands free, something between pulling his hair and scratching his eyes out. This fight started with me just goading him to get a sick satisfaction from his reaction, but now it's turned into a full-blown fury neither of us can control.

Somehow, his grip on my right wrist loosens and my hand twists free. My fist meets his jaw with a crunching sound. Nash rears up and flips me onto my back, before slamming both of my clenched fists against the mat. A cry of pain tears from my throat. His eyes are wild, gleaming dark like moonlight shining on the sea. His chest heaves as he breathes out shuddering breaths.

All at once, he backs away then puts his head between his hands.

A strangled sound of despair chokes out from deep within him, and he reaches for me. I roll off the mattress then dart out the doorway, running away.

He finds me a short time later at the Xtoloc cenote near the bathhouse. Women finish washing dishes and start packing them into their baskets. Men swim around in the water, washing the heat and toil of the day from their bodies. People cast me curious glances because I sit in silent stillness, my legs dangling over the edge and peering into the abyss of water. Tears streak my cheeks, but I make no move to wipe them away.

I am mad at him. I'm mad at myself. Both of us acted like a pair of wild animals. He was like an unleashed tiger I taunted and poked with a stick. It doesn't make what he did right, and his reaction doesn't excuse my wrong.

Nash comes next to me and sits at the edge, setting a basket of clean clothing between us to change into after our bath.

His gruff voice pitches low. "You didn't deserve to be treated like that, Ines. I'm sorry."

Turning my head, I meet his gaze. "I didn't sleep with him. It was wrong to make you think I did."

He squeezes his eyes shut then groans loudly, turning his face skyward. My eyes trace the slope of his forehead, down his nose, over his lips and chin. I ache to press my lips to all those places, and touch the smooth line of his throat. I hate myself for this helpless weakness I have for him. Even after he's shown me his bad temper.

Branches rustle in the distance and a small animal ambles out, his long nose sniffing. The anteater finds a spot and latches his attention to the ground.

Nash's head turns to me. Faint wetness shines in his reddened eyes. He sees the tears on my face, then drops his head in a sudden motion of shame. After a moment, he moves the basket from between us and scoots closer to wrap one arm around me. I lean into him, and the tears pour out fresh. His cheek presses to the top of my head and his arm tightens.

The last of the people leave, likely urged away on account of their moon goddess weeping in the arms of the sun god during their evening bath. Daylight fades and the sounds of the forest come alive as stars begin to wink dimly in the sky.

I sniffle and snuggle harder into his side. He smells like the wind, and earth, and man. "We're a wreck," I finally say with a short laugh. "I still like pushing buttons, and you ..." My words trail off. I don't want to finish.

But he finishes for me. "I still hurt women."

"Nash ..." I pull away from him, turning so I can look him in the eye. He doesn't want to meet my gaze and just stares in the blackness of the water below. "We were both in the wrong. I saw a weak spot in you, and I went for it. I mentally terrorized you, and you responded. It wasn't right for me to do that, and it wasn't right for you to use your strength against me. But we're okay. We're going to do better next time."

A half smile curves on his lips, and he nods. After a few moments, he exhales out a sharp breath. "So what happened with Lahun?"

"Same thing as you. Well ..." I remember the kiss, and backtrack. "Not exactly the same."

One heavy eyebrow raises as his head swings to me. "What do you mean?"

"Well he asked if I wanted to marry you. I gave him the same answer you did." I press my lips together. "And he kissed me."

Nash's features remain impassive. "And then?"

"We agreed we didn't feel anything special."

A smug look enters his eyes. "And what about with me? What do you feel with me?"

"That last one hurt."

"I wasn't trying to be nice there, Ines. But the other two?"

My heart dances in my throat. I lick my lips and glance down at my toes, giving a little kick. "I liked them," I finally say.

He scowls. "That's all? You liked them?"

I meet his eyes. "What do you want to hear, Nash?"

"The truth."

"Why?" I grate out, louder than I intend. He jerks back slightly, and I lean in, my words coming out in an angry snarl. "What if I said that ever since we kissed, there's this horrible, aching emptiness inside me? Like I'm starving." My voice softens as my eyes search his. "And maybe every time we're together, it fills in a little bit. Whenever you laugh, whenever you touch me. But it's never enough. And without it I think I might die."

His jaw slackens and his eyes go wide.

I continue. "Let's say I told you all of that. What then? You storm the altar at my arranged wedding, shouting "Itzalan, Itzalan!" like that Kaan Ek idiot from your story who single-handedly destroyed Chichen Itza because of an itch to scratch? Or we forget this whole thing and just go home, Nash? Our real home." My voice cracks on the last word.

More than anything, I want to get on my knees and plead with him to forget all of this. I want to beg him to return with me when I go back to our time, but I already know he can't directly follow. My foolish woman's pride won't allow me to humiliate myself by begging anyway.

My emotions shift from an oozing mess and solidify into a protective layer, turning hard and dark. I whip my head away from him to stare out toward nothing. I just cannot look at him any longer without stupid tears pouring from my eyes. The ache in my chest widens into a cavern I fear will never fill in again.

Nash unfolds himself from the sitting position, then reaches over to pull me to standing. Before I know what's happening, his large arms wrap around me. He pulls me tightly against him in a hug, but it's such an intimate feeling with my bare breasts against his chest. My hands tighten around his back, and that stupid, aching feeling of loneliness melts away. The relief of being held close by him is so exquisite that tears burn in my eyes.

"I really am sorry, Ines," he whispers.

"Me, too."

He releases his hold, stepping away, and my body protests the loss of his. I want to lunge forward and wrap myself around him. Instead, I fold my arms tightly around myself.

Nash removes his woven fiber belt, then the hipcloth and loincloth, before setting them down on the rocks next to the basket of our clean clothing. He reaches for me, and his fingers wrap around the knot at my waist as he pulls me closer. Nash kneels, then unravels the fabric holding everything in place. The skirt slides away, and he sets it down. Still kneeling, his hands return to my body, settling on the swell of my hips. His gaze is that of a starved man, roaming over my skin. Dark blue eyes trace my curves in a caress I can almost feel. I shiver from the promise of what hasn't even happened.

"I want to touch you," he says in a low, tense voice.

He's already touching me where his hands rest on my hips, but he's asking for more.

"I know," I reply shakily, then lift my chin in warning. "Don't."

His forehead falls against my belly, and he inhales deeply, before pressing his mouth to my skin. The heated contact feels like a brand searing my flesh. I stumble away from him, and away from the dangerous state of mind we're both in. The midnight blue of his eyes appears almost black, and he just looks at me with something between pained desperation and hatred. And then he stands, before smoothly pushing off the rocks and diving into the inky abyss below.

My breath releases on an exhale, and my lungs burn. I didn't even realize I'd stopped breathing. Hopefully he stays down in the depths long enough for the lack of oxygen to burn away his passionate state of mind. I need to bathe quickly. I follow the large, flat slabs of limestone spiraling down the cenote wall like a staircase until I reach the water. The staircase continues deeper in, making it easier for me to bathe, since I have something to stand on. I crouch low, rinsing the sweat and dirt from my body.

Moonlight casts a silvery, muted glow against the water. The sky above is so clear and brilliant, the stars reflect on the glassy surface. Gentle ripples move across from my slight movements. In the distance, the snarl of a jaguar can be heard, and then a high-pitched squeal of a peccary ends abruptly. At least someone is eating tonight, I think ruefully.

I finish my quick bird bath, then turn to go. Arms wrap viselike around my waist as Nash explodes from the water. A sound much like that slaughtered pig-like creature squeals out of me as he pulls me backward. Our bodies connect skin to skin, and we hit the water with a splash.

And no, the swim has done nothing to calm him down.

I quickly turn and push away, then grab onto the limestone ledge for security. Even though I know snakes won't pull me down unless the portals are open, these swimming holes still make me anxious. Nash treads water in front of me with a calculating look in his eye I don't trust.

"Did you mean what you said?" He comes closer and grabs onto the ledge next to me.

"Which part?" I carefully back away from him, hand over hand, moving closer to the bottom slabs of the limestone staircase. My escape.

Like a jaguar stalking prey, he moves forward. "That you feel you'll die if I don't touch you."

I swallow hard. My hand scrabbles on the ledge behind me, and I've reached a low enough step for me to roll onto it and run away. But I don't. He comes flush against me, the heat of his body connecting like a magnet to mine.

"Because I'm dying too, Ines." His gaze drops to my mouth, and he dips his head. "Itzalan," he whispers, then gently touches his lips to mine, teasingly soft.

Without thought, my mouth opens to his. My arms should be pulling me out of the water, but they wrap around his head instead. My legs should be running away from him, but they enclose around his hips and lock him against me, as if I could fuse him to me forever with my will alone. Frantic and savage, we collide on the flat rocks. I could kiss him into eternity, and it still wouldn't ever be enough. Our breathing is wild and ragged as we dissolve against one another, melding and merging. And then I feel heated pressure where I ache for him the most. A moment of clarity pulls in my brain like an errant thread.

"Stop, stop, stop," I whisper, then bring my arms between us. "Nash. We can't do this."

"We can," he insists, pushing forward again.

Shuddering, I close my eyes, gathering my inner strength to do the impossible. "Please stop."

His lips draw into a tight line, but he pulls away. I roll to the side and pull my knees together. His wide back expands and contracts with every breath. His head rests in his hands, and we sit in silence for several minutes.

I want to touch him again, but it'll be like dropping a spark into a vat of oil. And I know that with every bit of my body I surrender to him, I'll also be giving away irretrievable parts of my soul.

CHAPTER 17

STIFLING, DENSE HEAT AWAKENS me the next day. Sounds from the center of Itza drift through the trees. Dogs bark, children laugh, and merchants shout to people passing by. We are well into the day, and I've slept like the dead. I look around for Calalu but see Nash sitting near me. A sticky wetness lingers between my thighs, and a familiar cramping takes hold of my womb. I sit up with a low groan. A scrap of red cloth has been haphazardly placed near my bottom, but my blood stains the thatch of my mattress. My period has started.

"Damnation," I hiss.

Nash gives me a wary look. "I noticed the blood when I came in, and I tried waking you up, but you were like a dead woman. I figured that's what the cloths in that basket are for, so I tried to put one under you."

Some foreign feeling blooms in my chest at a man caring for me in such an elemental way. I pause and look at him. "Thank you."

I wad up the cloth and stuff it between my legs, then shuffle over to the basket for a fresh piece of fabric. Nash extends a gourd filled with water to me. After dipping a fresh rag in the water, I clean myself as best as I can, before leaving the soiled cloth in the wicker basket. I wonder where Calalu is, as I could really use her female knowledge at the moment. Carefully, I fold a red strip of fabric into a small rectangle, before placing it between my thighs. My helpless gaze sweeps the room. Am I just supposed to hold it in place with my hand? Nash looks up and snorts out a laugh.

Despite the cramps and bleeding, I laugh softly in return. "I don't know how to keep this here."

He scoots off the mattress covered platform, then rifles through clean pieces of fabric until he finds a red length of material similar to the one he uses for his loincloth. One finger beckons me over, so I move to stand between his spread thighs. Nash threads the material through my legs, then around my hips.

"Oh my gosh, I feel like a baby." My cheeks heat in embarrassment.

His face turns up to me with a soft smile, and I lean forward to press my lips to his. The need to kiss him goes beyond conscious thought. His hands stop their movement, and his mouth presses back against mine with gentleness.

"Thank you," I say, my eyes locked on his.

The urge to cry wells up, and I curse the hormones that have been making me an emotional mess with him lately. He murmurs a response, then finishes tying off the loincloth. I move away to rinse my hands and wipe them clean. After tying on a brilliant blue skirt, I move back to Nash, where a platter of food awaits me.

"Did Calalu bring this?" I gesture to the food as I tear off a piece of warm tortilla.

He shakes his head no. "She didn't come yesterday either. Her mother came. The woman refused to speak to me at first and was just giving me food and trying to do my hair"—he laughs—"and then I basically had to command her to speak to me. She said Calalu is very sick, and she will be coming in her daughter's place until she is well again. I sent her home and told her to take care of Calalu. Guess she's still sick."

My brow creases in worry. "Will you help me find her?"

"Of course."

We pass through the bustling market, where I see Tato packing up his things. He must've already sold out of all his roots and herbs for the day. The old healer gives me directions to Calalu's home. We thank him, then head down the sacbe Tato pointed us toward. The homes on either side of the road are just inside the copse of trees. They're similar to Tato's in that they're oval shaped and plastered with colorful stucco. But Tato said I won't find her in this section. We continue down the road for another ten minutes, until gradually the nicer homes disappear behind us. These ones are smaller with no color. And then the palapas start to have no stucco. They just become wooden shacks. Tato said once we reach this point, start asking for her.

Naked children dart around, giggling as they play. When they notice Nash and me, they run to us and start tugging on our colorful hipcloths. I crouch low and run my hands over their glossy black heads.

"Who can show me where Calalu lives?" I ask with a big smile.

They speak over one another, each of them yelling that they can do it. I grab two of their hands and stand, then two others run to Nash and grab his hands. I glance over my shoulder at him, and he's grinning down at the kids saying something that's making them giggle. A strange sensation hits me, and all of a sudden I wonder what our kids would look like. I blink and shake my head. We've kissed less than a handful of times, and I'm going full blown psycho already.

The children drag us forward. We weave through huts, careening around bewildered looking adults. Finally, we reach a hut with a small, dark-haired woman butchering a chicken outside. Her eyes widen when she sees us walking up.

"That's her," Nash says.

I step forward, giving my friendliest smile as I greet her. Calalu's mother lowers her head.

"Is Calalu home?"

She nods.

"May I see her?"

She shakes her head no.

"Speak, woman," Nash commands gruffly.

I shoot him a disapproving glare. He widens his eyes and shrugs his shoulders with a what-else-did-you-expect look.

"She is very, very sick, my lady." The woman doesn't look up and stumbles over her words as she wrings her hands. "Her—her blood was so hot for two nights. The heat went away this sun rise, but now she cannot walk, and she is in pain."

My eyebrows raise. Her illness sounds serious.

I raise my chin, using my best authoritative voice. "I insist on seeing her."

Calalu's mother steps aside from the door, allowing me to pass, then follows in behind me. The tiny hut holds two hammocks. I head to the one Calalu lies in. Her eyes appear glazed over and she breathes shallowly.

"Calalu?" I kneel next to the hammock.

Her eyes move to my face, and she gives a slight, pained smile. I grab her hand she cries out in pain.

"You can't walk?"

"N—no, my lady Chel." It seems like even the effort to speak is painful for her. "Everything hurts."

"I'm going to take you to see Tato," I say with a tight smile. I turn to her mother. "Is that okay?"

Calalu's mother nods her head. Tears of relief spring into her eyes. Bending, I slide my arms under the girl's shoulders and knees. She stifles a scream, and tears well up in her eyes. I cradle her close to my body and walk out of the hut.

Nash's eyes narrow in concern as he sees me carrying the crying girl out. "She's paralyzed." My voice trembles in fear. "Can you help me bring her to Tato?"

"How can I help this little one?" Tato says cheerily.

Nash settles Calalu into a hammock. The healer takes one look at Calalu's disposition, and his weathered brow immediately draws inward. While I give my limited information about her condition, he looks into her eyes, smells her mouth, and then two brown fingers press into the pulse at her wrist. His lips tighten as he concentrates on what he's feeling. Tato steps back, and his demeanor is no longer his usual light and playful. His dark eyes grow heavy with concern and his lips draw in tightly.

"This is a powerful sickness. It is beyond my skills."

"What? No." I shake my head and grab his arm. "Tato, you have to do something. You are the most powerful healer in Itza."

"That I may be, daughter, but I can't help her. There is one more powerful than me. My great grandmother lives some distance from

215

here. I can lead the way there, but I must return to my home immediately so I can be back before nightfall. And I will send word to Calalu's mother that she will not be home tonight."

I blink twice, certain I did not just hear him say great grandmother. But now is not the time to question him. I'm just anxious to get Calalu wherever we have to go. Tato helps Nash attach Calalu to his back for the two-hour walk using a tumpline. He then binds her tight to him using strips of cloth, softly apologizing for the pain he's causing the girl by the movement. Calalu doesn't complain, but tears drip down her round cheeks.

Clouds overhead keep us shaded during the hottest part of the day. Occasionally, I give Calalu sips of water to keep her hydrated, but eventually she falls asleep against Nash's broad back. I wonder if she draws as much comfort from his skin as I do.

Tato sets a quick pace. His long strides move rapidly down the smooth sacbe. Nash and I walk side by side behind him. For an old man, he is in remarkable health. I remember when I asked Tato his age the other day, and he used a word I didn't recognize.

"Nash, what is a bak'tun?

"Eh, almost 400 years. Why?"

I chuckle softly. "Yesterday, when I asked his age, he told me he's seen one bak'tun, and has stopped counting. And now he says we're going to see his great grandmother. Tato is officially nuts."

Nash makes a low sound in his throat. "Hmm. You never know. I mean, doesn't your Bible say Methuselah lived almost 1000 years?"

"I honestly don't know ... maybe."

His lips purse as his thick brows draw inward. "It's been assumed the various mentioning of the deities over hundreds and hundreds of years was different generations of them. But then there is also the belief among a few that the first generations just lived for hundreds of years."

"That's impossible."

"Mm." Nash shoots me a half smile. "It sounds impossible, but as we have both learned these past days, anything is possible."

I give a short laugh. Pretty much everything I've claimed is impossible has happened, starting with time travel. I wonder what more surprises await.

A light drizzle begins to splatter down from the slate gray clouds above. The rain is refreshing, but I'm grateful it's not a downpour. Either way, we'd have to keep moving. I peek behind Nash to check on Calalu. Her features are tightened in pain. Small moans come from her, though her deep breaths show she's asleep.

The afternoon rain lures a variety of animals out from the trees. A wild turkey pecks the ground off the side of the road, while a few deer emerge further up near Tato. The old man inclines his head to the animals. Their ears pull back slightly, but the creatures return their noses to the ground upon determining he is no threat.

A short time later, Tato comes to a halt turning halfway to watch us approach, gnarled fists on his hips. He greets us with a gap-toothed smile. "This old man walks faster than two young people. I may be old, but I am strong."

I smile fondly at the healer. "Yes, you are strong, Tato."

He puffs out his ropey chest in pride. "This is where I leave you. Come look at this tree."

Tato waves us to the side of the road. The bottom part of the tree looks like an elephant's leg, with its wrinkled gray bark. Green, torpedo shaped fruit hang down from the tree.

"This is the bonete tree. And on this side, the tree with the small yellow flowers is yellow hibiscus. Walk straight through these two

217

trees. You will reach a path, then see a cenote. Her palapa is right after. You should arrive before the sun goes below the trees." And with a grin, Tato turns to make the two-hour trip back to Itza.

A carefully laid, narrow pathway of stones cuts a trail through the dense jungle. It's taken another fifteen minutes from the white sacbe to reach this stone path. I pick up my pace, hoping this means we're almost there. Calalu hangs limply from Nash's back, and while she's breathing short, shallow breaths, the girl is unresponsive.

"I'm going to run ahead," I call back to Nash, then start running along the pathway in short, quick strides.

The sooner I can get this healer informed about our situation, the quicker we can start treatment for Calalu.

After a few minutes of running, the trail broaden further and signs of cultivation appear. Overhead, saplings form a high archway, with purple passiflora flowers twining around it. Thick, cactus looking pitaya vines rest atop small bushes, and yellow dragonfruit hang from the clawlike appendages. Butterflies flit about with their colorful, wide wings, drifting from flower to flower for nectar.

Further ahead, the path splits, forming a roundabout around a massive ceiba tree, with a smooth, gray trunk. I slow to a walk as I pass a wide, deep cenote, where flame-colored orioles and turquoise-feathered birds flap around, their twitters echoing in the hollow space. The entire place reminds me of a fairy garden.

Further up, a short rectangular stone platform holds two oval-shaped palapas. Both are stuccoed and colored a deep, indigo blue.

Stately palms cast shade all around.

An old woman sits outside, her back to me. She wears a one-piece cinnabar red dress, with yellow threads woven through. Long, silvery hair is twisted on top of her head, the length held in place with a jade serpent. In front of her, a wooden loom is attached to a nearby palm tree, stretched between with a belt around her waist. Her hands busily fly over the fibers, weaving and creating a colorful length of fabric.

I walk around the stone base, moving into her line of sight. I'd rather not startle her. Her bearing is straight, and she does not hunch over, but age and wisdom emanate from the woman much like daylight pulses forth from the sun. It's an undeniable mantle surrounding her. She looks to be about a hundred years old. It takes a brief second, but her eyes snap over to me without her hands ceasing their work.

"Tato sent me," I say in greeting.

She nods, hands moving over the loom. Her eyes squint slightly as she looks at me. "What is your name, child?"

For some reason, I can't bring myself to lie to her. "My name is Ines."

She smiles. "Welcome to my home, Ines. How can I be of service to you?"

"My servant girl is very sick," I say in a rush as I climb the short set of stairs and come to stand in front of her. "Heat burned in her body for two nights, and now she is in pain and cannot move her arms or legs. My friend is just behind me carrying her. Tato said you can help us."

The old woman ceases her work on the loom, removing the belted piece from around her waist, and then stands with a smooth grace that belies her age. She is the same height as me. A crook of her finger signals me to follow her. We enter the palapa that has a smoldering fire inside, and it's the first doorway I don't have to stoop to enter. On one side of this palapa is a cooking area, while the other side is a workspace. A wooden table runs along the entire wall. Attached to the wall above the table are shelves holding baskets of dried herbs, roots, and flowers. I imagine the other palapa is her living quarters.

"Attach this hammock." The aged woman hands me a length of ropey, woven fabric.

I tie up the hammock in the spots she indicates on the wooden beams then peek out the doorway to see Nash walking up with Calalu. He's untied her from his back and cradles her in his arms. Her hands and feet hang limply from her body. I wave him inside.

"They're here," I say to the woman. "I'm sorry, I didn't ask your name."

"My name is …" She turns around from the table just as Nash enters the doorway with Calalu. Her eyes settle on him, and the color drains from her face. One wrinkled hand flies to her mouth as it widens in shock. A change sweeps over the woman as her entire demeanor softens yet brightens at the same time. Tears fill her coffee brown eyes as she stares at Nash.

"How … how is this possible?" she asks to no one in particular.

Nash's eyes dart to me, and his mouth opens and closes in confusion. He's just as thrown off by her as I am.

The woman steps closer to him, one hand shaking as she reaches out as if to touch him, but she drops her arm at the last moment. Tears slip down her cheeks. "What is your name?" she asks in a harsh whisper.

Just like me, he doesn't have the heart to lie to her. "My name is Ignacio. What is your name, revered one?"

She pulls her frail shoulders back, lifting her chin and wiping tears from her cheeks. "I am known as the Lady Rainbow. But you may call me Ixchel."

CHAPTER 18

MIRRORED EXPRESSIONS OF SHOCK are frozen on our faces as we stare at the old woman. Seconds tick past and no one says or does anything. And then Calalu moans, snapping us all out of the moment.

"Lay her down in the hammock," Ixchel says, wiping the tears from under her eyes with one hand.

Nash complies, then steps back, arms folded over his chest.

"Are you *the* Ixchel?" I ask, voice lowered.

She cocks her head at me. "I know of no other Ixchel, do you?"

I shake my head. "Um, please forgive my rude question, but how old are you, revered one?"

"I have seen two bak'tuns, child. It is too long for one person to live," she says with a sigh.

800 years old. Ixchel closes her eyes and feels Calalu's pulse. Then she nods her head and clasps both hands over Calalu's wrist as her lips begin moving in hushed prayer. She does the same thing with the other wrist, then touches her hands to the girls forehead to finish off the litany of prayers.

"Tell me why you both are here." Ixchel pins both Nash and me with a look.

"For Calalu." I extend my hand to the girl.

"No, that's not why." She shakes her head, smiling grimly, but her eyes remain kind and patient. "You"—she points to me—"are the image of myself when I was a young woman. And you"—her gaze settles on Nash, her features softening—"your face resembles a man who will forever haunt my heart. But you are not him. You are you. And you are different."

Her words are spoken with a calm assurance. Nash immediately drops his gaze to the floor of her hut, swallowing hard. The knuckles on his fists whiten, and he takes a step back, squeezing his eyes shut as he drops his head against the wall behind him.

"Why are you here?" she asks again, adding various herbs into a stone mortar.

"We were birthed from the cenote," I say. "Our time is three bak'tuns in the future. You are my ancestor, and Kinich Ahau is his. We are supposed to change something here, but we don't know what yet."

Her brow creases as she grinds the herbs with a pestle. "It is tricky to meddle with things better left forgotten."

Nash speaks. "In our time, the great empire of the Maya is gone. We are all scattered, living like the lowest classes all over the peninsula. Our great cities are abandoned, the monuments swallowed up by the land and decaying, our culture destroyed by invaders. Why does the Whole One God allow us to come back if not to change something?"

The old woman purses her lips in thought, then shrugs her thin shoulders. "This I do not know. Maybe it is only yourselves who are meant to be changed by the journey."

She grabs a big stone vessel from the table, and Nash jumps in quickly to help her move it.

"Fill it with hot stones from the fire, then put it under the girl," Ixchel instructs, and Nash does as she says.

Once the large bowl is full of heated rocks, she scatters the mixture of herbs over the surface, then drapes a large piece of fabric over Calalu. The ends of the cloth puddle on the floor of the hut, and she ties knots down one of the opened sides to seal it. On the other side, she crouches low with a wooden bucket of water, and pours it all over the hot stones. The liquid begins to evaporate with a hiss. Herbal steam billows behind her as she retreats from under the cloth. With deft movements, Ixchel seals the other end to trap as much of the healing air inside with Calalu.

My ancestress stands, then looks at me. "Come, daughter. We have a plant to seek."

Ixchel heads down a manicured path, and I walk beside her. She is sure of foot and knows where to find what she's looking for.

Dark brown eyes move in my direction. "After all these years, just the image of Kinich Ahau still stirs my heart," she says wistfully. "I am an old, old woman, and still I have never loved a man like I love him."

That word again. I don't have the heart to tell her my thoughts on love. Part of me knows my negative experiences don't make an absolute rule of humanity. And yes, I know it's foolish of me to believe that in the first place, but my belief serves as a protection I'm unwilling to shed.

"I must tell you, Ixchel. Ignacio and I both have these … visions. But he says they are your and Kinich Ahau's memories that are part of our bodies."

She doesn't question the validity of what I say but listens and accepts it. Her eyes slant to mine. "What do you see?"

I inhale, the memories filling me again. They swirl within me like a vast cauldron of heat. "So much passion, Ixchel. It's almost scary how much passion existed between you two. It was consuming. It was frightening." I pause a beat, glancing at her. "And his violence."

She nods, pressing her lips into a thin line. Abruptly, the old woman grabs my wrist and stops, staring into the shrubbery. From the heavy green leaves, a pair of yellow eyes stare out at us.

My heart nearly stops as I realize the grave danger we're in. "It's a jaguar," I whisper in hushed hysteria.

Ixchel crouches low to the ground and holds out her hand to the creature. "Do not fear. He will not hurt you or me, daughter. He has promised."

The eyes come forward as the black nose of the jaguar pushes through the branches. My breathing goes shallow, and my instinct to scream and run begins to overpower reason, but Ixchel holds onto my wrist with a strength I didn't expect.

"B'aalam, in k'aat," she says in a low murmur.

Jaguar, my love.

The jaguar sniffs her hand, then rubs his head up her arm in a very catlike caress. His nose bumps against my thigh, and I imagine that powerful jaw clamping down on my leg. My eyes widen in terror. But the creature only presses his broad, spotted head and body against me as he continues past us then disappears in the greenery once more.

A small, squeaky exhalation release from me. "That thing could have killed us."

Ixchel laughs. "He would never."

"Is he yours?"

"He belongs to no one." The old woman begins leading the way down the path once more. "I never again knew a love like Kinich. No matter how many times I left him, he would find me. It was like we were two halves of a whole that needed to be together. He would say even though we were broken, we would always find our way back to one another. He said I could hide on the moon, and he would still find me." Ixchel chuckles out a weathered laugh. "I counted on it."

"Even after he hurt you so many times? Why?"

The aged woman inhales deeply and then shrugs, shaking her head. "Insanity perhaps. And yet ..." she glances at me. "He and I are done. What of you and Ignacio? What do you feel with him?"

I focus my attention on the footpath, chewing my lip for a moment, before exhaling the words out in a rush. "I feel everything. I feel too much with him. It scares me."

She smiles gently. "That is the start of love, Ines."

"I don't believe in love."

"It does not matter what you believe. It is what you are feeling. Love. Fear. The two are very much the same. You just have to learn their balance." Ixchel pulls up short and glances into the trees. "Ah, there it is."

We move through the undergrowth of vines, bushes, and fallen branches. Ixchel stops at a plant that is as tall as us and has a spray of small yellow flowers sitting up top like a hat. She gives thanks to the plant before gathering the long, narrow leaves, using the hem of her dress like a pouch.

"This is kayabim. We will toast the leaves, then make a tea for the girl to drink. It will clean the inside of her body."

"Will you be able to heal her?"

"It is not me that heals, daughter. It is the plant and the body. Both have to work together, and that's why you must always thank

226

the plant before you take it. Otherwise it will hold its healing power inside."

This is the same wisdom Tato, Ixchel's great-grandson and my ancestor, taught me. When we return to the hut, Ixchel has Nash remove the heavy blanket from Calalu. She keeps me busy toasting kayabim leaves on top of a flat rock resting on the fire.

Ixchel's gaze randomly settles on Nash, silvery eyebrows drawing together as she works. I can't imagine what it must be like to be in such close proximity to the near exact likeness of a man who once held her soul in the palms of his hands. In her memories, Kinich's smile, his laughter, his bearing, just the way he moved had been enough to get her heart pounding and head feeling dizzy. Simply looking at the man had been like a drug.

Ixchel moves over to me and sets a stone bowl filled with water in the coals, then starts crumbling the already toasted leaves to prepare the tea for Calalu. They make a satisfying crunching sound in her hands.

"Why are you and he not bound as one?" she murmurs softly.

My eyes flick over to Nash. He's trying to get Calalu to drink some water, but she's only moaning in pain.

"I'm staying away from men," I proclaim in a low-pitched voice. "They've given me nothing but trouble and hurt."

Ixchel murmurs a sound of agreement. "I know that feeling. I will never regret leaving him. But I will never regret loving him for as long as I have."

"Even still, you love him?"

"When your man walked through my door, I knew it was impossible it was my Kinich." She exhales on an almost reverent sigh. "But I knew if given a choice to do it all over again, I would. If it's true our memories have passed to you both, perhaps our love did too. You will not be able to stop it, daughter. Neither of you will."

Ixchel says it will take several days of treatment for Calalu to regain her strength, and she welcomes us to stay with her during that time. Nash and I agree that we don't want to leave Calalu alone here. And besides, it will be a great privilege for me to continue learning herbal medicine directly from my ancestress.

After giving us a basket filled with clean cloth and soap fruit, Ixchel tells us to go bathe before the sun is fully set. I rifle through the basket as we walk, and I see she did not forget to add the cloth for my monthly bleeding I requested. For the first time today, Nash and I are alone.

I follow Ixchel's direction and walk beyond the cenote, down the path where we found the kayabim plant. Further down, she said we'd find the entrance to a cave, which would take us deep down into one of the water systems that connect to the cenote, much like an underground river. Ixchel has a bucket system set up to collect her daily water from the deep cenote next to her home, but for bathing and laundry, she uses this other area.

Carefully, we pick our way into the cavern. The sound of water running over stones is just ahead, and we soon reach the river running beneath the earth.

Fading daylight pours in from a narrow opening above. Underneath is a tiny patch of greenery with a single thin tree reaching up its boughs out from the earth to the sky. Water trickles around the tiny island in a rocky stream. We follow the path of the water until it becomes deep enough to bathe and flows a bit more strongly. I set the basket of clean cloth off to the side.

"Can you believe it?" I grab a soap fruit and start lathering. "Ixchel in the flesh."

"It's amazing." Nash begins scrubbing his own cloth with the small yellow fruit. "Wasn't it weird how she looked at me?"

I incline my head in a half nod as I rinse out the soap. "Well, yes and no. You look almost exactly like the man she loved for so long."

He stops for a second and gives me a measured look. "But I am me. And I'm different," he repeats the same words she said to him. "I don't know how to tell her how much it meant to hear that. It felt like forgiveness for something I didn't do to her. Because it felt like I was doing those things to her." He wrings out his cloth and then pushes off the rocks to go stand in the waist deep water. "Throw me one of those yellow things."

After tossing him the soap fruit, my attention moves back to my cloth that needs rinsing. While I work, I steal glances as Nash lathers himself up. It feels almost sinful to watch his hands move over his magnificent body in such an intimate way. He catches me staring, and then flicks water at me with a grin.

"Come on in, Ines. I promise I'll behave."

"Well, I'd hope the fact that I'm bloody would be enough to slow you down." I wring out my cloths then lay them on the rocks.

He shrugs, flashing me a wicked smile. "No, it wouldn't slow me down. It's been a while for me, Ines. I'm getting pretty desperate."

"Man, it's been like four days for you. Calmaté." I laugh and bump my hip into him as I walk up, then start washing my hands with the fruit. "And it wouldn't slow you down? That's so gross, Nash. And not very comforting."

"I said, I promise." Nash moves behind me, then encloses me in his arms. I freeze. He speaks softly into my ear. "But it's going to happen, Ines. You already know it will. But I swear to you this: it will not happen until you ask it from me. Deal?"

"Deal." I swallow hard. He releases me from his arms, and I turn to him. "Not that I'm agreeing this is going to happen, okay?"

A cocky grin spreads on his lips. "Okay, Ines. Whatever you say."

I sit in the shallow pool and unravel my braid, then dunk myself backward to begin washing my hair.

His deep blue eyes grow curious, and he moves closer to me. "How much do I look like Kinich?"

"Almost exact." I move to stand in front of him and reach up to trace his eyebrow with my thumb. "Your eyebrows arch a little higher. His were straighter. Your lips are bit more full. His eyes were a lighter shade of blue. Yours are dark like the night sky."

He catches my hand then turns his head, bringing my palm to his mouth for a kiss. "You think this is how it started for them? Weeks of torture."

My eyes widen, and I laugh. "Torture? Is that what this has been?"

Nash nods seriously, entwining the fingers of our one hand together. "Absolute torture."

I shake my head. "They didn't wait weeks. Ixchel said the first time they were alone they had sex. She said they couldn't control themselves with one another. Ever."

"That's hot," he says in a deep voice, his thumb rubbing up and down the side of my palm.

"I mean, yeah, but look where lack of control got them. There has to be some control in life, Nash. Control is good."

Nash grabs my other hand, and then moves both behind my back, encircling my wrists in his fingers. "Control is good," he agrees.

"You are cra—"

He stops my lips with his mouth in a single featherlight kiss then pulls away, leaving me wanting more.

Ixchel hands us a single hammock to sleep in. "I only have the one for you to share," she says, a mischievous gleam in her aged eyes. "Unless you want to put the child on the floor."

We shake our heads no. The old lady shuffles out of the palapa, and Nash hangs up the hammock. It's really not a big deal. We've slept together plenty of times. And me being on my period, along with the fact that there is an old woman and child nearby makes this such a non-thing.

Nash settles into the hammock, then holds his arms out to me with a big smile. I grin at him, then roll in, my back landing neatly against his chest, and my bottom against his groin. He immediately wraps his arms around me and nuzzles his face into my neck. An electrical feeling moves through me at his touch.

"So what's your favorite memory of them?" I whisper to Nash in English.

"Besides the obvious hot sex all the time … hmm."

I giggle softly.

He's thoughtful for a moment. "They played pranks on one another a lot. Once she put a scorpion on his forehead while he slept. And he was deathly afraid of scorpions." Nash chuckles. "He cried afterward, and she laughed at him."

I snort out another laugh. Ixchel had been a stone-cold gangster.

"Poor guy."

"What about you?"

"I haven't been experiencing the memories as long as you … Wait, how long have you been having them?"

He inhales softly. "I think ever since I was about thirteen. But I started having dreams of a long-legged girl with black hair when I was twelve." Nash nuzzles into my neck, and I squeal softly at the tickling sensation.

Something twists in my heart at this admission, and I'm tempted to poke fun at him for it, but I don't. I wrap this moment into the precious recesses of my memory and store it away to remember one day when I'm missing him.

I sift through her memories and find my favorite one. "Okay, so my favorite is probably the first one I had. She was working at her table, sorting leaves, and he came in behind her. Like, she could *feel* him enter the room. And then he put his arms around her, and yeah, they got started from there. But it was just the safety in his arms, and the knowing, if that makes sense."

"Was that when we got to Playa del Carmen and you fell asleep in the car?"

"Wait, how—"

He laughs softly into my hair. "You are very vocal in your sleep, Ines."

"Oh wow." I shift in embarrassment. "So did you know the whole time I was seeing stuff, and what it meant?"

Nash throws one heavy thigh over my hip. "In a way. Remember when we were driving the first day, and you said something about the guy in the loincloth?"

"And if I wanted to pay to see you in one? And look, I didn't have to pay anything," I say smugly. Warm lips nip at my ear, and a moan nearly escapes me. I cough instead. "Yeah, that must have been the first one."

"And then the Kinich pyramid too, right?" he asks, his fingers grazing the underside of my breast.

I nod, and completely stop breathing.

"The way we would sleep a lot some days, that is because of the memories and the effect they have on our brains," he explains.

His mouth moves against the side of my neck. I close my eyes and reach back to grip his thigh. His hand slides up my chest and holds my throat just under my chin as his lips keep up their assault on my sensitive skin. "Oh my God, Nash," I whisper. "You keep that up, and you're gonna get what you want, regardless of blood, old ladies, or little girls. It's not gonna be pretty."

He laughs a low, throaty chuckle, but doesn't stop until I'm squirming under his heavy leg that has now conveniently pinned me in place. Little squeals escape my throat as I try to escape the delicious torture he's set himself to giving me.

"Shhh," he whispers.

I'm not able to stop the noises until he finally pulls his mouth away from my neck. We struggle to control our breathing. I pull his hand down from my throat, then interlace my fingers with his, willing the steady pound of my heart to slow. I want him to touch me again, but already this is getting too risky.

I clear my throat. "So you had to deal with seeing all of their action since you were thirteen?"

He sighs. "Sí. And I don't think it was healthy for me, if I'm being honest. I got started with girls around then and stayed busy. But nothing ever compared to their memories. It always felt so empty."

"Even with Alma?"

Nash's hand moves from my hip and reaches up to grab strands of my hair near my temple. He drags his fingers down the length of it. "I loved her. In my own way. But again, compared to what Ixchel and Kinich had, it was a candle to a bonfire. What about you?"

"No, not even with Jacob did it feel close to what they had."

"Jacob?" The pitch of his voice raises in interest.

"He was the first guy I said 'I love you' to ... remember, the one who broke my collarbone?"

Nash mumbles an affirmative, and then asks, "Did you really love him?"

"I thought I did. But Nash, I don't know if I believe in love anymore."

He snorts. "Yes, I've heard your opinion about it. Let's see if I'm remembering right. It's an ache that burns away and leaves you with ashes?"

"Yep. It's just a chemical reaction in the body. It's like drugs. It's not real."

Nash makes a soft sound of disappointment, clicking his tongue. "But what about love for your father. Is that real?"

"Of course. No drugs involved there."

"But love exists," he says with a stubborn edge to his voice.

The next morning, we awaken to Calalu staring at us from her hammock, smiling. Nash and I roll off our hammock and kneel next to hers. I rub the top of her head as we pester her with questions. She's regained movement in her hands and can wiggle her toes with much less pain.

Ixchel comes through the door several minutes later with a bucket of water from the cenote. She orders Nash and me to set up the steam bath again, and we quickly get to work.

"What else do we need to do?" I ask, once Calalu is set up inside the herbal steam bath.

"I'm going to get her to drink her tea once the bath is done. You two can go butcher one of my pigs and set a fire in the pib. There is a pile of wood right out there."

Cooking a whole animal in a pib, which is an ancient, in-ground oven, is usually reserved for celebrations.

Nash steps forward. "Are you certain, revered one? We don't need anything special to eat while we stay with you."

She waves him away with a knobby, wrinkled hand. "It is not every day an old lady gets the honor of caring for her future descendants. Allow me my honor. Now go." Her chin lifts in a stubborn tilt.

Nash laughs softly and grabs me by the shoulders, then maneuvers us to the door. I sneak a glance back at Ixchel, who stares at us with tenderness in her eyes.

"That look she gives when she lifts her chin," Nash says with a chuckle. "That is all you right there. I know not to argue with that look."

"Good to know," I say wryly, raising an eyebrow at him.

After we finish our tasks, we get more of the kayabim tincture into Calalu. She then falls asleep for an afternoon nap. Nash and I decide to find our way into the deep cenote to practice freediving for the rest of the afternoon. Ixchel tells us to follow the same cave path to the body of water we bathed in, but then we'll have to dive through an underwater opening to reach the actual cenote.

"You're really going to stay here after I leave?" I ask Nash as we follow the narrow path.

He gives a slow, measured nod of his head, but I see something like regret in his face. "I have to see this out, Ines. Whatever it is that needs to be done, I have to do it. I wish you would stay with me." He meets my eyes with a hopeful expression. "Is it really so bad here?"

The truth is, as angry as I've been at Nash about making this choice for me, it hasn't been so bad. The worst part was the arrival and walking through a village completely naked. But our life has been good and easy in Itza. However, I know it can't last.

Something major will have to happen soon, and we will have to be the ones forcing that change. It could be dangerous. I have no desire to die forgotten in a past of which no written record exists. And yet, I can't imagine leaving Nash behind, never seeing him again. Both options are an impossibility.

"No, it's not so bad here, Nash." I look sideways at him.

His dark hair falls forward over his profile, obscuring his face from my eyes. Even these seconds are too long without seeing him. How will I manage a lifetime? I stop and grab his arm, turning him to me, then push his hair behind his ear. I slip my arms around his ribs and pull him against me. He squeezes me tight, and I tilt my face up to his, then pull his head down to me.

Warm lips press against mine, and I respond with eagerness. Nash's hands grip my hips, and he yanks me firmly against him. We stand, bodies pressed together as close as we can get, French kissing like a pair of teenagers. His hand moves up my back, then threads through my hair before clenching it tight in his fist. I groan raggedly into his mouth, and he responds with a similar low sound. It's pure primal lust and passion.

Nothing more. Nothing less.

Our frantic kisses eventually slow to long, lazy strokes of our lips and tongues. He pulls away, pressing his lips to my cheek, then lips again, then nose. He frames my face with his hands, as his eyes roam over my face. When he returns his lips to mine, the kiss is so tender and slow that my heart aches with what I'm feeling for him. It's like his lips are worshiping mine. Finally he pulls away and just studies me, his thumb stroking my cheek.

"I don't care what you say, Ines, I know love is real."

Ixchel and I flatten pale yellow dough between our hands, then set the circles over the flat stone on top of the fire. Nash is busy removing the pig dinner from the pit oven.

She glances at me, her aged eyes smiling. "Tell me about your life back home."

In measured, careful words, I describe our cities, our home, the vehicles. I tell her about my dad dying, and being taken on this journey against my will.

"Do you have regret?" she asks, flipping a browned tortilla.

I gaze out the open doorway and watch Nash working in the hot sun to uncover the smoking pib. I don't think I'll ever tire of looking at him.

I shake my head. "I try to imagine what I'd be doing right now if I wasn't here with him." My eyes meet hers. "There is nothing I can think of that would be better than this." I shrug, laying it out as plainly as I can.

"When I see you two together, it warms my heart, daughter. You are true friends, which is the most important part of any bond. But respect one another's weaknesses, and build up one another's strengths. Don't focus on the bad. There is always bad to be found if you look for it."

Tears cloud my vision. "I'm scared, Ixchel. I'm terrified to give that power to someone. I don't know how to get over that." I sniff hard and rub my nose on my arm so as not to contaminate our dinner.

"One day, you won't be able to contain what you feel. And that's when any threat of pain will be worth it to have him. And yes, it will hurt. That is love. At its ultimate it is a wondrous thing. But in order to create something beautiful, sometimes it has to destroy. Be it pride, selfishness, or some other weakness. Love cannot live alongside those things. Our time to live is limited. I don't regret loving Kinich when I had the chance. When he left this world"—she inhales shakily, squeezing her wrinkled eyes shut—"I would have given anything to spend one more sunrise and sunset with him. Anything. There will always be fear and risk of loss, but don't waste the time you have."

After dinner, Nash and I bring the dishes to the river cavern to wash. I can't get Ixchel's words out of my mind.

We finish up and then wash ourselves for the night. I complain about my cramps, and he pulls me close so he can rub my lower back and squeeze my hips. Keeping my eyes closed, I relish in the feel of his hands on me, and our skin in close contact. All at once, the answer comes to me. My eyes spring open, and I pull back slightly.

"Marry me, Nash."

His eyes widen and meet mine, then he gives a short, nervous laugh. "The massage is that good, eh?"

"It's not the massage, tonto," I say, playfully calling him a fool. "Well, yeah, it's nice. But I've been thinking … Why can't we just tell Lahun we want to be married? Then I won't have to marry someone I don't really know."

Nash's expression is not what I hoped for. Rather than looking joyful, it's only a look of bewildered confusion.

"Why? Will you stay here with me then?"

I shake my head. "No. I don't want to stay here."

The thought of leaving him is painful, but the thought of staying in the past is terrifying.

His jaw tightens. "Then what's the point?" He releases his hands from me. "If it's just an itch you have, then I can help you scratch it. It seems that's what I'm good for, Ines, no?"

My eyebrows narrow. I don't understand his sudden hostility. I reach for him, but he steps away.

Forcefully, he points. "It is better for you to become Lahun's queen. He is the main ruler here. He needs a queen, and so that is your role now. My role is yet to be decided, but when that time comes, I will do it."

I fold my arms over my chest, putting up a measly defense to his words of rejection. "What's your deal anyway, Nash?" I spit out. "A couple days ago you freaked out when you thought I slept with him. And now you're okay with it? You do understand when I marry him, he will be expecting sons from me. You do know how that happens, right?"

Nash doesn't respond and just glares darkly into the water. I move in close again, getting my face in front of his.

"He has a penis, and from the looks of him, it's a big one."

Indigo eyes ignite at me, then he shuts it down, staring again at the water and stepping back away from me.

I move in front of him. "In order for me to get pregnant with his son, he will repeatedly put his penis inside me. Probably daily. I might even enjoy it."

"Stop," he warns, a dangerous gleam entering his eyes.

"Oh I'm sorry. You don't like hearing about it?" I shove him with both hands, but he doesn't budge. "Well I don't want to do it!" I shriek like a madwoman. "Damn it, Nash," I sob out. "Just marry me. You be the one to marry me. Please."

I've lost all pride, and I'm begging him in earnest now. Yet he stands immovable as stone, saying nothing, doing nothing. I feel myself gearing up, ready to do whatever it takes to get him to react. A sick part of me actually wants him to unleash his anger on me. I want him to hurt me, so that afterward, I can use his guilt to control him. I can make him do what I want him to do. It's a crystal-clear solution.

He's on the brink of exploding. His jaw is tense, nostrils flared, and he's breathing heavily. It would be so easy to push him over the edge.

But I don't. I won't.

He already loathes himself for his past actions. If he hurts me again, he'll be sad. And more than anything, even more than needing to get what I want, I hate seeing his sadness.

CHAPTER 19

"Lady Chel!" Calalu runs up the stairs to my house. "Lahun summons you and Kinich Ahau. Chaac returns today. We must get ready!"

I beam a smile at the girl. A week ago, we returned from Ixchel's palapa. Every day, Calalu has regained more and more use of her body, and today she's running. After handing me some food, the girl begins twisting my hair into an elaborate updo on top of my head. She finishes it off with the parting gift Ixchel gave me, the jade serpent. Its tail coils back and forth over the top of my head.

Nash and I have remained friendly, but after throwing myself at him at Ixchel's and begging him to marry me, the passion between us has lowered to a cautious simmer. Gone are the long talks, stolen kisses, and morning cuddles. In their place are seldom shared meals and brief nods as we pass one another on the sacbe. I spend many sunrises and sunsets with Lahun in his observatory and the two of us have become good friends. The king is a great man and a fine ruler. His greatest downfall is believing other people are also inherently good.

Nash spends much of his day in the Temple of the Warriors, training with the other fighting men and women, or going hunting. Sometimes I see him as I pass by during the day, sparring with spears, or shooting targets with bows and arrows. The warriors also spend a lot of time playing Pitz, the Mayan ball game, in a stone court with sloping walls behind the Temple of Warriors. The Great Ball Court we saw in Chichen Itza is not yet standing. I hate to admit how many times I've gone out of my way in order to catch secret glimpses of him playing the ball game. He moves with such raw, athletic grace, and I love watching him.

Calalu ties on my best skirt. The longer skirt's length reaches mid-calf on me. The cloth is a deep Mayan blue color with golden yellow vertical lines. An intricately colored band of red thread, with a white, notched fringe runs along the hem. This being a special occasion, we pull out my small stash of jewelry. Calalu layers on my jade necklaces. I also don my jade half-moon earrings and shiny tumbaga bangles. We sit on my thatch-covered porch while she paints intricate red designs on my forearms and then vertical lines down the middle of each eyelid from forehead to cheeks.

While I sit in the shade, the paint drying, Nash walks up, wet from a late afternoon bath. Calalu leaps up and runs to him. He grins down at the girl and catches her in a spinning hug. A brief feeling of jealousy pricks me, before I scoff at myself for feeling envious of a twelve-year-old girl. I drop my eyes, and from my peripheral, I see his gaze attach to me before swinging away again.

Calalu drags him up the stairs to get him ready for the evening. He emerges a mere ten minutes later, absolutely resplendent. Calalu has pulled his bronze hair back into a long braid that stops at the middle of his shoulder blades. The neutral colored loincloth has red lines running along the bottom hem. A bright yellow short cape is tied at his neck. Red designs are threaded all over the bright cape, and a white, notched hem finishes it off.

He sits on the steps while Calalu paints red bands around his ankles and vertical red lines down the center of each of his eyelids from forehead to cheekbones. While the paint dries, he leans back on one elbow, thighs spread, and the picture of masculine grace. It is unconscionable for a man to be so captivatingly beautiful.

The sun is setting when Chaac's traveling band enters the city. Nash and I stand with Lahun on the Venus platform as the group enters. People of Itza gather in the streets but keep a wide aisle to allow the arrivals to pass through.

Chaac leads the way. The god of rain appears slightly taller than Nash, and even wider of shoulder. His muscle strapped chest gives him the bearing of a warrior. Cold, onyx eyes stare straight ahead, not sparing a glance for the adoring crowd of people clamoring for his attention. He could be considered handsome, but the angles of his cheekbones and severe line of his lips belong to the face of a cruel man. The look of a predator blankets his features, and he moves with the prowling grace of an animal on a hunt.

Upon reaching the platform, he climbs the small stairs and spares a smile for Lahun in greeting. "Brother," he says in a low, broken tone, bending his head.

Lahun grips Chaac on the shoulder, grinning back at his friend, before directing Chaac's attention to Nash and me. "See, the cenote has given us Kinich Ahau and Lady Chel. They have agreed to rule alongside us. The Whole One God has shown favor to Itza."

Chaac's icy gaze settles on Nash first, and he inclines his head in a greeting. Black eyes slide over to me, and he studies me with a bit more interest. I raise my chin and stare back. A half smile breaks the

243

harsh line of his cheek, and he nods his head to me, then comes to stand on my right side. Next, he turns to the gathered crowd that has closed up behind the entourage.

"People of Itza!" Chaac shouts. "I have come from a place called Culhuacan. It is a city full of wealth, power, and riches beyond imagination." He extends his hand toward the group that arrived with him. "We have been blessed with the incredible beauty of princess Xochi who has agreed to the honor of being a bride of Itza. She will help our lowly city reach the same powerful heights as Culhuacan."

Chaac's eyes gleam as the petite young woman moves away from the crowd and climbs the stairs. She wears a short red skirt and a thick necklace of coiled strings of tiny, white beads. There is a girlish quality to her, with her slightly rounded, pink cheeks and long black hair that has been separated into low, looped pigtails. She looks to be no more than fifteen years old. And that's where the innocence ends. She has perfectly round, heavy breasts with upward facing, wine-colored nipples. Her full and naturally pouty lips spread in a pretty smile as she greets Lahun with wide, blinking doe eyes. Their hands briefly grip one another's in greeting. Her green eyes meet his as she gazes up at him through thick, black lashes. A pink tongue darts out to moisten her naturally red lips. Somehow, the young woman exudes eroticism with her eyes alone.

Xochi next moves to Nash, who keeps his arms crossed, but inclines his head to her. She smiles shyly and tugs at one of her hair loops before placing a small hand on his arm. He releases the tension in his arms and straightens them, gripping her hands with his as he gives another curt nod. If I blinked, I would have missed it. Xochi briefly raises his hands, brushing his knuckles over her nipples. Nash jerks away and recrosses his arms. Her eyes gaze at him with a secret smile.

She moves to me next, and a childlike grin comes onto her face. "Sister," she says with a light, breathy voice. I hold out my hands, and she responds by coming against me for a hug. Her height must be around five feet, making her feel like a child in my arms. She beams a smile up at me. "We will be great friends, I think," Xochi says in a lilting tone.

I smile back at her, utterly confused by the 180 she flipped between erotic enchantress and new BFF. Our group breaks away from the crowd and heads to the palace where we will dine. Xochi moves daintily alongside me and slips her arm in mine. We walk side by side like a pair of old friends.

The palace is bedecked with woven tapestries, potted palms, and banked pots of glowing fire for lighting. In the center of a great room is a low slab of limestone about a foot thick, draped with colorful fabric. It rests on an enormous thatched rug. On top of the dinner table is a gourmet assortment of food—an entire smoked peccary, clay pots filled with stewed pork and red sauce, another pot with a mixture of white beans, plantains, and eggs, whole avocados nearly as big as my head, along with sliced mangoes, dragonfruit, and bright orange mamey fruit. One wall is a line of columns leading out into an open-air patio framed by glowing pots of fire.

Everyone sits on colorful kapok filled cushions. Servants enter the room, bearing pitchers of balche, a Mayan beer, along with fruit water. They fill our jade goblets and place stacks of hot corn tortillas around the table.

I sit on one side of the table with Xochi, while Lahun sits directly across from me with Chaac opposite Xochi, and Nash on his other side. The men dig in, using a jadeite knife to carve into the roasted peccary. Everyone eats, while Chaac and Lahun converse in low tones. No doubt, Chaac is filling Lahun in on their journey.

Xochi turns to me, swallowing a dainty bite of mango. "How long have you been here in Itza?"

I quickly scan my brain for the correct term. "Almost one uinal," I respond, picking up a piece of the red chile pork with a tortilla. We've been here just over two weeks, and a uinal is twenty days. "How long was your journey from Culhuacan?"

"About one uinal of hard travel."

Chaac's attention slips over to her, and his lips slant into a knowing smile. Xochi meets his gaze directly. My eyes move between the two. I suspect they slept with one another at some point during the journey. Chaac crosses his arms and leans back, nodding at what Lahun is saying, but his eyes stay on Xochi.

After dinner, Nash and I slip away to the open alcove, sipping balche from our jade goblets. The moon is high and round against the ink blue sky. The fermented beverage tickles my throat, and I give a small choking cough. Nash glances aside at me and thumps my back. He's had much of the drink, and I see the loosening effect it has on him. His hand lingers at my back and strokes down my spine. A shiver passes through me at his touch, and his eyes immediately drop down to my breasts. A lazy smile spreads on his lips.

Across the room, Lahun and Chaac form a triangle with Xochi. Her diminutive form is barely visible beyond the span of their shoulders. Every now and again, the twinkle of her airy laughter spreads through the room. The men appear entranced with her. I scowl in their direction.

Nash raises his eyebrows at my expression. "What is it, muñeca?"

"Them." I wave my hand in the direction of the trio. "Clearly she's the more attractive woman here."

A low chuckle comes from Nash's throat. "No, you'd be wrong there. At least for me. Let me explain. Look at her."

One long, bronze finger points to Xochi, her face barely visible between the wall of masculine shoulders. Her head tilts back in a dainty laugh, and her green eyes glow bright with excitement. Both men are the recipients of her welcoming smiles. Her fingers trail down one man's arm, while the other man gets the direct attention of worshipful eyes. She effortlessly switches between the two, giving equal amounts of herself. The woman is a master at commanding men.

"Okay, so?" I cross my arms.

"So?" Nash smiles. "She looks at a man as if he's a hero. Her eyes are wide, bright, and she smiles easily."

I increase my glare upon hearing his words of appreciation.

Nash continues. "I can see how some men like that, but for me? Boring. Predictable." Nash then frames his attention to me. His eyes move up and down, studying me. "Now you, Ines, if you could see yourself in a mirror right now, this is how you look. You are not as inviting as she is."

He crosses his arms and hardens his face. His eyes turn dull and glaring, and his jaw squares off. I laugh at his exact mimicry of my resting face, because it's a mirror image.

"But that"—his mouth widens in a smile as his eyes roam my face—"that laugh makes me want to kiss you until you can no longer stand."

He has already kissed me until my knees grew weak. It was

heaven. My eyes grow heavy lidded and move to his mouth. I suck in my bottom lip, remembering our last kiss. It feels like it's been years.

"And that," he says, his eyes darkening. "That makes me want to take you to my bed until you don't know your name anymore."

I squeeze my eyes shut. He's willing to do all that, but he is unwilling to make me his wife. I'm not falling for this flirty banter again, especially when he's been drinking.

Lahun's voice booms out. "The matchmaker approaches. Come, friends!"

Nash's eyebrow arches in question. "Matchmaker?" he mouths silently to me.

I respond with a quick nod. Everyone reclines at the cleared table and our goblets are filled with balche once again. The men have all imbibed heavily in the beverage and are boisterous with laughter.

"Kinich," Lahun begins, focusing his eyes on him. "When we spoke, you said you were not interested in marriage. But what of now? Look at these beautiful women. Maybe the matchmaker will match you with one of them."

Nash doesn't mask his confusion. "I don't understand, my king. I thought you would be marrying Lady Chel, not leaving it up to chance."

Lahun sighs. "I am a romantic, but no one here has claimed a love match, so we will do it the traditional way with a matchmaker."

Chaac speaks. "I would have princess Xochi if she will have me." His gaze is heavy on the young woman.

She smiles tremulously. "You do me a great honor, my lord. But I happen to greatly respect the traditional wisdom, so I will allow the gods to decide my fate, if it pleases you, my lord." Green eyes flutter at him beneath heavy lashes. I imagine marriage to another man won't be enough to keep Xochi from Chaac's bed.

Chaac drains his balche then slams the goblet on the table. "So be it."

Nash's eyes settle on Chaac, then slide over to me. "I will allow the matchmaker to give me my destiny," he finally says, sending a thrill fluttering down my spine.

Sandaled feet shuffle as an aged woman takes small steps into the room. A servant directs her to sit between Xochi and me. She carries a cloth bag, and the sound of heavy stones clack inside. The woman wastes no time, and looks around the table at everyone.

Crinkled eyes settle on Xochi. "What is your day sign, princess?"

"A snake, oh revered one," Xochi replies in a sweet, low voice.

The woman rifles through her bag then pulls out a small, rectangular jade piece and hands it to Xochi.

"Hold it in your hands," she instructs.

The matchmaker's gaze moves next to Chaac, but she doesn't ask him. As town matchmaker, she already knows his sign.

"Crocodile," she mutters, and searches through her bag before handing him the green rectangle. Questioning eyes settle on Nash. "What is your day sign?"

"Serpent," Nash says, in a low, deep voice, his fingertips tapping on the table.

Another jade serpent comes from the cloth bag, and she hands it over to him. Next, a jade rectangle holds the seed sign for Lahun.

And last, a deer sign for me, hastily spoken by Nash. The woman holds out her hands, and we return our tokens to her. She sets my and Xochi's signs to the side and begins matching the men's signs to ours. She brings the seed next my deer. The pieces connect with a gentle sound, and her brows draw in.

"A good match, but may not be the best. We will remember it."

Next she puts Lahun's seed next to Xochi's serpent, and the two green pieces join with a stronger sound. The woman nods her head in satisfaction. "This one is better. We will remember this match."

Chaac's crocodile is matched against both my and Xochi's pieces next. They make a similar low sound of connection as they meet. The old woman makes no comments about these, and just keeps shuffling the pieces around as she frowns, then sometimes smiles.

Next, she brings my deer next to Nash's serpent. The pieces seem to leap out of her hands and unite in a loud clatter as if they were magnetized. My heart jumps into my throat, and I try hard to control my features. Dryness overtakes my mouth, and I swallow hard. I realize I'm leaning forward and probably glaring at the matchmaker like I'm going to attack her. Exhaling slowly, I force myself to take on a less aggressive pose, disentangling my hands from one another.

She stares at our day signs for a long time. Maybe only a minute, but it feels like hours pass. I sneak a glance at Nash, and he's also leaning forward with an intense stare at the woman.

Her eyebrows narrow, and she shakes her head. "This is a very powerful match." The matchmaker looks to her left at me, then her gaze sweeps over to Nash. "But neither of you are ready for it."

Sweeping the pieces aside, she straightens her shoulders and brings Chaac's serpent next to my deer, her wrinkled lips curving in a smile. "This one is better." Her eyes move up to Chaac. "She will make you a great ruler if you allow her influence."

Xochi and I stand to face our intended husbands—Xochi with Lahun, and me with Chaac. I try hard to force a smile to my face, but all I feel is despair. My lips tremble. This is not what I want.

Chaac gives me a calculating look then comes around the table to stand in front of me. I smile and hold out my hands. Rather than grabbing my hands, his gaze sweeps my body. Dark eyes study me much like a farmer would examine a horse he's about to purchase. I lick my lips nervously and drop my arms down to my sides. His hands move forward. Long fingers run over my hips then glide back to squeeze the curve of my bottom.

He stares at me, challenge clear in his onyx eyes. "These hips will give me sons." His hands slide up my body with cold familiarity, and he cups my breasts, then rubs his thumbs over my nipples. "From these my sons will be fed. And me."

My hand tightens into a fist. Nash exhales harshly through his nose, a fire blazing in his eyes. He moves as if to step forward, but Lahun's arm shoots out, stopping him.

"Brother," Lahun says to Chaac, admonishment clear in his voice. "You shame our sister and our queen. This is not the way of a ruler."

Chaac's expression remains impassive, but he doesn't remove his hands from my breasts. It seems he's waiting for me to push him away. I won't give him the satisfaction of his desired response, so I just lift my chin and stare him in the eyes.

"I am well equipped to care for any childish needs my king may have," I say, using my most bored tone. "But if you are through examining me, I am ready to retire."

He laughs, but the humor doesn't meet his eyes. Chaac's gaze moves to Xochi, and a brief look of hatred passes over his features. After what seems like an eternity, his hands drop away from my breasts. I resist the impulse to wrap my arms around my body like a shield.

My gaze passes over everyone, before I sweep out of the room with the regal bearing of my ancestress. The need to run away rises, but I force myself to calmly walk through the colorful halls, passing guards and servants with my features locked in a look of serenity.

The man examined me like I was nothing more than breeding stock. How humiliating. If he's willing to do something so crude in front of a room full of people, what will he do in private when he has unhindered access to my body? I feel trapped, like a wild animal about to be slaughtered. My heart pounds in my chest, and I want to scream until my vocal cords shatter. But I walk rapidly, exit the palace, and head straight to the safety of my own home. The heart of Chichen Itza passes in a blur.

"Ines," Nash whispers harshly. He comes beside me and wraps his hand around my arm, pulling me forward as he continues walking fast. The sobs start to come out of me in ragged breaths. "Hold it together." He firmly grips my arm with a tight hand.

I widen my eyes and sniff hard, attempting to calm myself until I get to the privacy of the copse of trees surrounding our homes. He's basically dragging me with his long-legged strides. We turn and head down the sacbe leading to our houses.

"I told Chaac I'll kill him if he ever treats you so dishonorably again."

"What did he say?"

Nash breathes out sharply through his nose. "He said when you are his wife, he can do whatever he wants to you."

We climb the stairs to my house and enter the doorway. He turns me to face him and pulls me against his chest, wrapping his arms around me, his hand gripping the back of my neck. "What have I done?" he whispers in a strangled voice. "What have I done?"

I pull strength from his body against mine. In these moments where he's mine, I only enjoy the warmth and scent of his skin. It has a calming effect on me.

"I'll be okay, Nash. I'm sure I've dealt with worse." I give a short, harsh laugh. "Chaac is about a thousand years behind on the cruelty of men. I can handle him."

Nash pulls away and grips my face between his hands. "I did this. I'll never forgive myself."

"Good," I say solemnly, pressing a soft kiss to his lips. "Now get out of here before Chaac has your head for attempting to defile his wife-to-be."

A deep look of pain enters Nash's eyes, and he presses his forehead to mine. "Let's just leave, Ines. Let's just go live in a hut somewhere. We'll go live with Ixchel until the portals open again. Let's forget this. None of this is important to me anymore."

"No." I shake my head and pull his hands down from my face. "We're doing this, Nash. This is our destiny and exactly why we are here. We can survive this for a couple months. I'm stronger than you think."

"I know, but you shouldn't have to be."

I try for a brave smile, but my lips tremble. "It's my choice. We're seeing this through. I'm sure it'll be worth it."

With a rough shake of his head, he stumbles away from me,

leaving me alone. Once he's gone, I sink to my knees atop my bed, releasing bitter tears of humiliation.

CHAPTER 20

THE SUN IS NOT yet up, and the faint grayness and stillness of impending dawn hangs in the air. I feel him enter the room before I hear him. And then his arms come around me. Relaxing against his body curved around mine, I squeeze my eyes shut again.

"You can't be doing this anymore," I whisper. "Xochi is probably in the other house."

"I know," Nash responds softly. "But I was thinking we should go talk to Lahun in the observatory this morning. I don't have a good feeling about Chaac. Maybe we can convince him to change something." Hope tinges his voice.

I sit up and turn to look at him. "Like what? Defy the matchmaker? You marry me?" I draw my knees to my chest and wrap my arms around them, leaning my cheek against my bent knees. "You heard her. We're not ready for each other. Is my sign really the deer?"

"You said July 2nd right?"

I nod.

"Yeah that's the right one." He pauses, then rolls onto his hands and knees. "I don't know, Ines. But I still just want to try talking to him."

We grab a basket of fresh cloth to change into after our morning bath but head to the observatory first. Purplish hues of dawn creep over the horizon. A cinnamon-colored bird with a gray breast hops from limb to limb of nearby trees, screeching out a *kip woo* sound, then whistling in long *wheep* noises.

The observatory looms ahead. After climbing the three flights of stairs, we walk in. A girlish giggle echoes from the uppermost heights of the nearly forty-foot building. Lahun must have brought his bride-to-be to watch the morning ascend.

Xochi's soft, feminine voice speaks. "Your knowledge of the heavens is impressive, my king. It is almost as good as mine."

"Almost?" I hear the smile in Lahun's voice.

"I am somewhat of an astronomer myself," Xochi admits with a ring of pride.

"Ah, must be why we matched so well," Lahun says in a lowered tone. There is a brief moment of silence then he says, "May I?" His voice comes out even quieter.

"Of course, my lord," she responds in softer tones.

I put my finger to my lips and try to redirect Nash back out, but the telescopes have caught his attention. Lahun is testing out the first kiss with Xochi. A big part of me knows I should give them their privacy, but another part can't help but wonder if my king will find the love spark he seeks. Listening, I crane my neck.

"Do I not satisfy you, my lord?" Xochi's soft voice trembles.

"It's not that, princess. We will grow to love one—What are you doing?" His gentle voice raises in slight alarm.

I grab Nash by the arm to steer him out, but a muffled sound from above makes him stop and cock his head.

"My queen, please don't."

"I can make you happy, my lord," comes Xochi's voice, now confident, but low and alluring.

"No, please. I don't want you to—"

Lahun's voice cuts off abruptly and turns into a soft groan.

Nash's eyes widen and his jaw drops open on a smile. I hastily reach for his hand, and he keeps pulling from my grasp. This is too personal to listen to. And I actually feel bad for Lahun. Even though it sounds like she's giving him a lot of pleasure at the moment, the guy repeatedly said no. I give Nash my best chola stare, squaring off my jaw and putting an intense glare into my eyes. He raises his hands in submission and waltzes around me. We walk out the door, just in time to hear the finale.

The Xtoloc cenote lays empty. Nash and I laugh chaotically between gasps of breath as we slow from our run. As soon as our feet had hit the steps of the observatory, we began running to get away from there as fast as we could.

"Duuuuude," I say to Nash, bending down with my hands on my knees while I try and catch my breath.

"Xochi knows what's up," he says, grinning. "Literally."

He begins to unwind his loincloth.

I shake my head. "That was wrong of her though. He said no a couple times. Poor Lahun."

"Poor Lahun?" Nash scoffs. "He is not feeling sorry for himself right now."

After removing my skirt and unraveling my braid, I follow Nash down the flat limestone steps.

"You don't understand. I've gotten to know him pretty well. He wants love. That's why he kissed her. He was looking for the spark."

"Well she found it."

I roll my eyes then watch as he dives into the cenote. He emerges again and climbs back on the rock, giving a shake of his head like a wet dog before wrapping his arms around me and pulling me in sideways.

People begin arriving for their own baths, and we take care to keep an appropriate distance from one another. After all, as Chaac's intended bride, it would be frowned upon for me to behave with Nash the way we are prone to behaving.

We get out of the cenote and dress ourselves, then return to the observatory. Lahun sits on the steps alone, his head in his hands.

"My king," Nash says in greeting.

Lahun's face gentles into a smile. "Brother," he says, then to me, "My queen. The sun is too high to see any stars now." He gives an apologetic shrug.

"That's not why we've come," Nash says in a deeper tone. "I have some concerns about Chaac and the way he treated Lady Chel last night. Are you certain it is a good idea to have him be a co-ruler?"

"Chaac has been a good friend for a long time. I trust him with my life. He drank too much balche last night. I apologize on his behalf."

"It would sound better coming from him," Nash says firmly.

Lahun nods. "I agree. I will speak with him." His eyes meet mine. "Lady Chel, you did not deserve to be treated in such a manner. He can do better. I have faith in my brother. You can be assured he will make you a good husband."

"And what of you, my king?" I ask gently. "Are you pleased with your bride?"

His eyebrows draw close together. "She is beautiful. What more could a king want?" He forces a smile, but his eyes seem sad.

Lahun then tells us that the king of Uxmal has invited Chichen

Itza rulers to celebrate his son's marriage. It would be a three-day journey there, then several days spent in the palace for the festivities, and finally a three day return trip home. Nash and I readily agree to accompany him.

"We leave in two days," Lahun says. His eyes brighten. "And the matchmaker has chosen the auspicious day for the marriages."

Anxiety rises in my throat. "When?"

"Three days after we return from Uxmal."

I exhale out a steadying breath as my shoulders fall in defeat. My fate is inescapable.

"My lady," Calalu's soft voice comes from the doorway. "Lord Chaac summons you to the palace."

"Thank you, Calalu."

I set down the pile of leaves I'd been sorting, then stand. I've been doing my best to go into the forest every morning to forage for roots, leaves, and healing flowers. Many times I'm even recognizing things I haven't been taught by Tato or Ixchel, and I know it's the work of my genetic memories.

"Shall I do your hair and provide your jewelry?"

I shake my head. "That won't be necessary."

I'd rather wear sackcloth and ashes if it were available. After tying on my most plain skirt, I head out the door. It'll be interesting to see what this meeting brings. My walk to the palace is quick, and I sneak a glance at The Warriors Temple as I pass, hoping to get a glimpse of Nash looking all sweaty and masculine. I frown in disappointment as I pass by. He must be further in the back.

"Chaac has summoned me," I say to the first guard I come upon.

I have no idea where I should go. The guard turns to lead the way, and I follow. We pass the banquet hall, then proceed down a long, colorful hallway with intricate friezes depicting jaguars. I wish I could study the detail and color more closely, but the guard moves too fast. He stops at a doorway then turns, pounding his spear on the smooth limestone floor.

"The Lady Chel," he announces loudly.

I enter the doorway, noticing I've been brought to Chaac's private chambers. Looking over my shoulder, I see the guard retreating down the hallway now that he's delivered me to my destination.

Chaac sits in front of what looks to be a mirror, but it's black, made from obsidian. The reflection is clear on the smooth surface. He runs a jadeite blade over his jaw, shaving stubble from his face.

"Please, give me one moment," he says, appearing momentarily flustered.

"Of course, my lord." I clasp my hands together then realize how the position lifts my breasts front and center, so I just drop my arms to my sides. My fingertips, feeling lost, tap against my skirt.

Chaac splashes water over his face then wipes it dry with a piece of fabric, before standing and coming toward me. A ghost of a smile crosses his face, though it seems forced.

"We had a bad start yesterday, my lady. I apologize," he says with a tight set to his lips. He extends his hand to a low table, where a meal has been set. "Please, join me."

I want nothing to do with him, but since he is to be my husband until I'm able to hightail it out of here, it's better I get to know him. Forcing a bright smile, I graciously accept and take a seat on a low cushion. Chaac sits across from me and pours a dark brown liquid into a jade cup, then pushes it to me before pouring his own drink. There are also several hard-baked eggs, and an array of mangoes, papaya, and sapodilla, which is a dark skinned fruit with a sweet, pulpy center.

I take a sip of the chocolate drink and blink hard as I swallow. There is no sweetness, but there is definitely spice. A smile plays on Chaac's lips as he watches me. The man could be considered handsome if he smiled more often.

"Have you not had xocolatl yet, my lady?" he asks, pronouncing it show-co-la-til.

I shake my head and press my lips together. The bitter drink will take some getting used to. Coughing, I cover my mouth. "What's in it?"

"Roasted cocoa beans, chili, and ground corn, I think." Chaac swirls the liquid in his cup around.

We eat in awkward silence, though I occasionally make asinine comments about the food. Chaac doesn't say much in reply, but nods. When we finish eating, servants appear from thin air to remove the remains of our breakfast.

With a heavy sigh, Chaac gives a tight smile. "Have you been happy here in Itza?"

He's trying to make small talk. While I respect that he's trying, the man looks in pain to be speaking in a friendly manner with me. I flash him my most genuine smile, hoping it reaches my eyes.

"It has been wonderful, my lord. You have a beautiful city. You have much to be proud of."

His jaw tightens, and he shakes his head in disappointment. "We could be so much greater. If you saw Culhuacan, you would not think this city so great. Their pyramids are the largest I've ever seen. They have so much wealth. The leaders are powerful."

261

"Do the people love their leaders?"

"Does it matter?"

I'm tempted to let it go, soothe him, and just allow his male ego to reign supreme. But the matchmaker did say he could be a great ruler if he accepts my influence. Maybe that will be my role here. I take a deep breath before continuing.

"I think it does, my lord. Your subjects would be the ones who build the pyramids, and the work is hard on their bodies. They have to believe in something to keep them going."

"Fear," is all he says with a blank look.

"What?"

"That is the surest way to control people. Fear. In Culhuacan, the priests sacrifice the slaves. If the work is going well, it is only one or two people. But if they are struggling to complete it, that means the gods require more people."

I struggle to keep my face impassive, but my right eye twitches with how casually he talks about humans being murdered.

Chaac continues. "It is considered a great honor to be sacrificed."

I pin him with a look then think better of my forward stare and lower my gaze. "Would you consider it an honor to be sacrificed yourself, my lord?"

He stays silent for a moment, so I chance a glance back up at him. He narrows his eyes, then a terrible smile moves across his face. There is nothing kind or mildly pleasant about the way he looks at me. Chaac reaches across the table, grips my wrists, and pulls me across the surface, sliding me onto his lap. I stiffen in his arms.

"My lord, this is not proper."

"I am doing nothing improper, Lady Chel. Holding my future

wife in my arms is not wrong." Chaac runs his fingers through my hair, yanking at the tangles none too gently, trying to get a reaction out of me. "See? I am only feeling the beauty of your hair. That is not wrong."

He runs his hand over my arm, and his long fingers graze the tip of my breast, but he acts like it didn't happen. There is a challenge in his eyes. This man seeks to dominate me. Unfortunately for him, and probably even more so for me, I'm not the subservient type.

"Would you like me to kiss you, my queen? A kiss is proper."

No, I don't want this idiot touching me for one second more. But I also need to try my hardest to make my next weeks here as pleasant as possible.

I smile sweetly. "I will kiss you, my lord."

Once I remove myself from his lap, I kneel in front of him. He reclines back on the floor, propped on one elbow, his long legs stretched out. I scoot closer, not willing to crawl over his large body in order to reach his head. Chaac's thin lips curl in a sneer as he waits for me to move close enough to kiss him.

I lean forward and press my lips gently to his. He smiles against my mouth, then deepens the kiss. I accept him for a few seconds then try to pull away, casting a demure look at him from beneath my lashes. He inhales sharply, then rears up, flipping me onto my back. My head cracks on the floor, and he smiles at my cry of pain.

"Chaac—"

I move to sit up, and then he covers me with his weight, kissing me in earnest. His hand moves between my legs, and I clamp my thighs tightly together. I twist sideways and try shoving against him, but he is a solid, unmovable mass. Chaac gets his knee between mine then unravels his loincloth, while keeping me pinned beneath one heavy hand.

"No, stop, please."

I struggle, fighting him as hard as I can, but it's useless. My strength is meager compared to his. And then I notice beneath his loincloth, he is completely limp. A brief feeling of relief washes through me, allowing me to relax slightly. His eyes meet mine, and he sees I've taken notice of his inadequacy. White teeth bare at me in a fierce growl of anger. Large fingers thrust roughly inside me, stretching me and hitting my cervix. I scream out in pain, and then I feel the pulse of him stiffening against my thigh. My eyes widen in shock as I come to the horrible realization that he must need to inflict a measure of pain in order to get it up.

"Oh Lady Chel, this is not proper," he says mockingly while shoving his hand impossibly further inside of me, while I push ineffectively against his arm.

The sharp rapping sound of a spear pounds on the floor outside the door. "My Lord Chaac," the guard says in a toneless voice. "Your presence is required at the Temple of the Warriors."

Chaac's black hair has fallen over his forehead, and he flips it back with a short twist of his head. "I am busy," he says to the guard, returning his attention to me. My legs shake with the effort of me trying to hold them closed against the rest of his torso moving in. I gulp in huge breaths of air, both of my hands gripping the wrist of the fingers buried inside me. Gratefully, I recognize he's already gone limp again.

"Lahun insists on your presence," the guard says with hesitation.

Black eyes squeeze shut in frustration. When they open again, a look of gentleness comes across his face. "I'm sorry, my bride. We will have to finish this later." He leans forward and presses his mouth to mine. I keep my lips firm and closed, then turn my head away.

Finally, he removes his fingers from my body and wipes them on his loincloth, staining the white cotton with a tinge of red. His eyes come alight upon seeing my blood.

After Chaac leaves the room without a second glance to me, I take a moment to compose myself. My hands tremble as I slide my fingers through my hair. I close my eyes and breathe slowly, trying to push down what feels to be an impending panic attack. I feel dizzy, and my lungs seem to be getting smaller. I've never had a man use a sexual act as punishment against me. My stomach turns, and I gulp down the bile that's threatening to leave it.

My head in my hands, I sit still, breathing slowly. A minute later, Chaac re-enters the room and comes to crouch next to me. I straighten my spine and turn to meet his cold gaze. One hand caresses over my hair, and his eyes move back and forth over mine. He's looking for tears. Thankfully, I can be pretty stone cold when I need to be.

"My lord?" is all I am able to say without my voice shaking. I force my expression to look utterly bored.

He presses his mouth to the side of my head as if to kiss me but whispers instead. "Let me make something clear to you. Neither Lahun nor Kinich can save you from me. Yes, they will both try, but you can be certain they will both fail. Do you understand?"

I turn to him once more, my eyes remaining blank. "I do not require someone to save me, my lord."

Chaac's meaning is clear. The man is ruthless and evil, but he's hidden his true self from Lahun for so long. And Lahun, in all his goodness of heart, remains utterly blind to what Chaac really is. He will never think the man he calls a brother to be a wicked person. Even if I'm able to convince him, Chaac seems like the vindictive sort, and I wouldn't put it past him to commit outright murder to retain his position.

And Nash … My Nash would try to kill him as he promised. Even though the two men are similar in size, Chaac's body is bigger and battle hardened. He has been training in ways to kill men for much longer than Nash has. I wouldn't have Nash risk his life for me. I'm willing to suffer this to keep him safe. This is my own sacrifice to make.

The guard's spear rings on the floor. "King Lahun Chan and Lord Kinich."

Chaac remains crouched next to me, his hand tenderly running over my hair. My intended husband's hulking build completely conceals my body from the view of the other men.

A deep chuckle comes from Chaac, as if I've said something funny. "Now smile," he whispers harshly, before standing.

He pulls me to my feet, then turns to the two men standing in the doorway. Nash's eyes narrow slightly as he sees me. I force myself to go stoic.

"I am sorry for making you wait at the temple, my brothers. I lost track of time this morning after making up for my bad behavior last night. Thank you for coming here to meet." He sets me in front of him, large hands possessive on my shoulders. "I am a lucky man to have been matched with a woman as forgiving as Lady Chel."

The viselike grip of Chaac's hands releases, and he turns, signaling to a servant. Nash keeps his gaze locked on me, eyes full of suspicion. He knows me, and he can read me better than anyone here. I have to find a line between making my behavior believable to Nash, while placating Chaac.

"We've sent a servant to tell Xochi to come here instead of the temple," Lahun says stepping forward. His eyes settle on me and the corners crinkle in a genuine smile. "And it's good Lady Chel is already here too. I'm happy you've given my brother a chance to show his softer side."

Yes. Yes, I've seen his softer side.

I choke on my own saliva and start coughing madly. My face turns red as I attempt to get my lungs working properly again. Chaac's gaze sharpens on me. He pulls me against him, fingers digging into my ribcage.

"I do have a soft side, and I will use it often with Lady Chel," he says with a forced lightness, but his meaning is clear to me.

I laugh up at him and give him my best look of admiration. "Your soft side is your best side."

Perhaps I've taken it too far. His nostrils flare, and the midnight black of his eyes goes even darker.

Nash's gaze move between us, confusion knit across his forehead. I'm not convincing enough yet. I shoot Nash a slight eye roll and half smile to let him know I'm putting on a small show, giving him enough truth to get him off my back. The set of his shoulders relaxes slightly. Chaac releases me and inclines his hand to the table in his room.

We all take a seat around the small rectangular table. The table is only meant for a few people, so we sit in close quarters. Servants return with pitchers of fruit water and more xocolatl, along with a platter of fruit.

A pounding spear announces the arrival of Xochi. The young woman sweeps into the room, and then rushes to Lahun's side.

Chaac spreads his hands on the table to begin. Tattoos cover his heavily muscled arms. If I hadn't experienced their ruthlessness firsthand, they'd be rather pleasing to look upon.

"Look at us," he says, glancing around the table with a rare, genuine smile. "We Itzaes are the beginning of greatness that will sweep these lands. I have learned much from our great Toltec neighbors." He inclines his head to Xochi in a gesture of respect. "I learned achieving greatness is no easy task. Much sacrifice is required. The gods demand our best."

I wait with bated breath. Is this where he tries to get everyone to agree to begin human sacrifices? I can't imagine anyone here agreeing outright, besides Xochi, to whom it's a normal thing.

Chaac continues, "I am happy to announce that Xochi's father, the great King Quetzalcoatl, has agreed to gift us enough wealth to build a new pyramid upon the marriage of his daughter."

A soft sound of surprise comes from Lahun, and Xochi beams up at him, clutching his arm happily. Chaac briefly glares at her before erasing the expression with a single blink of his obsidian eyes.

"As we know, the upcoming marriages call for sacrifice, which we usually do by letting our own blood onto sheets of bark to give back to the gods. But King Quetzalcoatl has given us a unique opportunity. He sent back with us a number of their people who have been suffering from an illness that causes extreme pain as they die. These people are asking us to end their lives in honor of our marriages." Chaac looks around the table, judging everyone's reaction. A sudden, sad expression passes over his face. He shakes his head. "At first, I refused the king, my brothers. I told him Itza would never do something so terrible as to end a person's life before their time. But then their priest explained that for people who face a long painful death, giving their life in sacrifice is considered a noble death. They will not have to journey the thirteen levels in the afterlife to get to the paradise of Tamoanchan. We would be helping these people go straight to paradise."

Xochi sighs reverently. "Yes, brother. It is a great honor for them. We would be helping them move on from this life. No more suffering. What a beautiful thing."

There is utter silence as they wait for the rest of us to speak. Lahun's eyes narrow to slits, and I can tell he does not agree with this.

Finally, he speaks. "You will thank King Quetzalcoatl for his ... hmm"—Lahun presses his lips together, searching for the proper word—"generosity. But this is something I cannot allow. The Whole One God is the one who decides when a person's journey on this level is done. I cannot take that from him. So we will help these people heal. We have powerful healers here in Itza."

A sad moan comes from Xochi. "The people suffered so much to take this long journey here, my king. Do not take this honor from them. We have had no marriages or temples dedicated in Culhuacan as of late, so there has been no opportunity for them to give their lives honorably. They suffer, my king."

Lahun shakes his head, folding his arms. "I have spoken, princess."

I see the proverbial air go out of Chaac's sails. For now, he is defeated. His eyes seek Xochi's, and something unspoken passes between them. She gives the slightest nod of her head.

CHAPTER 21

A PROCESSION OF PEOPLE leave Itza early in the morning to make the three day journey to Uxmal. Servants carry large baskets against their backs secured by tumpline. Supplies for the trip, along with wedding gifts comprised of turtle shells, quetzal feathers, and rare blue jade are stored inside the basket.

Itza rulers walk along the smooth path flanked by sixty armed warriors. The fighting men are a small fraction of Chichen Itza's army, but they accompany us for protection. These occasions, while often completely safe, can result in assassination attempts on kings, so the protection is well warranted.

Our pace is rapid, but we stop during the hottest hours of the day to rest in hammocks, bathe in cenotes, and eat hunted food or dried meat and fruit from the baskets. We continue moving well past sunset, and the sacbe gleams like moonstone as it reflects the lunar glow.

"Did Chaac ever apologize?" Nash asks quietly.

We've been apart for most of the day, but I've remained in constant awareness of him. Now that we've found one another again, our movement slows and we walk a few paces behind the last of our group. Ahead, I can't even see Lahun or Chaac, and both likely remain in the lead. I'd purposely avoided Nash in Itza the last couple days, which wasn't difficult with how busy he had been. I feared what Chaac did to me would be written on my face.

I breathe out a sigh. "In his own way."

"And in what way is that?"

Slivers of truth are the best way to disguise a lie.

"He tried to get frisky."

Nash's shoulders turn in my direction as one eyebrow raises. "Keep going."

"I faked it as much as possible—"

"Faked what?"

I can hear the dripping venom of jealousy in his voice.

"Enthusiasm. I acted like I liked it. But ..." I pause, searching for the right words.

The next words come out in a growl. "But what?"

"It's kind of embarrassing."

"Ines, I swear to God ..." He exhales a harsh breath. "Will you just tell me already?"

"He couldn't get it up."

Pressing my lips together, I peek a glance in his direction. A wide smile splits his face, and then he shouts out a loud laugh that spreads in the darkness around. A few people glance back at us, but no one continues watching.

A few hours before midnight, we stop to set up camp. Hammocks are strung side by side in trees. For my own safety, I have a servant set mine up near Nash and Lahun.

Chaac gives Xochi a meaningful look then heads deeper into the trees, disappearing into the darkness. She strings her hammock up on the other side of Lahun then eases herself into his. They speak in hushed tones, and a short time later, I hear the soft sounds of kissing.

I turn myself on my side, giving them privacy while facing Nash. He's lying on his back with one hand resting on his abdomen.

His head tilts in my direction. "Why did you say it was

embarrassing what happened with him?"

"I mean, yes, I'm glad he couldn't do it, but at the same time it's a blow to my ego, you know? Like I'm not attractive or something. Isn't that stupid?"

"Ay, Ines." He is silent for a few moments, long enough that I think he's done talking. But then he says, "He would have to be blind and deaf to not find you attractive. But if he doesn't, then I'm glad. Because you're mine."

I let out a loud sound of exasperation. "I don't belong to anyone, Nash. When will you learn that?"

"You belong to me as much as I belong to you. It doesn't matter who we've been with, or who we will ever be with. Our ancestor's blood makes sure of it. Whether you like it or not."

I can say with absolute certainty that even though Ixchel is over 800 years old, every cell of that woman still belongs to Kinich Ahau. But there's nothing to convince me an emotion can imprint in the genetic code.

And yet, something about Nash has always drawn me in. Even when we were children, and he was busy tormenting me because he thought I was pretty, while I just wanted to be around him. But if what he's saying is true, and their love did pass to us, perhaps their fate will as well.

I'm not willing to settle for a dysfunctional relationship. At most, I'm willing to fake a relationship, as I will be doing with Chaac.

Soon, silence descends over the camp as people succumb to sleep. I've never been much for sleeping beneath trees under an open sky, so dreams elude me, slipping from my grasp over and over again. Sometime later, the sound of rustling catches my attention. I open my eyes to see Xochi leaving her hammock and quietly walking in the direction Chaac went. It still takes me some time to fall asleep, but she doesn't return before I do.

The next morning, red horizontal lines visibly mark Xochi's neck. Not hickeys, but they resemble fingerprints.

"What happened to your neck, my queen?" Concern rings from Lahun as his heavy brows pull inward.

"Something bit me in the night, and I scratched in my sleep." Xochi stares up at him with wide, unblinking eyes.

In the distance, Chaac leans one shoulder against a tree watching her explanation, his expression lit in amusement. Xochi casts a brief look in his direction and angles her head as if she's stretching, running one finger across the lines on her throat. His chest seems to swell as his obsidian eyes become impossibly darker. Raw arousal flashes across his face.

Being in close quarters for several nights with Xochi is unsettling. The woman-child is a complete nymphomaniac. If she's able to fulfill Chaac's sexual needs, then she is also a masochist. Several times I hear her trying to start something with Lahun, who remains a gentleman in the face of her attempting to sexually assault him almost every night. I feel so much pity for my king, along with sorrow at the thought of his lifetime stuck with this unfaithful creature. It's only wishful thinking to hope I could do something to alter his future.

The next night, I try to wake Lahun after she heads to Chaac, but the poor guy curls his large body inward and shakes his head with a mumbled, "No, princess," and then falls immediately back to sleep. During the daytime, Xochi doesn't leave Lahun's side, so I have no opportunity to speak with him.

The third night, I am awakened by Nash saying my name in a low, drawn out tone. My eyes shoot open as I hear the unmistakable noises coming from the hammock next to me. A dark head is in his lap. I reach over and lightly tap his arm several times to wake him from whatever dream he thinks he's having. He hisses out a sound of anger, grips Xochi by the hair, and pulls her off.

"You touch me again, little girl, I will kill you," he grates out, before shoving her away.

She stumbles backward and hits the ground, but then crawls forward to him again.

"My lord," she whispers in low, seductive voice, "you were enjoying it."

"I was asleep. And now I'm not."

She reaches for him.

"No." The glimmer of an obsidian blade flashes in the moonlight. "Do you want to die?"

Xochi backs up, her large doe eyes filling with tears. "I only wanted to make you feel good, my lord."

"You dishonor yourself and you dishonor my brother. Next time, there will be no warning, and the last thing you feel will be this blade in your neck."

With a strangled gasp, Xochi turns and rushes away, probably to whatever twisted comfort Chaac can provide. Briefly, I wonder if he knows what she's doing, and then I have a nagging feeling maybe he's behind it.

"Jee-zus," Nash says on a loud exhale, sheathing his knife against his calf as he turns to face me.

I laugh softly, looking at his shocked face, unable to help myself. "Now you understand how Lahun felt?"

His eyes are wide and bewildered. "It was a good way to get woken up until I realized it was her." He makes a low sound of disgust and scrubs his palms down his face. "I feel so dirty now."

My lips curve into a smile. I don't comment on the fact that it was my name he was saying in his sleep.

High city gates loom in the distance. Our traveling group got an early start and began moving several hours before sunrise. Over the last half hour or so, we've passed the homes of the lowest classes. At the sides of the road, they peddle their wares of woven cloth, simple jewelry, and carved wooden pieces to all who pass by. Groups of people converge and move along the intersecting sacbes into Uxmal from all directions.

The thinnest strip of yellow bands the horizon, but the sun is not yet up as we finally step inside the city. Lahun stops his servant and rifles through the basket hanging on the small woman's back before pulling out one of his leather wrapped crystal telescopes. Throughout our days of travel, his view of the sky has been limited to what's directly above us, so I know he's itching to get to a higher point to see his usual constellations.

"Do you want to come to the Nine Steps pyramid to study the sky before the sun rises?" Lahun asks his bride-to-be with unconcealed excitement.

Xochi shakes her head. "I am tired, my king."

No surprise there. He doesn't hide his disappointment, and his large shoulders slump.

"I'll go," I offer to Lahun, my voice bright.

He accepts me with a wide smile and wave of his hand. This may be my only chance to talk privately with him about the chaos going on with his intended wife. Maybe I should mind my own affairs, but it's concerning to think of him entering a lifelong alliance with someone of her proclivities.

Lahun heads east, guiding me through the city with his hand on the small of my back. People mill about everywhere as more and more crowds stream in through the open gates to celebrate the marriage of the king's son.

Uxmal is different from Itza. Lahun explains that unlike most cities, there are no cenotes nearby. He points out various circular platforms where they've dug into the ground, lined it with limestone, then hollowed it out in order to collect rainwater. My head cocks slightly as I see the error in this plan. A massive drought will end this city before long. But for now, Uxmal rivals Itza in its splendor.

Whereas Itza has angled edges and specific geometric planes, Uxmal's architectural design is smoother and more rounded. The buildings are all plastered in stucco and brightly colored. Etched in stone are many bas-reliefs of various gods with curving noses. I'd rather not advertise my ignorance, so I don't ask all the questions brewing in my head. I'll ask Nash later. We reach the Nine Steps pyramid and begin climbing. Up top is a short building built on the highest platform.

"I have not seen my morningstar for many days now," Lahun says. "And they don't have an observatory here, so this will be the best view."

After arriving at the top, we walk through the building to reach the east side of the pyramid. We are approximately ninety feet in the air, with the vast, flat expanse of the Yucatán stretching all around as a blanket of low trees. Lahun already has his eye trained on the eastern horizon where his morningstar, the planet Venus, has risen. Telescope raised, he remains still for a few moments, then makes a soft exclamation.

"All is well?" I ask.

He thrusts the telescope in my hands and points in the direction of the steady glow of the planet. "What do you see?"

Squeezing one eye shut, I raise the leather wrapped crystal disc to my opposite side. Venus emanates its warm light, and it's shrouded by the cluster of the flower constellation Lahun showed me my first few days in Itza. Back then, the flower had only been near the morningstar, but now the stars surround it.

"The flower is all around the morningstar." I hand him the telescope back. "What does it mean?"

Lahun's handsome face is pensive, eyebrows drawn in deep thought. "I don't know. But I think I will soon find out." He extends his hand back toward the rooftop building. "Come, Lady Chel, let us find our rooms."

Shade descends over us as we begin walking through the building. A small, young woman enters the doorway on the opposite side, eyes glued to the floor and moving through in a hurry. She wears a long white huipil, and her black hair hangs freely down her back, reaching almost to her knees. My mind races and my palms dampen with anxiety, but I know now may be the only chance I have to share my concerns.

"Lahun, the past few days, I've noticed something odd …"

My carefully rehearsed sentence trails off as I realize he's not listening. His attention has been fully caught by the young woman. The king's entire body turns as she passes us, as if he's trapped in some invisible orbit.

"I know her," he says softly, a note of awe in his voice.

"Well, go and give a greeting,"

My powerful king has turned into a mute, paralyzed man. My hand wraps around his much larger one, and I pull him back to the eastern side of the pyramid where we stood before. The young woman stands staring at the horizon, arms hugged around herself. I grab Lahun's telescope from him.

"Do you need a viewing instrument?" I offer it to her.

She turns to me and hastily wipes at her reddened eyes. Impossibly long black lashes nearly brush her cheeks when she blinks. There is an ethereal beauty to her delicate features. Lahun stands frozen at the doorway, peering out from behind the wall. I widen my eyes and make a quick jerking motion with my head for him to come here.

"I haven't seen one of these in a long time," she says with a note of melancholy in her voice. For a moment she just stares at the leather wrapped instrument, but then she reaches out and takes the telescope.

"What is your name?" I ask.

She moves the telescope to her eye, training her sight toward Venus. "I was born under the White Flower constellation, so I am named Sac Nicte."

The name is foreign, but I feel like I've heard it before. I turn, again trying to discreetly wave Lahun over. He is frozen at a distance.

"My friend over there knows much about the sky," I say helpfully.

Sac Nicte removes the telescope from her eye and turns. Her eyes widen when she sees Lahun. "It can't be," she says in a hushed voice, but then a brilliant smile blooms on her face, seemingly lighting up her entire body. "It's you!"

Lahun gives her a gentle smile as he emerges from the safety of the wall. "So it is."

The king stands in front of her, and the top of her head reaches only to his chest. He is a massive man, yet he seems to shrink with uncertainty.

I decide to give introductions. "Sac Nicte, this is Lahun, king of Itza."

Shock floods her face. "You are the king? Oh …" One small hand flutters up to her mouth. "I must apologize. I feel shame for my behavior when I was in your city. I—I have never done that before—"

Lahun shakes his head with fierce adamance. "No, no. Please don't feel shame. I know you had not done that before." His eyes narrow with conviction. "That behavior was also not like myself."

Sac Nicte steps closer to Lahun and blinks slowly. Her eyes lift to his as she reaches for his hand with one of hers. "I do not regret it, King Lahun."

Strong fingers enclose around her small hand. "I also have no regret. Only that I did not hold you the entire night. You were gone in the morning." His voice is gruff and full of emotion as his gaze sweeps over her like a man seeing color for the first time. "I would have married you."

Her eyes fill with tears. I look back and forth between the two. This is the young mystery woman Lahun said he met when he became king of Itza. The one with whom he said he felt love at their first kiss.

Lahun leans down, closing the distance between them as he pulls her against him. She clings to him, and tears slide down her cheeks. Straightening to standing, he holds her in his arms as their lips meet.

I glance around nervously, but we are completely alone on this pyramid, with nothing but trees out to the east. With a quiet sob, Sac Nicte breaks the kiss and pulls away, trembling fingers tracing the line of his jaw, tear-filled eyes moving over his features.

"We can't, my love," she whispers. "The wedding here in Uxmal is mine. I am to marry the prince."

Lahun sits on the pyramid stairs, head resting in his large hands. Sac Nicte has left to finish getting ready for the planned pre-wedding activities. The wedding isn't for two more days, but each day has a variety of dances, games, and musical exhibitions in honor of the impending union.

"This hurts," Lahun says in a hollow voice.

He presses his palms roughly against his eyes then rubs them down his face. I sit next to him and put my arm around his broad shoulders, barely able to reach his other side.

"That one night has never left me," he finally says after some time. "We belonged to one another for that moment. I thought it would be enough to get me through my life. But now, knowing she will be with another"—he inhales deeply—"it hurts. She gave me her virginity, Chel. What if her husband punishes her when she doesn't bleed their first night together?" He drops his head in his hands again, a strangled sound coming from his throat. "I can't bear the thought of her with another man. Who am I?" His normally calm demeanor is erratic and hysteria tinges his voice.

I make hushed sounds meant to soothe, trying to impart some

comfort, but I know there is nothing I can say to change what he's feeling.

"Suddenly, I don't care for honor, I don't care for kingship. I just want her beside me." He turns to me, his eyes filled with tears. "I am willing to abandon the name of my forefathers, leave Itza, and return to the name I was given at birth."

"What name is that?"

He grabs the necklace that always hangs on his chest and lifts the black snake emblem. "Kaan Ek."

CHAPTER 22

"Lady Chel for Kinich Ahau," I say to one of the guards once I've entered the palace that is to be our home while we stay in Uxmal.

Eleven doorways line each long side of the building, with two unique arrow-shaped hallways near the ends. The guard leads the way past a dizzying array of doors, each filled with travelers settling in from their long journey. This impressive building holds more than twenty rooms inside.

"Lady Chel," the guard intones, announcing my arrival to Nash's chamber.

In one sudden realization, the impropriety of this meeting place dawns on me, so I just peek around the doorframe and beckon to Nash with my hand. "Let's go for a walk."

He smiles and leaves his chamber, and I lead him to a spot near the palace that caught my interest as Lahun and I passed through earlier. A lush botanical garden blooms in a large parklike area. We enter under a heavy arch of a blooming vine. Dark leafed copal trees and heavily scented frangipani line the walkway. Beyond are an incredible variety of medicinal plants, and I happily realize I'm able to recognize many of their names and uses.

We follow the winding path deep into the garden and sounds from the city soon grow muffled from within the blanket of green, imparting a sense of privacy. The path leads to a roundabout, where in the center lies a chultún, one of the rainwater collection cisterns. The circular limestone apron surrounding the hole is stuccoed and painted a bright shade of yellow.

I turn to Nash, who regards me with a curious look. My heart pounds as the need to touch him becomes my singular purpose. With intention, he hooks one finger in the waist of my skirt and tugs me closer. My hips bump against his, and my hands settle on his biceps as we meet in a crush of limbs, and mouths, and tongues. Our bodies grow heavy and we sink to our knees on the ground, frantically touching and gripping one another. It feels as if it's been a lifetime since we've been like this.

His hands thread through my hair, pulling me tightly against him, while I dig my fingers into the muscles banding his shoulders. He's gotten even bigger with all the training he's been doing in the Warrior Temple at Itza. I've missed this. I've missed his mouth, I've missed feeling his body against mine. But even more than that, I've missed him and our simple mornings of coffee with breakfast tacos. I've missed his insistent hand holding, even when it used to make me so uncomfortable. Now, my fingers just feel bereft without his between them.

Our bodies feel as if they weld together, and being in his arms again makes me realize how much I need him. It's somehow become something more than physical. We lose ourselves in the wonder and sensation of this now forbidden kiss. Thinking about forbidden things brings the reason I brought him to this private place back to mind, and I pull away.

"Nash, listen—"

He moves forward and presses his mouth to mine again. I smile inwardly as sunlight blooms within me, before returning his ferocity with my own pent up passion. His touch seems to wash away the filth I've felt staining my skin since Chaac assaulted me. Our kisses slow, then we open our eyes and stare at one another with wide, silly smiles in between the soft meeting and parting of our lips.

"Remember that story you told me about Kaan Ek and Sac Nicte?"

"Mmm," he says, touching his lips to mine, then softly nibbling my lower lip before he pulls away. "The lust filled idiot who shouted, 'Itzalan?'"

I smile as he parrots my earlier words, and I look up at him. "Yes, that one. He is Lahun."

"What?" Nash says, finally moving his attention from my body to focus on my words.

We sit on the ground, arm pressed against arm. Briefly, I tell him the first kiss story Lahun told me back in Itza. The one night our king had with the mystery woman a year ago. Then, I fill him in on what just happened at the top of the Nine Steps pyramid.

"It's his mystery woman, that first kiss where he says he felt love, and her name is Sac Nicte!" I explain excitedly. "She was born under the White Flower constellation. He's been obsessed with that constellation, because it's been close to his morningstar. Today, that constellation of stars was surrounding Venus. Like, it's destiny or something!"

"What part of it is destiny?"

"Them. Their relationship."

"The … eh, how did you say it? Lust filled …"

"Ache," I supply helpfully.

"… that burns away, right?" He raises an eyebrow at me. "And leaves you with ashes. You aren't starting to believe in love, are you, my cold-hearted muñeca?"

I grin and shrug. "I've been doing some growing, okay? And get this, remember how you told me kings just continue taking on the names of gods when they're inaugurated?"

Nash nods.

"Lahun's name given at birth was … wait for it," I say dramatically.

"Kaan Ek," Nash breathes out.

"That's why he wears that black snake pendant. That's what Kaan Ek translates to, right?"

Nash nods as understanding enters his eyes.

"Can you believe we're here for that? And we have sixty warriors from Itza with us just like in the story. What the heck do we do?"

Nash's brow narrows in thought. "If the legend is true, Itza will fall after this. We are here to prevent the fall of Itza, so we can't let him do it."

"But the difference is you and I are here. Can't we assume rule and let Lahun have his love story?"

Nash shakes his head. "It would go to Chaac. We haven't been officially made rulers yet. There is a ceremony, and priests, and rituals."

"Why does Itza fall, then, if Chaac takes over?"

"I'm not sure. But we cannot allow Lahun to abandon his rule."

My heart sinks. I can't imagine sentencing Lahun to a lifetime of crazy, unfaithful Xochi. This should be an easy choice, considering how much I've preached about not believing in love. But what I saw between them … If love exists, that's what it looks like. It didn't burn away. It grew stronger.

"There's gotta be another way," I mutter.

"Come up with one. If we can save Lahun from marrying that witch, then we will. But I don't see how it's possible, Ines. Even if

285

we save him from Xochi, for him to take another man's wife will start a war. Itza will fall."

The next morning, I head to the Nine Steps pyramid to meet Lahun, knowing he'll be there, and having the same certainty she, too, will be there. They sit facing the east, but they are not looking at the sky. They only fill their vision with each other. Her knees are pressed against his long legs, and their hands rest atop one another between them.

I wait, keeping an eye out for other people who may be coming to the pyramid. But these dim hours before sunrise seem to be reserved for sky watchers and forbidden lovers.

The sun peeks the curve of its bright face over the horizon, and Sac Nicte stands to go. Lahun pulls her into his lap, and she wraps her small arms around his broad shoulders. Their lips meet as both of them make equal sounds of desperation.

I turn away, pressing my back against the interior wall, giving them some privacy. A short time later, Sac Nicte passes in a hurry, sniffling and wiping her eyes. Lahun remains seated, facing east, and I move to sit next to him. He turns to me, eyes reddened and full of tears.

"I knew you would come," he says with a sad smile, then he turns to face the rising sun. "If I have one day of this life left, I want it to be with her. If I have fifty years left, I want every single one of them to be with her."

"How does she feel?"

"Helpless. The arranged marriage creates a powerful alliance both families want. She felt willing before, but now …" He shrugs. "She feels trapped." Lahun pins me with a pointed look. "Do you believe in destiny, Lady Chel?"

Destiny … The idea that our lives have been written with no will of our own. Was it my destiny to walk into Casa Mestizo during the five minutes Nash's father left? Did that moment seal my fate? Was I guided there at that exact moment by some meddling force?

I shake my head. "I believe we are free to make choices, but …" I try to think of a way to describe a pawn, since chess doesn't exist in ancient Maya. "But I think it's like warriors on a battlefield, and the king can direct their movement."

"Like the gods can direct ours?"

"I really don't know, but I do believe there are things beyond our control or design. And then there are things you can control. What can you control here?"

Lahun lets out a mirthless chuckle. "I can walk up to her, take her by the hand, and walk out of those gates." His eyes stare grimly to the east, back to Itza.

"And what would be the consequences of that choice?"

"War. Pain for my brothers. But happiness for me."

"You have to decide if it's worth that. You love her, yes, but you love your brothers too. Would Chaac take care of the people of Itza the way you do? Or would Xochi's influence lead to human sacrifice like the Toltecs?"

His lips press into a grim line. "I hope not."

"Either way, you would have no say in what he chooses to do when you're gone."

Lahun ponders my words for a moment, then gives me a half smile. "You have given sound council, Lady Chel. But tell me this.

287

How do I walk away from her?"

"We leave now. Say we've gotten word of something urgent from Itza, and we just go."

He inhales sharply through his nose. "Even thinking of walking away, I cannot do it."

"Will it be easier to watch her be married to another man, and then go? King Lahun, the choice you make regarding this is heavy. It can mean the collapse of Itza. The city needs you. This will be one of many times during your rule that what you want and what you need come second. Itza comes first."

"What if I offer my hand to her father? And more of everything the other city offers?"

"And what of Xochi? What of your alliance with her family? What of the other city? None of it is good. It is just all bad timing."

A strange look comes into his eye. "If I am being honest with myself and with you, Lady Chel, I don't care about any of it anymore. Itzalan would be anywhere we make it."

"Itzalan?"

The word had been Kaan Ek's battle cry when legend says he stormed the altar during the wedding.

My eyebrows knit together. "What does Itzalan mean?"

"The land of the Itzas. Itza is home, but I can make a new home with her. Anywhere she is with me will be my Itzalan."

"We're still back at square one," I say to Nash later that evening. "I talked to him this morning, but he seems set in his way. If we fail at this, we fail at saving Itza."

"Should we drug him and drag him back home?" Nash says, half laughing.

It's barely a joke, because I know he's partly serious. And I've already considered it. Dinner that evening only fueled my conviction, because Lahun did not take his eyes off of Sac Nicte the entire night. He boldly stared at her from across the room, not caring who noticed. Thankfully, balche was flowing in abundance, so perhaps only I saw his fierce attention.

Before coming to talk with Nash, I walked through the medicinal garden again, looking for plants for that exact purpose. But how to explain our comatose king to everyone else, including Chaac? And what happens when Lahun wakes from a drugged sleep? There would be consequences for me. It feels like our only option, though.

"We have to do it," I say firmly. "The wedding is tomorrow, and we need to be far away from here by then. I can't think of anything else to do."

"Gather the plants you need. We'll just say he fell sick, and we need to get him back to our healers at Itza."

The greenery of the medicinal garden encloses me in its shadowed cover and my mind stretches to commune with the plants. I remember watching both Ixchel and Tato walk through the forests, both of them seemingly drawn to the exact plant they searched for. My time with Ixchel was invaluable in activating the genetic memory of herbal medicine. Alone, that knowledge is pointless, but she taught me how to allow the plants to do their work of healing.

First I see Numay Pim with its reddish orange flowers. Crouching next to the low-lying plant, I collect the pointy oval leaves giving thanks while asking my friend to impart its wisdom and best use. The road forks, and it's as if I am swept along, my body guiding me to the next offering. An evergreen shrub with salmon pink flowers catches my attention. Kandel Che offers her glossy green leaves, and I gratefully accept. I then gather brilliant yellow thorny flowers as the final ingredient for my sedative mix.

Upon returning to my room, I prepare the herbal infusion with careful diligence. The mixture will steep for several hours, allowing its strength to increase. While I seek to merely knock Lahun out, too strong a dosage or too potent of a mixture could kill him.

Before sunset, I find the king of Itza darkly brooding on the Nine Steps pyramid. Sac Nicte will not be able to come tonight, and he knows this. I don't want this role. I want him to say he won't pursue her. I don't want to have to drug my friend in order to prevent the fall of Itza. But we've come to this. The fate of Itza, and maybe the entire Mayan empire, rests on what happens here. Itza serves as an important hub for all surrounding cities, and if left abandoned for the love of its king, a ripple effect will ensue, spreading out and touching every connected city.

I sit beside Lahun, giving him one last chance to do the right thing. "What have you decided, my king?"

His jaw tightens. "Nothing yet."

At this point, deciding nothing is not enough. In my mind, "nothing" means he's as good as chosen to proceed with taking her. We have to get him far enough from here that he is physically unable to return. Our plan must be set into motion.

I rest my fingertips on his forearm. "I've prepared an herbal tea to help you sleep tonight and ease your mind."

Lahun drops his head and turns his face to me. "You are a good friend, Lady Chel." One large arm wraps around my shoulders, and he presses his lips to the side of my head.

Tears prickle behind my eyes. I feel like the worst friend in the world right now. I repay his friendship with deceit and can only hope he will one day see the wisdom of my actions.

We walk back to the palace, and I hold onto Lahun's arm as if he were the one escorting me. In reality, I'm hoping to prevent him from dragging me toward wherever Sac Nicte resides, though I'm sure my weight will be as insignificant to him as toilet paper stuck to someone's foot.

Once I get Lahun back to his room, I grab the tea from where I've left the stone cup warming in smoldering coals in my chamber. Steam billows from the tannin colored liquid, and Lahun sips cautiously at the hot drink. His features twist at the bitter taste, but he swallows every drop down. My throat constricts realizing this will be the last time he ever fully trusts me. Lahun leans against the wall, deep in thought.

"In the morning, I'm going to take her, Lady Chel," he says quietly. "I'm going to command the warriors to action. They will not disobey their king."

"I know."

His eyes move over to me. "And yet you do nothing?"

"I pray you will forgive me." My vague words leave him to figure out whether I'm referring to what I've already done, or my seeming inaction.

Lahun closes his eyes. "It does not matter, Lady Chel. She is my destiny. The heavens have formed it, so it shall be."

A lump forms in my throat, but I swallow it down. Thirty minutes later, he begins nodding out. I leave his room and head down the fire lit hallway. Guards ignore my passing. After all, there is no reason for them to suspect anything of me.

I find Nash's room where he lies resting in preparation for our overnight journey. Everything might change for the worse after this. I kneel next to him, gently tracing his temple with my fingertips, then press my lips to his. He turns to me and slides his hands behind my neck, holding me in place as he returns the kiss.

After a moment, I pull away. "He's ready."

Together, we walk the hallways to find Chaac. Surprisingly he is alone. Satisfaction flashes in his dark eyes when he sees me, but then they narrow once he catches sight of Nash.

"I thought you were coming to finish our conversation from before, my bride." A smile meant to look alluring plays on his lips.

I cast my eyes downward. "Kinich went to speak with Lahun and could not wake him, so I checked him and something is wrong."

Chaac is quick to move, and he follows us down the hall to Lahun's room.

"Brother." Chaac crouches next to Lahun, giving him a rough shake.

Lahun doesn't respond, but just continues breathing short, shallow breaths. I kneel beside him and make a show of checking his pulse and opening his eyelids, while making grim, worried facial expressions. Chaac retreats to the door, his dark eyes full of genuine concern.

"Perhaps an evil wind has touched him," Nash suggests.

The Winds are considered beings of their own right and are known to be equally intelligent and dangerous. It's a brilliant suggestion for Nash to make, as the illnesses resulting from The Winds can be deadly.

I glance up at Chaac in alarm. "If so, then we need Tato. He will know how to help him."

"Why not ask the healers here?" Chaac leans against the doorframe, crossing his arms over his massive chest.

"Their healers are not as powerful as ours," Nash says.

"And what if this sickness has been called by them?" I stand and shake my head. "They will make him worse."

Chaac considers my words for a few nerve-wracking moments. "We will go back to Itza then. Kinich, gather our servants and our warriors. And you"—he directs his attention to me—"get Xochi. I will speak with the king of Uxmal to explain our departure, and to get a litter to carry our brother."

We three leave the room and scatter in opposite directions. Until Lahun awakes from the sedation, our journey will be difficult. But we have sixty strong warriors who will be able to take turns bearing the weight of our king. Guilt weighs heavy in my gut, pulling down my spirits like a stone, but I know we're doing the right thing.

CHAPTER 23

UPON SUNRISE, AFTER ONLY several hours of sleep under the Mayan sky, a swell of commotion forces my bleary eyes open. Nash rushes over to where I lie. With a quick beckoning wave of his hand and jerk of his head, he silently motions me to follow. I roll off my hammock and come to stand next to him.

"He's gone." His lips are set in a grim line as we make our way to the edge of the sacbe where Chaac waits.

"Gone?" I whisper in hushed shock. "How?"

Nash's jaw clenches and unclenches. "After everyone fell asleep, he woke up and had fifty warriors follow him back to Uxmal. This is bad, Ines. We weren't supposed to let this happen. I should have stayed awake." He curses himself softly.

Our group left Uxmal in a hurry well before midnight, with Lahun's weight shared by Itza warriors. For the next six hours, we travelled quick, which left everyone, save for those keeping watch, to fall into an exhausted sleep in roadside hammocks. What we failed to take into consideration was what would happen when Lahun awoke from his drugged sleep. Naively, I expected him to be confused, maybe angry, but I failed to understand how the depth of his love for Sac Nicte would make him take immediate action.

We reach the sacbe where Chaac stands, tattooed arms crossed over his wide chest. Xochi has taken a demure pose next to him, her small head lowered to the forest floor.

"He came to me while I slept. Said Itza and Xochi are now both mine as long as I give him my silence. What else could I do? I think he's in love." Chaac curls his lip in disgust.

My features remain locked, completely impassive. "In love with who?"

Chaac gives a short laugh. "That girl who's getting married today. Didn't you see the way he watched her at the evening meal?"

I shake my head, even though I definitely noticed and worried over Lahun's dark, impassioned stares across the room at the bowed head of the bride-to-be. Sac Nicte's eyes flicked up to his several times, and they had been brimming with tears every time.

"I think he's going to carry her off before the wedding." Chaac laughs. "I didn't think he had it in him."

Nash exhales harshly, narrowing his eyes at Chaac. "It's going to cause a war."

Chaac gives a quick shake of his head. "Not if I send word saying he has abandoned his throne and Itza, and the fifty warriors with him are no longer welcome to return. I'll send two warriors back there right now. They'll probably execute one of them as a form of payment, but at least the second one can bring us back news. Either way, we need to get moving in case they try catching up to detain us." Chaac regards me with a sideways look. "As further disappointment, I must advise you I will be making Xochi my queen instead."

Dropping my eyes, I press my lips together to prevent my features from revealing the absolute glee threatening to explode across my face. "Your happiness is important to me, my king." I am careful to use his new title.

Our much smaller party of people begins moving east, back home to Itza. The entire thing is slightly anti-climactic with how smoothly Chaac turns this disaster around and shifts events in our favor. Maybe he won't be such a terrible ruler after all.

We failed, but somehow we didn't. Chaac's quick action of sending word back to Uxmal prevents the second half of the story from coming true. Had the story of Kaan Ek and Sac Nicte played out as it did in legend, Lahun would have commanded all sixty warriors to rush the altar with him at the wedding, implicating the entire kingdom of Itza, including Chaac.

As it stands, according to the single guard who returned unharmed to us, Sac Nicte went missing before the wedding even took place. When the two guards arrived back at the city, a search was underway for the princess. It had been noted all of Itza left in the night, so already we were the most obvious suspects.

The Itza guards relayed Chaac's words to the king of Uxmal, saying that Lahun woke his brother, after gagging and tying him up, of course, and then told him he was abandoning his Itza rule and going back for Sac Nicte. Since we sent word as quickly as possible, the single executed guard was the only punishment they chose to exact. At least Itza is now safe from the retaliation of Uxmal along with Sac Nicte's city of Izamal.

I can't help but think about Lahun and Sac Nicte and hope their several hours head start is enough. I hope they will be happy, and I hope they will live long lives. Nash says some legends reveal the two of them will head south, and eventually settle in Peten Itza in what will be a small island named Flores in modern day northern Guatemala. Lahun will get his Itzalan, a home defined by the presence of the one he loves. Happiness glows in my chest knowing the two will get their happily ever after. I hope my friend finds it in his heart to forgive my betrayal.

After two days of keeping an impossibly quick pace, we arrive back at Itza late in the afternoon. The inauguration and wedding of King Chaac and Queen Xochi is announced and will proceed as planned within a few days time.

The next morning, sounds from the city awaken me. I've slept since we arrived back here yesterday. A busy flurry of activity has begun in preparation for the wedding. I smile when I see Calalu waiting for me. I've missed my girl.

"Calalu," I say, sitting up and opening my arms to her.

The small girl rushes into my arms. Smiling, I press my cheek to the top of her dark head. I worried for her while we were gone, knowing how much her mom relies on her service to the elite. But Lahun assured me she'd have work and would continue to be compensated while we were gone.

Nash walks through my doorway, grinning at Calalu. "Lulu!"

She beams a smile at him and throws herself into his arms for a hug. After pulling away, she goes to the door where our breakfast awaits. She hands us each a bowl of food then goes to wait on the terrace.

Nash and I eat in comfortable silence, every so often smiling stupidly at one another. It feels good to be able to have this simple friendship of ours back. I never told him what Chaac did to me, not feeling it's pertinent information. I have maybe another month left here, and I want it to pass as smoothly as possible.

Once we finish eating, Nash sets the bowls off to the side then comes to kneel in front of me, taking my hands in his. My lips quirk in endearment at the odd position. He clears his throat and then swallows hard, seeming nervous about something.

Dread settles in my bones as I run through all the possible scenarios of what has him behaving so oddly. It was foolish and wishful thinking on my part to believe for a moment that happiness could come easily. And then he speaks, interrupting my negative monologue.

"Ines, I've been thinking it's best we marry one another."

My heart leaps in my throat and my fingers twitch, gripping his hands tighter. "What?"

"For your safety," he clarifies. "At Chaac's whim, he can order you to marry anyone. But if we do this now, no one can do anything about it."

"For my safety," I repeat dumbly.

He nods. "As my wife, you will be under my full protection. My body and soul will be yours. I will protect you with my life."

I feel like I'm soaring above the clouds and drifting through a misty fog. An intense feeling of happiness had washed over me upon hearing him say we should get married, and yet at the same time there is a sadness I don't understand. It weighs me down.

Nash glances down at our hands before pinning me with a serious look. "And I won't make any ... any physical demands of you if you don't wish it, but at least in name you will be under my protection."

I swallow hard and lick my lips. "How do we ... how do we do it?"

"I have something for you." Nash lifts his eyes shyly to mine, then pulls a small object from the hip area of his loincloth and presses it into my hand.

The first thing I notice is the warmth from his body the small circle carries. I open my fingers, and my eyes widen upon seeing a simple ring carved from blue jade. I turn it over, running my fingers over the smoothness of the band.

"This isn't exactly a Mayan tradition," he explains, "but I remember how important a ring is to you."

Nash's eyebrows knit together and he studies my reaction. An intense ache unfurls in my chest at his thoughtfulness. I meet his gaze, pressing my lips together, still unable to understand the turmoil of emotions raging within me. I look back down at the ring. The blue jade is the exact color of his eyes and is already beloved to me by its default color alone.

"So … Ines de la Luz, will you marry me?"

Briefly, I consider he won't be marrying Ines de la Luz. He will be joined with Lady Chel as Kinich Ahau. The thought pricks my pride, but then I realize I truly don't care who we are, as long as we can be together for our time left. I cast pride aside like a heavy cloak that's been weighing me down.

I nod and beam a genuine smile at him. "Yes, of course. I would be honored to be your wife, Nash."

I absolutely mean every word I say. Nash pulls away then grabs the ring from my hand to move it onto my finger, where the dark blue symbol of our impending marriage slides smoothly into place. Something happens to my heart, as the secret hope I've cherished becomes reality. My hands reach for his face, and I pull him close to me, softly brushing my mouth against his. He responds briefly, but then stills for a moment before backing away.

"I need to get a few more things and find a priest to do the ceremony. We're going to do this today. I just had to make sure you'd say yes first."

His bronze hair falls adorably over his forehead as he grins at me. I brush the strands away and push them back behind his ear as that pained feeling rises in my chest again.

Nash looks down briefly, then back up at me. "I know I said I won't make physical demands of you, but you need to know I'm only human. If we start kissing and touching every night, it's going to be difficult to stop every time."

I drop my eyes to my hands, twisting the blue jade around my finger, then look back up at him. "I don't want you to stop, Nash."

My heart thunders so hard he must be able to hear it. I've just admitted something I haven't even been honest with myself about.

A muscle in his cheek ticks as he clenches his jaw for a moment. "But what if you get pregnant, Ines? You would still take my child and leave me when the portals open? If we have a child, that will change things."

With or without child, the thought of leaving him is getting more and more difficult to consider. But my selfish heart wants him for as long as I'm able to have him, so I don't answer his question directly.

"Tato gave me a tea. I drank it every day when I got my period. He said it would be enough to make me barren for like six months or something like that. I'll just make sure I drink it every month to be safe."

Relief floods his eyes. He doesn't respond with words but leans forward and presses his lips to mine. My arms wrap around his neck as I return the kiss with a boldness I've never used before. An urgent hunger rises in him, and I welcome it. My own barriers I've held in place quickly dissolve, replaced by the simple, human need a woman has for a man. His hands roam my body, tender and familiar. I'm seconds away from begging him to forget the blasted ceremony and let's just do this. But he pulls away and presses his forehead to mine, breathing unsteadily.

"Soon, mi amor," he promises.

My love.

My heart expands with heat. I hate the weakness that overtakes me upon hearing his tender words. I'm simply going to be his wife, and it's a pretty common thing for a husband to say to his wife. But he's called me "my love" in both Mayan and Spanish now. The little girl in me who used to believe in love is reading way too much into this.

"I'll be back soon," Nash promises, then he leaves for the center of the city.

Calalu and I head to the Xtoloc cenote for my morning bath. The ring is a comforting pressure, and I extend my fingers to admire the striking color more times than I can keep track of. I've actually never taken the time to fantasize about what my ideal engagement or wedding ring would look like, but I could have never imagined this. The blue jade is so unique and reminds me of lapis lazuli.

Once I finish washing, we head back to the colorful houses to wait for Nash's return. Calalu braids my hair. I imagine he might enjoy unraveling it later. After she leaves for home, I loosen the plait, thinking it might look more appealing hanging long down my back. Glancing at my skirt, I can't help but wonder if I have time to find something nicer to wear. I stand, ready to head to the market, when I see Nash returning. He is holding a tied bundle of cloth in his hands, but his expression is grim. He meets me on the shady terrace.

"Chaac has asked to see us," Nash says, setting the cloth package down near the doorway.

That explains the look on his face.

"Well, let's just do this. Can we just do it before we go?"

"The priest won't act without the king's permission, so either way we have to talk to him first. I don't think Chaac knows we're planning this, and all I asked the priest is how to go about it. Then I ran into Chaac and Xochi, and he asked me to get you so we could talk with him together."

My nose wrinkles in worry. "What do you think he wants?"

"My mind is coming up with all sorts of wild things right now, but hopefully nothing major."

Worry is clear in his eyes even though he's trying to guard his expression. I raise my hand to rest on the side of his face, stroking my thumb over his chin. He grabs my wrist and turns his head, pressing his lips to my palm.

"No matter what, Nash, I'm yours and you are mine. Okay?"

He squeezes his eyes tightly shut and nods his head. "Let's go."

The king of Itza sits on his throne, a red seat in the form of a jaguar with jade stones embedded throughout to represent the spots of the large cat. Narcissistic as always, he holds a ceramic cup carved with the likeness of himself, Chaac god of rain. No doubt there is xocolatl in that cup. He greets Nash and me with a tilt of his head. Two servants stand near Chaac, fanning him with palm fronds.

Chaac gets straight to the point. "In two days, I will be sworn in as king of Itza, and Xochi will become my wife. My brother made me agree to one thing before he left." His gaze moves between Nash and me. "I promised him both of you would be made rulers, and preferably as husband and wife. Is that agreeable?"

Nash and I look at one another with clear expressions of surprise. His eyes narrow slightly with a hidden message. I see the warning he's trying to send: don't act happy about it. I turn back to Chaac, crossing my arms.

"Is that really necessary? I mean, before all this, Nash was going to be a co-ruler without a wife. Why can't it remain the same for both of us?"

"Because you are the descendent of the moon goddess and he is of the sun god. It is a match the people want to see, and one that will inspire their devotion." He looks between Nash and me. "Are we in agreement?"

Nash looks at me, then back at Chaac before giving a single nod of his head. "For the good of Itza, we will do whatever is necessary."

"For the good of Itza," I repeat.

Nash and I walk quietly back to our houses. Neither of us dare to speak and ruin this moment where it feels like everything has fallen in place. I move my head in a minute tilt toward him, my eyes making a secret glance at his profile. As if he can feel my attention, he looks back at me and smiles widely. Happiness lights up his face, and I return the smile as a sense of joy and completeness fills my heart.

"We're going to be okay," I say softly as we enter the copse of trees around the colorful houses.

I link my arm in his as we climb the stairs to my terrace. Nash tugs on my hand to stop me from entering the house, pulling me to sit cross legged on the woven, cushioned mat with him. He leans over and grabs the cloth package he brought by earlier, then unties it.

"This package is called a muhul. It is tradition for the groom to present it to his bride before the wedding." He pulls out a pair of ornate hair barrettes carved from wood. "For my bride," he says, glancing up at me as he extends them in his hands as an offering.

My fingers wrap around the smooth wood, and then I set them in my lap before twisting my hair up and securing it with the carved teeth. Nash smiles and leans forward, his hand resting on the side of my neck and his thumb stroking my cheek. I close my eyes and lean against his hand.

"I don't want to wait two more days, Nash."

He drops his hand. "Me either, but we have to."

I'm currently a risky combination of impetuous and desperate. The memory of our kiss from this morning has steady heat flickering in my belly. Reaching back inside the cloth package, he next pulls out a long gold chain.

"This we would wrap around our hands as a symbol that binds us together."

"Show me," I say in a low voice, my eyes trained on him, fully intent on seduction.

Nash glances up, hearing the change in my tone, and a nervous expression moves across his face. "Ah, okay."

I scoot in closer—much closer than I need to be—and my knee rests on his calf. He loops one end of the necklace over my thumb, then starts wrapping around my wrist. I lean my upper body into him so with every rotation around my wrist, his hand brushes against my breast.

He laughs softly, an adorable blush climbing his neck. "Stop it, Ines."

"Come on, Nash. Let's just have some fun."

His hands pause for a moment, but he shakes his head, then starts wrapping the chain around his own wrist before looping the end over his thumb. Holding up our bound hands, he gives me a heavy stare. Our fingers entwine together.

"Mix bil kiin," he says, switching to Mayan.

My brain automatically translates his spoken words.

Forever.

He switches back to English. "If we do this now, it is true, we will be married that way. But if we wait two days, our marriage will be blessed by a holy man. For me, this"—he tightens the grip of his hand on mine—"means forever. And I want us to have the best start. Yes, I am marrying you to protect you, but mostly I am marrying you because I love you."

My lungs seize and the blood drains from my head upon hearing this unexpected confession of love. I swallow hard and stare at him, my throat completely closed up with emotion.

Nash gives me a lopsided smile. "You freaking out yet, my cold-hearted muñeca?" His eyes scan mine, which are frozen wide and still just staring at him. "Yes, you are. I know you don't believe in love, but I do. And I love you, Ines de la Luz. Is that okay with you?"

Is he asking for permission to love me? Everything I've ever believed has been challenged and proven to be different. I manage to give a quick nod as tears well up in my eyes. His words are like a

305

battering ram against my carefully barricaded heart.

"Nash, I …" Pausing, I squeeze my eyes shut for a moment, gathering my thoughts, then open them to see him watching me and waiting. "Everything I know has only been proof love doesn't exist for me. But I'm willing to let you prove different."

He nods solemnly. "Thank you for giving me that chance. And this is my first way to prove it." He smiles. "Not letting you tempt me into your bed tonight."

I scrunch my face into a scowling pout then give him a calculated look. "I haven't even started trying hard yet, Nash. You sure you're strong enough to resist?"

He chuckles as he begins to remove the gold chain from our entwined hands. "If there is even a tiny part of your heart that feels the same way about me, Ines … you won't do it."

CHAPTER 24

THE MORNING OF OUR wedding dawns, and I've surrendered to my failure. Instead of full on seducing Nash in order to prove I don't love him, my inaction, I fear, demonstrates the opposite. Part of me wants to defy the notion that the blessing from a holy man will make a difference, while the other half clings to the fantasy of happiness.

Much of the previous two days were spent with women holding lengths of cloth against my body. Weavers have worked at non-stop speeds to produce an intricately woven huipil worthy of elite royalty. Marriage clothing is uniquely designed to represent each partner, so the gown created for my previously planned marriage to Chaac will not do for my marriage to Kinich Ahau. New designs with brightly colored thread will be stitched into the white fabric.

The rest of my time, I've turned back into my nine-year-old self and stalked my future husband as I watched him play the Mayan Ball Game and train at the Warriors Temple. Nash is a natural, charismatic leader who inspires his team to absolute loyalty. For someone who didn't spend his entire life training to play Pitz, his skill is near unrivaled on the court.

I've lived and experienced lust, obsession, and all the desperate convolutions in between. The tempo of my heart for Nash is the same … but on a different arc. I'm finally allowing myself to be consumed by this feeling I've secretly nurtured. It's all combining into an intricate, sticky web I'm sinking into. And it's a terrifying bliss to be caught.

"Come, Lady Chel!" Calalu bounds into my room and grabs me by the hand. "Your wedding day starts with a temazcal."

Every wedding begins with a ceremonial steam bath. The temazcal ritual purifies and cleanses the body and mind. We've only been in Itza for a month, and what I used to consider 'their' strange customs are fast becoming 'mine.' I've grown to appreciate the Maya's connection to the earth and their attention to sacred things. The importance of both have been absent in my own life, and now that I've experienced their benefit, I don't want to know any other way.

Once Calalu braids my hair, I tie on a simple skirt, slide into my woven sandals, and head outside. My husband-to-be waits on the terrace. A gentleness brims at the forefront of the way he looks at me, leaving me feeling cherished.

Nash extends his hand to me, and I fit my fingers between his, right where they belong.

"I have to admit, Ines," he speaks in a low tone, "I've never been more happy to have a woman give up on me."

I raise an eyebrow at him. "The day is young. We're going to be alone in the steam bath, yeah?"

A loud shout of laughter bursts out of him, and I smile as my heart glows in response. I hope I never take for granted the simple pleasure his happiness brings me.

We turn right from our homes and follow the south sacbe to reach the ceremonial steam bath site. My interest piques. We've never come this way before. Even when we toured Chichen Itza, this area had been off limits. I vaguely remember Nash talking about Chichen Viejo, the Old Chichen, and how this area puzzled archeologists as its use wasn't clear.

Tall, dark wooded trees with small leaves crowd the sacbe and shade the white path. My fingers tighten involuntarily around his, and he returns the pressure, glancing in my direction.

"Nervous?"

I shrug, then give a silent nod. Nervous doesn't even begin to describe my state of mind. Forever, he said two days ago. I'm giving him a month. And yet, every minute we spend together from this day forward will take me years to get over. Marrying him is going to be bittersweet. He will be mine, and then I will be choosing to leave him behind to return … To return to what life? To who? I have no one waiting for me in 2012. This entire thing is quickly becoming more complicated than I ever anticipated. I no longer have the will nor means to protect myself from whatever may result from this surrender.

The fragrant scent of peach comes with the breeze that lifts my hair and cools my neck. Already, I am sweating as both the humidity and my anxiety rise as if they are one entwined being. Splashes of color fill the path ahead, as the typical thin-limbed Yucatán trees are replaced by graceful plumeria shrubs. Long oval leaves frame bouquets of delicate golden-white and coral-pink blooms. The rich, sweet fragrance becomes the very air we breathe, and peace blossoms in my body.

Ahead, colorful large buildings peek out from beyond the greenery. A high, yellow wall looms in front of us, stretching out to both sides. We pass under a golden colored stone archway, with the ceiling vaulted into the shape of an arrowhead. The massive entrance could fit about six men walking through side by side.

Chichen Viejo opens up before us. Various buildings of blue and purple with their columns and terraces stand like silent sentinels. I long to explore and touch and inhale these treasures. This ancient place simmers with something holy and otherworldly, and it's as if the weight and splendor of the universe rests within these barricaded stone walls.

If I'm not mistaken, the structure ahead looks exactly like a turtle, complete with a large, rounded shell on top. In front stands a priest. The man's body is mostly bare, with his face, arms, and torso painted with intricate red designs. However, he is wearing one of the most massive headdresses I've ever seen. An intricate stone image of Chaac sits directly atop the priest's head. A woven strap attaches a large, rectangular sheet of painted thatch behind the statue. Green snakes are painted around the frame, and fanning out from the top and sides are at least a hundred long quetzal feathers. He'd do well to walk through the entrance archway by himself.

"The turtle signifies resurrection and rebirth," Nash explains. "We go in as who we were and come out as who we will be."

Scattered around the base of the turtle altar are dozens of white water lilies. The priest holds out two delicate ceramic vessels, which are also covered by a design resembling the white lily. Nash grabs one and hands it to me, then takes the other for himself.

The warm, cloudy white drink goes down smooth, leaving behind a sweet, woodsy taste on my tongue. The priest chants, invoking the four directions while patting our heads and bodies with a bundle of leaves. Then he turns around, climbs the turtle altar, and removes a woven sheet of thatch from a small opening to reveal the ceremonial steam bath.

Once we remove our clothing, we crawl into the dark dome. Faint light filters through the opening. We sit cross-legged on either side of a shallow, indented pit.

A woman comes through the opening using a forked stick to push along a large stone. The heat coming from the rock is scorching. Once the stone settles into the pit, she pours water over, filling the small space with heat and steam then backs out of the chamber, sealing it closed with an inner screen of thatch. A gentle glow of reassuring light seeps through the weaves, but then we are immersed in absolute blackness as something more opaque is placed over the outside. I am no longer a child, but the pitch-black dark still causes anxiety to expand in my chest.

"Finally got you alone and naked." I attempt to distract myself from my rising fear.

"Mmm, save it for later, mi amor. Do yourself a favor and lie down on your side. That drink is laced with a morphine derivative."

Ignoring him, I move to my hands and knees, then carefully shift myself around the heated core of the dome. He's not going to trick me that easily. My hand finds the warm muscle of his thigh. But as I slide my palm higher, my limbs begin to grow heavy and relaxed.

Nash grabs me by the shoulders, forcing me to lie sideways on the ground. Confusion fills me as some subconscious wall inside me crumbles. It feels very much like I'm sinking into a pit of mud. Darkness fills my ears then covers my face and nose. Hidden thoughts and fears float up from where they've been buried deep in my consciousness. I am so alone.

"Don't let go of me." The high tone of my voice sounds childlike to my own ears.

"I won't."

Our bodies curve around each side of the heated center, with our hands holding tightly together up top.

"It's hot. I can't breathe."

"You can, mi amor. In. Out. In."

Nash's voice soothes me as my body grows heavier and heavier. Light trickles through the opening as the woman rolls in a second stone. More water poured over the top heats and thickens the air further. She backs out, leaving us in the pitch-black humidity again. There is nothing to distract me from drowning within my own mind.

"What is happening?" I moan softly.

The trauma that has lingered in my soul filters out from the recesses of my bones and I feel smothered by it. Whatever was in that drink has pulled down the barriers that have kept me safe. I hear a low noise come from Nash, and his fingers tighten around mine. He is facing his own demons as well. Again and again, the woman returns with stones and water, pushing the air to impossible temperatures and drenching our bodies with sweat. And perhaps our very souls are weeping.

My emotions reach near frantic heights, and combined with the intense heat and steam, I can no longer take it. I try to disentangle my hand from Nash's so I can crawl out of the steam bath, but he makes a negative sound with his throat and grips my hands even tighter.

"Trust me. Wait. Almost there." His voice sounds as pained as I feel.

Wait for what? A sob tears out of my throat. Memories of hurt, betrayal, and pain flood me, and I'm unable to shut it down. I have no choice but to stand face to face with the past, letting it rip through and decimate me once again.

Tears and sweat mingle on my face. "What did they give us?" My voice sounds far away, helpless and weak even to my own ears.

"The white water lilies. You'll feel peace soon."

Peace? All I feel now is despair. Every ounce of sadness and torment I've ever felt piles onto my body. And yet, if I concentrate ...

There.

Around the jagged edges of memories, a white mist seeps in,

softening the sharp areas, smoothing the hurt. The fog expands in my mind, much like the steam, then combusts, flooding my body with a pure sensation of bliss. My hands relax, and I uncurl from the fetal position to lie on my back, arms loose by my sides. I sigh as pleasure replaces the pain. Even the damp heat on my skin feels like a lover's caress.

"Oh my God, what is this?"

My nerve endings grow warm and pulsate with every heartbeat.

"Kind of like an opiate, but it's not. Forces dopamine through the body."

Both of our voices are strained and low. I laugh softly, feeling as if sunlight shines through each of my pores.

"We're high, aren't we?"

"Something like that."

"Fantastic," I breathe out.

The first layer of my wedding gown is a simple off-white sleeveless dress that is actually long enough for the bottom to cover my ankles. Embroidered patterns line the hem in blue, orange, and red. The second layer reaches my knees and drapes over the first layer of the dress like a poncho, but the top hem rests perfectly on my upper arms, exposing my shoulders. Long, open slits run down the sides, creating a sleeve-like section with an embroidered hem of green and red bands. A stunning piece of needlework decorates the front, and I recognize the depiction of the sun god, Kinich Ahau, outlined in golden thread and complete with deep blue eyes.

Our wedding takes place on the Ossuary pyramid, which is a

structure almost identical to the great pyramid in the center of the city, except much smaller. The city gathers in silence as respectful observers. We sit on a thatched mat facing one another. Nash wears a simple white cape and hip cloth. Both have an embroidered hem that match the hem of my dress.

The same priest who began our ritual steam bath again invokes the cardinal directions, along with the elements—earth, water, fire, and air—asking their energy to center on this union. Smoke from sacred copal resin drifts throughout the open space, covering the terrace with its woodsy pine scent. The holy man moves back and forth from between us and then over to a small wooden altar holding cacao beans, corn, flowers, and fruit. He speaks of Heart of Sky and Mother Earth, and so much of what he's saying is lost to me. I'd normally write it off as mystical mumbo jumbo, but I want to understand. I wish to believe something like this could be everlasting.

Finally, the priest takes the gold chain and wraps it around our wrists, entwining it between our hands, symbolically binding us together under the energetic focus of the elements. As he prays, I look up to see Nash's eyes closed, while he moves his lips to repeat the same words under his breath. I try to do the same, and initially stumble on the strange wording. Essentially we are asking for wisdom to dawn within us, then ripen and transform into the right action. We recite the same prayer three times, and by the last one, I'm able to say all the words smoothly.

My eyes open to meet Nash's on the last sentence, and a smile lights up his face as we repeat the last words of the prayer to one another, "May everything be known as the light of mutual love."

Nash grabs my hand, and before I realize what he's doing, he draws his obsidian knife over my thumb. Blood immediately wells from the cut, but he catches the red drops on a length of tree bark. After wrapping my finger in a strip of cloth to staunch the flow, he hands the knife over to me, handle first, before offering his own hand up for the bloodletting. The blade is sharp, and I barely have to apply pressure. Once his blood has dripped sufficiently over the bark, we rest it on top of the smoking copal incense. The thin piece of wood smokes, then erupts in a small flame as our sacrifice burns away, its smoke reaching up to the heavens.

My husband stands first then pulls me to standing. We face one another, hands clasped between us, pressing our foreheads together as the priest moves the copal smoke around our bodies while reciting one last prayer over our union. The priest ends his prayers and raises his hands skyward, presenting us to The Whole One God, then outward, presenting us to Itza. He lifts a conch shell to his lips and blows. The deep, trumpeting sound signals the end to the ceremony.

The people had been silent the entire time, but now the crowd erupts in cheers. Nash and I beam wide, silly smiles at one another. He bends forward, wraps one arm around my waist, and pulls me against him for our first kiss as husband and wife.

Itza whoops, hollers, and whistles, and our kiss grows deeper as their enthusiasm gets louder. Apparently the goal here is for them to outlast us. Minutes pass, and they don't desist, but we aren't quitters. If anything, we begin to forget about the people watching us. My knees grow weak, and I just want to sink to the ground. Then Nash reaches down, and his fingers start lifting the skirt part of my dress. I play along and lift my thigh, wrapping one leg around his hip. The people burst into laughter, shouting their approval. We separate from one another, laughing. Clearly, we've won.

Chaac and Xochi's ceremony follows ours, and then the priests inaugurate them as king and queen of Itza, with Nash and I as co-rulers. I prepare myself for one more round of bloodletting, but the priests head down the steps of the small pyramid after a final prayer and the blowing of the conch. Maybe the blood from our wedding ceremony had been enough.

A celebratory meal is set in the Thousand Columns. All of Itza are invited to partake, but Nash and I slip away from the Ossuary, hand in hand, and head back to the colorful houses. Any hunger we have isn't for food. The walk isn't far, and soon we're alone in my house.

Our house.

I pull him to me, and he presses me against the wall, his hips tight against mine. Our lips meet and spark, starting the slow, lazy burn of a fuse. I raise my arms, and the dress lifts off my body, then falls forgotten to the floor. His hipcloth is the next to go, and then the loincloth. I push him backward, guiding him to the platform covered by the thatched mattress. We'll try out the hammock another time, but for now, I prefer the familiarity of a flat surface.

Nash turns me to face away from him, and his hands move to my head to tug the wooden combs free one by one. My hair falls in heavy coils down my back. He unravels the thick twists, then runs his fingers through the entire length, spreading the curls around me.

"I've fantasized about you like this," he says in a low, controlled voice. "Naked, your hair hanging loose down your back. And mine." Turning me to face him, he leans forward and touches his lips softly

316

to my forehead, then cheek, then mouth. "In my thoughts, when I was alone over there, and you were over here, there was nothing to stop me from doing what I wanted."

"Show me everything."

Indigo heat flares in his eyes upon hearing my words, and he pulls my hips tight against his. My fingertips trace the lines of his broad, smooth chest. We tumble onto the platform, and his large hands shape the curves of my body, paying repeated attention to the parts that draw the best reaction. He takes a brief lesson of me, studying and figuring out what I like and don't like. I guide him at times, showing that I find featherlight contact unpleasant, and more often prefer a firmer touch. He takes his time learning my every peak and valley, until the need coiling inside has me ready to burst from my skin.

The constant low flame that has always burned between us rises. There is no stopping this ancient rite, one of the oldest human acts in existence. Our movement matches the rhythm of heartbeat, starting slowly, then rising in speed.

Our eyes meet for a moment and he grins, hair falling loose over his forehead. My hands tighten in his hair, and his lips move to my neck. If he is the sun, then I am his moon, pulling and drawing waves from endless seas to crash on the shore, pushing us both to soul-shattering completion.

Hours later, we lie side by side, sweat-covered and working hard to catch our breath. I'm near catatonic. It's quite possible drool is coming from the side of my mouth, but my muscles and mind have not recovered enough for me to even have the care to check.

"Oh, my God," I gasp out.

He tilts his head toward me, eyes half closed and lips curved in a smile. "I knew you'd come around to calling me that eventually."

My brain is mush, and I don't even have the intelligence to come up with a good retort. All I'm able to do is snort out a laugh.

Nash turns to me, studying my face, then rolls his body against me, pressing his lips to mine again. Neither of us are ready to stop, and so much has built up between us for so long now. We have a lot of time to make up for, both for the past and for an uncertain future. The dying flame in my body flickers to life, and I reach my hand to the side of his face as I return the energy of his kiss.

Several minutes later, I have the nerve to ask the question weighing on my mind. "Are you happy, Nash?"

He looks slightly taken aback by my question for a moment, but then responds, "Yeah. Completely." His lips purse slightly. "Are you? Do you regret this?"

"I am happy." My chin tilts up as I meet his eyes. "And no, I don't regret it. I might later, but right now I don't."

Dark eyebrows narrow, but he doesn't ask anything more. He only rolls onto his knees, then looks down at both of us awash in the glow of flickering firelight and grimaces slightly.

"We need to bathe, come on."

Itza is silent and still, save for the invisible guards in shadow patrolling the city. A sliver crescent of moonlight shines above, and the stars lay thick and heavy like a blanket of fireflies. The impossible curve of the Milky Way is visible overhead as a thick, glowing band of purple and blue light. Our hands find one another in the dark as we walk, and a happy ache twists in my chest.

My husband, Nash Dominguez. Does that make me Ines Dominguez when I return to my own time? Or is this entire thing an illusion in the grand scheme of things, where I will remain Ines de la Luz, Nash's cold-hearted muñeca who doesn't believe in love?

I believe in him. For now, that's all I can say. Pain at the thought of leaving him here in this time has intensified exponentially in just these past hours. Before, it was his friendship, his laughter, and his stolen kisses I would miss. But now, I've drowned in torrents of what it means to have him belonging to me and me to him. The knowledge of that intimacy has permanently shifted something inside of me. I fear I will never be the same again.

We move carefully down the stairs of the Xtoloc cenote. Nash immediately dives into the water, and I can't imagine how he doesn't get nervous being in that blackness. I sit on a low ledge waist deep in the water as I take a soap fruit and begin washing myself. Nash's head emerges silently in front of me, then he pulls himself onto the ledge to sit. I move behind him, enclosing him between my legs and pressing my chest and cheek against his back. It's already been too long since we've touched. I lather the yellow fruit between my palms, and then begin spreading the suds as an excuse to have my hands on him. The ridges of his abdomen and the muscular curves of his chest get soaped up first.

"I've never had a woman wash me," Nash says with a note of surprise in his voice.

"And I've never washed a man." I move to his arms next. "But I've also never had a husband."

"It's nice."

I make a sound of agreement low in my throat and continue my ministrations. Nash reaches down and grabs my left hand, his thumb and forefinger tracing the curve of my ring.

"I love you, Ines."

My movements still, and my fingers convulsively tighten around his hand. That word again. I lean my forehead against his back, resisting the urge to press my lips to his skin to lick and taste him. It's just sex. Infatuation. Lust. That's what this feeling is. And yet, I can't explain why tears pool in my eyes or why my heart feels as though it's ripping and expanding.

"Is that stupid to you?" he asks, a note of hesitation in his voice.

Nodding my head wordlessly, I kiss between his shoulder blades then move my head to the side and nip at him with my teeth, trying to distract him from saying anything more. He shudders out a breath, before turning to me and laying me back on the smooth stone.

He is a skilled and generous lover, setting himself to the task as if his sole purpose is to bring my repeated satisfaction. Being with him in this way is entirely catastrophic to the careful walls I've built. Brick by brick, kiss by kiss, he's pulling them down and leaving me raw and bare. It's exhilarating, wonderful, and utterly terrifying.

I stare up at the slow rotation of the vast galactic expanse above and wonder if anyone has ever been as entirely happy as I am in this moment. A cold-hearted muñeca hopelessly mired in lust.

CHAPTER 25

A LINE OF FLICKERING torches passes silently through the center of Itza then disappears through the north sacbe leading to the Cenote Sagrado. Nash and I notice the odd procession at the same time. Once we tie our clothing back onto our hips, we leave the Xtoloc cenote and follow.

There's always some random ritual or ceremony happening in this city. We've seen our share of priestesses in hallucinogenic trances, along with ritualistic bloodletting. Neither of our ancestral memories take place in Itza, so we are learning several of these customs as we go. Since intruding on a ritual without invitation is frowned upon, we stick to the heavily shadowed edge of the tree line.

Firelight illuminates the still water in the cenote. Several priests, including a priestess and a priest from Xochi's city, stand waiting as the high priest of Itza addresses the group. We head deeper into the trees and pick our way closer to the edge of the sacred pool to watch. The smoky scent of burning copal wood drifts on the midnight breeze. Our vantage point gives us a perspective that now reveals Chaac and Xochi seated behind the red altar. The king and queen must be having their own special ceremony for their union.

Hearing the priest's words is difficult, since he's facing away from us. I lean forward, resting my elbows on the Y-shaped boughs of a tree, thinking I can close my eyes for a moment. We've had a long day. Nash's arms frame mine as he leans against me, his hips pressing against my bottom with the unmistakable pressure of something else. I cannot believe the stamina this man has, but it'll be a fun way to keep ourselves entertained while watching this secret ceremony.

His lips find my neck, and I close my eyes, enjoying the promise of what's to come. I turn so my hands can reach him, and he lifts me onto the branch, perching my butt between the Y. I giggle watching him make quick work of unwinding his loincloth.

Identical sounds of relief come from our throats as we reconnect as one flesh. I clamp my teeth together, attempting to remain silent as the pressure begins to climb. His mouth teases my neck in gentle, suctioning nibbles. Just as everything inside is coiling tighter and tighter, he freezes, his motions coming to an abrupt halt.

Impatient, I nudge my hips forward, but he remains statue still, staring over my shoulder. I'd almost forgotten we were watching a clandestine ceremony while engaging in our own clandestine activities. I crane my neck around to get a glimpse of whatever he's seeing. Nash steps back, lifting me off the intersecting boughs of the tree.

"No, no, no." He wipes one hand over his eyes as if attempting to remove a veil.

While engaging in our tryst, we missed the sight of five people approaching the altar. Blue-green paint covers their bodies from head to toe, and rope binds their wrists in front of them. Thick necklaces hang from their necks, and their arms and legs are also weighed down with various heavy metal bangles reaching to their elbows and knees. A priest stands in front of each bound person, shaking a bundled bunch of leaves over their bare bodies.

Nash makes a frantic grab for his loincloth and begins wrapping it around himself while moving in a rush toward the cenote. I follow behind, slipping through the narrow spaces between the trees and climbing over fallen trunks. Our trek through the trees is too slow, and we're still about twenty-five yards away, when we see obsidian blades glimmer in the firelight, then find their new homes as the priests drive the knives into each person's heart. Strangled groans from dying humans come from the altar.

I've stopped moving, hand over my mouth as I drop to my knees in disbelief. The priests guide the dying to the edge of the cenote and push them backward. The blue bodies splash into the sacred water one by one and disappear into the murky deep.

"Brother." My husband's voice rings in the air that now hangs heavy with death.

Chaac's eyes move from staring into the cenote and raise to where Nash stands on the opposite side of the sacred pool. The expression on the king's face doesn't change.

"Oh, no," I whisper, lifting myself from the ground on shaky legs and moving in closer.

"I would speak in private with you," Nash says in a firm voice.

Chaac directs his attention to the priests. "Return to the temple."

"But my king, we must wait to see if any return," says one of the Toltec priests. "For their spoken words will be law from He Who Makes Things Sprout.

With a wave of his hand, Chaac gives one last silent command to the priests, then motions Nash forward. "Come and speak with me, brother. My wife remains by my side."

Nash picks his way around the edge of the cenote as the priests walk single file back to the city. Xochi raises her chin but keeps her lashes lowered as he approaches.

"We agreed to no human sacrifices." Nash stands before the king and queen, crossing his arms.

"My brother's decision. And he is no longer here."

"Why wasn't this brought to Lady Chel and me first?"

"The sacrifices had to be done before the end of the day, and you two were nowhere to be found." Chaac raises an eyebrow. "You must have been enjoying your wife. And yet you are here." He nudges Xochi forward with his arm. "If your woman didn't satisfy you, we can share our women, brother. What's mine is yours."

Xochi bows her head and sinks to her knees in front of Nash, then raises her eyes to him. "Whatever you desire, my lord."

"No." Nash takes a step back, his gaze swinging to Chaac. "And my wife will not be shared. She is mine alone."

Chaac chuckles. "That woman is too cold to keep a man happy for long."

The muscles of Nash's forearm ripple as his fist tightens. Mentally, I will him to drop it, to let it go. Chaac's opinion of me is not important. Nash's shoulders relax as he releases a breath.

"We will continue this conversation tomorrow, my king. Please"—he extends his hand to the sacbe—"don't let me keep you and your wife from your home."

The king inclines his head with a smirk. Xochi stands, and then they make their way down the road. I pick my way out of the thicket of trees and walk around the edge of the pool to the altar where Nash sits, staring into the murky water. It's doubtful the knives alone killed them quickly, and I imagine their lungs filled with water as the weight of their jewelry pulled them to the bottommost parts of the watery pit. My own memories of drowning in cenotes rise up sharp in my mind, and I struggle to swallow down the urge to scream at the horror we just witnessed.

"So much wrong just happened. What do we do now?" Nash

rubs his forehead with his thumb and forefinger.

I hug my arms around myself, feeling a sudden chill even in the thick heat of the night. "I don't know. You think this is the next thing we have to change?"

"I wouldn't even begin to know how," Nash says softly, dropping his head into his hands. Despair rolls from the sinking curve of his shoulders. He glances up at me, eyes filled with regret. "And I shouldn't have let him speak of you like that."

"Oh, please. Promise me you'll never stand up to him for something so stupid, Nash."

"Why?"

"Chaac is dangerous. It's not worth it to go against him."

"You think I can't handle him?"

"It's not that, Nash. The man is evil. Pure evil."

"Where is this coming from? You were about to marry him and you didn't act like it was so bad."

I exhale and cross my arms. "I chose to protect you from the truth."

"Protect me? Do I look like I need protection?" He stands, his full height towering over mine.

"Yes, you idiot. Look at you even now. Your testosterone is raging at the thought of someone thinking of you as anything less than an all-powerful man."

His eyes widen. "Wow, Ines. You really have a way to make a man feel good about himself."

I roll my eyes at his sarcasm. "And that's exactly what Chaac doesn't like about me. I can be cutting when I need to be. I can be stone cold when I need to be. He thrives off of fear and pain. If you even knew—"

I stop myself before I go too far. But he's heard it.

325

"What? If I knew what?"

"Nothing."

"Tell me, Ines. We are one now. Don't start our marriage by keeping secrets."

I remain silent, staring into his eyes. He's going to flip if I tell him what Chaac did. But at the same time, he needs to be fully aware what that man is capable of.

"Promise you won't do anything crazy, okay?"

He narrows his eyes. "Why?"

"Because. It's exactly why I didn't tell you in the first place. I don't want you to defend my honor and get hurt or killed in the process."

"Tell me."

"Promise first."

"Fine. I promise."

I relay the story of Chaac assaulting me with his fingers, making me bleed, and the look on his face when he saw my blood. And then the chilling words he spoke about Lahun and Nash trying to save me, and failing.

Pain and regret fill Nash's eyes. He holds me by the shoulders and presses his forehead to mine, inhaling deeply. "Ay, mi amor. You should have told me."

"I knew I could handle him. It was mine to bear."

"If he touches you again, I'll—"

"No, you won't." I pull away and look up at him. "What happens to me if you get yourself killed in the process? Think about that. I'll be completely alone."

"You heard him offer the queen to me, right? So you're saying I just let him treat my wife like a whore too?"

Squaring my jaw, I look him in the eye. "I don't give a damn what Chaac does or says, and you shouldn't either. He is nothing. But you mean everything—" I squeeze my eyes shut and take a half step back.

He tightens his hands on my shoulders. "Keep going."

My lips press into a thin line as I stare down at the drops of blood staining the altar floor. Those people are gone. They cease to exist. They're now only memories.

"You're everything to me, Nash." My eyes fill with helpless tears. "We need to survive Chaac. Together. Don't let him use me so he has reason to hurt you."

"As you know, we are nearing the end of K'atun One," Chaac says, spearing a piece of meat with a jadeite blade. "The twenty years end, and change must come, brother. It is our obligation to lead it."

We've spent the hottest part of the day learning our new duties as rulers of Itza, and now we recline at an afternoon meal with the king and queen. If Chaac and Xochi do not listen to our council, it seems inevitable human sacrifice will continue. My husband takes a deep swallow of balche, giving himself time to formulate a response. Xochi nibbles a section of fruit, watching Nash in wide-eyed expectation of his response. The air is tense and thick with the weight of our husbands' disagreement.

Nash sets his cup on the low table. "It is a dangerous course to put yourself in the position of The Whole One God and remove his will in deciding when a person's journey is over."

"Dangerous?" Chaac's eyes gleam. "We court danger by hunting the jaguar in order to take the splendor of its spotted skin upon our shoulders. What could be more worthy of danger than reaching for the glory of the gods?"

"The glory does not belong to us."

"But it does, and it shall."

Xochi speaks up. "K'awiil is moving in opposition to the stars. A sign from the heavens that our king is on the right course."

I remember enough from my time in the observatory with Lahun to understand K'awiil is the planet Jupiter, which is considered Chaac's celestial body. All of these signs and symbols from the heavens are at the whim of the interpreter. How Xochi interprets Jupiter's retrograde is likely completely different from how Lahun would comprehend the same event.

Nash shakes his head. "Lahun did not agree to it. I will not agree to it, brother. I will oppose you every step of the way in this."

"Are you happy in your new marriage, my lady?" Chaac asks, directing his attention to me.

Happy? Happiness due to a person can be taken away. This is a human truth even black-hearted Chaac surely knows and seeks to exploit.

I choose my words with care. "Kinich and I will adjust to our new role."

"If your husband is ever not to your liking, just say the word." Chaac gives me a wink. "I'm sure I can easily find reason to have him executed."

He drains the rest of his balche, then shifts his eyes to Nash, a half smile cutting through the curve of his cheek. The intended sign of jest doesn't meet his eyes.

"I wonder, Lady Chel," the king finally says after several beats. "Are you the sort of ruler who will go the way of least resistance, or do you see the value of what is gained by sacrifice?"

My shoulders square as I raise my chin. "Any sacrifice the gods require is mine alone to fulfill. No one else."

Chaac regards me thoughtfully as a servant refills his ceramic goblet. "Mm, but sometimes the gods require something that is not yours to give. I wonder who or what that is for you?"

Following the early dinner and a quick bath, Nash and I go home and tire ourselves out even more with our newest favorite activity. Afterwards I nearly fall asleep while still atop him, but he rolls me sideways and curls himself around me. A warm breeze drifts through, cooling our sweaty skin.

Later, I am awoken by warm lips spreading a trail up the inside of my thigh. I smile, sinking into the sensation of being loved so thoroughly by him. Once he has me decidedly awakened, we leave to explore Old Chichen. Yesterday, we only spent a brief time in that ancient part of Itza for our pre-wedding steam bath.

We walk hand in hand as a gentle drizzle cools the hot, late afternoon air. My entire body is sore and feels like I've been beat with a blunt object. I glance over at the owner of said object and chuckle softly at the thought.

Nash smiles. "What? You got that look in your eye like you're ready for more of this."

I laugh loudly and jab my elbow into his ribcage. "I can barely walk straight. Give me like fifteen minutes to recover."

He looks at an imaginary watch on his wrist then holds up four fingers. "Four-minute warning."

"I wasn't imagining how magical this place is, was I?" My gaze sweeps the interior of Old Chichen.

Nash murmurs out a negative sound as he looks around.

"It wasn't the drugs either?"

He laughs and shakes his head. There is some undeniable energy in this place. The only way I can describe it is that it feels like home. Sunlight streams through the trees, sending dappled shadows to dance on the forest floor. Even though the brightly colored buildings lie empty, each one seems to have its arms open in invitation. *Explore*, they seem to say, *live here, love here.*

To the left of the turtle altar is what resembles a huge house. Columns support a beautiful thatched roof, and the stucco is painted in blue and yellow. But we don't turn that way, we continue straight ahead past the stone turtle.

"There's a temple here I've only heard of," Nash says. "Really want to see it."

His eyes sweep the structures ahead, and then he begins heading to a two-story yellow building. We walk through the low doorway just as rain begins falling more heavily. Stone hallways twist to the courtyard out back, and a vaulted thatched roof soars up high in the center, shading the interior. Nash chuckles as he walks across the courtyard, then pulls me forward.

"Welcome to the Temple of the Phallus."

He points to an obvious penis sticking straight out of one of the walls. I laugh and lean my elbow on the mushroom-shaped end.

"Really? We've come all the way here to see a short, fat dick?"

"No, there's more, I think."

We leave the courtyard, and briefly duck back out into the rain to find another entrance with columns of Atlantean figures holding up the lintel. High above the door are various snail shells painted different colors, but lining the top of the doorframe are a great variety of penises. Wide ones, longer ones, short ones, and bulbous ones.

"What in the world?" Laughing, I step closer to study each one, then wrap my hand around the longest, thickest one. "This one is my favorite."

"Looks familiar." Nash steps in closer and lifts his imaginary wristwatch again. "Oh look, time's up."

I giggle as he wraps his arms around me from behind. "I've always wanted to be banged inside a penis temple."

"I am only here to serve you, my goddess." Nash guides me through the low doorway, and we move through the hallways until we find a room with a thatched covered pallet.

We surrender to the mindless oblivion the joining of our bodies provides. Tension heightens, builds, then spills over into an energy that expands from my center, flooding my veins with pure and utter bliss.

When I open my eyes, it's as if the roof above has fallen away. The sky is clear and blue, but thunder rumbles and I can hear the steady sound of heavy raindrops plopping on stone. And then Nash's arms tighten around me as he finds his own release, blocking my view of the sky. I press gentle kisses to the salty skin at the base of his neck, and he trembles in response. He lifts up onto his elbows, and behind him the vaulted stone ceiling is visible again.

My eyebrows narrow. "Something weird just happened up there.

The ceiling disappeared. I saw the sky. It was blue and clear, but I can hear the rain right now. And look, the ceiling is there. It was like my visions of the past, but in reverse."

He sits back on his heels, confusion clear in his eyes. "The portals don't open for another month. For me, the visions increase about two weeks before the zeniths and equinoxes. It's definitely a signal it's coming. But it's too early."

I think for a few moments. "Unless there's an eclipse coming."

Nash uses the hem of his loincloth to clean between my legs, then he sits back, resting one arm on his knee. He is silent, and his demeanor shadowed as he stares at the floor.

"So you'll go then?"

His words hit me like a punch to the gut. I imagine myself being dragged back to our time, kicking and screaming. My reticence is not due to fear of the method of travel, it's the thought of being forced to leave him. Everything has changed. I wrap my arms around my knees, feeling the ripping agony of myself being torn in two. My mind in one direction, and my heart in the other.

"Do I have to?" I whisper, tears clogging my throat.

His attention slides from the floor to me. The carefully placed shield over his eyes drops away to reveal first hope, then wild emotion. Strong hands enclose my arms and he pulls me across the thatch and tightly against him.

"Please don't," he says in a strangled tone.

I sit cradled between his spread thighs, and my tears spill over. He presses his cheek to the top of my head, exhaling in small gasps. Equal parts of relief and utter terror rise in me. Within the span of a few seconds, I've made the choice to stay by his side no matter what. But maybe it was already made the second I looked into his eyes at Casa Mestizo. Or maybe it was that night in Tulum when he howled love songs to the rising moon. All I know is my fate was sealed the moment I fell in love with him.

CHAPTER 26

THE VOICE OF THE king of Itza drones on throughout the morning. Nash and I sit, bleary-eyed and exhausted, as people come forward to have their issues heard. Clearly, there is no time for a honeymoon. As newlyweds, we don't sleep much at night due to our spending the majority of the time in a variety of horizontal and vertical positions. Even so, the city awaits its rulers to resume normal activity.

Every morning of the past week has been spent as judges in the city court, and each afternoon we spend with the priests in the temple learning Itza law. Mostly this is for my benefit, since Nash has the advantage of having been taught the oral history throughout his life. But he stays with me and poses intelligent questions, which help deepen both of our understanding. We're getting better able to pass fair judgment to the residents of our city.

Chaac and Nash sit in the center, with Xochi and me sitting on the ends next to our husbands. Servants use palms to fan the densely heated air. Two farmers argue while standing before us. One man accuses the other of stealing one of his fowls, while the other accuses him of sleeping with his wife.

"Off with their heads," I mutter while stifling a yawn.

Apparently I didn't say it as quietly as I thought I did, because Chaac leans forward grinning maniacally at me. "Do you have a solution, Lady Chel?"

Both farmers look at me with eyes widened in terror. I shrink back in my seat, shaking my head. My yawn must have amplified my whisper.

Nash gives me a disapproving head shake, then turns his attention to the men. "According to the law, adultery is punishable with death by stoning." His eyes sweep over to the fowl thief. "While theft is punishable with death by strangulation."

Chaac gives a satisfied sigh. "It is decided then; death for both."

"Unless, the men pardon one another," Nash says.

"This man filled your wife's womb with his seed." Chaac points to the accused adulterer, while staring at the fowl thief. "You would pardon him for such a disgrace?"

Reminded of the offense, the fowl thief's face grows reddened and his jaw clenches.

"Please keep in mind if you sentence him to death publicly, the likelihood is he will do the same to you." Nash remains the voice of reason. "But if you two can make amends and no longer assume ownership of the other's property or spouse, then no one dies today."

Both men quickly agree, and Chaac huffs out a disgruntled noise. The five sacrifices from last week must not have been enough to satiate the king's bloodlust.

Later that afternoon in the temple, we take a detour from the law books and seek out the astronomer-priest. It was disconcerting the other day to hear Xochi use the movement of Jupiter as a sign from the heavens to support human sacrifice. If we have any hope of making changes here, Nash and I need to gain even more understanding of the movement of the stars and planets, and how the

Maya relate these to their lives.

We enter the room where the priests who specialize in astronomy work. The interior is painted a dark blue, and constellations and planets are mapped out in detail. Splices of time show the difference of the same sky during the year. The intricacy of attention they pay to the variety of phases of each celestial body is apparent.

The Maya astronomer-priest is the same man who performed the marriage for Nash and me. His quetzal headdress is thankfully much smaller than the gigantic one he wore for our ceremonies. He stands with his Toltec counterpart, a priestess. She appears to be in her early forties, but her striking beauty is apparent. Her skin is pale like Xochi's, and she wears a long, blood red sleeveless gown. Bands of tumbaga metal inlaid with jade encircle her upper arms, and quetzal feathers hang from her long, wavy black hair. A rolled out piece of ficus tree bark covered in glossy lime lies on the table. The woman speaks in low tones, pointing to various glyphs on the paper, and the priest nods in understanding.

Nash clears his throat, and both of them look up from their study.

The Maya priest smiles. "Kinich Ahau and Lady Chel. What an honor. Please come in."

"Thank you, Alom," Nash says to the priest. "My wife and I seek to gain greater understanding of the heavens. Who better to learn from than you?"

Alom bows his head. "It would be my pleasure." He extends his hand to the Toltec priestess. "This is Cit'lalli, high priestess from Culhuacan. She is staying in our city for a short time, teaching me the Toltec wisdom."

Cit'lalli bows her head.

"The backward movement of K'awiil," I say, looking between the two. "How do you interpret it?"

Xochi interpreted Jupiter's retrograde as a sign that Chaac was on the right track in his bringing human sacrifice to Itza.

"K'awiil resides in the fifth layer of the heavens," Alom begins. "Above the sun, above the stars, and above the moon and clouds."

Cit'lalli speaks up. "And K'awiil being higher than those, we cannot ignore the importance of him moving against those objects of fixed motion."

"As Cit'lalli explained to me most graciously, since the movement of K'awiil coincides with Chaac's ascension to the throne, we believe this to mean that he must enforce a change against something that seems unchangeable."

The priestess's intelligent hazel eyes lock with Nash's. "You seemed to not agree with the sacrifices in honor of the king and queen."

"I do not believe that The Whole One God desires us to choose when a person's journey is ended."

Her eyes lower. "With respect, my lord, the heavens disagree. I understand your held belief is as unchangeable as the movement of the sun." Cit'lalli's eyebrow raises as her eyes meet his again. "But that is why K'awiil moves in opposition."

The explanation is so perfect and succinct. Nash's shoulders bow in defeat, as he gives a small shake of his head.

"My wife and I will not partake in human sacrifice." Nash crosses his arms.

"In avoiding this necessary ritual, the Itzas have lost the opportunity to receive communication directly from the gods," Cit'lalli says.

"What do you mean?" I ask.

Alom explains. "Sometimes the gods receive a sacrifice but return the person from Xibalba alive. The first words they utter then become unchangeable law."

A weight is off my shoulders with my decision to remain here in Itza, and I'm doing my best to make this time and place my home. Being Nash's wife makes the transition easier. Our days are filled with our ruler obligations, and our nights remain filled with one another. Every moment spent together lodges him deep in my heart and soul, a layer that reaches to my marrow. I've admitted to myself what I'm feeling for him is growing much closer to love than infatuation, but I've never uttered the words to him.

We remain uneasy under the mercurial rule of Chaac but do our best to stay on his good side. Nash and I begin seeing an increasing number of visions as we near the impending eclipse. Bright, colorful facades fade before our eyes, and one time we even awoke to see a section of our roof crumbled away. The future calls, but I cannot bear the thought of leaving him behind.

The planning phase for building the next layer of the great pyramid begins. This one will be dedicated to Kukulkan, the feathered serpent god. Chaac calls for a city-wide gathering to announce the plans.

At the top of the great pyramid, Chaac and Xochi sit on their jaguar thrones. Nash and I stand off to one side while the Maya and Toltec priests and priestess stand at the other. The thatched roof provides partial shade, but servants holding large palm leaves fill in the gaps.

Citizens of Itza wait shoulder to shoulder in the plaza below. The higher classes of people relax in shaded areas, lounging on cushioned seats while being fanned by servants. The middle and lower classes stand in the full heat of the sun, while children perch on the limbs of trees.

Chaac stands and gazes out over his people, prowling the width of the uppermost level of the pyramid. The people's attention stays locked on their king, and a heavy blanket of silence descends.

"People of Itza," Chaac's voice rings out over the crowd. "Are you ready for greatness?"

He extends his arms and his frenetic energy reaches the people. They respond with a deafening cheer. Itza's enthusiasm reaches a fever pitch as the crowd stamps and shouts their approval.

"Greatness requires sacrifice, my dear people. Do you agree?"

A murmur of agreement rolls through the crowd. Nash reaches for my hand, and I thread my fingers through his, tightening my grip for comfort. He squeezes my hand in return, but we make no move to look at one another.

"The gods require our blood, our life force, sent up to them. We strive for Itza to be as great as the Toltecs in the west. This reach for greatness calls for even more sacrifice. Are we willing to do what is required, my dear people?"

Itza responds with an affirmative shout.

Chaac's eyes gleam as he stares out over the sea of his subjects. "It is a rare opportunity to be able to offer your entire body, not just your blood to the gods. The priests have confirmed this sacrifice is equivalent to a man dying in battle, or a woman dying in childbirth. It is honorable, and your path to the paradise of Tamoanchan will be straight. A person who gives their body in this honorable sacrifice will not have to journey the thirteen levels of the afterlife. Paradise is yours upon arrival."

A sound of hushed awe moves through the spectators. They drink in every word dripping from their king's lips. Though venomous to Nash and me, they seem sweet as nectar to the people. Widened eyes stay glued to their king, and hands raise in reverence.

"We place the first foundation stone of the new pyramid in two days' time, so the sacrifices must coincide. We will consider the first thirteen people who show up to our court chamber."

"No one will show up," Nash murmurs, as we follow the sacbe to our shaded circle of trees.

"I'm not so sure about that. Didn't you see their faces?"

The glow of adoration coming from the people unsettled me. I had been certain the idea of human sacrifice would be met with revulsion. Rather it appears to have been met with avid acceptance.

My husband pulls me up the stairs our home and makes quick work of doing away with my skirt along with his hipcloth and loincloth. We stand for a moment, arms wrapped around one another, soaking in the sensation of our bodies pressed together. I breathe in the scent of his skin at the base of his neck and am immediately infused with spreading comfort. For a moment, neither of us move or do anything. The heaviness of the day creates a sinking helplessness inside me, and I know he must feel the same. There is nothing we can do to control what's about to happen here in Itza.

I lean back and reach one hand up to his jawline then rest my palm against his face, aching to give him the oblivion only my body can provide. His eyes meet mine and I pull him down to me. Our lips meet, blurring the world beyond, and we replace it with hands, and lips, and the heat of our merging bodies. I give myself to him, letting him use the only control he has in his armory.

And for that time, we forget. I am only sensation, reduced to some she-creature at the mercy of the male beast holding me tight around the waist, his teeth sinking into the skin at the back of my neck. We become a fierce, savage copulation of grunts and desperate whining noises. If I had any sense, I'd be ashamed of the sounds coming from my throat. But I am his, and he is mine, and this is ours.

And then behind me, his motion freezes. His fist releases the clenched handful of my hair. I look around in confusion, and my gaze meet the dark, obsidian eyes of the king. Chaac leans against our doorframe, arms crossed, watching us. In a hurried movement, I jerk one of our colorful blankets up in front of me. How long has he been there?

"Get out," Nash says in a low, harsh voice.

A smile curves on the king's cheek. "You are not finished, brother. It is not good for your health to stop halfway. Please, continue. I am a patient man."

Nash pulls back, not bothering to hide himself from the king's eyes, and straightens from his kneeling position on the bed to stand on the floor. He tosses me a skirt from our basket of clean fabric and wraps a loincloth around himself, then stands in front of Chaac, extending his hand to our terrace. Chaac shoots me one more lazy look tinged with both amusement and desire before he turns and walks outside.

After I drop the blanket, I tie a green skirt onto my hips, then sit waiting on the pallet. Their voices drift in.

"What brings you to our dwelling, my king?"

Chaac waits for a beat in silence, then says, "She is much more enthusiastic than I thought she would be."

"Do not speak of my wife. What do you need from me?"

Chaac's urge to continue goading him on is palpable, and I can just picture the grin he has on his face. Silence stretches between the two men to an uncomfortable degree.

"I wonder if you are you willing to provide anything I need, brother?"

"Within reason, my king."

"I require you and Lady Chel in court to witness the selection of the sacrifices."

"I will have nothing to do with it, and neither will she."

I stand and walk from the bed, then exit out onto the terrace to support my husband. Crossing my arms over my chest, I face Chaac. "It is not necessary for us to be present. You and the priests can witness the selections."

The king's eyebrow raises. "I see you are … adjusting … to your new role, as you said. The … ahh … position seems to suit you."

Raising my chin, I meet his eyes in silence, refusing to rise to his bait.

Chaac's eyes flash in response to my defiant stare. "You should see the people waiting to be chosen for the sacrifice. Some are ill, but many are healthy, and just want to be able to leave this level and move to the next."

"Why do you ask for thirteen? Why not just one?" Nash asks.

Chaac waves his hand casually. "It is a sacred number. It's a good start for the first level. I'll call for twenty-six for the second, and even more each level higher we go."

Nash's eyes narrow. "Why do you want so many people to give

their lives?"

"Why not allow more people to leave this level and journey to the next?"

"If everyone leaves, then who will be left to do the work, and to rule over?"

"People are born every day here. We will never lack for people. But if you are so concerned for them, brother, your body alone will cover the sacrifices needed for the foundation stone."

I step forward. "Don't."

Chaac's eyes come alight. Immediately, I catch my mistake. In showing concern for my husband, I've shown the king something I value.

In the space of a breath, I look between the men. "It hurts me to see the two of you argue." I force my eyes to grow tender as I focus on the king's face, then move to my husband's. "I have grown to care for the both of you. Please don't fight."

The Xtoloc cenote is still and quiet, and the sun shines high overhead. Most of Itza must still be gathered in the plaza. Nash immediately dives in, and I settle myself on the low stones, sitting waist deep in the water.

After Chaac left our house to return to the palace, we were able to finish what we'd started before being rudely watched by the king. A knot of discomfort forms in my belly upon remembering the look in his eyes. I could only imagine what he thought seeing the primal, rough way Nash and I were having sex, and even more so, my clear enjoyment. Shame washes over me. Chaac should not have been a voyeur to such a personal moment.

We finish washing then tie on our clothing. Curiosity pulls us back to the plaza to see if Chaac really was telling the truth about the number of people volunteering their lives in sacrifice for the foundation stone. Nash and I stay further back, hidden in the line of trees from the view of the waiting people. In no way do we want them to believe we support this.

But our eyes confirm what the king said. A line of about fifty people curves outside the palace. There are several elderly people, but also men, women, and some young people.

My eyes scan the line, and my mind whirls in confusion and disbelief at what I'm seeing. How quickly people sign up to give their lives for something that won't even benefit them. And it's blind faith taking the priest's word about what will happen to them afterward. I'm disheartened to see how readily the Mayans accept the change to human sacrifice. Perhaps they'll change their minds once they see it in action. But probably not.

A loud sound of disappointment comes from the crowd, and I see a guard waving the line of people away. The thirteen have been chosen.

Nash turns to me. "Once the people leave, let's go inside to see what's happening."

I nod and grip his hand tightly with both of mine. The line of people disperses, clear disappointment on many of their faces. Once the palace is only patrolled by guards, we leave our hiding spot within the shady trees.

Inside, servants bustle around with pitchers of balche and xocolatl, along with platters of delicacies. A feast is being set for the commoners who are giving their lives. Chaac and Xochi actually mingle with the people. Both the king and queen nod their heads and keep their attention fixed on each person who comes to speak with them. It is a rare occasion for commoners to even speak with a member of the elite, let alone share a meal. But Chaac has pulled out all the stops, giving them the best of what he has to offer.

Our entrance to the room has caught the people's attention, and they rush over. Tears fill my eyes as I embrace a small, elderly woman who says she is grateful to escape the daily pain ripping through her body. Next a man tells me he wishes to join his wife, who journeyed to the beyond a short time ago. Each person has their tale to tell, and my heart pains me to see how this is unraveling with everyone being an eager participant.

"They will be well cared for the next two days," Chaac says from behind me after I embrace the last person. "They will be fed the food of the gods and wear the finest fabrics they have ever worn in their lives. The men will have as many women as they wish, and the women will have as many warriors as they can handle."

Angrily, I swipe a tear from under my eye then turn to him. "What good is it?" I whisper. "The people who love them will miss them."

Chaac leans in then reaches forward to rest one hand on the side of my face. His thumb swipes at the wetness on my cheek. "The people who love them will be happy for them. Our ultimate goal is to get to the paradise of Tamoanchan, and they are going straight there. Why are you not happy for them?"

I have no answer for that. I stiffen and pull away from the king before reaching for Nash. My hand encloses around my husband's. "Let's go."

The king drops his eyes to our linked hands, then looks back up at us with amusement. "Kinich, I require your presence for the remainder of the afternoon. We have much important business to discuss in regard to the building of the pyramid. Lady Chel, you may stay if you'd like."

No, I do not want to stay. I want to escape this madness. I desire no part in any of this. Behind the king, the brilliant jaguar frieze painted on the wall fades, and then Chaac himself disappears from my view. I feel the pressure of Nash's hand squeezing mine, and I know he must be seeing the same thing. And then Chaac is there again, brows narrowed in confusion as he studies the blank look on my face.

"I'm sorry," I say, snapping back to the present. "No, I'm leaving."

Chaac inclines his head, then returns to his wife.

"I'm going to visit Ixchel," I say to Nash. "I'll be back before sunset."

CHAPTER 27

MY LUNGS BURN AS I race through the trees. Branches snap against the exposed skin of my belly and arms, and twigs and leaves crunch underfoot as I dart along the narrow pathway. I don't have much time, because the sun is sinking lower and lower in the sky. I've waited until too late in the day to visit Ixchel, but the urge to speak with her is unbearable. Why does the future call to me if I'm to remain here? In one of the dreams I had of her, she herself traveled through a cenote, but I hadn't understood it then.

The narrow pathway widens, and then staggered, flat stones replace the dirt under my feet. I slow my pace, gasping in ragged breaths. I pass under the velvety floral scent of the passiflora vine then curve around the wide, tenuous base of the ceiba tree. Echoing tweets drift up from the deep cenote, and warm, soft rays of sunlight illuminate the cavern with a golden glow.

"Ixchel," I call out, climbing the short stairs to reach the platform where the palapa sets.

I peer into the cooking hut and scan the interior of the sleeping hut, but she is nowhere to be found. The basket for dirty cloth is gone, so I head in the direction of the underground river where she must be washing. The well-worn path is easy to follow, and soon I find the entrance to the cave. Carefully, I pick my way through the rocky terrain then follow the babbling shallow stream of water.

My 800-year-old ancestress is crouched on a low rock, scrubbing cloth in the water. A small stone rolls along the path, loosened by my foot. She turns to me, and her aged eyes light up with surprise.

"Ines." Her lined face softens in a welcoming smile. "Come, help me clean these."

The woman never misses a beat. She motions to the pile of cloth next to her and then returns to her task. I squat beside her and take up the washing, and for several minutes, I lose myself in the repetitive motions of the rubbing, scrubbing, rinsing, and repeat. After a while, Ixchel turns to me with an expectant arch to her silvery brow.

"Tell me your thoughts, daughter."

I wring out a clean cloth before setting it in the empty basket. "You traveled through the cenote before, right?"

She nods.

"For what purpose? What did you have to change?"

Her eyebrows draw inward. "Change? My life was in shambles. I gave myself over to The Whole One God, and he gave me a different way. I didn't change anything. But I gained knowledge and understanding."

"Then what was the point?"

"Why do you ask these questions, Ines?"

"Ignacio says that is why we travelled here. We have to change something, make a difference."

"As I told you before, perhaps only you and he are the ones meant to be changed by this journey."

I ponder her cryptic words for a few moments of silent scrubbing. "The portal is opening again. Do you sense it?"

She shakes her head in the negative. "Xibalba is not calling to me this time. Sometimes it speaks gently, letting me know there may be a different path, and other times it has roared at me."

"It's calling me."

"What about him?"

I nod. "He is being called too."

"Then it is time to go." Ixchel slants a glance in my direction. "You are his now, yes?"

Is it that obvious? A blush creeps up my neck, and I nod wordlessly.

"I can see your happiness. I remember it well. How is life with him?"

"Consuming, passionate." I lift my shoulders in a helpless shrug. "I'm falling in love."

"I told you it would be impossible not to." She grins at me. "Enjoy it. Loving my Kinich was one of the best parts of my life."

A soft chuckle escapes me. "I found love where I swore I'd never find it. With him."

When we stayed here with Calalu those few days, Ixchel and I had plenty of conversations about Nash's past and my reticence to be with someone who's been violent with their partner. I'd even told her the times he and I lost control and got physically aggressive with each other. All of it pointed to a bad match. Even the matchmaker said we weren't ready for one another. I'm not sure what changed.

"Ines, most of the time people fall in love with the divine, perfect parts. That is the side of themselves people show. But perhaps you fell in love with his human part first. And now you get to find the divine."

I smile at the thought. We've only been married two weeks, and I know this intoxicating honeymoon phase will take years to pass. But if we retain even a fraction of this passion, I will be content.

I set my last clean piece of cloth in the basket before wrapping my arms around my knees. "And I've found love here, in this place that felt so foreign to me. Itza has begun to feel like home."

"Itza exists in your time too, no?"

"In a way. The structures are there, but it is a dead place. Not alive like this."

"Maybe it is time for Itza to be reborn there."

Ixchel wrings the last piece of cloth in silence.

"It's getting dangerous in Itza," I say. "Chaac is king now, and he's starting to call for human sacrifices."

My ancestress's eyes get a faraway look. "One of the last times I travelled through a cenote, I ended up beyond this time. I lived in Zama, all the way where the sun rises. I married a king named Chaac, probably a descendant of Itza's king. I remember the day he told me he was going to start using humans as sacrifice. Right then, I decided to leave Zama. I walked for three days, heading west. Xibalba started calling me as I walked. I found this cenote here and jumped in. My heart drew me north to a city of yellow, because the first thing I saw at the top of their golden pyramid was my Kinich." Ixchel draws in a shuddering breath, closing her eyes. "He was their god and shaman. I stood there in the midst of a town of people, and somehow he saw me from far away. I didn't have it in me to run. I surrendered to him again. We were happy for a while, but he hurt me again one day."

I listen intently, fearful to say anything, needing to hear every tragic detail of their story.

Ixchel continues, "He wept in my lap. Promised he would change for good. But I didn't know his words were literal. We made love one last time, and I was going to leave him in the night like I always did. But he never fell asleep. After a while, he whispered words of love in my ear and left the bed. As he stood outside in the light of the moon, I sat up and watched him. I could never not watch him. He fell to his knees, his back arched, and terrible sounds tore from his throat. I ran to him, and his eyes were no longer blue. They were wild and golden in color. His last words to me were, "I will never hurt you again." He transformed into a jaguar and ran off. I gave chase, but could never find him. I wandered for days, shouting his name. I returned to this cenote, waiting for Xibalba to take me again, but it stayed silent." Ixchel lifts her bowed shoulders in a shrug. "So here I am. For some time, I did live in Itza—got married again and had a child. I used to think Xibalba pulled me and him together again, because we belonged to one another. But now, I think Xibalba called me here to wait for you. If Xibalba calls again, I will answer, but it has stayed silent for me."

Nash and I eat breakfast in the palace with the king and queen, along with the thirteen commoners who will be sacrificed tomorrow. The people seem happy and relaxed from the past day of luxury and pampering.

Mentally, I make plans to visit Ixchel again tomorrow. I felt so much peace after talking with her. Confusion still clouds my mind, but I'm trying to trust things will work out.

I take a sip of xocolatl, enjoying the spicy cocoa flavor as it spreads on my tongue. Next to me, Nash eats his usual protein heavy breakfast of meat and eggs. Last night, he'd met me on the sacbe back from Ixchel's, and as we walked back I told him everything she said about her own travels. But he remains unconvinced it's our time to return. And so I will stay here, in this place where my heart beats in rhythm with his.

Alom, high priest of Itza rushes into the room. The king's eyes narrow upon his uninvited intrusion, but the high priest moves forward and whispers into Chaac's ear. Alarm fills the king's eyes, and then he stands.

"Everyone is dismissed but the rulers."

The thirteen people get up and leave the room as one obedient group. Alom remains next to the king with his head bowed in a submissive pose. Once the last of the people have exited, Chaac signals for us to follow. The colorful passages of the palace flash by as we move in a hurry.

We exit the palace and emerge into a bright, sunny heat. The sun climbs higher in the sky, so it must be close to noon. Waiting for us are the other Itza priests, along with the Toltec priests and high priestess.

"The eclipse," Nash says softly.

And then I notice the light is fading degree by degree, like a heavy layer of cloud is moving over the sun, casting the entirety of the land in shadow. As if some unspoken signal is given, everyone steps back inside the palace, and Nash pulls me inside the doorway. The Maya must believe something negative about the light from an eclipse.

"Chi'ibal kin," someone mutters.

To eat the sun.

"The gods did not send him to us to call him back so soon," Chaac says, his lips set tight.

We've returned to the common room inside the palace. Chaac

faces the priests, his heavily muscled arms crossed in front of him, and Xochi stands at his side. Nash and I remain by the entrance door.

Alom bows his head. "My king, we do not understand the ways of the gods. The sign from the heavens coincides with the foundation stone of the pyramid. The gods do not want thirteen commoners. They want the sun god, Kinich Ahau. The moon has swallowed the sun, and she alone was in the sky. He must leave his wife and return to the gods."

The king is not happy with this interpretation. His nostrils lift in disdain, as if some pungent odor has drifted in on the breeze. A lump expands in my throat and the tip of my nose tingles with unshed tears. Next to me, Nash remains still as a stone, barely breathing. In my periphery, I see the brief rippling of his forearm as his hands clench and unclench. I'm terrified to look at him, afraid to see the expression on his face. I am seconds away from losing it completely. The urge to lunge at the high priest and violently shake him is overwhelming.

"I will not allow it," Chaac says, a slight tremor to his voice.

My gaze shoots over to him in surprise. Of all people, I didn't expect bloodthirsty Chaac to protest.

"Then be prepared to anger the gods," Alom says, raising his eyes to the king's. "Are you ready to face their fury so soon in your rule? They will find a way to take him anyway. You cannot stop this, my king. The gods have spoken."

The gods. I want to rip my hair out and shriek like a madwoman. These signs still seem to be at the mercy of some arbitrary interpretation. Eclipses happen in a cyclical fashion. There is no way this one means my husband needs to be sacrificed.

I raise my eyes to the priest, careful to keep my expression neutral. "What did the last eating of the sun mean? What was done then?"

"Many times we just observe it and make a notation of it. The eclipse is a powerful sign from the sky that can also give us messages from the gods. Right now, we are sending them the first sacrifices. They have made a clear request, and it is our duty to fulfill it."

Chaac's gaze moves from the priest over to Nash. "Brother?"

"I seem to have no choice here. If I refuse?"

The priest speaks. "We will not allow you to refuse. We have our methods to keep you calm."

Hallucinogenic drugs.

My husband's throat moves as he swallows hard. "That will not be necessary. I will come willing. For now, I would spend the rest of my time alone with my wife."

Alom bows his head. "You have until the sun rises."

This is not happening. We didn't come all the way here for Nash to be sacrificed for some stupid pyramid. Guards trail behind as we walk back to our house. Normally, as a sacrifice, Nash would be under the control of a guard while being plied with delicacies and women. As a final favor, Chaac allowed us to return home, but still sent guards along with us.

"Let's run away, Nash," I whisper, gazing up at him with pleading eyes.

His lips tighten as he shakes his head. "I don't think we'll be able to escape this."

"But we can try."

He remains silent and we enter the copse of trees surrounding our house. Peering behind me, I see the guards stop at the end of the road, keeping their eyes trained on us.

I try again. "We can run away to Ixchel's. Hide out there until the portals open again."

"She has chosen to live away from the city for a reason. We would endanger her. I won't do it."

We climb the stairs to our house, and panicked breaths start coming from my chest. Tears soon follow, and I collapse on the thatch covered bed as soon as I enter the doorway. Gasping sobs wrack my body. Nash crouches behind me and pulls me against him. There is no escaping this. My cheek presses against the warm, smooth skin of his chest.

I can't live without this.

He sits back against the wall, holding me within his arms as I fall apart. I struggle hard to control myself. I need to be strong for him, especially since I'm not the one being sacrificed by Mayan priests in the morning. After a few minutes, I'm able to slow the tears to a trickle. I untie my skirt and use the fabric to wipe the wetness from my face and nose. His eyes are reddened, but dry. He has the look of a shell-shocked man.

Desperate to bring him back to me, I lean forward and press my lips to his. The taste of him almost brings me to tears again.

I cannot live without this.

The thought becomes an obsessive mantra as I straddle his spread thighs and do my best to give him a moment of peace. He sparks back to life, returning my kiss with a wild urgency. I loosen the knots of his loincloth and pull away the fabric. His hands roam my body and his fingers dig into my hips, as if memorizing the shape of my curves and the softness of my skin.

For a moment, he grips my face between his hands and pulls away, staring into my eyes with a pained desperation. "I wish I could put a child in you."

It would be the only thing left of him, and all he can give me. But it would mean everything to have a piece of him. I will it to be so.

"You will," I whisper, pushing him to lie back on our bed.

For a long time, I simply lie on top of him, belly to belly, hip to hip, using my lips to make up for the years we didn't have one another, and for the lifetime I will be forced to live without him. Unbidden, tears slip from the corners of my eyes and pool down to the space between our lips, spreading salt on our tongues.

"Stop crying," Nash says in a gruff voice, then he lifts up and rolls me onto my back. "I don't want you sad when I put my son in you."

I giggle softly, then my head arches back in a gasp as he moves forward. There is no space in our bodies for sadness, and we fill ourselves with loving, with the sensation of being one, and the all-consuming power of this beautiful, perfect moment. He is mine forever, flesh of my flesh, and bone of my bone. A fine trembling builds in my center, and then heat floods through me, sending powerful waves rippling through my body. The beautiful agony of the release comes sooner than I wanted it, but we have the rest of the day and all of the night. Yet it will never be enough.

It's been several hours since the eclipse, and we've filled all of that time with one another. But now, Nash holds my hand as we walk through the city, Itza guards trailing at a distance. The firm set to his shoulders and tense line of his lips reminds me of the way he acted when we were walking to the cenote that brought us here.

We take the north sacbe leading to the Cenote Sagrado. I don't want to be here. I don't want to see this place where he will die. My hand tenses in his as I try to slip from his grasp, but he tightens his grip around me.

"I don't want to come here, Nash. Please."

He's like a deaf man, making no indication he's heard me besides dragging me forward and gripping my hand even tighter. A quiet sob breaks past my lips as we move forward. We reach the thatch covered terrace where the altar lies, and then Nash turns to me.

"It's time for you to go back home, Ines."

I recoil from him, shock imprinting on my features. "No." I swallow hard. "I'm not leaving you."

My gaze darts to the smooth surface of the water, and it seems to pulsate like a beacon, one time, then goes still again.

"Our time here is done. Once I'm gone, there's nothing to stop them from sacrificing you if, gods forbid it, there's a lunar eclipse." He breathes out a harsh laugh and shakes his head.

My eyes narrow to slits as I take a step away. "I'm not running away. If anyone's leaving today, it's going to be you. So jump in."

His lips thin into a tight line, and he tilts his head down to me. "This ends now. You're going back. You have no choice. Sometime between now and when the sun sets, I will throw you into this water."

I step forward, putting myself nose to nose with him. "So you'll just drown me again? I have no idea what I'm doing."

"We practiced this so many times at Ixchel's. You've done it."

He's right, but I'm not going to admit that. The mention of Ixchel's cenote has an impossible idea brewing in my mind, but it will force me to play multiple roles that end in betrayal.

"What if we can make it so you don't die?"

He is silent for a few moments, staring over my shoulder at the guards standing just down the sacbe. "How?"

"The priest said anyone who returns from the cenote is considered to have been given power of prophecy, and the first words they utter will be law. What if I insist on being the one to stab you in the chest with the knife?"

Understanding comes into his eyes. "And you aim high."

I nod. "You'll have a wound, but you'll survive it. You find the cave again, hide out in there all night. And then when the sun rises, you come back. Speak the words that the gods do not want humans sacrificed. It will become unchangeable law."

Tentative hope springs in his eyes as he rubs his jaw with one hand. "It's a good plan, Ines."

Relief floods me as he turns away from the cenote. Our hands linked together, we head down the path and back to our home. The sun sets in five or six hours, and that will be all the time I have left with him. There is much to be done before then.

CHAPTER 28

THE KING OF ITZA regards me with a heavy stare. I can't interpret the look in his eyes. Nervously, I fidget with the hem of my skirt.

"You are certain of this?" he finally says.

I swallow hard and nod my head. "The gods want him before sunset today. This is why the moon ate the sun today, and not tomorrow. All we have to do is put him in the water, and Xibalba will swallow him down. You will see it, and the sacrifice will be better accepted because he is alive and whole."

Chaac's eyebrow curves up. "You want him gone that bad?"

"No, my king. He is my friend—"

"You looked like much more than friends earlier."

"We are husband and wife. It is expected, and he is pleasing to look upon. My needs have gone unmet for some time." I give Chaac a meaningful look.

What I'm doing right now is unforgivable and I never imagined I'd betray Nash in such a dishonorable way. While the plan I laid out to Nash successfully prevented him from forcibly returning me to 2012, I'm risking everything by coming to try and convince Chaac to set my own plan in motion. But I'm saving my husband's life, and for that, any cost is worth it.

"If you send him in tomorrow, he will return from Xibalba. How do you think Kinich Ahau has become one of the most revered gods of the people? He will take your throne, and the priests will support him in it."

"Why do you help me now, Lady Chel?"

"Our descendants will have a strong bond, King Chaac." I stare into his onyx eyes. "Do you not feel it? Even the matchmaker saw it."

His lips purse in thought. "I was cruel to you."

My lashes drop demurely. "As you saw, I enjoy that kind of love play."

Chaac sits forward, resting his elbows on his knees. "As a noble man, I am permitted multiple wives. Is this acceptable to you?"

"I would be honored, my king."

"Then I will gather the priests to complete the sacrifice before sunset."

My heart beats unsteadily in my chest as I return to our home. In my hands I hold a bowl full of blue paint. One of the priests mixed the concoction from indigo, clay mineral, and sacred copal resin. The vivid color resembles a cloudless sky. The king, queen, and a procession of priests trail behind me. I quicken my pace to put some distance between us.

Minutes later, I climb the stairs to our house. My husband lies sleeping, blessedly oblivious to what is about to happen. I set the bowl beside the bed and kneel on the ground next to him. His eyes open, and he stretches with a lazy yawn.

"Come back to bed, mi amor."

"Nash."

His head tilts in my direction. "What is it?"

"Our plan isn't going to work. It might, but that's not good enough for me. What if you get an infection? What if they don't let me be the one to put the knife in your chest? There are too many what ifs."

"It's all we have."

"No, it isn't. Listen, I love you." I swallow down the lump forming in my throat after speaking the words I never imagined I'd say.

A wide smile curves on his face.

I continue speaking. "I've convinced Chaac to do the sacrifice today, before the sun sets and the portals close. You're going home, because I love you, and I can't live in a world where you're only a memory. You'll go now, and I'll follow in two weeks. The priests and Chaac are right behind me."

"How long?"

"They're probably walking up right now—"

"No. How long have you loved me?"

I smile as tears fill my eyes. "I don't know. All I can say for certain is one day I knew you'd be part of me as long as I live, and probably even longer. You have changed me. Permanently. You've imprinted into my heart, my blood, and my cells."

He sits up, swinging his feet over the edge of the bed, and I move between his thighs. Strong arms enclose around me, and I kiss the smooth line of his throat.

"Ay, my cold-hearted muñeca … what have you done?"

I pull back. "I've made sure you'll survive this."

"At what cost?"

The words freeze on my tongue. I can't lie to him, and the truth will crush him.

"The only thing I have of value to the king." I lift my chin. "I've agreed to be his second wife."

Nash's eyes blaze. "You will have to kill me before I let that happen."

One side of my mouth curves in a sad, ironic smile. "Coincidentally, that has already been arranged, my love. If they kill you tomorrow, what do you think will happen to me anyway?"

His eyes drift to the doorway. I turn to look over my shoulder and see the small crowd of people gathered at the base of our house.

"Nash, if you fight me on this, he will know I've tricked him. He will punish me and perhaps kill me too. It will take time to make the announcement, weave a dress, pick an auspicious day. I will insist everything be done to perfection. By then, the portals will open again."

"And if he forces himself on you?"

I swallow hard and raise my palm to rest against his cheek, keeping my eyes on his. "It's just my body, Nash. You are the owner of my heart. I hope that's worth more to you. But I promise, amor, this will work."

Creamy, blue paint spreads over my husband's body. It still holds warmth from when the priest mixed the ingredients in the vessel over the fire. I smooth my hands over his skin, transforming it from the beautiful bronze tone I love to the azure color of the heavens beyond the clouds. Only then will the gods accept him to the uppermost levels. I cover every inch of his skin and don't bother tying his loincloth back on. A small part of me wants Chaac to see just how insufficient he will be when compared to my magnificent husband.

"This isn't right, Ines," Nash says through clenched teeth. "I'm supposed to be the one to stay here."

I smooth the last of the paint over a spot I missed on his neck. "I know. And I'm sorry I made this choice for you. But we're even Esteban now, sí?"

He narrows his eyes at me. "I don't want to leave you here, Ines. You're my wife … my heart. Everything in me is screaming to not let this happen. But you've neatly trapped me."

I rinse my hands in a bowl of water and use a cloth to dry them. After standing, I move in close to him, a hairsbreadth apart, unable to touch due to the wet paint.

"I love you. Remember that, okay?"

He nods solemnly.

An eerie reddish light spreads over Itza as the day fades. Chaac and Xochi lead the way to the Cenote Sagrado. Nash walks behind, hands bound in front of him. I follow with the group of priests. People from Itza take notice of the procession, and a few start to tentatively trail behind.

We reach the cenote, and the still, murky water now seems to glow iridescent in the fading light of the sun. My skin itches with the need to be in the water, enveloped by its cool, liquid embrace. The pine-scented smoke of copal incense fills the space, and one of the priests begins speaking, calling on Heart of Sky, Mother Earth, and the four directions. Nash stands at the edge of the cenote, his back to the water. I focus on my husband's face … that strong jaw, his eyes the color of the night sky, and those lips that worshipped my body through the long hours of the night. Two weeks isn't long, but it's going to feel like a lifetime.

Alom, the high priest, shakes a bundle of leaves over Nash's body then moves a plate of smoking incense around his form. Cit'lalli, the Toltec high priestess, comes forward with an obsidian blade.

My eyes shoot over to Chaac, but he only stares straight ahead, avoiding my gaze. Clearly he didn't fill the priests in on doing this without the whole stabbing in the heart part. Nash's jaw moves as he clenches his teeth. Alom, grabs the knife and speaks a prayer over the blade, then takes the killing stance.

"Wait," my voice rings out in the silence.

All eyes turn to me.

"Xibalba will take him as soon as he touches the water. There is no need for the knife."

Cit'lalli shakes her head. "We must put holes in everything we send to Xibalba. It allows the spirit to escape the body and return to the gods."

An unsteady breath releases from my lungs. We won't be able to escape this part.

I step forward. "The moon swallowed the sun, and so the moon must be the one who sends the sun to Xibalba."

My hand reaches for the blade, not waiting for approval. Under no circumstance can I allow any of them to use that knife on him. My heart thunders in my ears as I wait with my hand outstretched, my eyes pinned on the high priest. If he tries to put that knife in his chest, I'll have to move forward and push Nash in. Alom glances at

Cit'lalli. She gives a short nod of approval.

With a flick of his wrist, Alom extends the weapon in my direction. My fingers wrap around the gilded handle. The ceremonial tool is a display of remarkable workmanship. The handle is shaped with the curving nose of the rain god, formed by a mosaic tesserae of turquoise, dark green malachite, and iridescent white mother-of-pearl outlining and filling in his features. The shiny black blade tapers to a sharp point.

I turn to stand in front of my husband, eyes raising to meet his. He returns my gaze with a steady nod of acceptance. We didn't practice this part. I don't know where to stab him. Closing my eyes, I reach my hand out and lay it over the left side of his chest, pressing in to find the spaces between the upper ribs. His heart thumps in a quick rhythm under my hand.

"Breathe," I murmur softly, opening my eyes. "Calm down."

He nods, then drops his forehead to mine. "Even if you kill me, I love you, Ines. Just being your husband and friend has been worth it."

Tears drip from the corners of my eyes. "I'll see you in two weeks. I love you."

"Hold it with both hands," he whispers.

I nod my head and grip the handle tightly between my palms then take a step back to give me more momentum. I keep my eyes glued on the spot below his collarbone, but above his heart, and pray my aim will be true. It's a good thing we didn't travel to the time when they disemboweled the sacrifice victims, or we wouldn't stand a chance of this working. My eyes raise to his one last time.

"I don't have all day, gringa," he says with that arrogant smirk I used to hate, but now only love.

A single warm tear slides down my cheek, and I step forward, driving the knife into my husband's chest.

The impact sends a shockwave up my arms.

I've buried the blade hilt deep, just an inch below the spot I aimed for. I pray it was high enough. He exhales out a harsh breath then takes in several small breaths. With two hands, I shove him backward, and he falls. I drop to my knees at the edge, bracing my hands on the stone.

The glassy stillness of the cenote ripples before his body even hits the water. He rotates himself into diving form, then slices into the water, disappearing beneath the surface. Bubbles begin to erupt from the center, and then a sharp gust of wind blows, tearing leaves from the trees. My eyes widen as a downward pull, much like a whirlpool, appears. A noise like the sound of screeching, grinding gears rips through my head. I cover my ears with my hands, but the deafening vibration is coming from within. My body begins to arch toward the water, but I force myself to lie flat on the stones, keeping my eyes glued on the maelstrom below.

This will be an easy descent for him, but I remember how murky the bottom was. He'll need time to find the entrance to the underground cavern. Combined with the chest wound, I can only hope his body will be able to handle everything, including when he comes to on the other side. A sob escapes me as I think of him waking alone with the momentary loss of memory, a knife in his chest, and the pain. I shove my fist against my mouth to stifle the escaped sound.

All at once, it's as if the cenote exhales. A gust of air explodes from the deep, and then the surface is mirror smooth again. I push myself off the ground to stand on shaky legs. Clear awe shines from the rest of the onlooker's eyes at witnessing this acceptance of their sacrifice. Their combined expressions of religious fervor send a chill down my spine.

The king's attention shifts, and his head swings in my direction. "You have the night to mourn your husband. Then you will move into the palace tomorrow."

The splendor of Itza disappears behind me as I trade the colorful stone homes of the elite for simple wood and thatch dwellings of the poor. Before I do anything else, I need to ensure Calalu and her mother's safety. Very soon, the future will catch up to all of these people, bringing with it the same fate that befell Nash.

My heart throbs in pain. It's only been about twenty minutes since I forced him to leave me. I never wanted to remain in this place, and here I am without him, my entire reason for staying. I hurry along the white sacbe as the sky lights up in the indigo blue of nightfall.

The poorest citizens of Itza eye me warily as I enter their neighborhood. Seeing one of the elite seek out a member of the lowest class likely shocks them. I smile warmly, but as expected, all lower their gaze.

Calalu and her mother's eyes widen when they see me walking toward their palapa. I wordlessly gesture for them to enter their house, and I follow behind. Pressing my palms together, I pin my eyes on each of them, attempting to communicate the importance of what I'm about to say. Calalu's mother reaches out, and I extend my hand to hers.

"We need to leave Itza." My chin trembles slightly, but I clench my jaw to control its movement.

Calalu's wide brown eyes stare at me. "Where is Kinich Ahau?"

"That's why we need to leave. Instead of vessels and jewelry, the king has started to sacrifice people to the sacred well." My heartbeat thuds in my ears, the words paining me even as they rise up. "Kinich was the first."

Calalu's mother gasps loudly, while Calalu stares at me unblinking. "Where is he?"

"He's gone, my sweet girl. Where all the sacrifices go. In the sacred well." I kneel in front of them, tears filling my eyes. "King Chaac will be calling for more and more people and soon will start forcing you to sacrifice yourselves. You need to leave Itza before it starts happening."

"Where will we go?" Calalu's mother meets my eyes, her steady gaze filled with determination. My heart breaks as I hear Calalu's soft, gasping cries of grief for the man who cared so much for her and was unable to say goodbye.

"There are other cities around here. But the safest place will be a short walk away, at an old healer's house. I will bring you there."

A sudden thought flashes through my head. Tato. I need to warn him too. But is he at the market, or at home?

Decision made, I stand. "Get everything you own ready to go. Meet me at Tato's palapa."

Both of them begin moving around to gather their life's belongings into baskets. I rush away, heading back to the market. Most days, Tato stays as long as he has medicinal supplies to sell, and the need varies day to day. It's too risky to assume he's gone home already, because once I leave this city, I won't return. Ixchel's home will be a safe haven for the next two weeks. I move haphazardly through the merchants streaming from the center of the city, keeping my eyes out for Tato's tall, gangly frame.

Tato's stall is nearly empty, and the old man shuffles around, packing up the remainder of his roots, bark, and leaves into a basket. I breathe out a sigh of relief, hurrying toward him.

"Tato."

The healer looks up, his aged eyes coming alight as they connect with mine. Almost immediately after, his features droop in sadness. "My girl," he says softly. "I heard about your husband."

"You and your wife need to leave Itza, Tato. Calalu and her mother are waiting at your house. We can go to Ixchel's and be safe there. King Chaac plans on sacrificing thirteen people for every level of the new pyramid. Kinich alone served for the sum of the first level, and the next level will require twenty-six people, and the third level will need thirty-nine people. He's going to just keep going. Hundreds of people will die before the pyramid is done."

Tato shakes his head sadly, and then his eyes widen as he stares over my shoulder. "The king is walking straight to us."

My belly lurches in fear. Tato turns away, sifting through the contents of a basket. He makes a small sound of triumph, then sniffs the bundle of cloth before handing me a small package of roots. "This is powerful poison," he whispers. "Use it if you must." Tato's eyes crinkle in a forced smile as he waves. "Enjoy your tea, my lady."

I give him a shaky smile and turn away, hoping it's not me the king is seeking. But I already know.

"Lady Chel." Chaac's voice spreads through the mostly empty plaza.

There is no use pretending I can't hear him. No use running from him. I turn and face the king, keeping my features as neutral as possible.

"Yes, King Chaac."

He walks closer, and briefly I consider what a shame that such savage beauty in a man has been wasted on a person with an evil heart. I clench the bundle of roots in my hand, knowing I can't use it. Killing the king would ensure the pyramid of Kukulkan would never be built. I can't gamble with the past nor the future in such a reckless manner. My heartbeat quickens as the king moves closer, and for the first time in a very long time, I pray.

CHAPTER 29

Chichen Itza, 2012
Two weeks later

NASH

"Señor," comes a male voice behind me. "Estamos cerrando."

I glance down at my watch. It's almost 5 pm. I've been sitting here at the edge of Cenote Sagrado the entire day, and now they are closing, as the worker behind me is saying.

"Por favor, cinco minutos más," I say, begging for five more minutes.

Standing, I keep my eyes trained on the leaf littered water. I've felt its pull all morning, but a few hours ago, the feeling went away. There has been no indication she's come through. I have no way of knowing if she's run into trouble, or if she's struggling somewhere under that water. My jaw clenches as I run all the possible scenarios through my head for the hundredth time this day. Several times I've contemplated jumping in and going back, just so I can know she's safe. But then all of this will have been in vain.

Absentmindedly, I scratch at the healing wound on my chest. Waking up in that cave completely naked, hands bound, and painted blue was unsettling to say the least. Those long minutes where my mind was fractured and my brain felt on fire, combined with the knife sticking out of my chest, had been excruciating. I'd never felt more helpless in my entire life.

And then my memory trickled back bit by bit. Our time in ancient Itza, the incredible things we witnessed and learned.

My wife.

That memory of being with her was what finally broke me. That proud, stubborn woman loved me. Somehow, I'd earned what I knew I never deserved. I used trickery, deceit, and manipulation to get what I wanted from her. And yet, she still found it in her heart to love me back.

I shake my head, ashamed of my selfishness, loathing myself for everything I put her through. Would I change a single thing?

Probably not.

Perhaps I'd choose to not be stabbed through the chest at the end there, but I deserved to be the one sacrificed. It felt like the ultimate divine retribution for my sins. And maybe, just maybe, I could have a clean slate in the eyes of the gods.

"Señor," comes the tentative voice behind me. "Ahora, por favor."

At least he's being polite in asking me to leave now. Pressing my lips together in frustration, I turn away from the cenote and follow the worker down the path. I'll jump the fence once I get back to my truck. If she's not here before sunset, I'm diving in.

Thankfully, when I returned from the past two weeks ago, the sun had long set and the historical site of Chichen Itza was closed. I washed as much of the blue paint off my body as I could, pulled on my jeans in the cave, then shoved my shirt in my pocket. No one had been there to witness me emerging from the water then collapsing on the edge of the cenote. Only then did I grip the handle of the knife and pull it from my body, agonized groans coming from between my clenched teeth. I braced myself on my hands and knees, letting the wound bleed to help wash out bacteria, then stumbled into the trees.

Instead of using the main entrance to leave, I hopped the fence north of the cenote. Hopped isn't the right word. I fell over the fence in an ungraceful heap, clutching my balled-up shirt against the gaping wound on my chest. After crossing the highway, I made it to my friend's house where my Jeep was still parked. The older woman who owned the land there would be able to better care for my wound. I had no interest in going to a hospital and answering questions.

After spending most of that first week recovering, I went back to my home and lay low. There was no point in telling mi papá I'd returned, since he already knew I never planned on coming back. I'd avoid adding to his stress and wait until both Ines and I could see him in person.

And now, my own stress soars sky high as I walk past my Jeep in the Chichen Itza lot. I stop at the guard station near the exit and tell the man I've run out of gas and would be back. I briefly consider just driving my truck to my friend's lot, but if Ines comes out sometime before I'm able to get back over there, I need her to know I'm nearby. The guard at the entrance of the parking lot kindly offers to drive me to a gas station, but I reassure him a friend is coming to meet me. The man tells me just to move the cones when I'm ready to go, and then with a wave leaves the white station and hops on a moped parked off to the side.

I follow the long, brick-paved road to the highway then turn right to walk to the area leading to the fence outside of Cenote Sagrado. After hopping the fence, much more nimbly this time, I plod through the thicket of trees until I reach the edge of the sacred pool. Resuming my earlier post, I sit cross-legged, staring into the water.

Hours pass, and the sun sinks closer to the line of trees. If I'm going to jump in and go back for her, now is the time. Otherwise, I'll need to wait for the next equinox in September. Two months is too long to leave her there without me.

I stand, glaring into the water and willing her to appear. After a final harsh exhale, I suck in air, pulling oxygen deep into my lungs, then dive in.

I pull myself up the flat rocks around the edge of the cenote and stand there, dripping wet and pissed. Nothing happened when I dove in. No snakes, no pain, no unholy screaming noise. I wasn't able to pass through. Dropping to my knees, I press my forehead to the smooth rock. This is agony. Being without her for two weeks was too long, and now I have to wait two months to find out if she's even okay. Did Chaac imprison her somehow? The thought sends a ripple of dread through my body.

Clenching my hands into fists, I push off the rocks and make my way to the exit. At this point I don't care if I trigger alarms. I scramble over the high fence to the side of the main entrance then land lightly on my feet.

My Jeep stands solitary in the lot. I'd left my keys in the glove box, so I just pull the door open and climb in.

"Bueno," comes the feminine voice to my right.

Startling slightly, I turn to see my wife lying in the passenger seat. She is a vision to my starved eyes, wearing a sleeveless black, knee-length huipil.

Her eyes fill with tears as she smiles. "I'd like to get this tour over with if you could start driving already."

For a moment, I just stare at her, my eyes widened in surprise. Then in a rush, I explode from my seat and run to the passenger side. I yank open the door and drag her out of the car before wrapping my arms around her and lifting her against me. We stand glued together for a few moments.

"Jesus," I whisper into her hair.

She sniffles against my neck, and then I turn my head to her, needing to feel those lips on mine again. For several minutes, we get lost in the sensation of one another, pulled together by the same unseen force that has always drawn me to her. I pull away, breathing unsteadily as I set her down.

"What happened, Ines? I waited all day."

She smiles wryly, looking down at her now wet dress. "And I take it you jumped in the cenote too?"

"I didn't know what else to do. You didn't show. I had no choice but to try and go back for you. What happened?"

She swallows hard and shifts her gaze to look over my shoulder, avoiding my eyes. My brow creases as my eyes narrow to slits. I pray she's not about to say what I fear she's going to say. If she had to sleep with him, it's going to crush me.

"I did what I had to. Chaac commanded that I move into the palace in the morning. I immediately decided to leave and hide out at Ixchel's, but I stopped to get Calalu and her mother. Then I remembered that I'd need to tell Tato too. And Chaac found me there in the market. Tato gave me a package of poisonous roots that I could use to kill Chaac." She closes her eyes and shakes her head. "I didn't know what to do, Nash. If I killed him, it would change everything in Mayan history. The pyramid of Kukulkan wouldn't exist. So I ... I invited him back to our house. I thought it would be better if I took charge and didn't let him get the upper hand."

My jaw clenches so tight that I wouldn't be surprised to hear my back teeth crack from the pressure. But I let her finish.

"I did kiss him, but after a while I started crying because I could only think of you. And he tried to keep going, but I could tell that me being emotional was a big turnoff for him, so I just made myself go hysterical with crying. He couldn't do anything. He said he expected me to be done with my sadness when I move into the palace in the morning, then left me alone. I ran to Ixchel's right after."

My breath releases on an agonized exhale, and I pull her tightly against me. The relief of holding her again is so sweet that I want to cry.

She continues talking. "I waited at Ixchel's until the portals opened again. So when I came back, it was at Yokdzonot cenote east of here. It took me so long to feel right again. I just kept puking and felt horrible. One of the women working there found me lying on the dock. She acted like finding me there wearing only a Mayan skirt was totally normal. It was like she knew somehow. She insisted on giving me this dress and feeding me. Then I took a taxi here. Thank God you have the horrible habit of leaving your truck unlocked," she finishes with a muffled laugh against my chest.

"I have many horrible habits, as you will continue to learn." I pull away, then grip both of her hands in mine. Hope sparks in me when my fingers connect with the wedding ring I gave her. "But I promise to never stop trying to earn your love, even if we live to a hundred years."

"You already have it, Nash," she whispers.

"But I don't ever want to lose it." I pause for a moment, studying her features. "Will you marry me again, Ines? Here. In this time."

One side of her cheek curves in a smile, and her eyes glimmer with amusement. "Of course, mi amor. You're not getting rid of me that easy."

I tighten my arms around her, enjoying the feel of my wife in my arms. "What now?" I murmur. "Do you want to go see mi papá? Get your dad's letter? Or go home?"

She looks up at me. "Home? Cozumel?"

I nod. "That is where our home is, if that's where you want to live. But if you want to return to America, I will come with you."

She shakes her head. "I want to stay here. We weren't meant to prevent the fall of the Mayan empire, but like Ixchel said, *we* were the ones who changed. We can use the knowledge we learned and everything we lived, and teach it to all those who want to learn it here. I can teach herbalism, and you can teach the real rules to the Mayan ball game. We know more about the ancient law, astronomy, the food, the textiles. Let's bring it back to everyday life for the people here. It'll be a start to changing here and now."

We pull into the long sandy driveway of a two-story beach house in Telchac Puerto where mi papá lives. On the other side of the highway is the coral-colored Laguna Rosada, where the moment I'd felt her hand in mine, I knew I wasn't ever letting go. I battled back and forth against myself for days, knowing she didn't deserve to be with someone as messed up as me, but I craved the simple peace I felt in her presence.

After parking my truck next to his car, I knock on the front door. We wait for a few minutes, but there's no answer. It's ten at night, so either he's sleeping, or he's out by the ocean.

"Let's go around the back," I say, grabbing Ines' hand.

We slip past the side of the house, then I test the back door to see if it's locked. Grinning, I slide the glass door open. Many of my bad habits were inherited from mi papá.

The first floor is one large open room. The living room flows into the kitchen and eating area, then there are stairs off to the left next to the front door, and a bathroom to the right. Ines makes an immediate run for the restroom, marveling loudly at how much she's missed indoor plumbing. I smile as I brace my shoulder against the wall, looking out at the ocean where I can see the familiar shape of a man walking away from the water and toward the house.

Ines comes out of the restroom and leans against me. I wrap one arm around her and pull her against my ribcage. The door slides open and my father steps through.

"Papá," I say gently, hoping not to startle him too much.

Clear shock flashes across his face, and then his eyes fill with tears. "Ignacio. Ay, Dios."

I rush forward, and we meet in a hug, tightly gripping one another.

He holds me out at arm's length and looks me up and down. "Que pasó, hijo?" he asks, wondering what happened.

"Regresamos." I shrug, telling him we came back. Then I point over my shoulder. "Mira, su nuera."

His eyes light up to hear me call Ines his daughter-in-law.

He extends his arms out to her with a smile. "Ines, you married this fool?"

She laughs as she walks into his arms, returning his hug. "I did. No regrets. Yet."

My father shouts out a loud laugh, pleased at her response.

"We'll tell you about everything that happened, papá, but first, where is the letter from Ines' father?"

He rushes out to his car to get the letter from the glove box. Ines sits at the table, while I rifle through the fridge looking for food. I throw some tamales in the microwave, and then mi papá returns through the front door holding a white envelope. Dread flashes across Ines' face as he sets the letter in front of her.

"We'll talk in the morning, mis hijos. Good night."

I smile at hearing him call us his children.

Ines gives him a sad smile. "Good night, papá."

After grabbing my heated tamales from the microwave, I set the plate on the table and sit across from her. I'm not sure if she wants privacy to read the letter, but I'm not leaving unless she asks. She pushes the letter across the table.

"You read it to me."

I raise one eyebrow. "You sure?"

She nods.

Sliding my finger under the seal, I open the envelope and slip out the single folded sheet of paper. I unfold the page and scan the unfamiliar handwriting scrawled within the lines. I clear my throat then begin reading.

Mi hija, I love you and I miss you. I hope you will forgive me for sending you back to the Yucatán. Maybe I'm just crazy, but I think time travel is real and I think what happened to us in the cenote has something to do with it. Maybe you have the power to travel back and make a difference for our people.

It was difficult to piece together my own memories, combined with the visions (which I now believe were memories from our ancestors), and to put it together with the limited information Guillermo Dominguez revealed. I think he knows more about time travel than he let on. I don't think he felt comfortable trusting me with specifics, and I can't blame him. Too often our telephone conversations ended with my mind splitting apart again.

This will be the last letter I write. I pray you live a long life full of love and adventure. Mostly love. Don't live in fear. Be gentle with yourself and reach for happiness every day. I will never regret the moment you arrived on this earth. I have loved you every day since then, and will continue to love you in the hidden parts of my fragile brain. Te amo para siempre.

As I fold the letter up again, I study my wife's face. I can't tell if she's relieved or angry about her dad's words. She extends her hand, and I pass the letter to her. She sets the letter down then extends her hand again, reaching for me. I wrap my hand around hers and bring her fingers to my lips.

"You okay?"

She nods. "He knew." An exhale of breath expels from her lips. "I can't blame your dad for not telling him more. I should be angry that all of you seemed to be in on it." She pauses. "But more than anything, I understand."

We sit in silence for a few moments, just staring at one another. The face of that little girl I enjoyed provoking is still there, hidden in tiny facial expressions and genuine smiles. When I saw that same girl, turned woman, walk into the tour office two months ago, too many thoughts burst into my mind. I knew what her being there meant, and what I had to do. I hated to be the one to betray her in such a way. Telling the truth felt impossible, so I took the coward's way out. But my life led to it, and hers did as well.

Now here we are, husband and wife, modern descendants of the Ancient Ones, living their legacy and bringing their passion full circle. I'd once longed for greatness, a chance to experience what it meant to be an ancient god ruling over a forgotten civilization. All I wish for now is continued happiness with my wife at my side.

We were never supposed to save the ancient Maya, but maybe Ines and I needed to find each other and heal the break between our ancestors. And now, together we will be at the forefront of a Mayan rebirth. I marvel at the thought of the life we have ahead of us, and how a Day of No Shadows resulted in something even more important than my original goal.

I found the greatest love of my life.

EPILOGUE

Seven Years Later

Yucatán Destination Offers Unique Experience
By The Yucatán Post on May 13, 2019

The past two years, Mexico has seen a decrease in tourism due to a Travel Safety Alert issued by the US government in 2017. But business continues to boom for various tourism companies in the Yucatán. One such company is a unique adventure destination located in Yokdzonot.

According to the owners and founders of Aventura Itzalan, business steadily grows. Six years ago, husband and wife team, Ignacio and Ines Dominguez, purchased nearly a hundred acres of mostly forested land located between the historical ruins of Chichen Itza and Coba. After two years of construction, Aventura Itzalan opened to the public. Glowing online reviews say the retreat is like taking a step back in time.

"It's a return to Mayan culture," says Ignacio, the thirty-three-year-old co-founder, "with all the comfort of a five-star establishment if one desires."

Ignacio defers to his co-founder and wife, thirty-year old Ines, who is currently pregnant with their third child. "I teach classes on both weaving and herbalism, while my husband stays busy torturing the tourists."

Ignacio laughs. "Ancient Mayan warriors trained for hours every day, men along with women. Those who come here to train in the ways of our ancestors appreciate and respect the routines. We also have a Pitz league, and teams from all over the peninsula come to compete in the ancient Mayan ball game."

Dominguez insists his technique is the most consistent with how the game was played a thousand years ago. His charismatic nature along with natural leadership skills led to other leagues in the area quickly adopting his style. Their six-year-old son and four-year-old daughter actively participate in the junior leagues.

Tourists are drawn to the luxurious amenities, combined with unique lessons and experiences offered throughout the sprawling eco-retreat. Some choose to sleep on beds in air-conditioned rooms complete with indoor plumbing, while the more adventurous type sleep in thatch-covered palapas in hammocks. Meals served on the premises are grown and cooked according to traditional Mayan methods. The property also boasts its own cenote, which guests take full advantage of on hot days.

"We provide jobs for locals. They teach tourists how to create clothing, weapons, pottery or jewelry, all using the same methods our ancestors used," Ignacio says.

As demand steadily grows, more people from surrounding communities are able to secure the well-paying jobs available. In an effort to keep the culture alive on the peninsula, Aventura Itzalan invites all Yucatán residents to come learn, free of charge. Available classes include pottery, weaving, Mayan ball game, Warrior Temple training, herbalism, and cooking, along with many more.

When asked about their plans for the future, Ignacio speaks up. "Since the last bak'tun ended in 2012, many Yucatán Maya felt directionless. Our hope is that influential people in local villages take advantage of what we offer, then take that knowledge back to their own villages and encourage more people to come take our classes. Enriching the present with the past is what will lead to the best future for the Maya."

Next week, Aventura Itzalan celebrates Day of No Shadows, the solar zenith, which is a twice-yearly event. We've heard it also marks a special moment in the couple's history.

The cenote will be closed on that day.

THE END

AUTHOR'S NOTE

This story delves into the complexity of abuse that trickles down through generations. I didn't want Ines and Nash to be perfect characters. They needed to struggle and become better for it in the end. I hope I conveyed that in a realistic, sensitive manner.

While I had great fun writing this story, it took me about three years to complete it. I got the first five chapters down, then proceeded to put it away for almost two years. A vacation to the Yucatán in 2017 changed that. My fickle muse spoke again. Learning all of the incredible things the Mayans did long before anyone else astounded me. Being of Mayan descent myself, I couldn't help but think of my ancestors and how they lived.

Writing the remainder of the story was an interesting process. There were several things that I typed out, believing I was using my creative rights to invent something, and then weeks later, I'd find an article describing that exact thing. To mention one example, when Nash and Ines traveled back and there was an eclipse on the same day as the equinox, I made that up. Or so I thought. At that point in time, I had no title for the story. Around the 80% mark of writing, I found an article from 2012 describing the Day of No Shadows, and how the celebration that year was so unique *because an eclipse occurred the same day.*

That was just one mind-blowing discovery. Coincidence? I'm not sure, but let it be stated that I'll be staying out of cenotes if there are any celestial events occurring on my next Yucatán vacation. But if I see a 6'5 tall man with bronze-colored hair, all bets are off.

Do you enjoy unique love stories set in the Amazon rainforest? If so, check out my debut novel, The Blue Amaryllis.

Is romantic suspense more your thing? You'll enjoy my second novel, Embers of Starlight.

ACKNOWLEDGEMENTS

Firstly, I have to thank my critique partners and fellow authors. Ted Swanson, your male viewpoint was invaluable and helped me refine so many scenes. Denali Whitford, your sensitivity to details about character motivation and your recommendation on where to cut down scenes helped this story become what it is. Karen Wyle, your thoughtful commentary and eagle eye for details took this story to a different level. Nicole Fiorina, you entered late in the game, but helped me see inconsistencies and areas that needed clarification.

Secondly, my betas—Joy, Joannah, and Lilyana. Thank you guys for being my cheerleaders and fielding my endless random questions.

A great big thank you to my editor, Jennifer Clark-Sell. What would I be without you, woman? I'd appear illiterate, that's what. Thank you for removing my comma frenzy and fixing my tenses!

And to Lee Ching, cover designer extraordinaire, who gave me exactly what I requested, and then without complaint, made the changes when I realized what I asked for wasn't good enough. You rock!

Thank you to the bloggers and early reviewers who accepted an advanced copy of this story and posted their honest reviews. Without reviewers and bloggers, writers would be absolutely nothing. You all are the true VIPs.

Last but not least …

Four years ago, I gave up writing. When a story came to my mind a year later, my husband encouraged me to write it down. As I wrote, believing it led to nowhere, he continued to encourage me to keep writing. I know this passion for writing often pulls me away from my obligations of being a mother and wife, but if it weren't for him, this story wouldn't exist. So to the love of my life, thank you for encouraging me and supporting me. I love you.

Made in the USA
Columbia, SC
06 August 2019